THE HAVOC INSIDE US

Greg Juhn

Matt Yurina

D1566891

THE HAVOC INSIDE US

FUTURENESS

COVER DESIGN: GREG JUHN
COVER PRODUCTION: NESLIHAN YARDIMLI
INTERLUDE ILLUSTRATIONS: BARTEK BŁASZCZEĆ
EYE GRAPHIC: NEXUSPLEXUS
VR INTERFACE: PANUWAT SIKHAM
MOTHER ICON: CHANUT IS INDUSTRIES
ROLLING HILLS: VECTEEZY

PART ONE

"The technophiles are taking us all on an utterly reckless ride into the unknown. Many people understand something of what technological progress is doing to us, yet take a passive attitude toward it because they think it is inevitable. But we don't think it is inevitable. We think it can be stopped, and we will give here some indications of how to go about stopping it."

Theodore Kaczynski, the *Unabomber Manifesto*

CHAPTER 1

Snow fell in the quiet darkness. The flakes settled onto 20,000 cars in the stadium parking lot and dusted the footprints of the great crowds that had flowed to the entrance gates. Inside, the fans had bought their snacks and programs and branded shirts. They had taken selfies and found their seats. And now, they roared. The football season was making its drive to the end zone with an assault of lights and thundering noise. Crunch time. The Big Game.

Four minutes into the first quarter.

The air was electric as a punt sent the ball spinning over the running players. The receiver dropped the ball, and everyone piled on.

Burlie Brown stood on the sideline, watching and waiting. If the ball changed possession he'd be out there in a minute. High above the stands, the Jumbotron flashed an array of his biometrics – pulse, blink rate, sweat production.

From the great domed ceiling, the world's most powerful stadium lights illuminated the field. In the stands, spectators waved their arms and shoveled hotdogs. They hungered for human collisions and aggressive attacks and thrilling takedowns.

The broadcast booth jutted out from the tiers of spectators, providing the best seats in the house. Two commentators sat at the anchor desk.

Color commentator Scott Hopkins checked the stats. He looked at his partner and said, "Burlie's acting cool as usual, but his blood pressure is up and his heart rate's in a sprint. He wants out there."

When a player could dominate the game and the music charts at the same time, as Burlie had, everyone wanted to see him on the field making history on the big night… not standing on the sideline with a bunch of coaches, ball boys, and photographers.

Scott's partner, the other commentator, did not respond. As usual.

The man was a football legend, but Scott thought he was terrible at keeping up the banter. Not that anyone else seemed to mind – the guy had an effortless smile that covered a lot of flaws. Scott secretly called him Beamer.

"I'm a Burlie fan, and I can't wait," Beamer finally said. Stating the obvious.

Hell, *everyone* was a Burlie fan. The linebacker had delivered an exceptional rookie season with unearthly speed and flashy tackles, the kind you usually only saw in halftime demos by the augmented guys.

The refs pulled players off the pile.

"Miami has the ball," Scott said. "Burlie is heading onto the field."

The beat of the hot new single *Burlie Ball* blasted throughout the stadium.

"The crowd is singing along," Beamer said, as happy as if he had just sailed into the end zone, as he had in his own glory days. He swiveled his pudgy ass in a chair, tapping his finger on the table. "Burlie will join the cast of *Celebrity Island* in two weeks right here on T-Stream. By the way, thank you for joining us tonight for the final game of the postseason here in Nashville. Okay. Miami down at their forty-eight."

Scott handed his suit jacket to an assistant. The room was warm and he wouldn't be on-camera until the half-time recap. A bug flew past his eyes. He swished it away.

He knew Beamer would disapprove of him taking off his jacket. Scott didn't care. He wanted to be comfortable as he watched the monitors, consulted his laptop, and conferred with the production team. He leaned into his mic and spoke in a soothing baritone. "Rumor has it that Burlie might make an appearance in the half-time show. What do you think, any chance?"

"No," Beamer said. "I don't think so."

Scott forced a laugh. This sucked – to be always carrying the ball, always keeping the viewers entertained, but paid less than his do-nothing partner.

Burlie's InstaStat page flickered with blinking icons. Scott was growing concerned, but his analytical support team hadn't sent him any notes. He tapped off his broadcast audio. "Burlie's blood pressure is dropping in his arms and legs. How is that possible?"

Their lead producer shrugged. Scott tapped audio back on. "For those of you diving deeper into Burlie's InstaStats, he has a couple of warning flags. Something's probably wrong with his data feed. A lot of people say the league should go back to the pre-chip days. Chip errors have taken more than one healthy player out of the game."

Miami threw a nine-yard pass and Burlie tackled the receiver.

"How is he looking down there?" Scott pressed binoculars to his eyes.

"Burlie looks fine to me," Beamer said.

Beamer sipped water. An assistant primped his hair. The man's laptop had dropped into sleep mode. The diamond football on his massive ring glittered in the studio lights, tight on his finger.

Scott's college ring slid under its weight, refusing to stay put.

Beamer popped a chicken nugget into his mouth during a commercial break and whispered, "Put your jacket on." As the time-out ended, he leaned into his mic. "Hello, we're back, first down."

Scott watched Burlie through the binoculars as he lined up for the play. Returning to the InstaStats, he saw blood pressure rising in Burlie's head, but falling in his legs. And Burlie's heartbeat spiked randomly. Scott turned to the producers, pointed at the laptop, and mouthed the words "What the –?"

They didn't have a chance to respond. Miami prepared to snap the ball, but Burlie dropped to his knees, clutching his chest.

"Hold on," Beamer said.

Burlie's teammates rushed to his side as he collapsed to the turf. They motioned to the emergency crew. The players made room for two medics with a stretcher.

Scott handed the binoculars to a producer.

"Taylor seems ill, too," Beamer said, watching another player. "He's sitting on the field."

The broadcast booth burst into shouting and movement.

More medics advanced onto the field. They removed Taylor's helmet and checked his pulse. Fans jumped to their feet. Drones scanned worried faces.

Burlie appeared on the Jumbotron and waved. The crowd cheered. He lifted his right sleeve, flashing a tattoo on his massive forearm: *Strength.* He patted it and pointed toward the sky. But as they carried him into the crowd on the sidelines, his face contorted.

"Our prayers are with him," Scott said.

Screams erupted from the stands below the booth. Scott checked the drone cams and muted his mic. "Get a close-up. Who is that guy lying in the sidelines? Did someone faint?"

Frightened outbursts ripped through the stadium. A drone hanging over the crowd zoomed in on an elderly woman and positioned its shotgun mic. "My husband's not breathing!" she screamed. "Someone get a doctor!"

"What's happening?" Scott hissed. He took a slow breath and enabled audio. "Folks, a fan seems to have fainted. We are taking a brief break. We will return shortly."

The monitor with the broadcast feed switched to a commercial: A man sat in his home wearing a virtual reality headset, mouth agape. Behind him, robbers tiptoed around, stealing all his furniture.

Scott ripped his headphones off. "What the hell is going on? Talk to me!"

Most of the production crew had raced to the window. A secondary director said, "Zoom in over the thirty-yard line. Is that another fan down?"

"Live in fifteen... ten..."

"Damn, the medics are running around like crazy."

As the commercial ended, the virtual reality guy's house had been cleaned out, and still he played. A deep voiceover said, *The new K System. It's all you need.*

Someone shoved a sheet into Scott's hand and he scanned the page.

"We're back with several updates. Players Jackson Taylor and Burlie Brown are in serious condition. They are en route to the hospital."

A few feet away, Beamer touched his earpiece and said, "And at least two fans are being treated."

Lacking additional information, Scott winged it. "This is unprecedented. All we can do is wait for news from the medics."

Beamer looked down at the field. "Another fan has jumped from the stands and is running along the sideline. He's grabbing his chest. I don't want to be alarmist, but could this be a deliberate attack of some sort?"

Scott wiped sweat from his forehead. "We can't jump to that conclusion. Everyone, stay calm."

Too late for that. Below and all around, the fans were on their feet, pushing, screaming, and stampeding for the exits. Scanning the monitors, Scott saw people collapse amid the crushing throngs. He ripped off his headset and shouted, "Can we please get some facts about what's going on? People are in full-blown panic!"

On the field, at least three other players were down and surrounded by teammates, but not medics.

"The stadium doesn't have enough emergency personnel," Beamer said, almost to himself.

Scott swiveled back to his laptop and checked Burlie's blood pressure. 10/40. Almost dead.

The crowd had bottlenecked at the stairwells. Scott wiped a hand over his mouth.

"It's pandemonium down there," Beamer said. "Where's security?"

Scott felt disembodied.

"Get a shot down there–"

"Over there, Brian, the twenty-yard line."

"People are being crushed."

"The entire place is descending into chaos."

"People are jumping from the second level."

An assistant handed Scott another briefing. The news team was going live in thirty seconds to take over the broadcast. "I don't feel so good,"

Scott said.

He faced the camera. "Folks, we are witnessing a major disaster. We do not yet know–"

Pain pulsed in his chest. An odd sensation too… maybe warm water streaming through his upper body. He tumbled from his chair onto the floor.

An assistant rushed to help. Scott grabbed at her arm and experienced a shockwave of paralyzing pain. The room disappeared into a strange dark hole. He gulped for air, but each inhalation burned and suffocated.

What was happening?

Oblivion.

A woman lay on her bed gazing into a tablet in semi-darkness. Her eyes darted back and forth, hungry for information. The muscles at the corners of her mouth tightened. Not her most attractive look, the man thought, studying her as she gazed into the screen. Zoom in: she had pretty eyes, though.

Sensing that she was being watched, the woman paused.

Her lips puckered slightly. Were they quivering? Yes. She felt fear.

Fear, confusion, sadness, and anger.

The man smiled as FaceLab recognized these emotions and labeled them in capital letters that scrolled across his vision. SHOCK... DISGUST... ANXIETY... FEAR.

She had reason to be afraid, he thought.

The word SADNESS appeared and faded. He wanted to reach out and hug her, to comfort her.

He focused on each area of her face, his pupils expanding and contracting, seeking a view that would read further into her expression. He wished the software could read her thoughts. What machinations lumbered in her mind? But FaceLab only divulged the same basic information: ANGER... FEAR.

The woman sat only a few feet away, next to him in bed. He smiled. She ignored him.

Ronan Flynn sighed. "Honey, could you look more depressed? I'm calibrating."

She tapped from one website to another, searching for information about what had just happened at the game. Lisa had been doing this for over an hour.

"What?" Lisa raised the tablet and waved it. "Don't you want to know what's going on?"

"They don't have answers this soon. I don't care about speculation."

She sighed and narrowed her eyes. "Stop looking at me like that."

"Pretend you're about to cry, then maybe squint like you're in pain… just for a moment?" Ronan tapped his thumb and index finger together, then rubbed them twice.

Lisa noticed these movements. "Seriously? Can't you ever shut that stuff off? Have you called work?"

IRRITATION. That was a new one. FaceLab nailed it.

"That's a lot of questions," he said. With a tap of his fingers, the data overlays retreated into the background and disappeared. "Yes, I called. I'm on standby."

Her eyes fell. "Our vacation is out the window, isn't it? Experts are calling this a terrorist attack. You'll soon be off to help investigate. We may only have a couple of hours together before you have to leave, and all you can do is play with your toys."

He leaned against the headboard and adjusted his large frame, a feat that was always a bit of a challenge. He had lost his legs below the knees in an accident a few years before, and he still found it awkward to do simple acts like repositioning himself. He pushed with his arms and wiggled his torso. "These are not toys. Once voice analysis is ready, I'll be able to triangulate the human mind. I'm already detecting lies and emotions pretty well."

"Ronan, I can do those already without turning myself into a computer. Will you pay attention to me?"

His shoulders slouched. "But that's what I've been doing."

She snatched the TV's remote and turned up the volume. She was going to ignore him again. This was obvious, even without FaceLab.

"Calibration is important," he said, taking up his prosthetic legs, which he'd removed earlier for comfort. "I can't go out in the field with all my readings off. It's part of my job."

"Job? You do it for fun!"

"You know that's not true."

"Okay. I'm sorry. What did your office say?"

"Not much. We're waiting for answers like everyone else." Ronan smiled. "Don't worry. Something crazy is always happening in the world. No big deal. Let's iron out our vacation." He pulled a laptop from the bedside table. "I've done some planning."

With a slight twitch of his fingers, trying not to arouse her suspicions, he brought up the Defense Intelligence Agency's internal alert feed on his ocular. The trick was to read the updates while pretending to look her way, reading the words without focusing on them. There was a real art to it.

He got the gist of the alerts. No one knew a damn thing.

CHAPTER 3

Robert Saddler, Secretary of Homeland Security, rubbed his eyes. The action did nothing to clear the fogginess from his head. *I am alert and ready for action*, he told himself. The gentle swirling of the room suggested otherwise.

He squinted at his phone, then looked from face to face at those gathered around the table – advisors, intelligence officials, department heads. They had all been watching the game, just as he had, and based on the unfocused gazes on some of their faces, at least a few had been drinking heavily – as he had. They shifted uncomfortably. Were they prepared for a meeting of this magnitude? He needed a top-notch team right now. Instead, he had a collection of nervous drunks.

Saddler spoke in his most commanding voice, knocking them to attention. "The game was aborted in the first quarter. At least thirty-seven people are confirmed dead. Social media is thermonuclear. One of the top trending topics right now is Nashville Attack." He held up a finger. "Did you catch that? *Attack.*"

They were gathered at Joint Base Andrews, an Air Force facility in Maryland fifteen miles from the White House. The barren yellow walls and cheap rolling tables were no different than the conference rooms at thousands of hotels across the country, except that the uncomfortable office chairs were padded with brown camouflage cloth. The team had been summoned from their living rooms, where they left friends and popcorn bowls behind to speed across the suburban landscape for this emergency briefing. Several had thrown on a tie or nice blouse, but many wore T-shirts and sweatpants, and two still wore Detroit face paint. The tables were scattered with paper pads, yellow briefing sheets, Cokes, and coffees.

Thirty minutes from now, Saddler would fly to the stadium to see the pandemonium first-hand. He turned back to his phone. "Who wants to guess the *number one* trending topic?"

No one ventured an answer, so he said, "DHS Fail."

His team stared in shame, trying to focus their beer-addled minds. He tossed his phone on the table and paced. "Do you know what our problem is right now? Both are probably correct. It was an attack. And we failed."

He pointed at his chief advisor. "How many people exited the stadium, and how many are still inside?"

A pudgy man pushed his glasses up his nose and straightened in his chair. "About ten thousand individuals left the stadium in the initial stampede. The parking lot is a disaster – accidents, gridlock, fighting, lost kids, vandalism. We don't know how many people have left the area entirely. The National Security Force is on-scene and beginning to establish order, but things are still chaotic. The stadium stairs, escalators, and exits are all under control by armed security. Thirty thousand people are still inside. They will be held until we know the best way to deal with them. We don't know if they are infected, or if there are terrorists among them."

Stephanie Andrews, the senior analyst, pinched a cotton pad to remove paint from her face. "If terrorists were on site," she said, "they would have been the first ones out before the doors shut."

"Probably true," the chief advisor agreed, peering over his glasses. "But we can't be sure. Meanwhile, there is panic among those trapped inside. Rumors are spreading like viruses. The detainees believe they are all going to die, that the government is experimenting on them, that terrorists deployed advanced chemical weapons."

A young woman spoke. She was flipping through her phone. "People are saying it's Russia, it's China, it's Iran, it's... whatever. Many are predicting the attack used some kind of invisible weapon. Everyone is slamming us. Listen to this: 'Where is Homeland Security? We give them billions in taxes – for what?'"

Saddler looked at his watch. "The president is in Japan. He wants me at the stadium to represent Washington. What do you think? Should I hold a press conference?"

"Absolutely not," Stephanie said. "You can't go out half-baked. We need to get a handle on the situation."

"I disagree completely," another advisor said. "We need to control the messaging. All this speculation is just making things worse. We need to calm everyone down."

The others fidgeted with their pens. They nodded at both points.

Saddler held up his arms like a referee signaling a touchdown. "Raise your hand if you think I should do a press conference."

A few people raised their hands.

"How many think I shouldn't?"

The majority raised their hands.

Their boss mulled over the two options. He studied his chief advisor, who sat with fixed gaze and confident posture, but whose comb-over was dotted in sweat.

"I'd love to debate this," Saddler said, "but we don't have time. Tell the press I'll give them a statement upon my arrival."

Stephanie raised her eyebrows in alarm. Sighs and murmurs crisscrossed the room.

"Quiet! I've made my decision. Sharpen your pencils and get to work. I want a simple message."

On the table to his right, three monitors relayed the chaos unfolding at the stadium. He shook his head. What had happened? And how did they let it happen?

"Your message to the nation must convey order and control," his chief advisor began. "We must calm everyone down. Explain our process to address incidents like this and our timeline for letting everyone out of the stadium."

Saddler wrote a note on the pad in front of him. "Good. Keep going."

Stephanie spoke next. She had instantly aligned herself to Saddler's decision. "You need to mention a plan. Make it both specific and vague. You could say there are three steps that will be carried out immediately."

"I like that." Saddler gulped coffee. "Let's review our actual contingency plans and distill out three great-sounding points that don't mean anything."

"How about this," a man yelled from the back of the room. "Step one: every department of the intelligence community will make the investigation their top priority."

"I can't say that," Saddler said. "The president could authorize that before I get there, but I won't be the one to communicate it. Give me something else."

"Step one," someone else yelled. "We are confident that everyone on the inside is safe and that every contingency plan is currently being followed to the letter."

"That's on the right track," Saddler said. "But be more vague. And more concrete."

He smiled. His best people were proving their worth. A solution was close at hand. He glanced at his watch. They'd have to continue their discussion en route. He held up his hand and shouted. "Great start, team. Let's continue on the plane."

Groans. No one was going home tonight.

An alert popped up on Ronan's ocular: the head of Homeland Security was going to hold a press conference in ten minutes… at "ground zero." The same information now streamed across the TV.

Lisa noticed the announcement, too. The laptop and the vacation plans lay next to her on the bed. "You'll be called in. They'll want everyone in every department chasing every lead." Her dog, Ziggy, licked her hand.

"I don't think so," Ronan said. "The victims were accidentally poisoned by spoiled food or something, and even if this was an intentional act, poisoning isn't my area of expertise. Its got nothing to do with the DIA, certainly nothing to do with emerging technology."

Ronan adjusted the fit on his prosthetic legs while waiting for the press conference to start. He was rugged and broad-shouldered, an ex-military guy. Though once solidly built, his muscles had softened in recent years. His job was no longer physically demanding. These days, he did little more than drive around interviewing people and gathering intel for a variety of security investigations. Nothing too strenuous. Furthermore, he just wasn't very active since losing his legs.

A man in a black suit appeared on the TV before a crowd of journalists. He was inside the stadium in a meeting room that had been arranged to convey order and control. A line of armed guards and security personnel stood along the walls. The room fell to a hush.

"Good evening, I'm Robert Saddler, Secretary of Homeland Security. Tonight, we witnessed a tragedy that resulted in thirty-seven deaths. We mourn for those who lost their lives and pray for their families and loved ones. All deaths occurred within a short timeframe. There have been no new deaths or illnesses in the past three hours. We want to reassure the country that the situation is stable, and we detect no further threat. We have the stadium locked down and we're screening the vital signs of every person inside. Everyone in the parking lot has been detained and moved to safe facilities. Some people left the site, but they are all being located."

"The good news is that no one is exhibiting any signs of poisoning or infection. We are still pinpointing the precise cause of the deaths. The FBI, CDC, and Homeland Security are all onsite and we're taking careful steps to determine exactly what happened. We suspect a toxic agent, perhaps food poisoning, but we don't have conclusive evidence yet. We'll know much more in the next few hours. The smartest and most capable people are working on this. That's where we are currently. I've got a full plan of action that details how my department will move forward, but before I get to that, I'll take some questions."

Saddler pointed at someone off-camera. The TV cut to the gathered group.

A journalist in the front row stood. "We know that a lot of the spectators made it out of the stadium, and many of those went home or elsewhere. What if they are contagious?"

Saddler's face showed no change in emotion. "As I said, we will locate them all soon. There is no evidence that this is contagious, but we are implementing quarantine for anyone they come into contact with."

"But what if a contagion spreads quickly, and it is already too late to contain?"

Ronan turned up the volume.

Saddler shook his head. "We are on top of this." His voice took an edgy tone. "There is no reason for anyone to panic."

"I'm concerned this might be a targeted attack," another journalist said. "And if that's the case–"

"Listen," Saddler said. "We'll know more soon. It is *not* time for panic or conspiracy theories. Let's wait for the facts."

"What facts do we have?" a third journalist asked.

"Hold on." Saddler leaned on the podium. He took a deep breath.

"Please let me finish. We are initiating a three-part plan that will address these concerns. It covers exactly how we will determine the cause of this tragedy. This plan will reassure everyone that there is nothing to worry about."

Saddler cleared his throat, took another deep breath, and looked down. He turned to his advisors.

"What's he up to?" Lisa said, leaning toward Ronan's ear, unable to take her eyes off the TV.

Ronan shrugged.

As Saddler spoke with his advisors, they reached toward him, but he pushed their hands away. He nodded reassuringly, then approached the microphone again.

Instead of speaking, his face went white. He pulled at his collar. His aides ran to him and caught him as he collapsed to his knees.

"He's hyperventilating. Do something!" an aide yelled, and everyone in the world heard it.

"Like what?"

"Give him a bag to breathe into!"

Someone shoved a purse over Saddler's face, which he smacked away. His arms flailed for a moment as he clutched at his throat.

Medics pushed their way through the crowd and mounted the small stage. Saddler fell to all fours.

Lisa sat upright on the bed. Ronan squeezed her hand.

On the TV, Saddler jerked and screamed. The journalists yelled over each other, a rising din of questions and commands. They grasped at each other to pull themselves toward a better view of the podium, now completely blocked from the view of the cameras. Ronan muted the TV.

He and Lisa looked at each other. Ronan's phone buzzed. The caller was Edward Foster, his boss. He picked it up. "Got it," he said. "I understand." He ended the call.

"Well?" Lisa asked, fingers pressed to lips.

"You were right."

"They called you in?"

He nodded. "Edward's on his way to Nashville. I have to go, too. They don't know what's going on, but it's bad, Lisa. Saddler is dying, and that looked like a targeted act." He scooted to the edge of the bed and verified that his legs were securely fastened.

Lisa hugged him. "Don't forget about me, okay? I'm crazy scared. Let me know what's happening as soon as you can."

"I will." He kissed her. Always ready to travel at a moment's notice, he grabbed his pre-packed suitcase, and within five minutes had left the house.

Snow hit the windshield as Ronan left the suburbs behind. He pressed the accelerator with the heel of his prosthetic, feeling only the pressure against his thighs. When driving, he sometimes imagined he could feel his feet, especially when he was intensely concentrating on operating the car. Was it an illusion, or were the legs beginning to integrate into his physical identity? He moved his thigh again and the car gained speed.

Adrenaline kept him alert. He felt the thrill of heading toward the action, but at the same time, he had no interest in walking around a contaminated zone infected with a deadly pathogen. Surely, the high-risk areas would be off limits.

No doubt half the intel community would be there by the time he arrived: hundreds of officers from dozens of departments across all of the major U.S. intelligence services.

Ronan was just a single processing node in a massively complex system. In the military, he had completed three tours in Afghanistan until an accident while on leave cost him his legs, now he was a technical officer specializing in interrogations. Not that he was really good at that; he tended to be impulsive and impatient. No matter. His value during an investigation was to "record everything." Detect lies, link data, process the environment. He was mostly just a big data collection device.

The cornea of each of his eyes contained several tiny components. A camera recorded his surroundings, a chip analyzed everything, and a micro-LED panel projected words and data inward, through the pupil and onto the back surface of each eyeball. His brain then perceived those words hovering over their associated real-world objects. Various modules could tell him someone was ANGRY, for example, or identify millions of possible objects in his immediate environment, like a GLOCK 19 SEMI-AUTOMATIC PISTOL or an ANTIQUE SPOON or a BAG OF COTTON BALLS. Some of the information was more useful than others.

When he no longer needed these labels and words, he'd tap his fingers and they would whisk away like clever spirits. His ocular system also had some pretty handy hardware. A subtle electric current, when applied, extended the implant slightly into a sharp optical zoom. To someone looking at him, this made his eyes bulge a little, which was noticeable and unsettling.

He'd been slowly incorporating all of these physical and cognitive enhancements over the past year. Until now, he'd only used them in mundane assignments. This investigation was the big moment to prove the value.

He was excited, but nervous. He had too much personally at stake for this to fail, including his sanity.

On the road ahead, a large green highway sign announced the on-ramp to the expressway. He could head north to Dulles and wait for the earliest morning flight, or go south and drive the nine hours to the attack site.

He glanced at the time.

It was a long drive. He tapped his thumb, activated voice control, and called out a search of all flights with seat availability leaving Dulles.

ZERO.

Maybe the search missed an available flight. Probably not. And even so, the lousy weather might delay departure.

If he drove the entire way, the weather would clear as he got further south. And, of course, Driver Assist would keep him on the road if he dozed off.

That settled it. He took the expressway heading south and surrendered control. The car took over, easing away from the slushy edges of the road.

He relaxed into the seat, arms at his sides, leg sliding off the accelerator.

For Ronan, Driver Assist was more than a useful tool for someone with prosthetics. The feature represented an entire set of values – an endpoint and an ideal.

An hour later, he was asleep at the wheel and safely heading toward chaos.

While Ronan was en route, his boss was already in Nashville getting his first look at the victims. Edward Foster pulled into the back lot of a hospital just two miles from the attack and immediately felt the drag and friction of the lockdown. Two NSF officers blocked the entrance, checking the identity of anyone attempting to enter. A line of cars backed up in several directions.

As he waited his turn, he watched the two officers deny entrance to most of the vehicles. The National Security Force represented all the bullshit security machinery that he loathed. A lockdown was supposed to stabilize and control crowds in terrorist situations, but Edward considered them a charade – all for show. He inched his car to the closest officer, lowered the window, and showed his phone.

The officers wore the familiar outfit and gear of the NSF: brown camo, helmet with center cam and mic, automatic pistol on belt, automatic rifle slung over the shoulder.

"Do we really need a security force to guard a morgue?" Edward asked.

The officer scanned the Personal Identity Code on Edward's phone. *Bonk!*

A red light blinked on the scanner.

"Sorry, you're not authorized. Please turn the car around."

"Can you try again?"

The officer scanned Edward's code a second time. *Bonk!*

"Sorry, you have to turn the car around."

Edward leaned out so they could get a better look at him. "Please look at my credentials. I'm with MET."

The officer stared at Edward's phone.

Despite the cold night air, Edward could feel his temple begin to burn, sarcastic comments forming in his mind. The card identified him as the head of Management of Emerging Technologies, or MET, a relatively new division of the Defense Intelligence Agency. The officer handed Edward's phone to his partner. They whispered. The first officer spoke Edward's name into his mic, then said, "Office of... excuse me, *Management* of Emerging Technologies."

"Thank you for getting the name right," Edward mumbled, not caring if the officers heard him through the open window. He'd had no sleep, and a third coffee was getting cold in the cup tray. No chance of rest tonight. He needed to get through this morgue visit quickly. Ronan and Deanna were on the way to meet him for a debrief.

"Sir," one of the officers said. "You're not on the list. We'd like you to turn your car around immediately."

"Please call Jim Turlington. He's inside with Homeland Security."

This brought results. After a brief call, the officer returned Edward's phone. "You are cleared. Move forward."

Edward accelerated into the lot and parked.

A crowd waited outside the building's rear entrance. Thankfully, he saw no reporters or photographers. He pushed his way inside and a weary officer didn't protest.

"I'm glad you're here," a voice called. Jim Turlington, a Senior Investigator for Homeland Security, was built solid – the opposite of most Homeland Security officials Edward regularly dealt with. An old friend. Turlington smiled but his face betrayed anxiety.

They squeezed through the lobby and down an adjacent hall, where the crowd thinned.

"What's the verdict?" Edward asked, voice low. He assumed they were dealing with terrorism, maybe homegrown, maybe not. The method of death was strange. If he had to guess at this point, the victims had died from a fast-acting poison. Probably not a nerve agent; the symptoms didn't fit. Edward guessed cyanide or ricin. But there was a problem with that theory, too. How did the terrorists engineer a hit on the Secretary of

Homeland Security, just at the right moment, live on TV in front of millions of viewers, with no visible weapon?

"I can't say anything here. You need to see it," Turlington replied.

The cryptic response spooked Edward. If his colleague had simply said "cyanide" and left it at that, all would be well. Regardless, Edward was pretty sure the cause of death wasn't some kind of new weapon. This investigation wasn't going to fall into his department.

Turlington led him into a service elevator, built wide for gurneys to be maneuvered in and out. "Wait until the country gets its hands on whoever did this. No mercy."

Edward nodded.

They dropped a floor to the basement. In the dark hallways below, a handful of police walked from the opposite direction, heading back up. Storage and supply rooms lined both sides.

A sign taped to the wall at an intersection said *PATHOLOGY*. A red arrow pointed left. They went in that direction and arrived at a door with another sign: *NO UNAUTHORIZED PERSONNEL*.

They had arrived at the hospital morgue.

Here's the fun part, Edward said to himself.

The first thing that hit Edward was the sheer size of the room. Three of the morgue's walls had cold storage chambers from floor to ceiling. If war broke out right here in the city, they'd be ready for the bodies. Stainless steel sinks and glass cabinets lined the fourth wall. Large lamps hung from the ceiling in neatly spaced rows, ready to swing into position.

The second thing that hit him was the overpowering antiseptic smell. Edward felt a little nauseated. It was too soon for noticeable odors of decomposition from the game's victims, but he imagined that subtle death-smells must be starting to emerge from all those cadavers. He breathed through his mouth.

Four men in medical gowns conversed in the middle of the room, face masks down, and several police officers milled along the periphery, still wearing their coats. While the air was warmer in here than outside, it was chilly. The police looked like they were trying to concentrate on anything other than their surroundings, and several seemed about to vomit. The room was exceptionally clean and well lit. The bodies had been stored in the wall coolers.

"Watch your step," Turlington said, indicating a splash of vomit on the floor. He gestured to an assistant scrubbing a sink. "Can you get some absorbent on this?"

A short man talking to the group noticed their arrival. "Hi. Roberto Cevelas, Chief Medical Examiner." Though it was only 1 a.m., he'd already had a long night.

Edward cautiously shook the medical examiner's gloved hand.

Dr. Cevelas noticed Edward's hesitation and jumped. "Damn, I need to remove these." He snapped off the latex gloves and threw them into a biohazard container.

Edward glanced at his hand.

"Don't touch anything," Dr. Cevelas said. "Gonzalo, show Mr. Foster to the sink and disinfect his hands for two minutes with chlorhexidine."

After the assistant gave Edward's hand a quick scrub, which Edward thought was no more than thirty seconds at best, Dr. Cevelas brought him a gown and mask. "Keep this mask on at all times. Unless you are going to puke. In that case, please try to make it to the sink."

Edward surveyed the room. "How many of the victims are here?"

Dr. Cevelas ignored the question. "If you feel faint, sit on the floor and take deep breaths. Allow time to compose yourself. Take all the time you need. I don't want you falling on this hard floor and hurting yourself."

Turlington answered Edward's question about the number of victims. "We have thirty-four from the stadium, which is almost all of the victims. This is the largest morgue in the city, so they brought them here."

Like Turlington, Edward was outraged by the senseless attack and loss of life at the game, but he wanted to keep his emotions in check. He surveyed the room again and considered how many of those drawers were full. Men, women, and children had gone to the game excited for the biggest sporting event of the year, fans with their friends and families, and now here they were, housed in cold chambers to be analyzed and deciphered like coded mysteries.

He fixed on Turlington and the doctor. "What do we know so far?"

"Let's take a look." The medical examiner opened one of the cold chambers and slid a draped body onto a gurney. He wheeled it to the center of the room and positioned an overhead lamp.

"Where's the biosafety equipment?" Edward asked.

"On loan, but coming back on an overnight flight. We can't wait for it. Triple gloves and N95 masks are fine."

A tall, tanned man in a perfect suit seemed to notice Edward for the first time. He scanned Edward up and down. "Who are you?" he asked.

"Edward Foster, DIA. Management of Emerging Technologies."

"Haven't heard of that."

"You have now." Edward smiled.

"I'm Nicholas Click," the man said, extending his hand. "Central Intelligence Agency."

"How long have you been here?"

"Forty minutes."

"Good, I'm not too late."

"Wrong. You missed a good discussion," Click said.

"I'm sorry to hear that."

While DHS and CIA would likely take the lead on this op, covering both domestic and international investigations until it was determined where the attackers originated, Edward's group in the DIA would spearhead a parallel investigation, if appropriate – though that still seemed unlikely. The mission of his group, MET, was to predict how terrorists around the world might launch attacks on U.S. soil with new exponential technologies. Cheap weapons of mass chaos. Since Edward's group had expertise in this area, any incident along these lines would require his agency's help to get to the bottom of it. Edward hoped for a collaborative approach.

"What does the autopsy show?" he asked.

As Dr. Cevelas pulled back the sheet, Edward braced himself. He'd seen a few morgue autopsies and they hadn't been too hard to stomach. Six hours after death, the internal organs would be turning thick and dull as blood settled to the lowest point. Still, lifeless organs provoked a strong primal feeling of revulsion that was hard to overcome.

Dr. Cevelas had carved up the enormous body and studied every crevice. The primary incision sliced its way from the base of the neck to the groin, cutting through skin, fascia, and ribcage. The flaps were peeled back, opening the body wide for inspection. The ribs, pulled apart to expose the chest cavity, reminded Edward of alien jaws closing on a mouthful of organs. He leaned closer and saw deflated lungs, stomach, coiled intestines, and blobs of fat pushed to the side.

The victim's head remained covered by the sheet, but the arms, exposed and bare, were waxy. Edward could tell that he was a black male.

With Turlington and Click at his side, Edward felt compelled to ask the victim's identity, to hear the name, to assign a life to the body. Then he recognized a tattoo on the right bicep: *Strength*. He swallowed.

This cold, opened-up corpse, resembling a movie prop more than a man, could not be the vibrant, exciting, and beloved linebacker that everyone in the country had been cheering for seven hours earlier. It didn't seem possible.

"Damn, I hate to see him like that," Edward said. "That man was a warrior on the field."

"Dope rapper, too," the morgue assistant said.

As Dr. Cevelas began a didactic tour of Burlie's insides, using a scalpel to push here and there against pale tissue, Edward put a shaking hand to his stomach, attempting to subdue the growing nausea. He was glad he hadn't eaten anything. To get past the moment, he stared at the ceiling on the far side of the room. A fluorescent light flickered. That didn't help. His stomach fluttered.

"For the most part, his organs didn't sustain any damage and they all look healthy," Dr. Cevelas said. "But there is one obvious exception. Check out the heart."

The doctor used a tongue depressor to carefully lift a spongy glob of tissue – a mess that stretched as he pulled, much like melted cheese on a pizza slice.

Edward looked under the goopy blob but could not see the heart. "Can you scrape more of that off?" he asked.

Dr. Cevelas scraped the remaining gelatinous ooze into a specimen jar. He was wearing gloves again and, Edward noticed, had two or three pairs on top of each other. Edward still didn't see the heart. "Where is it?"

The doctor held up the specimen jar of ooze. "Here."

"Holy Jesus," Edward whispered.

Turlington interrupted before the doctor could respond. "They all look like that. Every one of the bodies is fine, except for the heart, which – well, all I can say is we have a whole bunch of specimen jars. We don't really have any hearts per se."

Edward stepped back from the cadaver, the entrails, the gloves, the specimen jar. He caught a glimpse of the flickering fluorescent light again, and, feeling unsteady, gripped the gurney. After a few deep breaths, he spoke, but didn't look again. "My God. It's like someone poured Drano into his heart. It just – *dissolved*."

The doctor started to speak, but Edward backed away, left the gurney, and headed toward the wall. The police officers watched.

Edward collapsed against the wall, breathless, and slid to a seated position. Damn, he thought, and cursed himself for not handling this better.

"Take your time," the doctor said. "You're fine. This is a normal reaction. You haven't been the first tonight."

Edward nodded.

"The morphology is disturbing and unusual," Dr. Cevelas continued. "The heart has no structure. It's almost liquid."

Edward held up a hand to indicate *shut up*. "What could do this?"

Click spoke. "We are looking at something like Streptococcus, which can cause necrotizing fasciitis, or another flesh-eating bacteria, like Klebsiella, or a virus, like Ebola or SP2.1."

"SP 2.1?"

"That's a weaponized version of smallpox discovered in the Middle East during the war in Syria, when rebels took control of one of Bashar al Assad's government buildings. Rumored to have been created in a Russian-Syrian collaboration. It's suspected to have a ninety-nine percent fatality rate inside twenty-four hours. I wouldn't be surprised if that's what we have here. Regardless, we think it was a bacteria or virus juiced up by a military somewhere."

"Maybe," Edward said.

"Not *maybe*." Click stared. "A bacteria or virus is the obvious explanation. This certainly wasn't caused by a poison. The damage was confined to the heart. A poison wouldn't do that."

"There are other possibilities."

Click smirked and looked down at Edward. "Of course. That's why you are here. There are already a ton of conspiracy theories, and you are welcome to check them all out."

So that's how it is going to be, Edward thought. *NOT collaborative.* He let the comment slide and got back on his feet. "The deaths started four minutes into game time. They ended six minutes later. Assuming all the victims were exposed at the stadium, that means extremely rapid onset and death. I am not aware of any weaponized bacteria or virus that acts so soon after infection. Do we have a good handle on the capabilities of bioweapons from other countries? How fast can the latest viral weapons replicate?"

"We don't have all the intel gathered from our internal sources yet," Click said.

"How do you think the victims were infected?"

"Chairs, drinks, railings. We are checking the entire facility, top to bottom."

Edward's shoulders trembled and he felt the cold of the exam room. But his reaction was caused by more than the chilliness. He was realizing with growing concern that the agency heads had already discussed their options and drawn the wrong conclusions.

He pressed on. "If this was on a surface like a chair or railing, how did they attack Bob Saddler so precisely?"

"That was a coincidence," Turlington said, revealing that he was on board with Click's theories. "Look, there are some unknowns right now, but let the experts work out the details. We don't know which bug we're dealing with yet. Any foreign military could have reduced the incubation period and boosted the fatality rate of a naturally occurring lethal microorganism. We'll know a lot more soon. Let our people do their job. We have the best infectious disease teams in the world."

Edward nodded, but only to acknowledge he was conceding to authority, not that he agreed. "One other thing is bothering me."

"And what would that be?" Click asked.

"How did the deaths all occur within a couple of minutes, then stop just as suddenly? What prevented further infections?"

At this, Click narrowed his eyes. "I don't know what you want me to say. This wasn't caused by a poison. The experts tell me this is the work of a genetically enhanced bacteria or virus. I know there are all kinds of crazy theories flying around already, and you are free to explore any and all of them. I want you to do that. Leave no stone unturned."

Edward couldn't keep the sarcasm from lacing his words. "Terrific. We are on the same page. I will take this to my team to explore other options."

"Please do that."

Edward had to leave, fast. Their theory didn't match enough of the key details to be plausible. The deaths all started together, then abruptly stopped at the same time. The internal damage was highly targeted. Edward realized the entire investigation across multiple departments was heading down the wrong path.

At this very moment, the entire DHS, FBI, CIA, and CDC apparatus, thousands of people strong, was moving into gear. MET was marginalized. Unless the leadership changed their thinking soon, they were going to lose a lot of valuable time. They had already convinced themselves they were on the right track. That was dangerous. Their mistaken theory would be institutionalized by daybreak.

Furthermore, he already had some theories of his own. If he was right, the future he dreaded was already upon them.

Edward would have to move forward with limited support. *I've got to get this information to Ronan and Deanna,* he thought.

CHAPTER 8

In the noisy industrial section of Johannesburg, a man in a lab coat emerged from a car, locked it, and set off down a trash-strewn road. Several steps later, he came to an abrupt stop. He returned to the car and threw his lab coat in the back seat. *No point in bringing that,* he thought. Besides, it was damn hot out.

He had parked five blocks from his destination. The scientist didn't come to this part of town often. If he didn't have an important delivery to make, he would not have come. Too unsafe. Sure, there were plenty of people around – factory workers, aimless druggies, a few dealers – and many of them were harmless enough. But even among the hardscrabble workers, some of them had undoubtedly spent their paycheck already and might be desperate for cash. It wasn't uncommon to be yanked into an alley for illegitimate purposes.

The scientist was here to meet people more dangerous than street thugs, of course – they were cold-blooded murderers – but at least his partners didn't want to kill *him*. He hoped.

At the end of a cracked and crumbled sidewalk, he arrived at an empty parking lot and abandoned warehouse.

The view from the street offered no clues that anything was happening inside, but the man knew that a lot *was* going on. The workers in the warehouse were accustomed to secrecy. They didn't appreciate visitors, but his role was important to them.

He heard the pit bulls barking deep in the building, ready to attack if needed, and wondered if this entire endeavor was worth the risk. So many things could go wrong. He was a nanobiologist, for God's sake. What was he doing here?

If today's delivery was their last requirement from him, he might not make it out alive.

I'm just paranoid because they have started their attacks, he thought. The Nashville attack was just the beginning.

As he made his way across the parking lot, he glimpsed a large man behind him. His heart pounded. He glanced at his pursuer, a guy with scraggly white hair and a wide toothless smile, and their eyes met.

He picked up his pace across the lot, which was empty except for a banged-up car or two. He realized the two of them were alone. Just another thirty feet or so...

The toothless man was directly behind him now, their steps almost in sync. Would Toothless attack him right here in daylight? The warehouse windows were boarded up; if he was attacked, no one inside would hear or come to his aid. He prepared himself for a fight. Fifteen feet.

He sensed the man right behind him.

Toothless arrived at the door at the same time he did. They looked directly at each other from just a few feet apart. The man's eyes were wild and intense, staring through a matte of hair. Though he looked to be in his sixties, his heavily tattooed arms were thick and muscular; he glistened with sweat and reeked of arm pit. Toothless raised a beefy hand, but instead of grabbing the scientist, he opened the door for him.

"Cape Buffalo?" the toothless man asked, addressing him with a code name. The man's mouth contorted as he spoke, overcoming the lack of teeth to deliver his fricatives.

The scientist nodded, clutching his hands to prevent them from shaking.

They entered a tiny lobby with an empty receptionist's desk. Toothless stared at him, then grinned with his empty mouth hole. "The boss is waiting. He's on the video feed. Follow me."

The scientist followed the imposing man down the hall, through a heavy steel door and into a noisy manufacturing area. Rows of industrial fabricators churned at top speed. Each machine had a chute at the side. Bins of empty plastic tubes lay on the floor. Neatly stacked tubes lined the ends of the tables. The fabricators cranked out tiny biting machines – and the scientist wasn't in the loop on that.

Then he passed the chemical synthesis machines, just before they reached the far side of the room. The synthesizers were lined in neat rows, like the fabricators, but these machines were much quieter and identical to the ones he had in his own lab. *They're producing the instruction sets I gave them last time*, the scientist thought.

His role in the Nashville attack was now tangibly real. Everything unfolding was his fault. He put his worries aside for a moment and continued to follow his toothless escort. Best to look calm and detached when he was face to face with the boss.

Toothless led him into an office behind the manufacturing area and shut the door. The scientist took a seat and felt a welcome blast of air conditioning. A laptop rested on a table. On the screen, a bug-eyed man leaned forward, the skin of his face cured into a deep brown by countless days in the tropics. A crude sun was tattooed on his cheek, etched in blazing orange ink, a symbol, perhaps, of domination and unrelenting power. This man was the boss of the entire terrorist operation being conducted inside the warehouse. *Thank God he was thousands of miles away.*

"Ah, Cape Buffalo," the man on the screen said, his hair hanging in tangled strands across his enormous eyes. "Thank you for coming. I am always excited by your visits. Did you bring me anything new?"

The scientist fished into his back pocket and held up a small drive. "Yes."

A man screamed from somewhere in the warehouse, and the scientist jerked.

The boss in the computer smiled. "Don't mind the noise. We're conducting some fun trials. You seem unable to verify the function of each batch, so we experiment on test subjects. Our lab is in the right part of town for finding volunteers."

The scream trailed into a wail of agony.

The boss gave a thumb's up. "I can't wait to try out your new ones."

"I've detailed the effects on rats and rabbits, Mr. Harper…"

"Don't say my name!"

The man on the laptop was crazy, no doubt. He was the leader of a group of social rejects who hated modern life. They lived in a rainforest and called themselves the Kazites, after Ted Kaczynski, the Unabomber. The scientist had never met the boss, but knew his full name – Jonathan James Harper. "Speaking of my name," Harper continued. "From now on, you will address me as *My Beloved*. Understand?"

The scientist forced a faint smile. He had a moment of doubt, as he had many times before, about partnering with such an unstable person. "Why do you want people to call you... *My Beloved*?"

"I don't."

The scientist was annoyed. "I'm not following, sir."

"Not people. Only you." Harper leered through a scraggly lock of hair. "Go ahead, try it."

The scientist stared at the screen for a moment. He cleared his throat. "My Beloved."

Harper clasped his hands together and collapsed into a laugh. "Wonderful. In time, you will see me as such." He leaned closer and pointed with a middle finger caked in dirt. "The words *My Beloved* will keep you in a loving mind toward me and loyal to the Kazites. In short, it's for your safety. Remember that."

Fuck this, the scientist thought. He composed himself and nodded toward his thumb drive. "Here are three new instruction sets."

"Three?"

The scientist nodded.

Silence.

"Three?"

"Yes, My Beloved."

Harper leaned back and seemed lost in thought. "I am very happy with the first attack."

"We have their attention."

"Agreed, and we did it with less than fifty biters. Do you know how many biters we have in that room you just walked through?"

The scientist had no idea. Obviously, a lot. He shook his head.

"Three million," Harper said.

"Three... *million?*"

"And we are just getting started."

The scientist's stomach sank, a hopeless feeling, like seeing a car accident happen right before his eyes. "At a certain point, it starts to defeat the purpose."

"We may disagree at a few ideological junctures. But you miss my meaning. My men are working day and night. All you must do is log into a computer. Do we agree on that?"

The scientist sensed the toothless man watching him. "Yes."

"So, why is it any harder to copy a dozen instruction sets, or a thousand? Do you think I am a damn idiot?"

"No, of course not. But I was trying to get the most impactful ones... and I need to login at times that won't draw attention."

"I'm so frustrated with you." Onscreen, Harper leaned back.

The scientist tried to think of something that might explain the situation but sensed there was no point in trying. He steadied his hands.

"We need to go big," Harper said. "The attacks must re-orient the worldview of every man, woman, and child. Nothing short of God-like power is going to do that. And any minute now, the planet will be crawling with defense intelligence assholes. The U.S. will launch counterterrorist operations. We have a very short window. Do you get this?"

"I do." The scientist gripped his knees.

"Three files. As in, one... two... three?" Harper moved close to the screen, his teeth as dark as a tannin-stained river. "I want everything on your network. I will decide what is useful. We tried one batch that left a guy vibrating like a jack hammer. Didn't kill him at first. He eventually died because he couldn't eat. I'm not a sadist, but this is powerful. This is exactly our point, right?"

The scientist listened to the hum of the fabricators as they churned out the attack vectors in various shapes and forms... the biters, as Harper had called them. The sheer volume of production output, if Harper was telling the truth, had shocked him.

"This can really change the framework, Cape Buffalo. This may be the last chance."

"I understand the vision," the scientist said and panicked, realizing he had almost said *your* vision.

"Good. I just need a simple yes or no. Can you bring me at least five hundred files next time?"

"Yes."

"I won't let anything ruin this opportunity. The world is awakening within its virtual cocoon. Breakout is coming. There is one chance left."

The screaming man in the nearby room was pleading now, the kind of hopeless, primitive pleading that doesn't expect any mercy.

The scientist's hands trembled.

"Are we in this together, Cape Buffalo?"

"One hundred percent."

"Take yourself back to work, then, and get what we need. We are out of time."

The scientist stood, stiff and damp, and hurried back into the manufacturing room. The large steel door shut behind him, muffling the man who was being experimented on, now moaning, past the point of fight or hope.

The scientist returned to the empty lot. Even among the growing noises of the city, he thought he still heard the last sounds of death emanating from inside.

What would happen when Harper no longer needed him? He didn't know. Therefore, he would get Harper the requested files, but he would also plan a safe exit from this relationship.

Several flies buzzed around his head. He jerked away. Nearby, a dead dog lay in the hot sun, plagued by a cloud of flies. For a moment he had a chilling vision of a swarm, not of real flies, but something far worse.

Ronan had almost reached his destination and was back at the wheel, speeding through the sparse early morning traffic. He'd left the snowy roads behind, and the eastern sky was brightening. His phone warbled, interrupting Burlie's *Take Back the Ball.*

"Yes, boss."

"Get online." Edward's voice boomed from the car's speakers. "There's a live feed on Kaleidoscope. Someone's claiming responsibility for the attacks."

"What's Kaleidoscope?"

"Search for the app."

"It's not coming up," Ronan said, tapping his thumb against his index finger. "Hold on." He pulled his Elano Flexdrive into a convenience store lot and braked.

"Got it?"

"Not yet."

"Go to XN. They're streaming it, too. Hurry."

A few seconds later Ronan had the feed on his right ocular. Floating in his vision, two news anchors sat behind a desk. An inline video showed a wild-haired man on a horse positioned against a rainforest or similar tropical environment.

"...he appears to be warning about technology," one anchor said.

"Yes, Anika, *if* this is the group responsible – we don't know that yet."

Ronan heard a snippet of the wild man's speech: "– a bit about what is happening. Again, we can kill anyone we want, at any–"

"He's threatening to attack again and seems to be claiming the ability to do so at will."

Ronan banged the steering wheel. "Stop talking, you imbeciles."

The two anchors did stop talking and the terrorist's video went full screen. With two taps, Ronan expanded the view. Beyond the ghosted video images floating in his vision, people in the parking lot strolled in and out of the store.

The man in the video slid off his horse. "You will never see us coming. Your beloved technology allows us to dominate you. Your hyper-socialization makes it impossible for you to comprehend how weak you are. See how easy it is for a little group like us to strike terror into the entire industrialized world?"

A crude leather garment wrapped the man's upper and lower face, but crazy eyes peered through, and a hole had been cut for his mouth. Dirty dark hair sprouted from the top of the leather mask and poured over his face in tangled mats, like a filthy mop. The rest of his body was concealed in a drape of enormous, loose-fitting leaves. The man and the horse stood before a dense growth of tropical trees and bushes. Nothing except the occasional bird moved in the forest.

"We're just getting started," he continued. "We took down the United States' Secretary of Homeland Security while you sat at home wetting your pants. How many of you are on anti-depressants just to cope with a society you can hardly stomach? Now you look at me, your *savior*, and think, 'oh, he's just another guy with another opinion. I don't want to hear any more opinions. I'm happy where I am now.' Well, my friends, I've got the courage to stand up for us."

Ronan dimmed the feed in his left eye and glanced at his surroundings. A small crowd inside the convenience store watched the news on an overhanging TV. He returned his attention to the video.

The man outstretched his cloaked arms. In the mask hole, the mouth grinned. "It was easy! And we're primitives! Imagine what people who *like* technology could do."

Although most of the man's body was deliberately covered, his hands were bare, revealing several tattoos, which Ronan expanded and enhanced: a Celtic sun and waves, crudely drawn.

"This was your wake-up call. You've had many warnings in the past, but you won't be able to ignore the message any longer. Technology is destroying you. It owns you. It controls you. We are here to demonstrate what happens when your society – *my* society – is completely infected with technology on every level. You love technology in your heart, and now you have it in your bloodstream."

The horse stamped as the man yanked its reins.

"What's he got against technology?" Ronan wondered aloud.

The man bent down and dug his hands into the loose ground. "How can you avoid damning yourself? It's easy. Get back to the earth. Grow your own food. Use simple tools. Don't let technology ensnare you. You were born to live in the earth, not in a machine." He paused to swat at a bug in front of his eyes. "But let's be honest, most of you are pretty stupid and won't understand what I am talking about."

The man did a herky-jerky movement and said, "The monkey needs terry cloth. Reality not technology."

The video went black.

The speech was automatically saved to Ronan's cloud drive. Well, he thought, that was a crazy motherfucker. Was that really the guy who orchestrated these attacks?

Ronan wondered what the world would do with this insane information, and then Edward's voice boomed again.

"Ronan, where are you? Hurry the hell up!"

"On my way." He threw the Elano into gear and blasted back onto the road, where traffic was beginning to pick up.

Ronan arrived at a lonely industrial complex and found the nondescript building where Edward had arranged the meeting. He swung into one of the many empty spots and cut the engine. Emerging from the car, he stretched. His back hurt. At six feet two, he was a big guy, but not as solid as he used to be in his army days.

A sparkling silver Porsche occupied the space directly in front of the doors. Odd. Edward avoided flashy vehicles, so who was this?

He shielded his eyes and peered through the Porsche's tinted windows. There were several sheets of paper on the passenger seat. Out of habit, he tapped his fingers and snapped a few pics with his ocular. He liked to know as much as possible about anyone he might be working with.

Inside, the single hallway was was dark. Light shone from a room at the far end. He entered and found a woman sitting with papers scattered on a table in front of her.

"Hi, I'm Ronan Flynn," he said.

"Deanna Pirelli."

"Nice to meet you. Where's Edward?"

She nodded. "Getting coffee."

Ronan threw his bag on the table and unzipped it. He pulled out a keyboard. "Just drove in from Virginia. I slept most of the way."

"Lucky you. I never went to sleep."

Ronan noticed a dark shadow under her eyes. "Sorry. I can see you've had a long night. I'm looking forward to getting filled in."

He synced the keyboard with his ocular and darkened the lower half of his vision to make a workspace.

As Deanna studied her laptop, he wondered about her role. She reminded him of the women he'd served beside in the military – serious, tough, disciplined. Shoulder-length hair pulled into a pony tail. Eyes cool and confident. With a shock, he realized she resembled a woman he had known once – but he didn't want to go there, and he forced it out of his mind immediately.

Her gaze drifted toward a bank of monitors at the front of the room. Each had a frozen video still from the game. Several monitors were zoomed in on something, but the resolution was poor.

"When did you get here?" he asked.

She clicked a pen. "Two thirty. I was only a few hours away. Edward flew in from Washington and went to the morgue. He filled me in on your background. He speaks very highly of you." She eyed him with a hint of a tired smile. "Former Sergeant in the Army, three tours of duty in Afghanistan. Honorable discharge after losing your legs. Now at MET, doing field intel. Testing body augmentations. He said not to get freaked out if you sometimes extend your eyes slightly."

"All true." Ronan paused on the keyboard and gestured to his eyes. "500:1 zoom, radar-based PulseView, micro-LED display projecting onto the fovea at the back of each eye, data overlay controlled by my fingers. I also have prosthetic legs with boosted strength and a few other augs. Testing it all for field use."

She stared at him.

Taken aback by what he thought might be a smirk, he returned to his typing. "It's all a bit wonky. I wouldn't run out and get yourself any of this yet."

"No worries." She smiled. "There's Edward."

Edward rationed his movement with slow and deliberate steps. Ronan recognized the walk. When his boss worked long hours, he switched into something Ronan called Energy Saving Mode – by restricting his calorie burn, Edward could stay active around the clock for a week, relying only on short naps. Edward's mind wasn't razor-sharp in this mode, but it helped him power through crises. He gave Ronan a warm nod.

"Here's where things stand," Edward said. "The CIA and Homeland Security have large teams moving into action. They will run a face ID and license plate scan on every individual and vehicle who was within five miles of the stadium yesterday. That will check employees, delivery trucks, security, foot traffic, and every car that passed through the area."

"Good start," Ronan said.

Edward nodded. "And maybe they'll find something."

"What's our mission?"

They both knew that MET was always a sort of backup plan on any op, a hedging of the bets. The agency's mandate was to monitor, track, and evaluate developing technologies for terrorist potential, especially systems that could be cobbled together at low-cost, with the assumption that all reasonably dangerous technologies would eventually be used to wreak violence and havoc in the public sphere.

Edward said, "We need to generate and investigate theories. The entire intelligence and security community is engaged. We'll collaborate and share progress, but I have to tell you, the other departments are way off base. They believe we are dealing with a conventional bioweapon. I don't agree. I think we are in strange new territory. Deanna and I have made some progress." Edward fussed with a remote and rewound the footage on one of the screens.

Ronan laughed to himself. The guy who headed up one of the most cutting-edge divisions of the intel community often had trouble with basic technology. But Edward had a gift. He could see a path through the noise, a way of connecting data points that often looked haphazard and ridiculous to everyone else, but which in retrospect was glaringly obvious and simple. Edward kept MET aimed in the right direction.

Edward continued. "The chief medical examiner has opened most of the victims. A couple of the families didn't cooperate, but the others consented. We've done thirty autopsies, including Robert Saddler, the Secretary of Homeland Security. I saw one of the victims a few hours ago, just before Deanna arrived. In each case, something got into their body and mucked up their heart. And when I say mucked up, I'm not exaggerating."

Ronan glanced at Deanna. "Mucked up? Like filled with sludge or something?"

"No," Edward said. "Like when you melt cheese in the microwave."

Ronan was baffled. "What happened to the rest of the body?"

"No trace of damage anywhere else." Edward slurped from his cup. "Coffee, Ronan?"

Ronan wanted coffee in his veins but wanted the debrief more. "Not yet, thank you."

"Take a look at this." Edward slid a photo across the table. The image showed a flask with something red in it.

Ronan zeroed in on the photo and did a quick search of any known substance with the same color and consistency as the contents of the flask, and a ghosted image popped up in his field of view. The image showed a strawberry banana smoothie. What a crappy match – he needed an upgrade. "Let me guess. Is that a heart?"

"Bingo," Deanna said.

"What could do this?"

Deanna picked up another document from the table. "Edward and I suspect that the internal damage was caused by a nanoweapon. Militaries all around the world are experimenting with them."

She handed this second document to him, a diagram of an object he didn't recognize. The thing looked like a biomolecule, maybe an enzyme or other protein.

Edward watched him, waiting for a reaction.

Finally, Ronan spoke. "I could stare at this all morning, but unless I get that coffee, my brain just isn't going to register anything." He excused himself.

...

He found the coffee machine in a small room across the hallway. The brew had been cooking on the burner for quite some time. He poured a dollop into a foam cup; the smell was awful. However, the caffeine was still in there, so down it went.

Now, Ronan thought, *a quick search on nanoweapons.* He tapped his fingers and bright blue text scrolled across his vision. He tried a few links, but they led to information-dense PowerPoints. A quick overview or fact sheet would have been nice.

Deanna strolled in and picked up the pot, sloshing the black poison around. "You didn't drink this, did you? I'm going to need you alive if we are going to get our hands on the Timeout Terrorists."

He forced down a few gulps. "Is that what people are calling them?"

"Yeah, pretty lame if you ask me. I'm sure the growing hurricane of tweets and posts will settle on something catchier."

"I can think of a few names for them. But I will keep those to myself."

She had a hint of an up-turned eyebrow and seemed to pick up on his anger. "Yeah, we are dealing with a pretty sick group. Only the best intelligence and analysis will give us any chance of staying ahead of the next attack."

Ronan nodded. "My enhancements allow me to analyze everything, all the time. I've just added more software. There are kinks to work out, but I believe this will help when we start interviewing people."

"I'm glad we are trying it."

They headed back to the meeting room, coffee in hand. Edward appeared ready to continue.

...

Ronan settled back into his seat. "Did this molecule come from a military lab?"

"I don't think so," Deanna said. "Let's assume the crazy guy in the video was directly involved in the attack. If so, this is do-it-yourself terrorism. Dozens of companies and university labs are conducting nanotech research. Maybe a rotten apple in the civilian sector went rogue."

"I follow you, more or less. How does that thing get inside you?"

"To be accurate, *billions* of molecules of it get inside you. But you're right, they need a delivery mechanism, an attack vector. Edward and I have reviewed footage from the attacks. The answer is right there." She gestured to the front of the room.

Edward was cueing images on the monitors but having trouble freezing them where he wanted. Every image was a blur. "Take this one, for example," he said.

Ronan squinted and boosted sharpness with his ocular, but neither helped.

"I apologize for the blurriness. You'll get hands-on with them in Taipei. That's a mosquito sitting on someone's neck."

"It looks like a dark blur sitting on a less dark blur."

Deanna aimed a laser pointer at the screen. "Look. Six legs, wings, eyes, proboscis… but everything is a bit off."

"I'll take your word for it," Ronan said. "Hold on. Taipei? As in Taiwan?"

"We suspect this is a microdrone," Edward said. "Used for spying and other types of data collection. Deanna wants you to go with her to check out a company in Taiwan called LikeLife. They've become the largest manufacturer of microdrones and microbots in the world."

"What is your role in this investigation?" Ronan asked her.

"I'm leading it."

Ronan turned back to Edward. "You're sending me to Taiwan? Because there was a mosquito or two in the stadium? I've got these in my back yard. I'm sure they've got them in Taipei too, but jet fuel's expensive these days. Seems kind of far to hunt mosquitos."

Edward rubbed his forehead. "You know we don't have any mosquitos here in February. I'm putting Deanna in charge because she is much more familiar with this market. Visit LikeLife. I want you to find out if they make this microdrone, and who buys it."

"Let me summarize," Ronan said. "Those blurry blobs there…" he waved toward the monitors, "…bit people and injected them with these artist's renditions here?" He flapped the molecule drawing.

"Exactly. As flimsy as that theory may seem at first, I think it's a strong one. Regardless, those mosquitos are the best lead we have at this point. LikeLife makes machines like that."

"I drove down here to interview people. You want me to rush to the opposite side of the world when at least some of the terrorists may still be here in Nashville?"

"Exactly. Deanna has good instincts. It's worth the gamble. You're going."

Deanna stared at Ronan, unblinking.

"Fine. Sorry for the tone. For the record, I don't think this is the best use of our time."

"Noted." Deanna smiled.

Edward clapped his hands. "We're fueling up Khatib's plane right now. You get to fly in luxury."

Chapter 11

Lisa's phone buzzed from the back pocket of her jeans as she fumbled with the keys to get inside the apartment. Ziggy pushed inside, his leash tangling around her leg. Her phone buzzed again.

She threw the keys on the counter, tossed the leash, and grabbed the phone. "Hey, babe."

"Honey, how are you?"

"I'm fine. Today was hectic. Ziggy has stomach issues. I've taken him out three times, but he still made a mess in the front room."

"Did you let him eat fatty beef from your plate again?"

"I suppose that could have happened."

Lisa settled on the sofa and the dog joined her, resting his head between his paws. She ran a hand along his back.

"I miss you," Ronan said.

"Well, *you* left *me*."

"What are you doing now?"

"Petting Ziggy. Getting ready to clean the kitchen, take the garbage out, check the bills. The usual fun. Have you learned anything? What's going on?"

"You know I can't tell you."

"I know... they don't have any clue who killed those people, do they?"

"You're on the right track," he said.

She wished they wouldn't have to play these games. He knew he could trust her with any information. Maybe if she could tell what he was thinking, he wouldn't have to *tell* her anything. But she never knew what he was thinking.

"Listen, honey," he said. "I have to take a trip. For a week or so."

"Where?"

"I can't tell you the country, but it's on the other side of the planet."

"You don't sound happy."

"I was outgunned. I didn't think this trip was the best use of my time, but I have to follow orders."

She heard commotion in the background. Men shouting instructions in what sounded like a big space, maybe an airplane hangar. She kicked off her shoes and propped her legs on the coffee table. Beside her, Ziggy wheezed in semi-sleep. Leaning back with eyes shut, she asked, "Are they pairing you up again?"

On the other end of the connection, he hesitated. "Yes, I'm going with an analyst from another department within the DIA. An expert on – an area related to our investigation."

"That's nice. Have you worked with him before?"

"The analyst is a she – Deanna Pirelli."

Lisa opened her eyes and raised an eyebrow. "You're going with a woman?"

"I'm going with a female DIA officer, yes."

Lisa hated to ask more questions but couldn't help herself. She'd always been a little insecure, even though Ronan had never given her any reason to worry. But in the past, she'd been blindsided when she least expected it, from boyfriends she had trusted. So who could blame her?

"Just the two of you?"

She heard more yelling, something about a plane. They must be fueling or loading it. He was going to be gone awhile.

He hadn't answered her yet.

Was he indifferent to the question... or pretending to be? She caught herself in the wall mirror. A lifetime of self-doubt flooded back. Almost getting married. The discovery of cheating.

After a moment he responded, as though he had just realized they were talking. "Yes, just the two of us."

She tried to be funny. "So, you are running around with a hot secret agent?"

"Umm..."

"Or would you say she is unattractive?"

"I wouldn't call her ugly, no."

"I see..."

Lisa shook her head. She knew she was out of line.

The silence grew and stretched into awkwardness and finally Ronan spoke. "Can we change the subject? Let's talk about vacation."

This was just like Ronan to take off for God knows how long, to God knows where, with no information on who he was with, except that the "he" was a "she." Lisa opened her laptop and typed in D-e-a-n-n-a P-i-r-e-l-l-i. *Tap. Search.*

"She's gorgeous."

And Deanna looked a lot like someone else... which she found disconcerting.

When he spoke again, Lisa noted irritation. "Gorgeous is too strong a word. I'm not going to argue about something this ridiculous. I don't even get along with her. She's got an attitude. We need to talk about our vacation. Did you look at the info I left?"

"Yes, and it is full of bird pictures and bird notes and birding locations. We're looking for birds again? What happened to the beach?"

"We can go to the beach," he answered. "I'm good with that. Los Lances Beach is known for Audouin's Gull. It's one of their specialties."

Lisa scratched Ziggy behind the ear, searching for inner calm. "What's with you and birding?"

He sounded relieved that the conversation had shifted to birds. "I've seen 8,679 birds. Less than fifty people in the world have that many birds on their list. It's almost unheard of."

She smiled. "Yeah, but you can zoom in on any bird, take a photo, and then your head chip identifies the species. That seems like cheating."

"You know how to take the fun out of a guy's hobby."

"Speaking of cheating..."

"God, what?"

She was pacing the room now, one hand jammed into her arm pit. "I can trust you, right? With this Deanna woman?"

His voice sounded far away and mingled with the background noises. "Yes. You can trust me. For God's sake, Lisa."

CHAPTER 12

As soon as the Windslicer was airborne for the fifteen-hour trip to Taipei, Ronan fell asleep.

The plane was larger than the average private jet, designed for speed and luxury. The plane's owner, Nazia Khatib, was an Israeli billionaire who had helped launch MET as a fledgling agency within the DIA. She had simply pulled some legislative strings and moved money around in ambiguous ways.

Now that MET had an upper hand in something for once, as Edward had explained to her, she had a strong incentive to make this mission a success: if MET could get more influence within the intelligence community's decision game board, she could start funneling all of her company's high-tech products into government contracts. She had funded all of Ronan's software and hardware – the ocular surveillance system, the prosthetic legs, an oxygen boost – but these were just the beginning of all the systems she had to sell.

Khatib had provided her plane to make it harder for the CIA and other departments to track their progress and get the scoop before MET did. Khatib was paranoid. She thought this might be their big moment. She was taking every step to ensure success.

Of course, the fact that Khatib expected a return on her investment put additional pressure on Ronan, and it disturbed his dreams.

When he awoke, his keyboard had slid off his legs to the carpeted floor. Deanna tapped on her laptop. Outside, he saw a vast urban sprawl approaching in the distance. His ocular flashed a confirmation: TAIPEI CITY.

"That was fast," he mumbled. He wandered up to the cockpit to chat with the pilot but found an empty seat. He returned and said, "Where's

Joe?"

Deanna pointed to the back of the cabin. "Bedroom."

At the back, Ronan knocked once and opened door. "Hey," he said to the sleeping man. "Hate to disturb your dreams, but were you planning to land this thing?"

The pilot rubbed his eyes. He staggered into the adjoining bathroom and shut the door.

"Just thought it might be nice," Ronan said.

He plopped down next to Deanna. "What have you learned?"

Turning her laptop's screen to face him, she said, "This is a recent analysis of LikeLife's market position. They're privately owned, so they don't disclose much."

He retrieved his keyboard from the floor. "Did you notice that we've arrived, and the pilot doesn't show much interest in landing?"

"He and I were chatting," Deanna said. "The autopilot is going to land it."

"Ah. Good." Ronan glanced out the window as their altitude dropped. The edge of the dense city was almost below them.

"Jin Li, LikeLife's CEO, is waiting for us," she said. "He's well known in military contracting circles and there's nothing particularly suspicious about him. He's an interesting man and should be cooperative. But anything is–"

The plane began a rapid, steep descent. Joe stumbled by, gripping the seats as he made his way to the cockpit. "I should have said earlier. Stay in your seats until we land. Keep your seat belts on, too." Then he was gone.

They clicked their belts. The Windslicer went into a deep downward turn.

"Uh… wow," Deanna said under her breath and leaned back.

She turned away from the window. "Sorry. I'm old-school when it comes to landing planes."

Ronan nodded. "It will all be over soon." As the roar of the engines grew, he shouted, "Last year, a test plane in Omaha came in for an automated landing and – never mind."

The wheels hit the runway and they pitched forward as the plane slowed to a long bouncing stop.

Deanna sighed in relief. The plane angled toward the private aircraft stands.

She regained her composure and smiled. "Tell me about yourself. Girlfriend? Wife?"

"Yes and no."

She lingered for a moment before looking away. Another label flashed into Ronan's view: INTEREST.

...

They passed through a clearance gate and were met by two Taiwanese intelligence officials who ushered them to a waiting sedan. The four were soon heading away from the city. The officials spoke fluent English and were willing to help facilitate the trip, but they stressed the need for being courteous with the LikeLife employees. After the third request not to distract the company's workers, Ronan cut them off. "Got it," he said.

The Taiwanese officials had blank expressions, but their eyes drilled deep. "Thank you," one of them answered.

Deanna chimed in. "Don't worry. Our investigation won't disrupt the employees. We just want to learn about the industry."

Ronan glanced at Deanna.

Her stare said, *don't piss them off.*

...

LikeLife's corporate headquarters was a half hour south of the airport, in the heart of the Hsinchu Science Park. The main building was a colossal structure that appeared to break out of the ground from below, thrusting upward in an explosion of trees and vegetation. The surrounding campus swirled with flowing canopies that provided shade and color along the garden trails.

Ronan could see his breath in the cool air. There was a crystalline beauty in the way the light gleamed from the damp surfaces of the building's steel and glass. Cherry trees at the base of the building were at the start of their bloom, an explosion of pink beauty. Two plump gray birds fluttered up from the bushes. SPOTTED DOVES.

Unfortunately, he didn't have time to admire the surroundings.

Just inside the doors, two men in black tactical uniforms manned a security station. Deanna smiled but they did not return the courtesy. They moved her to the side and had a few words in Mandarin with the Taiwanese escorts. Ronan didn't bother viewing a translation. The guards gestured toward a line on the floor and Deanna stepped up to it. They waved a screening wand along her body, tapped a console, and allowed her to pass.

One of the guards motioned for Ronan to step up.

"I'm going to set this off," Ronan said. His foot touched the line on the floor. *Beeeep*.

The guards approached with their wands. "Legs," one said. "Knuckles," said the other. They were more careful than with Deanna.

Ronan pointed to his left arm. "Here's a medication port."

They nodded and kept inspecting.

From behind, one of the men asked, "Box about two inches over the kidneys – is this for dialysis?"

"No. Oxygen boost." The boost was designed to combat the effects of blood loss, smothering, smoke-filled rooms, and submersion. He never got into sticky situations, but it was handy for going on long morning runs. He added, "I also have sensors in my thumb and forefinger to control an ocular interface."

A guard leaned in for a closer look at his eyes. Ronan expanded the lens and the man recoiled.

The man composed himself.

"What else?" the other guard snapped.

"That's all of my augs... so far."

"Go ahead. Ignore the alarm."

Ronan set off a barrage of squeals and beeps as he passed to the far side of the room.

In the foyer beyond, Ronan saw Jin Li, the company's CEO, waiting for them. Short and thin, Li was both dorky and debonair: hair slicked back, pants hiked up and cinched tight, all bespoke, all carefully cultivated for maximum personality impact.

Li adjusted a thick pair of glasses. "Welcome to LikeLife."

"Mr. Li, we appreciate your time," Deanna said. "We are familiar with your products, especially the AutoSurveyor and the LikeLife microdrone. We've been keeping up with you for years. As you know, we came here to learn more about the leading edge of micro-flight technology. We hope you can help."

"Leading edge?" Li produced the hint of a smile, vaguely genuine, but maybe condescending. "I am flattered. And to be somewhat, ah, less than humble shall we say – I think you will be amazed by our capabilities." Li gestured to a kiosk. "But first, can you put your Johnny H. on this nondisclosure agreement? You will be seeing things we haven't made public."

While they flipped through ten or twelve dense forms on the kiosk panel, Li waited nearby. There was no small talk. Li's bio had said he was a self-assured genius, so Ronan kept quiet, not wanting to say something foolish. They signed the forms, and Li gave a big wide swing of an arm and led them down the hall. He abruptly stopped at a windowless door.

"This is our demonstration room," Li said. He rested his hand on the door handle and smiled fully, eyes excited. "Ready? I like to make a big impact right away."

"You've got our attention," Deanna said.

He opened the door. Inside, a dense cloud of flying objects swarmed and buzzed, as thick as a sandstorm. Each object changed course at the periphery, staying inside the room and, collectively through their mad flights, created an almost tangible wall where the door had been.

Li's smile disappeared. Then he stepped into the cloud and was gone.

CHAPTER 13

Ronan took stock of the buzzing mass before them. "Okay," he said, "now we know Jin Li is a showman."

Deanna shrugged. "Can't hurt to play along. Here goes." She stepped into the swarm.

Ronan thumbed into UltraTrack mode and tried to assess what the flying objects looked like, but they were too quick. He wondered whether all this would interfere with his electronics. No way to know. He followed them into the room.

The buzz was all-encompassing. Tiny objects shot in front of his eyes in such numbers and speeds that he couldn't differentiate one from the other. It was like walking into a world of background static or statistical noise.

Deanna and Li were gone. There was nothing but movement swirling around him, obscuring the view in all directions. Looking at his arms and chest, he saw that nothing had landed on him.

Nothing touched him, and nothing collided. On the floor, larger, slower objects moved around his legs. Some resembled cockroaches. Others looked more like vipers or rats. They appeared out of the noise and then disappeared back into it again. Nothing brushed his feet.

Sweeping his hand around, he couldn't feel anything in the air, although he sensed a vague bitter taste of soap on his lips. These things were leaving residue in the air. And strange smells too. Freon? Ozone? Burnt plastic?

He realized he was disoriented, unsure which way was forward, or whether he was even supposed to move forward. He did not call out.

Flashing a compass bearing – NE – and comparing it to when he entered the room, he took steps in the direction that kept him in a straight line. He extended his hand so as not to bump into anything.

He emerged from the kinetic specks and saw Deanna and Li waiting. Behind him, the flying chaos stretched from floor to ceiling, one wall to the other. A flying metal rod shot out, flipped, and disappeared back into the mass.

"Well?" Li asked. "What do you think? That's our product line, as well as a few prototypes."

"Consider me shocked," Ronan said.

"And awed," Deanna agreed.

"I'm so happy," Li said. He gestured to a table.

The remainder of the room was nearly empty, occupied only by the single table and a clustered mass of flies crawling on an otherwise bare portion of wall.

The table had a statue of the Buddha and a small control pad.

"What's this?" Ronan asked.

"A game," Li answered. "I like our site tours to be fun for visitors. Interactive. Which one of you would like to play?"

Deanna nudged Ronan forward.

"I will."

"Wonderful. I am showcasing two products here. One is for spying on you and one is for attacking you. But which is which? You tell me."

A game? Ronan had not expected any of this. He stepped toward the table for a better look at the objects resting there. But as he did so, the flies on the wall stopped moving.

Ronan studied the flies. They were now fixed in place, but clearly monitoring his actions. He looked back at the table.

The Buddha seemed innocent enough.

He figured that the control pad had settings to play with. But as he lifted the controller off the table, the flies left the wall. He froze.

The flies hovered but did not come any closer. He touched the dark glass on the controller. This activated the screen, which displayed a single button: "Awaken."

What the hell. He pressed the button.

The Buddha didn't move. Its eyes remained shut.

"Nothing happened," he said.

"Can you tell what is hunting you, Ronan, and what is simply watching?"

"I think the flies are just watching me."

"Correct."

Ronan took a long look at the Buddha. "Therefore, I don't think I will get too close to the statue."

"Why not?"

"Because I don't trust it."

"You can trust it. This is only a statue of the Buddha."

"Should I trust you?"

"I wouldn't lie about the Buddha."

Ronan looked around. "I give up. I don't see what is going to attack. You got me."

"Yes, I did."

An electrifying shudder passed through Ronan's right hand and Deanna gasped. He tried to drop the controller, but it stuck with him. A small wire had wrapped around his pinky from underneath. He flapped his hand, but more wires slid effortlessly over his skin, and soon had his hand trapped like a fly in a spider's web. The tips of the wires poked into his skin.

Li smiled. "We go out of our way to build things that are not what you expect."

Ronan's bound fingers were turning white.

"Off," Li said, and the mass of wires loosened and dropped to the floor.

Ronan massaged his fingers and tried to look as though he enjoyed these weird activities.

"That concludes the demo," Li said. He pulled one of the flies from the air, where it had hovered in place. "Relax, no more tricks. Let's chat. You're here because of the attack at your big football game."

"Yes."

Li held the fly between pinched fingers. "This is a SpyFly. It is only for surveillance. You want to know if anything as tiny as this can be used to kill someone."

"I already know it can," Deanna said. "I am more interested in the specifics. I couldn't see what was in that swarm we just walked through. Do you have a model that looks like a mosquito?"

"Ah. That would be hard, wouldn't it? Even for us. Challenging flight dynamics. Let's finish the tour. You want to see the state of the art, right?"

He gave the fly a toss.

...

Machines of every sort were on display in testing rooms, innovation labs, QA cubicles, workshops, courtyards, break rooms, and just plain snaking down the damn hallway. They were everywhere.

Ronan understood the equation: Money + Superior Engineering + Imagination = Cambrian Explosion of Robotics.

"No photos with those, please," Li said to Ronan, indicating Ronan's eyes. "Be good."

Even Deanna, who had extensive background on LikeLife, was not prepared for so much robo-diversity at once.

As they passed one room, Ronan glimpsed a rabbit as it jumped into the corner of a plexiglass cage. Something inside the cage rose from the floor, starting flat and reaching a foot in height. The thing had many legs and claws. It lunged. Ronan looked away to follow Li, but thought he saw the rabbit's head fly off. It must not have been a real rabbit.

Deanna hadn't noticed.

They stopped. "What is this?" Ronan asked.

A small machine rested on a desk in the hallway, the size of a photocopier but with no lid or tray. Ronan had noticed similar machines in previous rooms.

"Our fabricator," Li said. "We don't make much money by producing the bots and drones themselves. We license the *plans* for them." He slapped his hand on top. "We give our clients a printer like this one, which can make 500 different bots, all micros. Every time a client prints a bot, a little money drops into our bank account."

Ronan examined the front and back. "Can you show us?"

"Resins go in back." Li hit a touchscreen. "You download the plans, tap a few buttons, and it starts cranking them out. The tiny ones take less than a second." Li withdrew a tube from the back, popped off the top and shook something into Deanna's hand. As soon as it tumbled out, the thing began wiggling.

"An ant? I've seen plenty of microbots, but this is incredibly small."

"We are the best," Li replied. "That thin strip on the top is a simple polymer battery. Just plastic." He flipped the bot, squinting for a closer look. "This one has small scrapers. Maybe it cleans industrial sewage pipes. Only three or four moving pieces. You'd use thousands of these bots, crawling through the pipes. Then you flush them out and re-use the resin to make more."

As they moved on, Ronan took another look at the fabricator. Li had said it made 500 different microbot models. Some scraped. Some flew. Maybe some bit. It just stamped them out. *Pop, pop, pop.* He wondered how many of these fabricators were out in the world.

Chapter 14

A bug peered through the darkness. Ronan studied its thick tangle of legs and eye stalks, crammed under an enormous hunched carapace and rising two feet above the surface of the table. The sculpture seemed to have no purpose, decorative or otherwise.

After the tour, Li had brought them to a typical corporate conference room. Ronan and Deanna sat at the large table that dominated the room, watching a video that a marketing guy was playing for them.

The video celebrated LikeLife's history of innovation, starting as a supplier of autonomous cargo vehicles and large agricultural drones, then becoming a developer of small, inconspicuous machines that blended into the natural world. The company's new strategy was to plagiarize the functionality of living creatures. LikeLife's bots could navigate the rubble of an earthquake or bombing, analyze inaccessible spaces, sneak under leaves and down chimneys, leap onto things, attach to clothing, whatever might be useful. Not only did the company's new machines leverage nature's ability to design for a task, but by mimicking insects and small animals, those designs allowed the machines to hide in plain sight. At first, the company had focused on industrial applications. But as the demand for micro surveillance systems had taken off, especially through government contracts, it had decided to specialize in that market.

Ronan sighed. The video was informative, but maybe Li was just chewing up time, preventing them from asking questions. His eyes rested on the statue again, the leggy bug thing, which stood in the middle of the table, pointed his way.

As the video played, Li flipped his finger across his phone, but once it was over, he snapped back to attention and the smile returned. His hands rested on a small plastic container, light aqua with a thin pink lid, about the size of a pack of playing cards.

Meanwhile, the bug stared.

Marketing Guy was delivering well-rehearsed talking points. "After Rob Wood at Harvard built that first m-drone that could fly – the first microdrone – the race was on. It took years for us to make our first breakthroughs in micro. Then we made a lot of breakthroughs. Now we invent something cool almost every day."

Ronan's ocular scanned up-down, left-right for muscular cues on Marketing Guy's face, but little emerged. Marketing Guy was nothing but packaged spin. *No point trying to read him,* Ronan thought. *He's a parrot.*

"Who are you selling to?" Deanna asked.

"Scientists, non-scientists," Li said. "Governments, businesses. And distributors who have their own clientele. It's not possible in most cases for our company to know precisely who is using the fabricators. We do know, of course, where we ship them. I must admit that Russia and Iran are on that list. Pakistan as well."

The bug's exposed underbelly was covered in black spots. Did the pattern look the same when he had entered the room? Ronan wasn't sure. He zipped back through his running footage, which he had kept going despite Li's request. *Several black belly spots had shifted position.*

The thing was watching him.

There were raps on the door and a man's head poked in. He said, "Client?"

Li seemed annoyed by the intrusion. "No. American investigators."

"Oh really?" the man said. "I wasn't aware of this."

Ronan's ocular flashed: HE ALREADY KNEW.

The man entered and extended a hand. "I'm Siyu Chen. LikeLife's biggest investor."

"They suspect m-drones were involved in the Nashville attack," Li said, playing with the small aqua box.

Siyu feigned surprise. He was middle-aged, ashen, tense. Limp hair clung to the side of his head and his pale skin hinted at many hours in front of a computer, tweaking financial formulas on spreadsheets. His suit was a loose mistake on his thin frame.

"I want to hear this."

"And I asked you to stay out. They just want information, Siyu."

"Is that right?"

Li seemed flustered. He spun the aqua box.

"What do you have there?" Deanna asked.

Li opened the container, tipped it carefully, and poured a small pile of black dust onto the table's surface. He gestured at the pile with both hands. The dust had a fuzzy quality, as though clinging to itself.

Ronan leaned in.

"Touch it," Li urged.

"I'd rather not," Ronan said.

"Go on!"

Ronan pushed his index finger into the dust just far enough to break the surface. As he held his finger in place a few seconds, a creepy tingling sensation spread across the submerged tip. He withdrew it. His fingertip was black, like ink.

"Those haven't entered production yet. Mighty Mites."

Ronan bent his eye toward the black mass. Zooming to 200x, he saw a sea of movement. Tiny creatures. *Holy shit.*

"Do they bite?"

"No," Li said. "I don't think that batch bites." He pulled a plastic warning label off the box and used it to sweep the pile back inside. "But they can do whatever we need them to do."

Ronan held his black-tipped finger in Siyu's face. "Please get these off my finger."

The investor leaned back. "Hey. I don't… Li?"

Li scooted the label across the table. Ronan scraped the mites off, letting them fall into the box. Some landed on the table.

Ronan stared at his fingertip. Were these games just Li showing off, or was Li trying to keep him off-balance?

"Getting back to my question," Deanna said. "Here's a photo taken at the game." She held up her phone. "You can see a mosquito. Have you designed something like this that can deliver a liquid payload?"

Siyu leaned in for a closer look. "It's blurry. It could be anything."

Li ignored his investor. "If this is a drone, it's hard to say where it came from." He held the phone close to his eyes. "I mean, it *could* be one of ours."

Siyu went silent.

"Is that a yes?" Deanna asked. "Some of your technology looks like this?"

"Yes."

Ronan's fingertip tingled with mites or imagination.

"I will show you something," Li said. "But this is under the strictest confidentiality." He grabbed Marketing Guy's laptop. "You can go," he told the man.

Marketing Guy picked up his things and left; the door clicked shut behind him.

Deanna said, "We believe this photo from the night of the attack shows a microdrone with a biting or stinging injection mechanism. Is that possible?"

Li tapped on the keypad and swung the laptop around. "In the interests of world security, I want to show you this."

"We should have lawyers present!" Siyu complained.

Li waved his hand. "I don't want to drag this out and I'm not going to lie. They can call a few of our clients and get the answer, anyway. Look." He tapped the screen. Ronan and Deanna saw a wireframe model of a mosquito, white polygons against a dark blue background. Li rotated the model and zoomed in on the head, which had a long proboscis. "The injection mechanism mimics a real mosquito. Two outer shanks cut the skin. A vibrating middle tube slides in. But unlike a real mosquito, the target's skin doesn't itch. That's because no bacteria are introduced at the puncture site. This m-drone uses a sterile needle."

"You were right," Ronan said to Deanna.

Siyu shook his head in frustrated disgust.

Deanna's voice took a hardened edge. "What triggers it to bite?"

"The mechanism is simple. Just program the bug to fly around and land on people. When the m-drone touches skin, the head bends forward and the needle extends. The biting is automatic. Without the itch, most people never notice."

Deanna and Ronan exchanged a lingering look.

Ronan was careful with his next words. "You build tiny drones that bite."

"We do. Injectors are an obvious feature for our clients to request. There are military applications."

"I appreciate your honesty," Deanna said.

"Like everyone else," Li said, "I've been watching the news and reading rumors. What do you think was transmitted by the mosquitos at the game in Nashville?"

Deanna tapped her phone. She had brought a confidentiality agreement of her own.

Li signed the form with his finger and gave it to Siyu, who spent considerably more time reading it. He signed.

"Maybe a nanoweapon," Deanna answered when she had her phone back.

Li raised his eyebrows. "What brought you to that conclusion?"

"The victim's hearts were completely destroyed, but nothing else. The evidence points to a sophisticated weapon with extremely tight organ specificity. So how do we determine if these m-drones came from one of your clients?"

"That would be very hard."

"We could start with a list of any client who has produced your mosquito design with their fabricator," Ronan said. "You said that any time a design is printed, it sends you money."

Li seemed caught, then shook his head. "The callback could be disabled. They wouldn't be that stupid."

"Still, that would be an excellent list."

"You're talking about my book of business... but I will give it some thought. Maybe, if the U.S. pays me enough money, I will sell you the data buffet."

Deanna fixed on Li. "Unfortunately, we don't have a budget for that. As a next step, we would have to get an injunction that orders you to comply. Our governments are cooperating, so you can expect that would happen. Isn't there a way we can just get the necessary leads and be on our way? Give us the non-disclosure paperwork. We'll get it signed by the head of our agency."

"Let's say you get my list. What then? You might take the next three years trying to conduct meaningful audits of all my clients. You'd waste a lot of time. In my opinion, you are going about this backwards." Li's smile returned. "I suggest we take a brief break. Anyone want a drink? When we get back, I'll explain how there is a much faster way for you to go about this investigation."

CHAPTER 15

Li and Siyu had left the room.

Deanna leaned close and said in a low voice, "What do you think?"

Ronan shook his head and pointed to the beetle. They sat in silence.

After a few minutes, the two men returned. Siyu handed out bottles of Bogari sparkling water.

"If we don't go through your client list," Ronan said, "how, in your opinion, do we get to the bottom of this?"

"You need to focus on the payload."

"We will get to that, don't worry."

Li leaned back, cracked the cap and took a swig. "You've been assuming you need to identify who might have created an attack vector like the one you see in the game footage. But we've sold thousands of our fabricators. That's too many people to rule out. On the other hand, whatever substance was delivered into these people, few labs make something that could kill like that. That fact really narrows down your options."

Deanna shook her head. "There are a lot of government and military labs doing nanotechnology and we'll never get a straight answer out of them."

"Maybe it's not from a secretive military lab. Maybe the lab is right out in the open, looking innocent. When you said the heart had been destroyed, something jumped to mind. There is a lab in Johannesburg that develops targeted medicines to treat heart problems. I am not suggesting that they have anything to do with this, but their technology is in the right ballpark. They have this — framework, I guess you'd call it. A molecule that serves as a kind of chassis. They stick a specific functional group on the front of the chassis to react with target body tissues."

"What is this place?"

"Sanar Nanomed. It's run by Niko March. You should interview him."

"Medical researchers don't develop weapons," Deanna said, tapping on her phone.

"Maybe not," Li replied. "But there's something else you might not know. Their lead scientist is very concerned about the use of nanotechnology for military purposes. A couple years ago, he wrote a report for government advisory groups. Most haven't heard of the report because he didn't want the ideas getting widespread attention. The report specifically called me out, saying LikeLife products could be the vector for delivering nanoweapons into people. I took some heat from the Taiwanese Technology Safety Oversight Committee. If I were you, I would speak with Niko March."

"I haven't heard of this report, but we can check it out." She tapped, taking notes.

Ronan wasn't in the mood for another trip. "I don't know. Sounds like LikeLife and Sanar have a bit of a grudge."

"Mr. Flynn, I am not hiding anything. I opened the kimono. I'll tell you what. Go talk to Niko. If you don't have an obvious lead after that, come back here, and we'll talk next steps. If you ask me, I don't think it is a coincidence that their lead scientist is so concerned."

...

Deanna and Ronan re-grouped in a small conference room to discuss their options in private. A visit to Sanar Nanomed would require Edward to contact the State Security Agency in South Africa to make the necessary arrangements. While Li had appeared to be extraordinarily open about LikeLife's technological capabilities, they couldn't expect the same level of cooperation everywhere they went. Johannesburg was a sixteen-hour flight. After arrival, they might be denied access or interviews with the senior team. Then they'd have to wait while the DoD tried to get the

Security Agency to force the matter. That could take weeks.

"I don't have any record of this report," Deanna said. "But that doesn't mean anything if it had limited distribution. We need to get a copy from Li."

In Ronan's opinion, the report was just a misdirect. "He's trying to get rid of us. I don't suspect him, but one of his clients is surely involved. We need to start going through his client list today."

Deanna drummed her fingers on her chin. "I tend to agree with Li's argument. If he has a thousand clients, we might be better off looking into Sanar's nanoweapon capabilities."

"I don't see the benefit of flying that far to talk to one of Li's hunches, when there is productive work we could do right here. He seems to have a vendetta against this guy."

Deanna continued drumming her fingers.

Ronan noticed a beetle crawling on the window. He inspected it.

After a moment, Deanna asked, "Well?"

"It looks like a normal beetle."

She paced.

Finally, Ronan said, "I'll do what you decide, obviously. You're the boss."

"Let's call Edward. Unless he wants us to stay here, we're going to Johannesburg."

CHAPTER 16

"What's the verdict?" Li asked when they re-entered the gleaming conference room.

"We're heading to South Africa," Deanna replied.

Siyu, the investor, exhaled audibly. Ronan saw him smile for the first time since the man had poked his head through the doorway. Now that his investment seemed to have dodged a nasty legal problem, he relaxed.

Li also was pleased. "You're doing the right thing. In the meantime, I had my people get you a to-go box."

Li lifted a box off the table and handed it to Ronan. It weighed at least forty pounds. "There's a variety of larger stuff in here. Show your management. I have been trying to get contracts with the U.S. armed forces. I haven't found the right person to get my foot in the door. One look at these, and your president will get us on the fast track. You need what I'm selling."

Deanna offered a polite smile. "What's in there?"

"Rollers, flyers, bomb bots, a menagerie of test products," Li said. He pointed his finger over his temple. "Just to get the ideas flowing. They make great demonstrations to military decision-makers. But use them only in controlled internal environments. No vents, no escape holes. Strengthen door hinges and window seals. No one should be in the room with these devices. I just texted you a link to the app that unlocks them. They are perfectly safe until you start using the app."

Ronan hefted the box into his arms, resigned to leave and not liking the decision.

"I guess it is time to show you this." From another pocket, Li withdrew a small black box with a hinged lid, much like a ring case. He opened it. Inside, nestled in protective padding, Ronan spied a glass vial. Li extended the case.

Ronan removed the vial and held it aloft, catching the light. The vial contained a mosquito, glimmering and new, as immobile as if trapped in fossilized amber.

Deanna said, "Is that...?"

Li nodded. Although he didn't smile, he seemed proud. "Yes. There, I have nothing to hide. Take it. Study it. Use the same app to control it. Just identify the target and press the button. Or put it on random mode and let it drift around and find its own targets. Great for stealth surveillance."

"Or killing people," Deanna said.

Li fumbled for words and cut his eyes toward the investor. "Attacking soldiers. Naturally."

Deanna's eyes grew intense. "Be honest. You've known this whole time that this is exactly what happened at the football game."

"Maybe," Li said. "I don't know. I hope not."

Ronan stared at Li as if to say, *we could have a hundred investigators swarming your lab by the end of the afternoon.*

Li's tone grew patronizing. "Defense departments around the world are funding this technology. These vectors are perfect for urban and guerrilla warfare. You could program them to attack adults but not children, or anyone with a gun, or people wearing military uniforms. But the question remains, what substance do these vectors inject? Go find the bioweapon."

He snapped the case closed, and the mosquito disappeared, an insect entombed not in amber but glass, not forever but until the moment it was shaken free and activated.

He pressed it into Ronan's hand.

...

Deanna wrote final notes on her phone. Siyu hovered nearby. Ronan could feel the investor watching, no doubt wondering if a PR disaster had been averted or still hung in the balance. He must have been shocked that Li gave them a working unit of the machine that had apparently been used in a major terrorist attack.

The Taiwanese escorts were back. They had been diverted at the check-in desk, and Ronan had forgotten all about them.

Siyu tried to sound more friendly than he had been so far. "I'm headed to the airport myself. I can give you a ride. I'm sure our good officials here would like to get back to their regular duties."

Ronan thought this was a great idea. More time in the car with the investor. No doubt he would try to influence their opinion of the company, but even with deliberate spin-washing, he might accidentally say something useful.

"I think that would be fine," one of the escorts said. They were merely providing a diplomatic courtesy, not security. They seemed eager to get back to their normal business, to end this day of tedious waiting.

At Siyu's car in the employee parking deck, Ronan offered the front passenger seat to Deanna, but once they were on the road, realized his mistake. Sitting in back, he could only see Siyu's eyes through the rearview mirror. FaceLab could not accurately read expressions and body cues from this angle.

With one hand on the wheel and the other resting on the passenger seat, Siyu seemed relaxed.

"My kids spend all of their free time on Youku, Weibo, QQ, TopChart, video games," he said. "The whole country is like that. All of China. Taiwan too. They let their phones tell them what to do."

Deanna smiled. "You sound like every parent in America."

"Our world is in transition," Ronan said. "As we merge with machines, our lives will get better."

"Merge? Isn't that a little extreme?" From the front seat, Deanna turned to look back at him.

"No. It's already happening."

"Maybe you're right," Siyu said. As if to cut short the chit chat, he abruptly changed topics. "I want to say something about Li. He works hard, always on the move. Always building. He's a good man."

"He seemed transparent," Deanna said.

Siyu's tone was measured. "Unfortunately, he can be hard to manage. My firm has a controlling interest in the company. I believe in corporate responsibility to the investors. Li makes statements that sound bad and leave a false impression. Regarding your investigation, did he make matters worse for the company?"

Ronan shrugged. "Too soon to tell."

Siyu nodded. "I understand. I hope the media doesn't discover that one of our machines could have been used in the attack. You agree that this should stay quiet, right?"

"No worries. We don't talk to the media."

…

Ronan could see the planes approaching across the sky, banking in for their landing at Taiwan Taoyuan International Airport. Siyu pulled off the thruway and headed toward the private hangars. The conversation with him had yielded nothing useful – no small insights, no hints of a lie. Riding with Siyu had provided no more information than if they had travelled with the Taiwanese authorities.

Siyu parked next to the plane, popped the back trunk, and helped carry their suitcases on board. He tried to present a happy mood, chatting casually again about the terrible epidemic of idle children, their addictions to the latest focus drugs, and, he said with all due respect to Ronan, their dependency on technology.

Joe, the pilot who liked to sleep during flights, greeted them at the foot of the boarding stairs. He had been waiting in the hangar and seemed eager to get moving again. He grabbed a box of food from a cart and hustled up to the cabin. The three of them still had Khatib's jet to themselves.

Siyu dropped Deanna's bags on a leather sofa and gazed around the cabin, amazed at the luxury interior. He ran his hand along the chairs and tabletops. Ronan guessed Siyu could imagine the day when he would have his own private jet, just like this one.

Siyu grasped Ronan's arm. "You are doing the right thing."

Deanna noticed Siyu's serious tone again. She stopped to listen.

"The m-drones and robotics are just tools," Siyu continued, keeping his voice low so the pilot couldn't hear. "The payload – that's where you have to worry."

Siyu turned and left the plane.

Fourteen hours later, they were passing near Madagascar and maintaining their cruising altitude. Ronan was stir-crazy. Most of the trip had been over clouds and water, a long stretch of the Indian Ocean, but now he could see the enormous island below, the fourth largest in the world. Soon the southeastern face of Africa would come into view, and they would pass over Mozambique en route to Johannesburg.

Ronan had spent much of the time studying articles on the nanotech industry and the research conducted at Sanar. Deanna had sent briefing papers on terrorist scenarios, and he was annoyed by their detached tone; the authors didn't believe nanoweapons would be used by terrorists anytime soon. Nevertheless, the experts clearly thought certain scenarios were *possible*, at least in theory.

Deanna had talked at length about a burgeoning industry that so far had flown under the radar of almost everyone, including the alarmists. Eventually his brain was full and they had both lapsed into silence. Hours passed and she fell asleep.

He stared out the window. What was Lisa doing right now? Maybe she was at the spa for a massage or doing yoga. Or at the gym. She spent so much time there, always trying to lose weight, never making much headway. He tried to tell her he didn't care, just enjoy life, stop fighting for perfect health. But she just kept going. Recently she had looked in a mirror and said to herself, loud enough for him to hear: "I'm forty and fat."

He was in no position to judge her emotional baggage. Ronan was never truly happy, either. Deep inside, something from his past was tearing him up, and it was the whole reason he had started down a techno-utopian path in the first place. We all have our scars, he thought.

So, yes, she was probably working out. He had to admit that she was trying. This thought made his heart ache. When was the last time he'd taken her out to show the world how beautiful she was? Last summer they'd taken a couple days off and gone to the beach.

Damn, he thought. *Last summer.* What did this mean? Had he lost interest in her? Had he become too tied up in his own interests?

Ronan glanced at Deanna, then lingered. She was deep in dreamland.

She had subtle creases around the eyes and mouth. She was about the same age as Lisa, but Deanna's devotion to her job, her acceptance of danger, and the way she handled herself under pressure made her seem older and wiser.

He paced up and down the short central aisle, from the cockpit to the room at the tail end, which had a bathroom and a couple beds. The seats in the cabin were spacious. The plane's interior was designed for small groups of wealthy business folk. Several tables allowed people to meet and discuss projects. He sat at one, drummed his fingers, and checked the time on his ocular. He studied Deanna again.

She was a damn good investigator, and she had downplayed the boss-role with him. He was grateful for that.

She stirred and he looked away. He pretended to notice her and smiled. She joined him at the table, rubbing her eyes. He handed her a water bottle and she unscrewed the cap.

The pilot emerged from the cockpit. "Deanna, I heard you didn't like that last landing. If it makes you feel any better, I plan to land it this time."

"Thank you, Joe."

"How you guys doing?" he asked.

"Great," she said. "How much longer?"

The pilot paused next to their table, placed his fingers on the surface carefully like two small tripods, and sat down. "You guys feel okay?"

A look of concern crossed Deanna's face. "I'm fine… you?"

The pilot nodded but said nothing. His eyes looked distant.

"You don't look so well," Ronan said.

The pilot fell forward, his head landing with a *clunk* on the table.

"What the hell?" Ronan asked.

They grabbed Joe's arms and lowered his limp body to the floor. Ronan loosened his collar and belt, while Deanna checked his neck. "God – no pulse."

Deanna removed an ID card clipped to the pilot's front pocket and opened his shirt, buttons popping, to administer CPR. The man's eyes rolled upward.

A bug, a small wasp maybe, took flight from the man's neck. A moment later, another shot through the air.

"What's that?" She ducked her head, then looked at Ronan. For a moment, neither moved.

Scrambling to their feet and banging into each other, they stumbled madly toward the back of the plane, reaching the door to the small bedroom in a matter of seconds.

"Close it!" Deanna said, slapping at her arms and neck as Ronan slammed the door. He tested the knob with a pull.

"Did you see them?"

"Something fast was flying around in there."

"Yeah, but… maybe he just had a heart attack."

Ronan shook his head. "I'm sure something killed him." He brushed his arms, surveyed the air. "Well… ninety-eight percent sure."

"I don't know what I saw."

"Hold still." He scanned her arms, legs, back, then lifted her hair off her neck.

"See anything?"

"No. Any on me?" He turned around once.

"You look okay."

Gradually their breathing and heart rate slowed. They finished checking and double-checking and rubbing their clothes. They had retreated into the small back room intended for resting or sleeping, with two narrow beds that could fold into the wall. There was a short sofa, a tiny closet, and a sink with several cups and other items. Like the rest of the plane, everything was sleek plastic and metal lit by the aqua glow of embedded side lights.

"This room looks secure. I don't see any space around this door." Deanna slid a panel to reveal a small plexiglass window. She studied the cabin. "I don't see anything."

"We need to reach someone who knows how to fly this plane." Ronan tapped his phone. After several transfers, he was connected to the DIA's senior pilot in Washington.

Ronan got to the point. "The pilot's dead. It's just the two of us. How do we know if this thing will land itself? Neither of us has any flight experience." Ronan paused, held the phone away, and whispered to her. "Or do you?"

"No."

He continued. "We're in the back bedroom of the plane. The route to the cockpit through the cabin is blocked."

"What's going on?" the DIA pilot asked.

"We can't pass through the cabin. It's just not an option. We have a situation."

The man on the other end was quiet, possibly deciding whether to ask further questions. "Well, your plane has full autopilot and can land itself. But self-landing isn't currently activated. Without a pilot, your plane will maintain altitude, pass the airport and continue south until it crashes. You need to activate the landing sequence. I can tell you how to do that. Can you get to the cockpit?"

"Give us a minute."

Deanna was shaking her head. She gave the room another look, then dropped to the sofa and buried her fingers in her hair.

Ronan thought he heard a buzz, faint but deliberate, moving from somewhere nearby, maybe in the walls. He tapped her shoulder. "I heard something."

Deanna cocked her head, eyes focused on the door. "Your imagination."

The sound wasn't his imagination, but he couldn't hear it anymore, either. The room seemed well-sealed, but he gave the front wall another once-over, in case he'd missed any access points. In fact, he had – there was a short row of slits about a foot off the floor, blended into the striped pattern of the plastic, a vent no more than two inches long. He bent low and pressed his ear against it.

The buzzing was clear this time, echoing down a shaft of some sort, and getting closer. He glanced at Deanna and she knew instantly from the look on his face that they were in trouble. "Cover those slits with something!" she blurted.

After a befuddled moment, looking this way and that and finding nothing, Ronan lifted a foot and covered the vents with his shoe.

"Good thinking, partner."

"I can't stand like this all day while the plane crashes."

The room was almost entirely molded plastic, but Deanna noticed a rubber no-slide surface next to the sink. She attacked it with both hands, dug her fingers under the mat and yanked, ripping off a decent chunk, then flipped it over. "This is sticky on the back, slap it on."

Ronan lifted his foot a bit. Something flashed. He pushed back down, *crunch.*

"Hey – I got the fucker."

An insect was pinned under his shoe, a section poking out. It looked like a wasp, black and sleek, with narrow, delicate wings. He had crushed the stinger section, assuming it followed a wasp's body structure and function. Deanna bent for a look, inching closer. She gripped a plastic cup from the counter. As she hesitated, contemplating how to safely trap it, the winged section buzzed and vibrated, broke free and took flight.

"It's still going!" She swatted madly.

It arced through the air, disappeared, flew past, skimmed the ceiling, and landed on his leg.

Deanna swung the cup and covered the wasp. "Fast, it could bite you!"

"I'm fine," Ronan said. "My leg isn't real."

With a trembling hand, she slid a laminated drink menu under the cup, then lifted them together, trapping the wasp. The thing went haywire inside the cup, smacking the sides. *Thck thck thck.*

Ronan pressed the sticky cushion flap over the vent and gave it a gentle tug to verify the barrier would stay in place, preventing any further intruders.

Holding the cup aloft in the light, Deanna brought it close for inspection. The wasp landed on the wall of the cup inches from her eye, poking and prodding the cup with legs and tiny needles.

"The damn thing split in half and still managed to fly."

The wasp began buzzing again. She carried the cup into the bathroom. Ronan watched her shove the whole thing into the toilet, whisk the menu away and hit the lever with a loud sucking whoosh. She returned and fell against the sofa with a vague smile and crazy eyes.

"You just flushed our best evidence down the toilet."

"I wasn't taking any chances and we have bigger needs right now than evidence."

He nodded. "You're right. Back to the problem at hand: getting to the controls up front."

"We can figure this out. We're smart."

"If we're so smart, why did we run to the back of the plane instead of the cockpit?"

"Because it was closer…?"

"Let's think about this," he said, stating the obvious. "Start throwing some ideas out."

"How about this? You run like hell through the cabin."

"Me?"

"You're faster."

He squinted at her.

They brainstormed a few more minutes, but nothing jumped out as an obvious solution, and in the end, they had only generated three ideas:

1. Ronan wrap himself in a blanket and make a run for the cockpit. (Deanna's vote.)
2. Pull up the carpet and force one's way under it to the front of the plane. (Rejected when they remembered the carpet didn't go all the way to the cockpit – the pilot was lying on a slick floor.)
3. Send Deanna through the sub-floor space, assuming she could fit. (Ronan's vote.)

Ronan picked up the phone. "We're back."

"Thank God," the man said. "I was worried."

"We don't have many options. Is there a way to get under the floor?"

"Maybe. I'm looking at some diagrams. A small space for wires, pipes and equipment runs the length of the plane. It's not all one section, but if you are resourceful, maybe you can do it."

"We're resourceful."

"Look for a hatch in the floor of your bedroom. It may be covered by carpet or flooring. Open it, and you'll see a ladder. There are a lot of wires and electronics down there. You might need to rip out some of those to squeeze through. Just don't pull out anything important."

"How would we know that?"

The man on the other end of the phone didn't hear the question or ignored it. "Listen, when you get in the cockpit, activate the autopilot setting panel by tapping the blue auto button on the main screen of the pilot's monitor, then on the screen that comes up, find where it says full-a, tap that, and, wait, hold on. I'm sorry, it says full, just full – tap that. It will all be obvious."

"What?" Deanna asked. She was leaning close, trying to hear.

Ronan set the phone down. "I recorded it." He got his fingers under the carpet near the wall and began yanking, tugging, and ripping, until the hatch came into view.

Kneeling on the exposed steel floor, Deanna twisted the hatch's round lock and pulled open the lid.

The ladder was eighteen inches long with a single step. The space was excruciatingly tight.

"I can't make you do this," Ronan said. "But we have to decide. Either I run for the cockpit, or you do some scooching. I just want to say, as my closing arguments, that if the plan is for me to open two doors, that's going to let any poison wasps breach either room in the process."

She was down on her hands and knees, peering into the dark hole. "Well, maybe I can shimmy through this space." She didn't move, though.

"Relax, this will be easy."

"Even if I can make it all the way to the front, how will I get out?"

"He said there's another hatch in the cockpit." Ronan inspected the underside of the lid. "And the pin can be turned from underneath, too."

Now she was standing in the hole, having stepped into it without using the ladder. The floor was little more than halfway up her shins. She stared at him.

"Relax, you'll fit. You've got this."

She groaned and began to crawl into the narrow space. After some grunting and flopping and legs flailing, her body disappeared.

He heard banging.

There was some panting and cursing.

"You're doing good," he yelled. "Just keep moving forward."

"Shut the hell up," she yelled back, voice muffled. She had already made good progress.

He waited. The bumping and cursing grew fainter, more distant.

After some time, all was silent. He lay on the floor, leaning in, trying to hear.

He didn't want to aggravate her, but after another full minute went by, he bent his head further into the hole. "What's wrong?"

"Nothing," she replied.

"This is serious, Deanna."

"I know, you asshole. I'm hung up on something."

He waited a little, then asked hopefully, "Any progress?"

"No." Her voice was tired and exasperated. "My belt is caught on something. I can't move forward and I haven't been able to work my way back. I think I am completely snagged."

Shit, he thought. Another small wave of fear coursed through him as he glanced at the time.

He leaned in and yelled, "Any chance I can fit down there?" He regretted the words even as they left his mouth. If they *both* got stuck, they were screwed. What a way to go.

"Actually, yes," she yelled back. "I think you can make it."

He sighed and stepped into the hole, sank to his knees, and dropped onto his belly. He began wiggling.

The space was packed with equipment and tubes and wires. He found that the vertical space wasn't too bad, and although he couldn't do much but slowly inch forward with his arms crooked to either side, at least there was an inch or two above and below him. The horizontal space was another matter. He was squeezed tight. There was barely room for Deanna to pass between the clutter, but his body was much wider. His scrunched elbows banged the sides. There was no room for making body adjustments. Now that he was underway, he realized with another wave of concern, he was committed. Reverse was not an option.

He pushed forward, things poking him in the face, wires catching the bend of his elbows, slithering like a snake, no leverage, making tiny progress. The air was motionless. Hot.

Was that a buzzing? He paused and tried to quiet his breathing and listened above the hum of the engines. Yes. Buzzing, just above him. A wasp was seeking a way through the floor.

This prompted him to try to move faster, but the space prevented that, and he moved only a small bit. There was no running away down here.

A suffocating heat enveloped him. He was wedged into a tight, dark space, unable to retreat, under the floorboards of a plane with no pilot burning through the last of its fuel. Trapped.

Breathe slow, he told himself. *Deep calming breaths.*

After half a minute of that, he stopped trying. *Deep breathing didn't help jack.*

Full-on panic was fast approaching, and he worried that he was about to lose it. He no longer felt in control.

"Hey!" Deanna yelled.

This snapped him out of the paralysis, a little.

"What?"

"According to the time, we're over Johannesburg!"

"That's great news!" he yelled back. "Did you enjoy the flight?"

The banter boosted his spirits. He knew the feeling might not last long, so he began wriggling with renewed fervor.

Back, forth, back, forth, back–

He saw her shoes.

"Well, hi!" she called out in the dark. "I bet running through the cabin doesn't seem like such a bad idea anymore, huh?"

"I just realized I don't know how to help you. I don't have any leverage."

She seemed remarkably calm. "Relax. There is more room here. I've scrunched myself into a little pocket. You can get by me."

"You want me to go all the way to the cockpit?"

"I'm thinking that's better. I'm still worried it may be hard to get out of here."

Ronan didn't answer. He weighed this in his mind.

"You know," she continued. "We've got to get this plane turned around or we're going to get too far from the airport to make it back."

She was right. He shimmied his way along her legs. It grew tight, real tight, especially when he was even with her crotch. He flailed back and forth.

"Hmm," she said. "Time's wasting."

Good God, he thought. There's no way we can both fit.

He was smashed against her stomach, breathing hard into her shirt, grunting and pushing, inching up her body like a deranged python.

Exhausted, he paused next to her chest. He didn't want to – by all normal measures this was a bad place to stop without deliberate reason – but he had no choice.

"Don't go to sleep," she said.

He reached around her waist, feeling his way along her belt, until he found the problem. Something jagged and metal had embedded itself into the leather. He reached around her with his other arm, grabbed the metal and belt at the same time and yanked. It broke free, and he felt her sigh.

Back to the grunting and inching and pulling. They were face to face. "Hi," he said.

"Dude, your breath. Keep going."

After another five minutes of sheer agony, squeezing through spaces he never would have imagined he could possibly fit – and some that he wouldn't have, if he hadn't been able to shift the equipment – he arrived at another hatch. He felt he'd crawled the length of the plane. This had to be the right one.

He fumbled with the pin, wrenching his hand into an awkward position, rolling his body, until finally it turned. The hatch opened. Cool, fresh air billowed onto his face. If the cockpit door was open and a wasp awaited, he didn't care.

He pulled himself up and clawed his way forward onto the floor, collapsing. The cockpit door was shut; the pilot had followed protocol. They were safe.

Thumping noises came from the hole.

He reached in to help her out.

They were in the cockpit.

Landing this thing was going to be a snap compared to that hell.

They faced a panorama of digital screens – dozens of them, covering every surface of the instrument panel. Numbers and data everywhere. Real buttons, digital buttons. Real dials and digital dials.

Ronan did recognize a few controls. The wheel in front of the pilot's seat controlled pitch. And the lever to the right of the seat controlled speed. He pointed to it. "This is the throttle. I know that much."

"If you pull it back, does it speed up or slow down?"

"Slow down maybe."

"Should we do that to conserve fuel?"

"Wouldn't that also put us into descent?"

"How the hell would I know?" She slumped against the wall, hair plastered to her face, dripping sweat.

Ronan scanned the screens and dials, searching for the "Auto" button. The DIA pilot had said the button would be on the main screen. They needed to press it to pull up the landing settings. "I'm surprised they didn't teach you to fly at The Point."

"I learned to parachute. Did plenty of that. Never stepped into the cockpit."

Parachutes. Ronan straightened and glanced around the space.

"I've been looking for parachutes. There aren't any."

"You're sure?"

"How would we jump out? The door is in the cabin."

He nodded and continued searching the instrument panel. A mild level of panic swam around in his gut. There wasn't a damn "Auto" button. Maybe it was on some other screen. He'd also left his phone back in the bedroom, with the DIA pilot still waiting. He tapped a button to pull up a subpage, and they heard a *ping.*

"Watch what you press," she said.

"There's no Auto button!" Ronan yelled.

"What about this?" She pointed to a glowing green word on one of the monitors.

He bent close and read it: "Gaia."

"*Yes?*" A woman's voice said from overhead.

"Is this a voice assistant?"

"*Yes,*" came the voice, silky and authoritative.

"Here's the deal," Ronan said. "We passed our destination, Lanseria International Airport, and we're almost out of fuel. We need you to take over, turn this plane around, and land it."

They waited.

"*I don't understand that question.*"

Ronan looked at Deanna. "What was confusing about it?"

"Try shorter sentences."

He stared at the ceiling. "Gaia? We have no pilot. We need you to take over."

"*Autopilot is on.*"

"Is *full* autopilot on?"

Gaia was silent. Finally: "*Yes, autopilot is on.*"

Deanna furrowed her brow.

Clapping his hand on his forehead and trying not to notice the fuel indicator, which had started flashing red, Ronan tried again: "Gaia, is *full* autopilot on? Is the plane going to land itself?"

"*Could you please repeat your question?*"

"Oh my god." Ronan banged his fist on the panel. "I'm going to kill your product manager!"

A buzzer squealed.

"*Threats of violence are not allowed on the plane and are immediately reported to the FAA.*"

Deanna spoke. "Gaia, we need autopilot to land the plane."

"*To switch to auto-land, you will need the passcode, your authorized thumbprint, or the key card.*"

"Gaia, whose thumb print?"

"The pilot's right thumb."

"That doesn't make any sense!" Ronan blurted. "What if the pilot is dead or being held hostage?"

"Is there a hostage?"

Ronan threw his hands up and flopped down in the pilot's chair, cursing. He looked out the window and saw the world passing by below. The sight was terrifying. He had looked out plane windows a hundred times before, watching for breaks in the clouds, trying to identify mountains, looking for cars traveling in silence along lonely roads. It had always been a casual activity to pass the time on long flights, and he'd never given such terrible heights a second thought.

Behind him, her voice growing strained and fighting despair, Deanna tried to get the silky-smooth voice to clarify its point. "You're telling us we need to drag the pilot in here and press his thumb against the pad?"

"I don't understand the question."

"What was the other thing we can use... a key card...?"

"Correct. Please place the key card in the override slot."

Ronan rapped the panel. "Right here! It's right here." He tapped an opening about the width of a playing card, surrounded by dials and glowing screens.

Deanna scowled. "Great. We don't have a key card."

"The pilot probably has a key card. I think you unclipped it and set it on the floor."

"So after all this, we're back to running through the cabin?"

An emergency light blinked on and a siren wailed. Gaia joined in. *"The plane is low on fuel. You must land immediately at the nearest airport or runway."*

"Gaia." Ronan articulated his words as best he could under the circumstances. "If I move the control stick, does that disable autopilot?"

"Yes, manual adjustment of any flight control will immediately disengage autopilot."

Deanna nodded. "We have no choice. We have to try to land this thing. Get that guy back on the phone."

"No can do. I left it in the bathroom. We need autopilot. I think I can manually pitch us downward, then pull back on the throttle. The key card will slide to the door."

"Are you crazy?"

"The plunge should only take a few seconds. We grab the card, shut the door, turn on full auto, and let Gaia pull out of the dive and land. She's not going to let us die, will you, Gaia?"

"Ten minutes of fuel remaining. After that, the plane will remain aloft an additional twenty-eight seconds."

The red fuel light was flashing rapidly.

Deanna shook her head. "Sorry, no. I'm not letting you put this plane into a steep dive. That's dumber than crawling under the floor. I'm going out there and make a run for it."

"You'll get stung."

"I'm going. Shut the door behind me."

Ronan pushed the pitch control wheel and the plane nosed downward. His stomach lurched as he pulled back on the throttle, engines slowing. Deanna clutched her chair. Streets and trees rose in the window. Objects slammed into the door, one of which sounded large. He immediately increased thrust again and the engines whined in protest.

Ronan scrambled up the floor and reached for the door handle. He opened it. The pilot's body had slid into the wall, inches away. The man's eyes were blood red – the irises had disappeared into bleeding pools. Blood drizzled from his nose and mouth, rivulets streaming sideways across his cheek.

The key had slid with the body and was trapped under an arm.

"Watch out for wasps!" she yelled.

"I don't see any," he mumbled. "Oh shit!" A wasp was coming in fast.

Ronan grabbed the key and slammed the door.

He stumbled forward. Deanna steadied him as he shoved the key into the slot.

Nothing happened.

"Gaia, you there?" Ronan yelled.

Nothing.

"Gaia!" Deanna yelled, louder.

"This is Gaia."

Ronan tried to tilt the nose up. The plane veered and careened. The engines roared as the jet ripped through the clouds.

"Gaia, please land this plane, now!"

"Is this pilot DI-5786?" Gaia asked skeptically.

"I am pilot *DI-578... 6*," Ronan yelled. "Take over the controls!"

"Taking over controls," Gaia confirmed, and the plane soared, the throttle moving forward on its own, then back, nose slightly up.

"We are in a 180 and heading back. We have six minutes of fuel left. I am in communication with the control tower at Lanseria and beginning an emergency descent."

Ronan slid into the pilot's seat and let out a long, slow exhale.

"We are cleared to land."

The touchdown was smooth and flawless.

Lanseria International was smaller than O. R. Tambo, Johannesburg's busiest commercial airport, but it was ideal for wealthy jet owners and charter services. The private hangers, executive and security services, and exclusive lounges made Lanseria the preferred stopover for diplomats and elite business leaders.

Ronan and Deanna sat in a small glass-enclosed privacy booth in one of the airport's VIP lounges, courtesy of Nazia Khatib, MET's benefactor. Clearly, Khatib was sparing no expense when it came to helping MET get a big, splashy win. Through her ongoing intervention, the two were enjoying red-carpet service that few in the U.S. government enjoyed on their travels.

How was Khatib going to respond to the disastrous flight? She could be unpredictable. Sometimes she gave MET wide latitude to do anything they wanted, but other times she could wield power in scary ways. And they'd nearly crashed her jet.

Not to mention she could take away Ronan's technology anytime she wanted. She had Edward by the nuts.

Khatib was powerful within certain intelligence circles. Her company, Lekham Technologies, developed surveillance and security software. By helping top officers in the intelligence community secure lucrative positions in the private sector, she had got what she wanted – the creation of MET, which she regarded as *her* agency. At the very least, it was her brainchild.

Like many divisions of the sprawling Federal intelligence bureaucracy, MET's mission overlapped with the missions of other departments. In theory, MET was a small outpost, a bit player in the Defense Intelligence Agency. In reality, MET was one of Khatib's monopoly board pieces, waiting for a chance to become relevant.

Her endgame was to position MET as a key division of the DIA, and for her company, Leckham Technologies, to be a chief supplier of expertise and technology to the military. Everything from Edward's appointment as Director to Ronan's augmentation technology to the use of her private plane and this VIP suite was just an investment for the day when MET broke through and transformed Khatib's wealth by another comma. All they needed was a major win, then she could secure massive government contracts for terrorist surveillance systems, transhuman military technologies, and automated weaponry. Leckham had a backlog of software for the intelligence community, including FaceLab – which Ronan used – and FaceFill, which could identify terrorists from a grainy photo. For the armed forces, the company had hands-free tactical rifles and prototype brain interfaces. There was no end to the software, hardware, and services they were ready to sell to the federal government, beginning with MET once the Center proved itself.

The world of the one-percenters was new to Ronan and getting a taste of it made him envy the lifestyle. But he wasn't in this business for the money. Technology was going to turn people into humans 2.0, and he knew the good guys needed to get there first.

Their booth had large windows overlooking the airstrip. Out on the tarmac, two private security guards stood near the plane, its sleek angles glinting in the sun.

Ronan had given Edward an update as soon as they touched down, even before the plane had pulled itself onto the apron. Deadly weapons had flown in the plane's cabin, so access was restricted until Edward and Khatib could decide how to proceed. They had not notified the local authorities that anything was amiss, wanting to prevent panic and a barrage of red tape that might hinder the investigation. Instead, they'd hired security under the pretense that the owner had expensive antiques on board.

Guess we're flying commercial from now on, Ronan thought, looking at the sleek, grey plane. The wasps were probably long gone, just as the mosquitoes had disappeared from the Nashville attack.

Looking at the plane and thinking about Khatib was just a distraction. He was feeling extremely uncomfortable. It wasn't because he was drenched in sweat – indeed he was, but the air conditioning was quickly drying him off. And it wasn't because killer wasps might be waiting outside. The problem was Deanna, sitting across the small table, eyes boring into him.

"You're not happy," Ronan observed, not bothering to engage FaceLab.

"Damn right, I'm not. You almost got us killed. You didn't listen to me. I'm in charge, remember?"

"With all due respect, you oversee the investigation. You aren't in charge of preventing airplane crashes. For that particular situation, you and I are on equal footing."

Her eyes cut away, giving him some relief. She tapped the table. Her phone lay inches away, screen dark.

A waiter approached their enclosure with the drinks they had ordered, and the door slid open. The waiter set a glass of bourbon on the table by her phone. He handed Ronan a lemonade. The man sensed a serious conversation underway and didn't linger. The door closed.

Deanna rustled the ice cubes and brought the drink to her lips, her eyes again fixing on him for a moment. Then she sighed. "How did that fiasco just happen?"

"We let our guard down."

"I didn't think we needed to have it up. But that's not what I'm asking. How did they know who we are, where we were going? Who put those weapons on the plane?"

"I don't know. I haven't had time to think this through."

"The obvious guess is that Li did it. He is involved. He wanted to get rid of us, so he had Siyu sabotage the plane." She was staring at him again, but the anger was disappearing, replaced with a cool reserve.

"That's one possibility. We'll soon have investigators crawling up their ass."

"It might be best if you go back and help interrogate."

Ronan straightened. "Why?"

"I don't trust the Taiwanese authorities to get to the bottom of this. If you are there, you can look for inconsistencies in Li's behavior. I'd like you to take the first flight back to Taipei."

"You want to split up?"

"At least for now. I'm going to ask for Edward's approval when he calls."

"Really?" Ronan sat back. "I was starting to think we made a solid team."

She sighed. "If I was completely honest…"

"Go ahead."

"First, I usually work as an independent consultant. I'm not used to someone tagging along."

"Tagging along!"

"That didn't come out right. Don't be offended. It's just that… you're a little unorthodox."

Ronan gritted his teeth. He took two full breaths before speaking. "What's that mean?"

"You fly by the seat of your pants. You're not very disciplined. Frankly, I'm a little surprised you have a combat background."

He watched her for a moment. At first, he couldn't think of a response. Her words had taken him by surprise. "Well, that hurt."

"Sorry."

An awkward silence followed.

"You're right about me being undisciplined. That's just who I am. There's a reason I didn't stay in the military. I have a reckless nature. More than you know. I'll be the first to admit that."

She raised her eyebrows. A hint of a smile. "I'm glad we're on the same page. I just need to go to Sanar and learn all I can, without a lot of drama."

"What if you miss something important? I can record everything."

"I'm sorry Ronan, I just don't think we both need to be there. I can ask the right questions."

"Hmm." He felt a pit in his stomach. "I will go where you and Edward want me to go. But I feel I am more useful here."

"You'd have to give me a good argument why."

"For one thing, if Li is the culprit, as you say, then he wouldn't have sent us anyplace useful to our investigation. He would throw us off the trail. That would make Sanar a waste of your time, meaning you should return to Taipei with me."

She nodded. "I agree he wouldn't direct us to the source of the terrorists' bioweapons. But I can learn useful background information from Sanar's research."

"I'm not convinced Li is one of the perpetrators. In that case, why would he try to kill us? That would just focus the investigation on him. Furthermore, I was running a behavior scan on him the whole time. I saw no red alerts or signs of lying."

"Those are good points. It doesn't all make sense yet." She glanced at her phone. "This is Edward calling."

"What if Siyu acted on his own?" Ronan asked.

She hesitated. The phone continued ringing.

"That makes sense, doesn't it?" Ronan said. "Maybe Li's instincts were dead-on. He knew that Sanar was conducting relevant biomedical research. In other words, Li had nothing to do with the attack. He just knew from his industry connections that Sanar was the right place for us to check out."

She set the phone down.

"When that happened, Siyu panicked. He sabotaged the plane, even though that itself would be suspicious. He took that risk because the alternative was worse. He had a bigger problem. He was terrified of what we would find here."

"But if we died traveling from LikeLife to Sanar," she countered, "others would come to investigate both labs. That doesn't solve his problem." Her tone had less conviction now.

"Siyu was just buying time. A day or two. That gives the conspirators at Sanar time to clean up their tracks and get away. Meanwhile, he leaves the country and disappears into China. We don't know anything about him. He may have a fake identity and background."

She said, "What if Siyu was simply trying to stop us before the world linked LikeLife's products to the attack?"

Ronan shook his head. "He was worried, but not about his investment in LikeLife. If he wanted to avoid attention and prevent a media mess, sabotaging our plane would be the dumbest thing to do. No, he was worried we would uncover something right here in Johannesburg. This was just a stall tactic, nothing more."

She took a sip of her drink. "That's a pretty good theory, Ronan. It's simple, and simple is good."

"I like to stay one step ahead of you."

"Let's not go that far."

"It's just a theory," Ronan said, "but you know in your gut that is exactly what happened. Now the two of us need to conduct a thorough look into the activities at Sanar and figure out what made Siyu so nervous."

He smiled.

"Okay, you win that debate." She tapped her phone to dial Edward. "We'll stay together for now. But if you get in my way or cause problems, I'm going to find a side project for you."

He felt a surge of anger but squelched it. Maybe she was deliberately rankling him to gauge his reaction. He thought he had been professional at LikeLife, but maybe she'd seen through his good behavior, saw the lack of discipline underneath.

She had recognized it, and she didn't like it.

The waiter caught Ronan's eye and headed toward their table. Ronan slid the Do Not Disturb sign across their door.

...

Deanna put Edward on speaker, keeping the volume low, and held it between their heads so Ronan could hear. Ronan had just spoken to Edward to engage airport security; this second call was a formal briefing on the overall investigation.

Edward's voice was small and fuzzy. Bad connection. "How are you both doing? Deanna, are you okay?"

"I'm a bit shaken, Edward, but we're safe. I'm eager for the next stage of this investigation. The attack gives us concrete interrogation targets and confirms that our initial hunches were correct."

"Absolutely. We are officially on someone's radar, and that is a good thing. We must be extra careful from now on, but the plane attack also fast-forwards our progress. The Taiwanese National Security Bureau is already talking to Li. We haven't located Siyu yet. I'll let you know how those developments proceed. In any event, I am overjoyed that you were able to get yourselves safely to the ground. Khatib sends her best wishes. Don't worry about her plane. She says she'll take care of matters."

Ronan glanced out at the tarmac. Someone – Ronan didn't know who – would have to go over every inch of that plane. He had no idea how they would verify that the plane was safe to use. What if something smaller than wasps was hiding in there? An ant, a flea, waiting for the motion of a nearby human to activate it? Khatib would probably offload the jet on some rich dude without disclosing the incident or the risks. Chances are, everything would be fine.

Edward continued. "As for the terrorist attack, our best guess is that one of the 80,000 game attendees brought in a handful of microdrones, which would be easy to hide. The drones could have emerged from a trash bin or some other place that wouldn't draw attention. After injecting a payload into someone, each drone simply left – flew out the door with the hordes of people, or maybe disappeared into the ductwork. None were recovered. We assume at least one of the drones was still onsite when the DHS arrived."

"They can attack randomly," Ronan said. "But the fancier ones have a camera and transmitter. You could land it on whoever you wish. Have you heard anything about the pilot?"

"As you noticed, the pilot was hemorrhaging from the eyes and nose. I just got off the phone with Dr. Cevelas, and he confirmed that none of the victims at the Nashville attack had external bleeding. The difference is unsettling. The terrorists must have a variety of injectable payloads available to them."

"Good point," Deanna said. "We'll keep that in mind when we talk to the Sanar researchers."

Ronan lowered his voice. "How's the video analysis coming? Has FaceFill identified anyone?"

"Unfortunately, no. The man on the horse may have worn multiple face wraps to throw off his contours."

"Any clues about where the video was shot?"

Edward sighed. "Again, no. The terrorist is standing in front of tropical plants found in the Americas. We have a few dozen species identified, and a few birds. It's rainforest."

"That's progress, right?"

"We have the location of the video narrowed down to about one million square miles."

Edward was being sarcastic? He must be frustrated with FaceFill's failure to score a win for MET. Ronan also knew that Khatib had promised Edward an easy board position at Lekham Technologies, if he could help grease a large contract.

Deanna ended the call. She glanced at her watch. "We're supposed to be at Sanar in an hour. The Director is Niko March. We can't be too heavy-handed. But we must also act quickly. As you said, someone may be preparing to cover their tracks and get out of town."

Ronan downed the last of his lemonade.

She slid open the booth. "Let's get to work."

Jonathan James Harper never had to wait for his followers to arrive at the morning meeting. They were always on time. Without a beeping alarm or buzzing alert or haptic brush of the skin, using only the position of the sun to notify them, they funneled in and took their seats on the tree stumps that passed for chairs. Even the guards, after checking the traps and, if necessary, resetting them, arrived promptly. Three days had passed since they had attacked Nashville. All of his followers were committed to their urgent goals, but Harper was the founder. He was the architect of the vision. And he was the spokesperson: Harper was the man on the video who had told the world to pay attention.

While they settled, his lips moved in silence: *all will attend the morning meeting.* He mouthed the words over and over.

Their gathering place was a cavernous room in the depths of their fortress, a hallowed, spartan space that resembled a primitive worship area, with dirt floors, dim natural lighting, hand-hewn stools, and a massive carved table for him at the front. The sturdy covers on the skylights hung open, but these could be snapped closed using a pulley system with stone-weights. Here, among the earthy smells that emanated from the damp walls, they discussed the cultivation of mushrooms, disposal of fecal waste and methods for carving bone hooks, and the next step in destroying the global techno-industrial framework. The rooms around them consisted of workshops and storage areas, mushroom farms, and sleeping cells.

Harper leaned forward on the table, which he had hacked and carved out of tigerwood and inlaid with the bones of sloths, both the animal and human varieties. He favored tigerwood over the wood of some of the other trees in the forest: tigerwood was hard and strong, resistant to fire and fungus, but also could be carved and cut without difficulty, and the grain had a deep striped beauty that symbolized the ferocity of their passion. Most of the walls and floors of the building were rock and clay, but the men had made clever use of tigerwood, ipe, and Jatoba wood throughout the corridors and crawlspaces on all three levels.

Harper stroked each of the items that rested on the table's surface. His fingers touched the cobwebbed glass of an ancient NuTablet, the logo of the manufacturer scratched off in furious gouges, a symbol of the black corruption that threatened to engulf and extinguish his race; a clay bowl of soil taken from his garden, which he loved to run his fingers through, as this helped center his mind on the bare facts of the world; an old piece of terry cloth, which he used to remind himself, and his followers, of the differences between mother and mother earth. A flame flickered from a small lamp – a jambo fruit sliced across the top, hollowed out, and filled with pacu fish oil, creating a glowing rose-pink orb. Beautiful!

As the last of his followers took their seat, Harper reflected on their future plans. They had more attacks coming. They were working with a scientist who would soon provide a thousand more payload recipes, and each recipe was a new way to tear into people's bodies. Harper's team would arm swarms of biters with these payloads and release them into crowds, eliminating large swaths of human dander with little effort or expense. The payloads were not a contagion, so there was no chance of it escaping Harper's control. Such attacks were a bit ghoulish, he admitted to himself, but that's what made them the perfect way to get attention.

Harper had given the scientist three days to deliver the requested payloads. The man had been visibly nervous during their recent online call and might now regret his role in their first attack. Harper was glad the man was afraid. As long as the scientist felt fear, he would cooperate with Harper for the sake of his own survival.

The position of the sun's rays against the skylight shafts overhead told Harper it was time for the meeting to start. To bring the room to attention, he lifted the bowl and brought it down, rapping three times on the table.

Sixty men fixed their full attention on him and he felt a familiar wonderful feeling: they were one, a whole far more than the sum of their parts, a noble collection of revolutionaries like nothing the world had ever seen. Most wore their hair long, nearly all had full beards, and they were heavily decorated with tattoos from their former lives. These were the Kazites living at the compound who farmed, built, and maintained everything around them. Their counterparts, the Outsiders, moved in the world beyond and used technology according to his orders to raise awareness of the mad evils of Silicon Valley, strike hard at the drunken idiots mesmerized by the glow of their screens, and build the framework for the sustainable natural world to come.

All of them were radically committed to the same goal as their hero, Theodore Kaczynski. Terminate the industrial age.

The Kazites waited, some clutching gourds of a bitter, steaming tea brewed from yerba leaves, a concoction they learned from the locals, their Indian friends, the bright orange warriors who hid among the leaves. Harper closed his eyes and stuck fingers into his bowl of soil. Worms in the cool depths wiggled. Opening his eyes again after a period of contemplation, which may have been a minute or five, he focused on his men.

He stood, throwing his hands into the air. "Ripped from its mother's arms and thrown into hell!"

"The monkey prefers the cloth!" the Kazites roared back.

Harper gripped the edge of the table and adjusted his focus. "You are all aware of our mission status. Many of you have asked to play a larger role in the war. You must understand that for now I need you to maintain our home, keep ready for reprisal. The world won't be happy when we rattle the cage. The Outsiders have kept us updated. They've followed my commands. And what tremendous success! I've written a full account of the insights we provided to a sleeping world via the attendees at the Nashville game and the world's reactions to those insights. It's posted on the board in the common area. Read it over and over. Digest. Absorb. Relish. Give thanks. Graham, what news?"

First Lieutenant Graham Bolton, a large man who had grown so dark and hairy in the long months of jungle life that he now seemed carved out of a rotting Brazil nut tree, stood up.

Harper nodded for him to begin.

"Sir, two American officers were snooping around LikeLife in Taiwan."

Harper raised his eyebrows. "The Outsiders recovered every m-drone from the game. How did the enemy connect things so quickly?"

"Maybe someone got a good photograph that identified the manufacturer."

Harper's eyes flared but he composed himself. "Yes, yes, fine." He waved his hand. "They won't suspect Siyu."

The Lieutenant shifted. "There's more. According to Siyu, Li made an accurate guess about the source of the payload…"

Harper's eyes flared again.

"…and he sent them straight to Sanar."

Wow, Harper thought, fists clenched. *Siyu is an idiot for thinking he can run this operation right under Li's nose. Li is too damn smart. But there's no need to worry.* "We will lay low for now. They won't find anything."

"It gets worse. When Siyu realized the investigators were headed to Niko's lab, he attempted to kill them. Maybe he panicked. We don't know whether Siyu acted on his own or from orders of…"

"I fail to believe what I am hearing."

"The investigators survived the attack and are in South Africa. It's certain that they are heading for Sanar. They will be on their guard and suspicious now, and more likely to identify our source… the worst possible outcome."

Harper stepped backward until the back of his knees touched his chair. He reached for the armrests. Once he could feel them beneath his fingers, he eased himself into the seat.

"It's going to be okay," one of the men growled.

"Of course it is!" Harper slammed his fist down on the table. "I'm not worried about our future. Our plans are perfect. The future will happen. It cannot be otherwise. The problem, it seems, is that our allies made the mistake of thinking for themselves. Well, they need me. I have all the vision. I am the one making things happen. They are the idiots."

"We need to keep the initiative," Lieutenant Bolton said.

Harper thought about that, and after a moment, while the rest of the Kazites waited, his thin lips split into a wicked grin. "No worries," he said. "I'll handle it."

"Can we help you plan?" the lieutenant asked.

Harper wiped his hands one finger at a time. Action was required – immediately. The American investigators had to be eliminated, quietly, without the slightest hint of anything that could be tracked back to the Kazites. Make them disappear. Leave no trail. Siyu also must be dealt with. Harper could not, however, chance dispiriting his men by striking too hard against a key ally in the cause. Best to keep that part quiet.

"Lieutenant, how many Outsiders do we have at the Johannesburg warehouse?"

"Ten, including that toothless guy."

"Set up a call."

"Yes, sir." The lieutenant nodded. But he did not sit.

"Graham, what is the matter?"

"There's one more thing."

"What? What else?"

"Siyu said one of the U.S. intelligence officers is augmented. A guy named Ronan Flynn."

CHAPTER 22
SANAR NANOMED
JOHANNESBURG, SOUTH AFRICA

Ronan and Deanna drove toward Sanar Nanomed. Someone from the airport had loaded their luggage into a sleek black T7 Kargaan, a roomy personal transport they had at their disposal for as long as they needed. They left the airport and headed north to the Sanar campus to meet the company's founder.

Niko March was a British citizen educated at Oxford who now lived and worked in South Africa. They'd found plenty of public information on him: thirty-seven years old, fit and healthy, dedicated to science and human rights, fashionable and well groomed, a frequent supporter of charity events. He was widely respected for evangelizing the potential of automated medicine; in keynote speeches, he captivated his audiences with visions of a disease-free future. He had no wife or kids.

South African officials had notified him that American investigators needed his help. He had been instructed to answer their questions. He met them in the foyer, his face blank.

"Thank you for supporting the investigation," Deanna said. "Jin Li suggested that we visit you."

"Jin Li?" Niko asked.

"He's the CEO of–"

"I know him. One of our scientists wrote a paper that threw some heat on his business. I didn't realize he was behind this. The agency's request seemed to come out of the blue. What are we trying to achieve here?"

"Our theory," Deanna said, "is that a synthetic bioweapon was deployed at the stadium in Nashville during the game. We would like your expertise and insight."

"We don't make weapons here. Our products are for the medical industry."

"Understood. But that paper you just mentioned is highly relevant. Can you at least explain what you do here?"

Niko smiled for the first time, but he did not look happy. "Of course." No doubt, he had not enjoyed being approached by the State Security Agency to assist with an international terrorist investigation. Ronan wondered what pressure they had placed on him. Maybe his lab had a history with the authorities. Maybe he knew the best approach was full cooperation and transparency.

He led them down an empty corridor. Wide windows gave a generous view of the sky; a thick cloud hung over the city, dulling the interior light.

"There's not a lot to see. Upstairs we have a server room, finance, administration, and a kitchen. Down here, labs and offices for the researchers." They entered a room full of whiteboards and sticky notes. "We meet here to discuss ideas. It's a multidisciplinary team with specialists in molecular robotics, nano-biochemistry, synthetic organ printing, nerve genesis, and other fields. We cross-fertilize. We help each other see outside the blinders of each discipline."

"You better write all this down," Ronan whispered to Deanna as Niko headed into the next room.

She gave him the finger and whispered, "My guy's recording it."

Ronan was still rattled by their near-death experience and was pleased that she seemed to be in a teasing mood. Humor was a common reaction to almost getting killed.

They entered a lab. A row of instruments sat on a bench, most about the size of a microwave oven. They looked a lot like Li's microbot production machines.

"Our process is an assembly line," Niko said. "Step one, step two, bingo – new drug. What can I explain further to help you folks?"

"I read that your therapies target specific cells in the body," Deanna said. "Please explain, if you don't mind."

"They are made right here, in these synthesizers. The molecules are smaller than a virus, about twenty or thirty nanometers long. We call them nanites."

Niko scribbled on a whiteboard. "Our lab came up with the idea of a straight carbon chain that serves as a chassis. On the front, we stick little molecular claws or other tools depending on what we need the nanite to do. But nanites don't look like a typical machine, there aren't any wires or gears or anything like that."

Ronan's ocular flashed. SCIENTIST IS EXPLAINING.

He clicked it away.

Niko said, "Three things make the nanite far better than an ordinary drug: one, extreme tissue specificity, which reduces side effects; two, ability to model the entire thing from scratch; and three, the ability to execute multiple functions in a coordinated fashion."

With a few deft strokes of his marker, Niko drew something that looked like a lunar landing module. "Nature builds stuff like this too. This is a T4 bacteriophage, a virus that infects bacteria. It's about 200 nanometers long, with a polyhedral head sitting on a coiled tail. It's a four-function machine. Smart prongs on the tail latch on to the bacterium's cell membrane, which triggers the tail to contract, which injects DNA instructions from the T4's protective head down into the bacterium. The T4 is simple and efficient, designed by natural processes. That's similar to what we build. Tiny molecular machines that act on a specific target."

"How do they move around the body?" Ronan asked.

"Great question."

Ronan smiled at Deanna, tapped his head, and winked. She rolled her eyes.

Niko drew a blood vessel around his scribbled nanite. "They flow around in the blood. In thirty seconds, they've travelled the entire body." He drew branches from his blood vessel and something that looked like a stomach, which he circled. "The nanites have built-in tissue detectors. Blood vessels in the brain are not like blood vessels in the stomach or the heart or the kidney. They all have different receptors, chemical environments, and other triggers. The nanites don't control where they are going, but they know when they've arrived."

"Like an antibody," Deanna said.

"Ja! Perfect analogy."

Deanna winked at Ronan and tapped her head.

"I find it odd you call these machines," Ronan said. "A nanite sounds more like a man-made protein."

Niko pointed at him. "Agreed. When you build smaller and smaller machines, at some point they are just chemistry. At the molecular level, there is no difference between life and non-life, enzyme or machine."

Ronan winked at Deanna and nodded.

"Fascinating," Deanna said. "Come to think of it, I never considered what makes something a machine."

Niko wagged his marker. "Everything is a machine. Me, bugs, plants, computers. You two can stop winking at each other. If you want to get a room, I can find some splendid accommodations."

"I'm so sorry, we've had a long flight," Deanna stammered. "We're unwinding a lot of stress."

"I am joking. Water, food, snack?"

"We're good. Keep going."

Ronan had been recording everything since the beginning of the investigation and realized there was a lot of interesting stuff written on the whiteboards he had seen at LikeLife and Sanar. He initiated a program to analyze all of it and check for anything suspicious. It would take awhile to get back any results.

"Our process is simple." Niko patted a laptop. "We have a huge database of cell receptors and other biological factors… a massive catalogue of keyholes in the human body. We model a small key for any keyhole, then come in here–" Niko pointed to the instruments surrounding them, "–and crank out a million variations of the key."

"Forgive me for all these questions," Deanna said. "How do you test this stuff?"

"Rapid assay screening. I can show you in the next room."

Ronan soon found himself peering into a large incubator at rows and rows of shallow dishes sitting on angled shelves. A monitor read 36.1C. Stuff was growing in the dishes, a gelatinous material covered in blue dots.

Niko consulted a label on the incubator. "Brain tissue on a vascular matrix. Each blue dot is an injection point of a nanite variant. The tissue is sliced up and laser-scanned for macro-level impact."

Ronan saw hundreds of incubators, each with thousands of dishes, each with tens of thousands of blue dots.

"Every step is automated," Niko said. "Robotics run the whole thing – moving, slicing, packing, prepping. My researchers don't even model anything on the computer. We wrote scripts that find their own keyholes. Downstream, software analyzes all the data."

Deanna exhaled. "Then what do your scientists do?"

"They optimize the automation. Tweak it. The nanites coming out the other end are incredibly potent. The whole process is almost too efficient…" he stopped, creating an awkward pause.

"What do you mean?" Deanna asked.

Niko tried to sound cavalier. "The nanites we single out are extremely powerful. When injecting animals, we use very low doses or look for less-effective versions."

"I'm not following," Ronan said, although he was indeed following, and they all seemed to understand that a significant fact had been revealed.

"A lot of our research focuses on destroying bad stuff – cancer, diseased tissue. We aren't trying to harm healthy organs. But let's say we want to treat atherosclerosis and we develop a nanite that strips off arterial plaque. The problem is, we could inject just a little dose and discover it tears right through the walls of the arteries."

Ronan and Deanna exchanged glances.

"Really…?" she asked.

"It turns out then when you have severe plaque, you have to keep a little – it's helping hold the artery together. In the old days we spent years blindly testing potential therapeutics, but now we can target almost any cell type in the human body with ease. It's like we're holding a powerful laser and trying to find the right settings so we don't destroy the target. To be clear, that's the purpose of lab testing."

"I guess that's the better problem," she said.

"Ja. Keep in mind how fantastic this is for the health of the world. We have a deep pipeline of therapies. We are making amazing progress on cancer, heart disease, TB, and many other conditions, but it still takes years to push our discoveries through the drug approval process. First animal testing, then human clinical trials. We don't actually have anything close to market yet. The country's regulatory system is clogged up like an artery, I like to say."

As they walked down a main hall, Niko tapped security panels to give them a glimpse into various rooms.

"Cold storage," he said, pushing a door open to reveal a large, refrigerated room.

At the next room, he said, "This is frozen storage. We never dispose of the nanites. The laws and regulations are still evolving. Some officials are afraid the nanites could wreak havoc if they got into the water supply. These folks don't even want our samples getting into the landfills. We proposed incinerating everything, but they didn't like that idea, either. So all of it is right here until the regulations are worked out – I'm probably boring you, aren't I?"

"Not at all," Ronan said. "You're getting to the good parts. Keep going."

The freezer room looked even bigger than cold storage.

"Anyway, this is where we freeze our nanites." Moving down the hall, Niko reached the next door. He grasped the handle, then let it go. "This room doesn't have much to show." He rubbed his hands together and said, "Let's go meet a few of our researchers."

...

Dozens of researchers and engineers milled about the facilities.

Everyone they met was the same: busy scientists who smiled, answered a few questions, then resumed their work. Ronan assumed they'd been told ahead of time that officers were on site, investigating the Nashville attack. They were a quiet bunch.

But back in the lab, two of them were arguing. "It's my business," a young man said, "and I'm not asking for your input."

"I'm only trying to help," an older man grumbled.

"It doesn't affect you or anyone else."

"You're going to get yourself in–"

"Pieter," Niko interrupted. He gestured to the older man. "I want you to meet Ronan Flynn and Deanna Pirelli, from the states."

The two men, who hadn't seen the group enter, synthesized smiles.

"As I told all of our staff this morning," Niko continued, "our visitors are doing research to understand what might have caused the death of those victims in the recent U.S. attack. I'm not entirely sure how we can help, but we should do what we can to explain our work." Niko clamped a hand on the older scientist. "This is Dr. Pieter Heynes. He has been doing nanomedicine longer than any of us. He was one of my inspirations for going into the field. And this is Jeboko Kahn, who did his thesis work here."

No one said anything.

To address the sudden awkwardness, Ronan explained further. "We don't know what killed the victims, but nanoweapons are one possibility. We knew your lab is doing interesting research and wanted a little background."

Pieter nodded. "You are right to be concerned."

"Pieter wrote that paper on the dangers of nanotechnology," Niko said. "But we love him anyway."

"Is there anything going on here that could be used as a weapon?" Deanna asked.

Pieter hesitated.

"As I said, we don't do military work here," Niko answered.

Deanna nodded but said, "Pieter, what were you going to say?"

Pieter rubbed his chin. "There is material here that could be dangerous in the wrong hands. But we are a medical research facility. If you want to find terrorists, you'll have to look under a lot of rocks. Automated labs are popping up in all kinds of remote places. You'd want to look into a lot of state actors, hostile nations that want to disrupt democracy. Where to begin?"

"I want to get back to your point about the nanite's targeting capability," Ronan said. "The terrorists used an agent that chewed up heart tissue, leaving nothing but goo. Is it possible to create something like that here at Sanar?"

Niko didn't hesitate. "Ja, but as I said, we call those failures. No one here is actually trying to *attack* heart muscle."

"And even the failures are in the freezers? The overly reactive stuff?" Deanna asked.

"Yes," Niko said. "But we monitor who goes into the freezers and what they take out. Few people have access."

"Come with me," Ronan said.

"Where are you going?" Deanna and Niko chimed at the same time.

Ronan returned to the frozen storage room, tapped at the keypad and held up his phone. After a light beep, he swung the door open and stepped inside. The freezer was vast, with many corridors of racks.

Niko hustled to the door. "How did you get the password? The pad switches the number locations every time and the security combines an iris scan."

"I zoomed in and recorded the numbers when you entered them. I also took a high-def photo of your eyes with my ocular, added 3D and tissue filters, and pulled up your eye on my phone." He scanned the rows of vials. "I'm making a point. What's the craziest stuff you've got in here?"

Deanna tried to apologize, but Niko held up a hand. "Maybe this isn't the most secure place in the world. But none of my staff are terrorists. Don't touch anything. You aren't trained to handle this material. We have strict protocols – gloves, coats, all that."

"Shouldn't this be Biosafety Level 4 or something?"

"That's mainly for biological pathogens. These don't fall into a definite regulated category yet. What do you call atherosclerosis treatment with potentially deadly consequences? Think about it. Many drugs can cause lethal side effects. These nanites are not infectious, and they aren't airborne. For now, we aren't held to that standard."

"So, anyone can just walk in here and grab one of these?" Ronan asked. Some of the samples were simply available for the taking, while others were locked in steel canisters or other containers. All were labeled on tape with various handwriting.

"Ronan–" Deanna said.

Niko put his hand firmly on Ronan's shoulder and stared intently. "You totally missed the point. These nanites are all made with simple recipe instructions. No one needs these physical samples. All they need is one of those synthesizers out there. And those synthesizers are for sale. You can just buy one."

Ronan pulled away from Niko's hand. "Then describe some of the potent stuff a person could make with your recipes, so we can wrap up this visit and go home. What's the worst stuff in here?"

Niko didn't respond. He seemed to be debating his answers.

Ronan tried to sound supportive, but his words came out stern. "Look, I'm not a health inspector. I'm not interested in South African regulations or politics. But I do want to know what can kill people, and I intend to find out one way or another."

Deanna added, "Our investigation is limited to the Nashville attack. You could be drinking this stuff and we don't care."

"Who will you share this information with?"

"U.S. intelligence officials, but only if it is pertinent to the investigation. Depending on where this goes, we may need to share our findings with the South African intelligence community."

Niko shifted. "Please know that we'd *never* put anything dangerous in a human, but we've had some nasty things happen in our – you guys aren't animal rights activists or anything?"

"No."

Niko raised his hand and pointed to one of the sample racks. He tried to sound matter-of-fact. "That's one of the really harmful ones, for example."

A handful of tubes had red labels printed with skulls. They were inside an acrylic box, which itself had been wrapped many times with skull tape. Ronan asked, "What's it do?"

Niko sighed. "The nanites in those tubes react to a protein found on the surface of all mammalian cells, so they attack everything. Heart, lungs, face, hands, eyes."

A shadow crossed Deanna's face. "The label says 'Groot Gemors.'"

"That's Afrikaans for *Big Mess*."

Deanna rubbed her hand over her face. "Did you inject this into an animal?"

"We did. Unfortunately."

"And...?"

"One minute we had a rat, and then..."

"This is all a bit concerning," Ronan said. "You have some nasty stuff in here. Would you be willing to provide logs of everyone who has used your synthesizers and anyone with access to all the recipes, as you call them, and the effects of each recipe?"

Niko didn't answer for a moment. "Let me give that request some thought. You claimed you were here to learn about nanotech. This has become a different conversation. Are you saying that the real reason for your visit is that our lab is under formal investigation?"

"No," Deanna said. "But some of the stuff you make here is interesting."

Niko stared off at a far wall. "I want to cooperate. We have nothing to hide. I'll see if we can get you that information. For now, that's all I have to show."

Retracing their route, they passed the door Niko had skipped. Ronan said, "I'd like to see what's in here. That okay?"

Niko tapped on the room's security keypad. Opening the door, the lights activated. They revealed row after row of cages – rats, mice, guinea pigs, rabbits. In the back, a monkey sat in a cage, its head secured.

"You test on all these?" Ronan asked.

"I was hoping not to upset you. We do what we have to do."

Exchanging glances with Deanna, Ronan felt a bit sickened, but he knew this kind of testing was necessary before you injected humans with test drugs. He stepped back out into the hall.

"Niko, you have been extremely gracious and forthcoming." Ronan glanced at Deanna. "I'd like to suggest we all go to dinner. I'd like to meet some of your scientists. A good turnout will help keep everything friendly. Would you be interested?" He hoped Niko would understand that this was more of a demand than a request. He wanted to know more about these "failures," as Niko called them. Most were probably trivial, but at least some were extremely dangerous.

Niko accepted the dinner invitation. He would round up some of the staff to join them.

Ronan felt a sense of clarity and mission. Sanar might not house the terrorists themselves, but the nanites were a viable candidate for the weapon used at the football game. His hunch was proving correct.

Deanna seemed a little irritated, he thought, that he hadn't asked her to discuss next steps. The dinner idea had been spontaneous.

Back outside, Ronan and Deanna headed to their hotel. "Sorry to wing it in there," he said. "But they are going to clam up quickly. Niko is probably meeting with his staff right now, telling them that we might close the lab down. We could interview them for weeks and not uncover anything else."

"Probably right."

Ronan said, "We need to liquor these folks up and get them talking."

They took the elevator to their suite at the Michelangelo Hotel. The lights clicked on. The suite had two rooms separated by a common area.

They had time to settle in before dinner.

Deanna disappeared into one of the rooms. "I'll take this one."

Ronan surveyed the suite.

TROUSER PRESS, $650.

ORIENTAL CARPET, $2,500.

PLASTIC COFFEEMAKER, $5.

The balcony caught his eye. He opened the sliding door and stepped into a warm breeze. Up here, the sounds of the street were muffled and lights glittered throughout the city. He sat at a small table to absorb the view.

He activated PulseView, a visual layer powered by a thin device embedded in the skin over his right eyebrow, which emitted radio waves and used the reflection pattern to detect the distance, shape, and movement of objects, then converted this data into a dynamic image. The resulting display on his ocular turned the dark night to full daylight.

The transformation was far superior to old-school night vision, though still with no sense of color. As he scanned the nearby buildings, their lights and windows appeared in stark gray detail. Flipping to action mode, he watched the bustling streets below. The sidewalks faded onto a background layer while cars and people popped with movement.

He shut it off. Playing with PulseView was just a stall tactic. He needed to talk to Deanna. The Sanar team were going to clam up, and he wanted to tag them with geo trackers in case any left town. She might not like the idea.

"Yo, boss," he yelled into the suite, "check out the view."

She joined him.

"I want to discuss something," he said.

"Yes, we need to talk."

"Oh?"

"You embarrassed me. Breaking into the freezer. As Niko pointed out, the physical samples are irrelevant."

Ronan felt foolish.

"Stop the stunts."

"Okay."

For a while, neither spoke.

Then she said, "What did you want to talk to me about?"

"I don't remember," he lied. He stood.

She said, "If anyone knows how to target organs with ruthless efficiency, it's these guys."

"You got that right." He was a little angry himself, now.

He went to his room and unzipped his suitcase. A guy in a hazmat suit had boarded the plane during the night and retrieved their stuff. Their luggage was zipped up, so probably no worries. Nonetheless, he inspected every side of his suitcase. Finding nothing lurking on it, he flipped it open.

After removing a pair of folded pants and two shirts, he carefully withdrew a slim silver tube. Inside, there was a spool of transparent tape, as thin as tissue paper and spotted with black dots. The smallest location trackers available in the DIA, informally known as ticks. Stick 'em anywhere. He smiled, closed the lid, and started thinking about how to get them on the smartest team of scientists in the world.

CHAPTER 24

An hour later Ronan and Deanna joined twelve of Sanar's key employees for dinner at Belvedere's, a popular seafood joint on the outskirts of the city. Once they were settled into their seats, Ronan began to have doubts about his plan: buy them drinks, ask questions, record everything, then plaster the team with ticks. He touched the right-hand pocket of his blazer, where he had placed the small roll of ticks and a pack of mints.

Each tick had to be peeled off without drawing attention from the group. He planned to remove the mints from his pocket along with the roll, using the mints as a pretense for working his hands while he discretely removed a tick. Once on a fingertip, he could stick it anywhere, although finding a good spot would be difficult. Clothing would not work; they wouldn't be wearing the same shirts and pants every day. Bare skin wouldn't work either. The ticks would wash off.

The most obvious target was scattered right in front of him on the table – their cell phones. He needed to get his hands on every one of those phones, just for a few seconds, and if he could get them drunk enough, perhaps he wouldn't have any problems.

"Thank you for coming," Deanna announced to everyone at the table. "We wanted to show our appreciation. We know it isn't easy having people walking around disrupting your work."

Ronan raised his glass of sweet tea. "And don't forget that the U.S. government is paying for this, so don't hold back. Enjoy yourselves."

The scientists raised their glasses.

"You are gracious," Niko said unconvincingly.

"I've got a question," Pieter blurted, leaning forward so they could see him. He was the older guy who had written about the dangers of combining microbots with nanoweapons.

"What happened to the people at your big game? Organ failure?"

"I'm sorry, we aren't releasing any details at this time." Ronan glanced at his ocular recording of the conversation so far. No red flags yet, though there was one alert from the text analysis he had initiated of all of the investigation's video footage, which he hadn't looked at yet.

Pieter continued. "I have to ask. Are the employees of Sanar potential suspects in any way?"

"Fair question," Ronan answered. "It's obvious that some of the materials you develop at Sanar could be used to kill people. We don't suspect any of you are terrorists, but if there is anything you have heard in your professional circles that might be a little suspicious, please tell us. Someone could have got their hands on the kind of stuff you make."

Niko grunted. Everyone was tense.

Appetizers and drinks arrived soon after, and gradually the group began to relax and fall into natural conversation. As soon as anyone's glass was empty, Ronan ordered a refill.

"This pinot looks good," Deanna said and handed the wine list to Pieter. "Should we try it out?"

Pieter smiled. "This one is wonderful. A magnificent year. I had just joined Sanar and everything was looking up. Let's have some."

Ronan started his plan with the bold approach. "May I look at your phone?" he asked Jeboko, the young grad student who had been arguing with Pieter back at the lab.

Jeboko handed it over.

Ronan made a show of weighing the device in his hand. "It's feels like holding a pen." He turned to Pieter, "What phone do you use? I need a new one."

"The Ojo," Pieter said. He didn't make any effort to hand it to Ronan. He was studying his wine, holding the glass to the light.

Pieter turned and stared deeply at Ronan.

Ronan shifted. "Yes?"

Pieter leaned closer.

Ronan glanced sideways, then back at Pieter. "What?"

"You have a chip in your eye?"

"Oh, right. I forget to tell people. Want to see it move?"

Wondering what had gripped Pieter's attention, everyone twisted in their seats or stood for a better look.

With an unseen tap of his thumb, Ronan extended the lenses of both eyes a few millimeters, then retracted them.

Pieter smiled. "Fascinating. I've not seen those up close."

Ronan took Pieter's Ojo. "Selfie time. I'll push 'em out the whole way."

As the night proceeded, through a variety of subtle moves, Ronan touched every one of their phones. He congratulated himself. No one seemed to notice he was slapping ticks everywhere. Pieter had poured himself more wine, and Ronan thought he'd be loosening up. Addressing Pieter, he said, "Earlier today, Niko mentioned a report you wrote about nanotechnology. What was that about?"

"I wrote a position paper for a U.S. congressman who headed up a subcommittee on nanoweapons. I am concerned about the dangers." Pieter took a long drink.

Deanna scooted over. "Tell us about that."

"I'm more concerned than ever, but not about nations using the weapons on each other. I'm worried about fringe groups getting their hands on the synthesizers. Even the scariest stuff can be produced with ease. Commodity terrorism."

"Any ideas who might have used such weapons in Nashville?"

"No, but I hope the genie isn't loose."

"Do you think that's happened?"

"Maybe. Ronan, the danger is that once the instructions to make something harmful are out there, there is no going back. Any dumb asshole can make it. You can't stamp out the knowledge. And then the next set of instructions comes along, and the next one, and the next."

"You would be a good consultant for MET," Ronan said. He checked the time on his ocular. It was getting late. He remembered the alert from the text analysis and tapped *expand* for details.

The software had flagged – Deanna.

That's odd.

The alert was simple: Terrorist connection – Ladislav Kos.

Why would the analysis connect Deanna to a terrorist group?

The software must be drawing the wrong conclusion.

Still, a quick background check would cross the T's.

According to a quick search, Deanna Pirelli had been a contract analyst with the DIA a few months, and before that, a senior analyst in the Army. He knew that already.

He retrieved the investigation footage where the text had been flagged.

It was from their initial meeting: the folders and papers in the passenger seat of her car, which he'd recorded through her car window. He had forgotten about that. He retrieved the footage. There were several folders. A label on the top folder read: Ronan Flynn. Of course, she'd looked into his background. No big deal.

Beneath that, several sheets of paper had slid out of another folder. He saw a few handwritten words on them.

Zoom in. Boost contrast. De-pixelate.

The visible words were:

Ladislav Kos is

automate

What could that mean, and who was this "Ladislav Kos"?

He wasn't sure how the software connected people to terrorists – the algorithms could be maddeningly opaque – but he could try a search himself. He checked whether any employees at LikeLife or Sanar had any connection to this fellow Ladislav. Within seconds, the results played across his view.

One match.

Huh?

He pulled up the detail.

Siyu had worked with Ladislav Kos.

What was Deanna's connection to this guy, Kos? He did another quick check.

At one point, Deanna had been a contractor for Cyphertek Consulting, a Taiwanese software security firm that also hired Siyu. *Both she and Siyu had worked with Ladislav,* who was a prominent AI researcher for the firm based out of Slovenia.

What the hell?

"Where's your mind?" Deanna elbowed him gently. "You look troubled."

Ronan couldn't concentrate on the activity around him. *What am I supposed to do with this information?*

"Hello, Ronan," Deanna said, waving her hand before his eyes.

"Sorry," he replied. "Are you enjoying dinner?"

Her phone buzzed. "Hold on, I have to take this."

She hopped from her chair and headed toward the front lobby.

As he watched her walk away, he thought back on everything that had happened in the past few days. She had homed in on LikeLife within hours, and now they were possibly near a breakthrough. Just lucky? *Or did she know something? Was she involved somehow?* If so, why would she lead the investigation to the source? They had tried to kill her on the plane. Why would they do that if she was involved? To get rid of her?

He thought about that possibility. What if she was on their bankroll, but she was playing both sides? Maybe they realized she was betraying them.

Ronan agonized, weighing his options.

Deanna returned. "I have to go. Sorry to make it a short night. Are you all set here?"

"Yes."

She leaned to his ear. "You okay?"

"I'm fine."

"Should I stay?"

"No, go ahead."

Deanna gave him a puzzled look. "Let me know if you need to touch base later." She dropped her phone in her purse.

"You should say goodbye to Niko," he said.

Niko was telling the group a story. The only thing Ronan heard was "we killed it immediately." Everybody laughed. Deanna went over to say goodbye.

Ronan fished her phone out of her purse, flipped it over, and dabbed a tick on it. What was one more tiny black shape at the bottom of a phone? She'd never notice.

He was dropping it back in her purse as she returned.

Just in time. Maybe.

Deanna smiled briefly as she picked up her purse and hurried out.

Oh no, Ronan thought. *What have I done?*

CHAPTER 25

Ronan lay on his hotel bed, eyes shut. A map from his ocular floated in the darkness. It showed the pathways of the ticks throughout the city over the past hour, their locations tracing across his vision like wandering fireflies.

He felt energized. Sanar's research seemed related to the Nashville attack. The company was inventing dangerous stuff, intentionally or not. Someone, probably Siyu, had tried to kill them, possibly to derail the American investigation for a few days. If anyone at Sanar was involved in terrorist activity, they might rendezvous with other terrorists or leave the country.

Big *if*, though.

The tracking system showed that everyone he'd bugged was back at home, everyone except Niko, who had returned to work. The other tracker blips were relaxed, moving intermittently in the confines of suburban homes.

Ronan reviewed the various locations the Sanar employees had visited after dinner – a yoga center, a supermarket, a pediatric oncology center. Nothing suspicious. All he could do was watch and see if anything unusual happened.

At the moment, Pieter paced in his apartment. Odd, but maybe he was exercising. The bony old scientist did not seem like a person who worked out much, though.

Deanna, too, was pacing in her room, thirty feet from him.

How should he deal with this new information about her? She *couldn't* be guilty of anything. She seemed like a dedicated field operator driven to find these terrorists. He had to be careful not to jump to conclusions, even if the evidence looked bad. There could be a good reason for her secretive behavior and troubling background associations. Right?

Too many questions.

As Ronan watched, Niko left Sanar and headed down the street to an establishment called *Bro's*, a gay bar.

Ronan tapped his fingers twice, closing the map for the night.

Strange feeling, spying on people as they went about their lives.

First thing upon waking, Ronan checked the ticks again. Most of them were not in motion. The tagged phones, he surmised, were sitting around while their owners slept or prepared for the day. Deanna was in her room, phone stationary. Jeboko Kahn's tick was in the street outside an apartment building, which Ronan verified as his residence. Apparently, his tracker had already fallen off.

If caught placing ticks on everyone, he would be in big trouble. How would Deanna react if she learned he had done this without consulting her? She might not say anything if she had something to hide. Or she might notify Edward and send him home. Fortunately, the odds of discovery were low. The tiny stickers looked like holes or specks and had no noticeable weight.

When she emerged from her room, she didn't act any different than usual. She sipped coffee. "Another day of interviews," she said, looking at her phone.

"Yup."

"Did we learn anything at dinner?"

"Not sure," he said.

"Me either."

They arrived at Sanar before the building opened and waited in the parking lot. Deanna spent the time flipping through messages on her phone. He stared out the window, and neither said anything. He waited for her to display some emotion – a friendly joke, maybe, to show everything was normal – anything to give him a sign. Nope. When Niko arrived, the three of them went to his office to see if the IT data was ready and to discuss next steps. Sitting in silence as Niko clicked away at his computer, Ronan glanced at Deanna. No emotions. FaceLab gave him nothing.

A printer by Niko's desk came to life.

"This is the security report," Niko said, handing it to them from across his desk. "Over the past year, fifteen of us have used the synthesizers."

Ronan took the sheet, snapped a picture, and handed it to her.

"Have you looked at this yet?" Ronan asked Niko.

"No. Just received it."

"Why was Jeboko working late at night so much?" Deanna tapped the page with her index finger.

"I gave him permission to use the lab after hours. He was working on his thesis."

Ronan scanned down the log records. "How long ago was that?"

"He finished about three months back."

"This report shows Jeboko was staying late as recent as Monday night," Deanna said.

Niko studied the report. "Really? That surprises me."

She stood. "In that case, we need to talk to him. Where is he now?"

"University. He spends mornings there."

"Come on," Deanna said to Ronan.

"Jeboko's a great kid. I'm sure he was just working longer than expected on his thesis."

"Without your knowledge," Ronan added.

"He's not up to anything. But talk to him if you must."

They headed for the University of Johannesburg as quickly as the morning traffic would allow. While Deanna drove, Ronan activated *There's Waldo*, an app for locating people in a crowd. He loaded photos of Jeboko from the night before. This was going to be his first chance to use the app in the field.

As they pulled onto the campus, Ronan scanned the students. The buildings of the university formed a horseshoe-shaped complex muscled into the dense city. The structure held 25,000 students and faculty, and hundreds were outside on the sidewalks.

NO.

NO.

NO.

NO.

NO.

NO.

NO.

NO.

NO.

NO.

NO.

NO.

NO.

NO.

NO.

NO.

NO.

NO.

NO.

Damn program didn't need to tell him every time there was a non-match.

NO.

NO.

The labels were out of control, flying out of students' heads and blinking out a moment later. He paused the app.

"That sign says Molecular Biophysics," he said. "Let's try there."

After asking around inside the building, they soon found Jeboko's lab. A young man sat at a lab bench, donned in an unbuttoned white lab coat and wearing blue rubber gloves, clutching a device that looked like a plastic staple gun with a conical tip. He stared intently at row after row of tiny plastic tubes, squirting something into each. He glanced briefly at

Ronan and Deanna. They politely waited.

Ronan sighed. Deanna elbowed him.

Finally, the man finished. He set the device down and turned to them. No smile, blank face, and a hint of IRRITATION.

"Hi," Deanna said. "Does Jeboko work in this lab?"

"You just missed him."

"Know where he's going?"

"No idea."

Deanna flashed her U.S. security ID, which meant little in South Africa. "This is an urgent matter."

The student didn't look at the badge but stiffened. The display of authority had worked. "He got a call from his girlfriend. They often go to – don't tell anybody I told you this, okay? Especially not Jeboko. *Die roomys winkel.*"

Ronan ran the last few seconds through his translator. THE ICE CREAM SHOP.

"Where's that?"

"About three miles down the road. On the corner. A black building called *Singer's*. Please don't tell him I said anything."

"I don't even know who you are," Ronan said.

The young man smiled.

ETHAN CHETTY.

Ronan and Deanna turned and left Ethan to his tubes.

...

Seven minutes later, they pulled into *Singer's* and rushed inside.

The first thing Ronan saw were two enormous wooden boobs and a carved wooden belly. A sculpture of a pregnant woman towered at the entrance with a ceremonial mask draped on top. The room was full of masks: happy, blue, red, green, black, smooth, angry, abstract. Hooked on the walls and stacked on the floors. Blocking aisles. Drums and spears, too. Tourist artifacts from a distant sweatshop.

A young woman with a prominent nose ring sat behind the counter, red sneakers propped up, leaning back on her stool. Her eyes rolled up from a magazine. She saw that Ronan and Deanna had come straight to the counter and weren't buying anything.

"Ja?"

"Hi," Ronan said. "We're looking for someone."

She leaned forward and smiled. "Who?"

Ronan looked around at the masks. "We were told you sold ice cream. Is this the right place?"

"What?"

Deanna stepped to the counter. "We're trying to find a young man. Someone called this an ice cream shop."

The girl scratched her chin. She cracked open a door and yelled. "Broosh! *Twee Americkaners is opp-socken roomies!*"

A stern, commanding person emerged from the back room and addressed them in a thick accent. "Welcome," Broosh said. "How can I help you?"

Broosh had a wispy mustache, wide hips, muscular shoulders, and a square jaw.

AGE: 55-58.

"We are looking for a young man, a student…"

The door opened again. A burly old guy emerged and rounded the counter. He stood within breathing distance of Ronan and stared. His frost-white hair and beard looked striking against dark, weathered skin.

After an awkward moment, Ronan cleared his throat. "That's not him."

"I know," Broosh said.

"The guy we are looking for is in his early twenties, about five-ten, thin build, shaggy brown hair. Jeboko Kahn. A student from the university said we would find him here."

Broosh addressed the counter girl. "Juliet, anyone like that come in here?"

"I don't think so…"

"Maybe if you paid attention instead of reading *Femina* all the time, you'd know."

They jabbered at each other in Afrikaans.

The front door jingled and a skinny dude entered, walked past all of them without a sideways glance, and opened the back-room door.

"Son, you can't go in there," Broosh said.

The young man seemed perplexed. He had headed back there as if he had done it a hundred times, and now it was dawning on him that maybe something was up.

Ronan asked, "What's back there?"

"Nothing... I..." The young man hesitated then returned the way he had come, avoiding everyone's eyes.

Deanna raised an eyebrow. "Broosh, can we go in back?"

"I'm terribly sorry, but I'm not going to let strangers traipse around my storage area. What do you want?"

"We are investigators from the United States." Deanna flashed her ID card.

The old man aimed a lighted magnifying glass at the ID. He returned it with a grunt. Broosh shouted something in Afrikaans through the storage door.

Deanna said, "I'm going outside. Our man may be running out the back door."

Broosh sighed. "No need. Jeboko is here. Come on back. Let's talk to him."

Broosh waved them to follow into the storage area.

Ronan hesitated, then he and Deanna entered the corridor.

The door shut behind them.

CHAPTER 27

A hatchet whistled through the air.

Thunk!

It lodged in a slice of wood painted with a bullseye. The hatchet had just missed a cell phone adhered to the bullseye with a blob of *Hevea* sap.

The Kazites had gathered outside for a demonstration by their leader, Jonathan James Harper. They were taking advantage of a break in the afternoon rain. Everything was sopping wet and the hillside was full of puddles.

Crack! A second hatchet cut through the phone, chopping it almost in half and throwing shards into the air. Cheers erupted. Tattooed arms rose into the air, waving crossbows. Fifty voices roared as though they'd witnessed a miracle. The men thrashed their hair and clapped their hands and stomped the dirt. After a minute they settled down.

"We're driven to Surrogate Activity," Harper told his men, waving another hatchet. "There's no way to build shelter, start a family, or find a meaningful role within the modern technological community. The land for building houses is gone, unless you want to buy a house that's already been built for you, by someone you don't know and never will, with neighbors you barely know, and everyone shut in like criminals. You could start a family, but is it right to squeeze more children into more houses when none of it has any point? No. It's *cruel* to start a family."

A man raised a grimy finger and referenced the relevant section of the *Unabomber Manifesto*. "You got that right. Kaczynski Chapter 10, verse 20."

The men had studied every word of Theodore Kaczynski's manifesto against the industrial age. They had memorized it. They had numbered the chapters and verses, like a sacred text. And they had adopted

Kaczynski's name by calling themselves the Kazites.

Harper continued. "And how about a career? Everybody needs a career! Go ahead. Join ranks with other enslaved techno-men, glaring at a computer screen and talking into a headset, without a breath of fresh air, without exercise, without… *life*. What is this to you?"

"Cruelty!" shouted the Kazites.

"That's exactly what it is. Cruelty. People are prisoners. They've been conned. They believe their lack of self-sufficiency is a good thing. They believe it is normal to be trapped at a job, trapped in a little box in suburbia, completely dependent on a system that will crash at any moment. They are trapped inside their own self-justifying little heads. Yet despair will set in. They turn to anti-depressants and anti-anxiety medications. They struggle with strange attention disorders. Why? Because their actions are meaningless. They make money, but they don't achieve what they really desire. The Power Process. Survival skills and autonomy. Instead, their skills are abstract and worthless. What do we say to this?"

"Not on our watch!" shouted the Kazites.

Harper gazed with a hint of nostalgia at their muddy hillside. "Someday they'll come to us here. They will bring their automatic weapons. Are we worried?"

"Hell no!"

"And why aren't we worried?"

Several voices shouted memorized lines: "The over-socialized man is ignorant! He has outsourced every useful skill. He thinks he is in control! And he is not!"

"His life and his survival depend on technology," Harper growled, then pointed at an acolyte. "Will your weapon fail you?"

The acolyte held up his bow. "It will not!"

Pacing before his men, Harper noticed something and stopped. "What the hell is that?"

"It's a watch, sir," a man spouted without hesitation. "Wind-up. No electronics."

Harper tapped his scraggly chin and continued pacing. "And what of our home, here?"

"It's a trap!" the Kazites replied.

Harper grinned. "Is it what it seems?"

"It is not!"

"Our compound," Harper said, "which we built with our own hands, bends to our will, like a bow. Our compound is a weapon."

Harper stopped, lost in thought, studying the ground. He shook his head in frustration and walked back to the man with the watch. "Tell us about your watch."

"It's a mechanical wind-up. Over a hundred years old. My grandfather bought it. He gave it to my father, who gave it to me."

"May I see it?"

The acolyte paused, then unfastened it. He placed it carefully in Harper's waiting palm.

"How does it work?" Harper asked.

"It has a spring in it."

"How does a spring keep time?" Harper's voice was as taut as a crossbow.

The acolyte hesitated. "I'm not sure."

"You're not sure?" Harper faced the acolyte. "The sun tells you the time. How long have you been here?"

"Two weeks, sir."

"Do you realize that you've contaminated our sanctity?" Harper's lips had formed a snarl. "You were told not to bring technology into my presence!"

"Yes, sir," the acolyte stammered, "but I understood that to mean electronics."

Using his flint-knapped hatchet, Harper pried the back from the watch, pulled out the spring, and tapped out small gears and parts. He fumbled the pieces in his hand, examining them. He poured them into the hand of the acolyte. "If you can fix the watch, you can live. If not, you disobeyed the rules."

The acolyte stared back. A grin split his grimy face. He glanced left and right at his brethren to confirm that this was a joke. No one was smiling. He looked back at the mess in his hand.

"We're waiting." Harper tapped his foot in a muddy puddle.

The acolyte looked at the small objects in his hand. His eyes went wild. He leapt up, swinging at Harper, but two men grabbed him.

"This is crazy!" he shouted. "I'm on your side!"

"Give me his hatchet," Harper instructed.

"Let me go!" Bits of the acolyte's watch lay scattered at his feet, disappearing into the mud.

One of the Kazites gave Harper the hatchet. The two men restraining the watch owner swept his legs, knocking the troublemaker from his feet while they held him tight.

"You, sir," Harper said, pointing the hatchet in his face, "will be penitent."

"I'm sorry," the man shouted. "I didn't mean any harm. Please! I'll never do it again."

"You will be *silent!*"

The acolyte froze. Harper swung the hatchet into the man's shoulder. The acolyte screamed as bone crunched and blood splattered.

Harper examined the blade. "This is not sharp enough to do the job. So be it."

While the acolyte clenched his eyes, Harper began to chop.

The man screamed.

"Neither you," *whack* "nor your father," *whack* "nor your grandfather," *whack* "built this, nor do you" *whack* "know how it works, nor can you," *whack* "fix it. This is exactly what we are talking about! Who here agrees?"

After a moment of stunned silence, a wild roar rose among the stinking, tattooed crowd. A few Kazites were spattered in blood; they looked around before joining the cheers.

Harper severed the arm he'd started on, cutting collar bone to armpit. Then he began on the other. Blood poured forth, pooling around his feet.

When both arms lay beside the acolyte, the ruined body no longer upright, Harper finished with a single crunching blow to the skull.

Harper flung the hatchet away. "Sharpen your tools, gentlemen! Our lives depend on it! The Machination Men are coming."

"We'll be ready!"

Harper made a Kazite gesture that symbolized heart and mind. "The monkey prefers the cloth! Our benefactor looks to us for solutions. Failure to get our hands dirty would be shameful. We submit to no one."

Harper spat into the mud.

"All will submit to us!" his acolytes shouted back.

Harper stared into the wide eyes of the dead acolyte, then turned toward the compound. "Feed him to Alfie. Dismissed!"

Broosh had led Ronan and Deanna down the narrow corridor, single file, past closed doors and dark niches. Seconds felt like minutes. Ronan expected someone to jump from the darkness. The old man shuffled behind them, breathing heavy just a few inches away.

They entered a back room. With a quick scan, Ronan saw a half dozen men and women, piles of money, white powder, spoons. DRUG PARAPHERNALIA. The men scrambled things off their tables.

"Who are *they*?" one yelled.

There's Waldo found its target. A green light flashed and Ronan followed a trail of floating arrows until his gaze fell on Jeboko. The graduate student's head was bent close to the table, but he was looking up. *Waldo* surrounded him with a golden halo.

A wide-eyed woman embraced the young man.

"What's going on?" someone demanded.

Ronan and Deanna backed up, but the old man behind Ronan snatched a nearby gun. "We don't want trouble," the old guy said. "Who the hell are you?"

The others in the room drew their weapons.

Broosh lifted a hand. "Everyone take it easy."

Ronan sensed that Broosh was a third-rate drug dealer. If Jeboko was involved in global terrorism, these petty criminals probably had nothing to do with it.

Deanna raised her hands and nudged Ronan, who did the same. "We are here to investigate Jeboko's use of his employer's facilities," she said. "We are American. We don't care what you are doing here. We need to talk to Jeboko."

Broosh's voice turned aggressive. "Why should I cooperate with U.S.

investigators? You have no rights here."

"If you cooperate, we won't direct the local authorities to this room."

"That's a bold threat," Broosh responded. "There's nothing to find here, and even if there was, the local police are friendly with our establishment. College boy, come here."

Broosh ensnared Jeboko's neck in the crook of his arm. "What do you study at school?"

"Nanotechnology."

"What the hell is that?"

"Medical applications of very small molecules... uh, small things."

"You don't need to dumb it down; I know what a molecule is. So you're pretty smart?"

"I guess."

"Yes?"

"Yes."

"It looks like you've led some investigators to my business, right?"

"I guess."

"I guess? Tell me why they want you."

"Maybe because... I do drugs."

"Who said anything about drugs? What are you talking about?" Broosh gestured at Jeboko's girlfriend. "Come here."

She rose slowly and approached, and Broosh put an arm around her neck, too. "Tell me what is going on."

Awkward silence.

Deanna tugged a half dozen South African banknotes from her ID pouch, 200 Rand each. "I'd like to buy some time with him, what do you say?" She held them out. Broosh snatched the notes and thumbed through them. "This is all you have?"

She waved Broosh to bend close and whispered. Ronan couldn't get a read on her lips – the angle was wrong.

Broosh laughed and stuffed the money in a pocket. "I like you! Take this man and leave. Jeboko, get the hell out of here and don't come back."

"We appreciate your time, Broosh," Deanna said. "You have been very accommodating."

...

In the parking lot, they asked Jeboko's girlfriend to wait outside the Kargaan and directed the student to sit in the back seat.

"It's good to see you again," Ronan said.

"We just do a little blow." Jeboko's voice wavered. "We aren't into heroin and we don't sell anything."

"Relax," Deanna said from the driver's seat.

"Please don't tell Niko."

Ronan flexed out his eyes to keep the student off-balance. "Never mind your drug problem. You've been using the synthesizers at Sanar late at night, haven't you?" He activated Lie Check to analyze the young man's blink rate and pupil size, as well as any twitching, sniffing, scratching, shaking, or sweating that might indicate he was deviating from the truth.

"The synthesizers? Yes, they're part of my job. I don't understand what you…"

"Look directly into my eyes," Ronan instructed. "I'm recording our conversation and using software to detect bullshit."

"Yes, sir."

"How often do you use the equipment?"

"I used it every day until I finished my thesis. I haven't used it in months."

TRUE. 93% CERTAINTY.

Ronan paused.

"Is everything all right?" Deanna asked.

"This thing's not working," Ronan huffed. He made a series of flicking motions with his fingers. "Let's try this again."

"Do you think I'm a terrorist?" Jeboko put his hands on his temples. "I swear I'm not. I just like cocaine. I'll never do it again!"

"The security system indicates that you've been using the equipment almost every night after work. You didn't stop months ago, did you?"

"Yes. I *did* stop two months ago."

TRUE.

FEAR. CAUTION. FRUSTRATION.

Sweat glistened on Jeboko's forehead. His eyes darted between Ronan and Deanna.

"I think he's telling the truth," Deanna said.

Ronan narrowed his eyes. "How come the security system shows that you've been logging into the system after work more recently than that?"

"I don't know."

TRUE.

"Is it possible someone could log in as you?" Deanna asked.

Jeboko shook his head. "I don't share my passwords."

TRUE.

"How did someone get your passwords, then?" she asked.

"Why don't you ask our system administrator? Maybe someone used keystroke logging or set up a camera to steal my password. It's not hard."

TRUE.

"Let me double-check these settings," Ronan said, tapping his fingers.

"Huh?"

"Nothing," Ronan mumbled. "Oh, the hell with this."

Deanna pointed a finger. "Stay in town."

Jeboko nodded and pushed a lock of hair off his sweaty forehead. "I'm not leaving town."

TRUE.

"We'll need to talk to you again," Ronan said.

…

Jeboko jumped out of the car and wrapped his arm around his girlfriend's waist. They left.

"I don't know what to think," Ronan said.

"It seems someone logged in as him."

Ronan nodded, lost in thought. Then he asked, "What did you whisper to Broosh?"

"I noticed a glint in his eye, so I took a gamble that Broosh might be interested in you."

"What the hell are you talking about?'

"I said you were a passionate man with a bionic arm and that you were always looking for a new adventure, if he knew of anyone with compatible tastes."

"Wonderful. Thank you. Unfortunately, it's not true."

"Which part?"

"I'm not available and I don't have a bionic arm."

"But you're passionate?"

"Broosh better not call me."

"You'll probably need to make the first move."

Ronan moved to the front seat and they faced each other. Deanna said, "What do we do now?"

Indeed. What now? Ronan couldn't be sure. They had no obvious suspects or next steps. Sanar could be a dead end, but his instincts still told him something was up.

Time for more aggressive surveillance.

The camera began recording its surroundings, the first few seconds blocky and glitchy. Then the feed crystallized into high-resolution video.

Someone's palm dominated the shot, a vast plateau extending into blurry gray.

Motion. Buttons. Stripes. Antennae.

The palm lowered and objects tumbled into view: people, grass, clouds. The image stabilized. Delicate wings vibrated at the edges. Liftoff.

A foot below, a dark-haired man stared back, phone in hand, eyes narrowed in concentration. RONAN FLYNN.

"Go for it, little buddy," Ronan said. "It's all up to you."

The camera lifted higher and turned. The target stood on the far side of the soccer field with two other men.

Buzzing over blades of grass and patches of dirt along the side of the field, it navigated a path that avoided the locals watching the game. They were all enjoying the sun, rooting for friends, socializing. The hot season in Johannesburg meant the air was mean with mosquitos, real ones, and this one navigated its way through the air unnoticed.

Closer to the target.

Landing now on a handrail in the bleachers. Recalculating flight paths. The crowd was sweating in the heat. The men wore tank tops or no shirt at all. They yelled for their friends. They yelled for the love of the sport. They yelled just to yell.

Moving along, fluttering over people's heads. Behind the target now. Landing on his pant leg.

Audio quality poor… their voices too low and the background too high. Inching closer. Conversation emerged from the noise.

"This would lead to South America, but not to…"

"Watch what you say."

Detaching from the target's pant leg now and in the air, high enough to look down on him and the other speakers. TARGET: PIETER HEYNES. Camera rotating 360 degrees to record the surroundings. Ronan popped briefly into view on the other side of the field.

"Nothing's changed," a man said.

"But things will change," Pieter countered. "Sanar's under investigation. We have very little time."

"You worry too much."

"Hold on," a third man said.

"What?"

The men stopped speaking.

The bug maintained its height, waiting. Flying in a lazy circle, as mosquitos do. When the conversation did not continue, the bug dared to point at their faces. One was toothless.

Pieter was staring at the bug. "Don't move," he said to the others. He stepped forward. A great blurry shadow blocked everything.

A view between two massive fingers. A face bent close.

"Is that what I think it is?" Pieter asked.

The images erratic now. For a moment, the video caught Ronan again, on the far side of the field, breaking away from the crowd and heading in the opposite direction.

"Get rid of it."

The video feed stopped.

That night, Ronan reflected on the day's breakthroughs. First, someone seemed to have been logging into the synthesizers in the evening using Jeboko's account. Deanna had gone back to Sanar to request any available security camera footage. But the second breakthrough might make that unnecessary; Pieter seemed to be the guilty party. While Deanna was gone that afternoon, Ronan had used the tick to locate Pieter and Li's mosquito to do the spying. Now he had bombshell information, and he couldn't tell Deanna because he hadn't told her that he'd plastered everyone with trackers.

Even worse: he wasn't sure he could trust her.

Hopefully, in the morning he'd be refreshed and know what to do next. He fell asleep.

He woke when his phone buzzed. One of his trackers was on the move. The clock read 1:00 AM. Who could that be? He read the alert.

Deanna.

He opened the tracking app. She was at street level.

Ronan fell from the bed and attached his legs while tapping his fingers to transfer the tracker display to his ocular. As Deanna's location appeared on the display, he secured his legs, grabbed his pistol, found the car keys on the kitchen counter, and bolted for the door.

Where would she go without telling him? Maybe to a drugstore or something. He hoped for a mundane explanation.

She didn't take the Kargaan transport but caught a cab instead. It pulled away just as he reached the sidewalk. He paused to watch the car disappear down the road. Tailing her to a drugstore was a waste of time and risked a blowup if he was caught. But why did she take a cab?

Ronan ran to the adjoining parking garage, hopped into the Kargaan and was soon in pursuit. He kept her location on display and followed about a half mile behind. The roads were empty and he didn't want to reveal himself.

The cab stopped ten minutes later in a deserted section of downtown. Ronan pulled over on the opposite side of the road, a block away. They had arrived at a cluster of dilapidated buildings on a side street near the M31 highway. Deanna entered one of the many abandoned apartment complexes in the area. A small sign hung beside the door, too far away for him to read, even with zoom.

He shut off the Kargaan and slid out. In the moonlight he saw that most of the building's windows were broken, their dark interiors warning him away. Faded graffiti covered the grimy concrete walls; tangles of ancient wires hung from the roof. A strong smell of trash moved in the air. There was no turning back now – the situation had grown too unusual. Approaching the doorway, he saw the name on the sign: *Pinocchio's*. The sign featured a slim, cartoon man with a long nose, holding a drink.

How strange. He was growing angry but wasn't sure why. After all, she had the right to head off to a bar or club.

He went in and found himself alone in a dark room littered with cigarettes and debris. There was a small host station with a tiny lamp, and beyond that, a dark hallway leading a few paces to a black curtain. A faint murmur of voices came from within, but he heard no music. The sheer lack of sound was mystifying.

He tried to search "Pinocchio's" but couldn't get a connection.

While he debated whether to pass through the curtain, a young woman emerged, her hair tied in a bun. Her white shirt was decorated with the *Pinocchio's* logo, but still offered no clue to the nature of the business.

"Hello, sir. Are you alone?"

Ronan almost asked *what is this place* but feared she might kick him out. Better to go along with things and see where they led. He hoped to maintain distance from Deanna, allowing him to assess her moves in secrecy. He was tempted to go back to the hotel, look up *Pinocchio's*, satisfy his curiosity, and crawl back into bed.

The woman was staring at him.

"Yes, I'm here alone. Is that okay?"

She gave a big smile. "Of course! Most of our patrons come here alone."

She beckoned him down the corridor and through the black curtain.

Beyond, the corridor continued as before, just two beat-up unadorned walls and no clues whatsoever where they led.

They emerged into a dim room full of people sitting in booths, walled off from each other by waist-high partitions. The patrons all wore headsets and sat motionless. Most were alone. Scanning the room as discretely as possible, he located Deanna, already geared up and seated by herself.

He was beginning to form a theory that she was into virtual gaming, or cyber travel or, perhaps even more likely, meeting someone online. If that was the case, he would have no way to know who she was meeting – a friend, a lover, or someone suspicious.

Fortunately, the woman seated Ronan in a spot where he could keep an eye on Deanna without drawing her attention. The host handed Ronan a headset from the wall. Noticing his involuntary flinch, she said, "We clean these after each use." He reluctantly slid it on his head and over his ears. The unit was branded *K System*.

She waited until he pulled the mask over his eyes. "You're all set." He heard her flip a switch on the side. "I will be back in thirty minutes."

The screen turned from blackness to color video. An animated 3D man-puppet with an erect nose jumped in front of him, waved his hands with a flourish, and said, "Welcome to *Pinocchio's*!"

What the hell?

Pinocchio put his hands on his curvy hips. "You have been identified as Ronan Flynn. Is this correct? Just nod."

Ronan peeked out of the headset. Cutting his eyes to the left and right, he saw everyone still seated in their booths. He pulled the headset back into place, adjusted it for comfort, and nodded.

"Great! Just sit right there and enjoy. Bye for now!" Pinocchio did a kind of jig and danced off-screen to the left.

Tilting his head up and down, left and right, Ronan had no sense yet of the environment. Everything was a white void. Maybe they would drop him on the Great Wall of China or something.

An enormous panda sprung up from below. Ronan lurched back.

The panda backed away, wiggled its rump, and used both hands to blow him an enormous kiss. Hearts flew from its mouth like bubbles from a child's toy pipe. "I am Madam Panda. I'm glad you came."

She took a step closer and her face turned from white to pink. As she continued to advance, her face grew darker and redder.

"Nice," Ronan said. "Wonderful. What the fuck?"

"Now, now," the panda scolded. "No profanity."

She was inches away and wrapped her thick hairy arms around him on either side. He was startled to feel the panda's embrace. That damn host had draped a tactile cloth on him and he hadn't even noticed.

Panda pushed him down. Involuntarily, he leaned back and slid down in the booth. He didn't have much experience with these contraptions and couldn't control his reflexes.

Next thing Ronan knew, Panda had climbed on top, her weight pressing on his abdomen. She lifted her shirt.

"That does it," he said aloud. He raised the mask. Deanna was still in her booth, sitting stone-still with her headset.

The host appeared as if by magic. "I'm sorry, Mr. Flynn, you can't watch the other patrons. If you aren't going to participate, we will ask you to leave."

Ronan hesitated.

She didn't look angry, but it was clear that she wouldn't allow him to break the rules.

"Do you wish to continue?" she asked.

He nodded.

He slid the gear back over his eyes. Panda was undulating in sinuous curves, a beatific look on her face. She leaned in, nuzzling. The panting and snorting disgusted him. And something was snaking into his ear.

Like, REALLY sliding into his ear.

He grabbed the helmet's earpiece and tried to pull it away, but the thing was wiggling its wet way into his ear canal, spinning like a sopping wet Q-tip.

Madam Panda swelled like a balloon, face burnt red and baring her teeth and growling. The cloth thumped his crotch. Enormous hairy arms locked him on either side.

It's just a cartoon. It's just a cartoon.

He shut his eyes, but an alarm went off in his headset and a man's voice said, "Get those peepers open, princess."

Panda screamed bear-grunts in his ears and–

That's it. He unsnapped the mask.

He felt tapping on his shoulder. At first, he didn't notice because of all the panda grunting and bouncing, but the tapping continued, harder. He ripped the gear off his sweaty head.

Deanna was sitting next to him. Her face was as red as Madam Panda's. "What are you doing here?" She demanded.

"I..."

He couldn't think of an excuse. He sighed. "I'm following you."

"I know!" She lifted a hand and revealed a tracker resting on a fingertip, the tick he had pressed onto her phone. She fixed him with an evil glare. "Why?"

"I received an alert that you had... a connection to Siyu."

"What the hell are you talking about?"

"You and Siyu both worked with a man named Ladislav Kos, a prominent AI researcher based out of Slovenia."

"So what? Yeah, I worked for him. What are you implying?"

"Since you and Siyu both worked for this man–"

"For your information, Ladislav is a big name in micro-drone software. You can barely move in this field without interacting with him. Sure, we collaborated. He must have worked with a thousand other people, too. My connections in this field are exactly why I was hired by MET."

"It just seemed a little coincidental, is all. I felt I had to check into it."

Deanna sat back and looked at the ceiling. "I can't believe you let a software program drive you to do this." She shook her head. "You put a tick on me. Wow."

"I had to be sure. I made a split-second decision."

"Have you ever done a search for your own name against Siyu, Li, and Niko?"

Ronan didn't answer. He did a quick search.

He furrowed his brow. "I have two matches against Siyu."

"Lookee there." Deanna's eyelids fell to a droop. "You are twice as guilty as me."

"But how...?"

"Who are you connected to that knows Siyu?"

Ronan stared off, scanning information. He darted his eyes at Deanna a couple of times. He swallowed. "You made your point."

"Who is it?"

"Edward is one match. He hired a consulting company a few years ago to update a DOD team on the latest trends in mini-flight stabilization software. Siyu was associated with that consulting company. He was at the meeting."

"Who is the other?"

"Me. I am a direct connection to Siyu. I was at that meeting. There is a photo of a large group of us together. I don't remember the guy at all."

Deanna moved closer, arms folded. Even in the dim light, he could see the green in her eyes and the delicate lines of her lips. He detected a light fragrance.

"When we were at dinner with Niko's team," Ronan said, "you excused yourself to take a call, but seemed guarded about it. Why the secrecy? Who called you?"

"My boyfriend."

"Your...? I didn't know you had a boyfriend."

"I know. You never asked."

"When you asked if I had a girlfriend, I assumed you were scoping me out."

"It's called polite conversation. I was interested in getting to know you a little."

Ronan knew he had backed himself into a corner. "I guess I'm an ass."

Before Deanna could respond, the host was back. This time, her face was squeezed into a pinch. "You two need to take this outside. We aren't a bar. If you wanna get physical, you can't do it in here."

She headed toward the long hallway with the implication that they should follow.

Ronan rose. "I hate to ask, but were you... the panda?"

Deanna crinkled her brow. "Of course not. I was connected to Max, my boyfriend."

"I wonder who I was connected to?"

"Look in that booth. I figured you deserved a favor."

Ronan followed the direction of her finger and saw Broosh from the Ice Cream Shop, watching them. "Ronan!" Broosh yelled, waving. "What are you doing? We just got started!"

"Excuse me for a moment," Ronan said to Deanna.

He approached Broosh and leaned on the partition. "Broosh, nice to see you again."

"You don't like rough panda?"

Ronan's wince conveyed the answer.

"There's no need to apologize. I made assumptions."

"I'm more into kangaroos."

Broosh smiled. No longer in his drug den, Broosh had an odd sweetness about him, as though he were playful, maybe even affectionate. "You are more into women."

"Yes, that's accurate."

"Like her," Broosh said, nodding.

Ronan glanced at Deanna. Looking back at Broosh, he said, "I have to go now."

As he rejoined her, he weighed whether to be angry. They left. "That was a violation," he said.

"You could have stopped earlier. No one forced you."

He squinted at her.

She returned a glare. "Right?"

"Yeah."

"We need to be on the same team."

"I agree. I betrayed that. But it goes both ways. You don't think I contribute enough to this investigation."

"I think you offer plenty. You have certain talents."

They walked along the sidewalk in the shadows.

"All my talents are fake. Engineered. I stuck them in."

"Maybe you should switch that stuff off, a little."

"I'll think about it."

"Good." She put an arm around him, and for a moment he thought she might rest her head on his shoulder, but she didn't, and they headed back to the car.

CHAPTER 31

Ronan and Deanna were now on the same page. He'd told her about the trip to the soccer field. Pieter had clearly acted suspicious and the mention of South America was a significant red flag, given the tropical backdrop of the video.

It had been a week since the Nashville attack. They were making progress but there were still too many questions. Was Pieter the mastermind? Who was the guy in the video? And where was he?

Ronan texted Niko that they wanted to talk to him. Niko was at Sanar working, even though it was now the weekend. He sounded unnerved about the request for a Saturday meeting but told Ronan to swing by and check in at the security desk. Deanna stayed at the hotel to relay the latest news to Edward, catch up on paperwork for the investigation, and write status summaries for sending up the power chain.

When Ronan arrived, a guard said that Niko was in the animal testing room and led him there. The guard tapped the keypad and held the door.

Niko looked annoyed and simply nodded.

Ronan asked, "Any video footage yet?"

"C'mon Ronan. It takes time to get these things."

Ronan thought that was bullshit. It took ten minutes to look at surveillance footage matching any of Jeboko's recent evening logins.

"So you haven't seen any of it?"

"No."

"Fine. While we wait for that, I've got to talk to you about some new developments."

"Sure."

"We'd like to take you and Pieter out for lunch today."

"Another meal? I assume you'll explain what that means."

"We need to talk to the two of you, together. Something's up with Pieter. Yesterday I kept an eye on him. He met some people. These people were... different."

Niko laughed. "I don't know Pieter's friends, but keep in mind one thing. Pieter is a highly respected scientist. His goal is to fight disease. I don't have a shred of doubt about him."

Nearby, a rat stood on a platform. There were no visible barriers around the rat, which must have been surrounded by some kind of electric field that discouraged it from escaping. Dozens of wires emerged from the wall, snaked along the platform and entered the rat's anus. The animal's mid-section had been surgically replaced with plexiglas for convenient study, and Ronan could see that the wires penetrated its intestines, stomach, and heart. Niko studied a long glass monitor displaying various data displays of the rat's internal workings. He tapped the pane to move through the displays.

"Pieter met two men at a park yesterday afternoon. I dropped a bug on him and heard a bit of their conversation. They mentioned South America, which has rainforest matching the background of the terrorist's warning video..."

"You must be kidding. Pieter mentioned South America? He must be a terrorist, then."

"Please," Ronan held up his hand. "You know that I have to piece this puzzle together. This isn't ridiculous."

Niko took a bag of food and went to the monkey sitting silently in its cage. When Ronan had peered into the animal room previously, its head had been strapped. Now the head strap was gone, but it did not meet their eyes or move. The tag on its cage said R1167.

Niko sighed. "Fine, what else did they say?"

"They were concerned that Sanar is under investigation. They believe they are about to be caught. Those are their exact words."

Niko flinched but dug his hand into the bag of dried fruit and nuts. He sprinkled them in a bowl.

The monkey moved to the far corner of its cage, covered its head in its arms and bent down, trembling. It peed.

Unexpectedly, Ronan's ocular came to life and white labels blazed across his vision: JUMPY, AFRAID.

"How is R1167, anyway?" Ronan asked.

"He's fine," Niko replied, placing the bowl in the cage. "Back to Pieter. You're reading what you want into a casual conversation."

The monkey voided its bowels.

FECAL INCONTINENCE.

Ronan dismissed the label. "One of the men in the park saw the bug. They smashed it and left—quick. They were up to something."

Niko nudged the bowl closer to the monkey, which flinched and clawed its head.

POST-TRAUMATIC STRESS DISORDER.

Ronan dismissed this label, too. "Uh… your monkey is a wreck."

"Yes, I know. I feel terrible. This one is particularly skittish. The whole getup gives it anxiety."

Ronan stared at the monkey, having lost his train of thought.

Niko smiled at Ronan. "You're good at your job. I appreciate that. But Pieter's one of my heroes. He's one of the most dedicated and intelligent people on the planet. We're building, atom by atom, a cure for atherosclerosis, numerous cancers, and Rapier's disease. His knowledge and drive support this entire company. You should see how happy he is discussing treatments. He's too good a man to be slandered this way."

Ronan crossed his arms. "Look. Are you on for lunch? Deanna and I would like to ask Pieter a few questions, and I want you there, too."

As Niko headed back for the door, R1167 approached its food bowl. Another label popped up on Ronan's ocular: DESPONDENT.

Ronan shut off the labels. Too painful.

He followed Niko to the door.

"Sure," Niko forced a laugh. "You might as well call *me* a terrorist, but I'll play along."

"Excellent. Please tell Pieter to be at Blackjack's Steakhouse, twelve o'clock. A nice meal will keep it low key. We'll start off asking about his position paper, then casually ask about the men in the park. Catch him off guard. Gauge his reaction. He won't expect to be interrogated at a nice restaurant. Don't say anything to make him nervous."

Niko nodded. "Very well."

...

Pieter's phone vibrated. He read the message:

> *Ronan wants to meet us for lunch. Noon at Blackjack's. He has a lot of questions.*

Staring at the screen, willing a different interpretation, Pieter re-read the text several times. Panic set in.

He played out various scenarios in his mind and realized he might be in jail by midnight. He couldn't let everything go to hell. He dialed the men he had met at the park.

A man answered. "Why are you calling, Cape Buffalo? You know the rules."

"The American investigators are breathing down my neck. They're not going away until they get what they want. Do you understand?"

"I understand," the man said. "What do they know?"

"I haven't told them anything. The problem is they're not going to leave. The longer they're here, the more likely they'll figure things out."

"How can they figure things out if you keep quiet?"

"Don't put this on me, okay? You're supposed to solve this kind of problem. Get these people off me."

"Very well," the man grunted. "We can't just get rid of them, though. We'll have to interrogate them—find out what they know. It won't be pretty."

"Be careful. The guy is heavily augmented. You won't believe how much tech he's got."

"Siyu filled us in."

"Good," Pieter said. "I don't want to have to worry about them anymore."

"We'll take care of the matter. Don't call this number again."

"I understand and–"

The man ended the call.

Ronan and Deanna pulled into a charging station on the way to Blackjack's. As Ronan fed his card into the battery swapper, Deanna headed inside. She said, "I need a Coke. Want anything?"

"A coffee would be great."

While waiting for the batteries to rotate, Ronan wondered what drove people to dedicate their lives to crazy revolutionary ideals. He sometimes felt vengeful anger toward America's enemies. He got that. But he never felt like attacking any country's innocent civilians.

A man in a nearby car was staring. When Ronan glanced sideways and their eyes met, the young man looked away.

Ronan boosted overlays to medium sensitivity and scanned his surroundings. People milled about the lot, waiting for their car batteries. FEMALE, ~55... MALE, ~32... MALE ~28...

Someday soon, his ocular's labels would provide the individual's full name, with alerts on any criminal background, suspicious online activity, the whole business. Until then, the data was often worthless... like now.

...MALE, ~46... MALE, ~57. The ages were mere guesses. Each label faded out as he focused on someone new.

In the nearby car, the man was staring at him again, his eyebrows pinched. ANGER. Perhaps he had been arguing with the others in the car. He was in his mid-twenties and had a tattoo on his neck. The man looked down at his lap. He seemed to be typing, but sunlight glared off the window, making it difficult to be sure. Ronan casually readjusted to get a better look. Yes, he was working on a laptop.

Ronan noticed something odd... the man was typing with gloves on. He inched closer.

"All set?" Deanna asked, back with the drinks.

Ronan joined her in their Kargaan. As they returned to the highway and headed toward the restaurant, he kept his eyes on the traffic behind them. The car with the young man followed a short distance back.

"If Pieter trips up, we gotta press," Ronan said. "Who is going to play bad cop?"

"Me," she answered, as though it should be obvious.

He cut his eyes to the car behind them, then said to her, "You're too nice."

"Funny."

"I'll be the mean one, and you can do the warm fuzzies. A flirty smile wouldn't hurt."

"I'm not the flirty type," she said.

"Your eyes say otherwise."

When he glanced in the mirror again, he saw the other car close behind. The word TAIL hovered over it. Other nearby vehicles had the same tag: TAIL... TAIL...

He returned his eyes to the road and said, "Three cars and two motorcycles seem to be following us. They were all at the power station and left at the same time."

"Which ones?"

Ronan pointed them out.

"Take this exit coming up."

He didn't answer. The steering wheel seemed tighter than a moment before. Was it his imagination? He pulled into the right-hand lane and touched the brake. The car jerked ahead faster.

"What the..." he murmured.

"What are you doing?"

"The car is picking up speed."

"On its own?"

"Yes. I am applying the brakes."

"Can you take control?"

"Negative."

The doors locked.

"Dammit," she said. "Someone is taking over." She grabbed a pair of pocket binoculars from her bag and scanned the surrounding vehicles that were tailing them.

There was a short *bang* and their seat belts yanked them violently against their seats. Deanna had been turned half around and was pinned awkwardly.

Ronan tried to stay calm. "That was the pretensioner for the seat belts. It has a small explosive designed to detonate during a car crash and pin you in place. It's controlled by the central processor." He took his foot off the accelerator. The Kargaan moved with the traffic. "We're being kidnapped."

A vehicle pulled alongside them, keeping pace. Ronan saw the angry man from the power station. He raised his laptop and pointed to their car.

"That's the guy doing this," Ronan said, stating the obvious.

Deanna pressed the window button. Nothing happened.

She displayed her gun to the man in the adjoining car and tapped the barrel with her index finger. The man sneered.

"They're taking us somewhere," she said. "They probably want to know what the U.S. has learned in the investigation. They'll probably interrogate us, torture us if needed, and kill us."

They were surrounded and blocked in by a convoy of vehicles.

"Might have to jump out," he said.

"No way. We're going over eighty."

Ronan had a small fixed-blade knife strapped to his belt and he used it to cut through their seat straps. He inspected his pistol. "I have about fifteen rounds. How about you?"

"Same."

"Wherever they're taking us," Ronan said, "there will be more of them when we arrive. We have to escape now. I'll kick out our window."

She nodded.

He positioned himself on his back, then lifted his thighs and aimed his prosthetics at the window. His brain told his legs to kick at full strength and the muscles in his thighs conveyed the message to the prosthetics' sensors. With a massive, lithium-powered kick he smashed out the window glass. The pane pushed outward in one large sheet. He punched out the remaining shards with a heel.

"That car is pretty close," Ronan said. "If we can shoot out their back window, I could jump across, try to get inside, and take control. Then I could pull it over to get you."

She didn't have a better plan, so they unleashed their rounds on the nearest sedan. Nothing happened. Their kidnappers' windows stayed intact.

"Bulletproof glass," Deanna said. "And I'm already out of ammo."

"Me too."

She watched the vehicles tighten around them.

He reached between their seats and snatched his pack from the backseat. Unzipping it, he examined the contents. "I didn't bring anything useful."

"Is there anything in the very back of the car?"

"Maybe a lug wrench," he said. He scrambled until he could see into the cargo area. "Hey!"

"What?"

"You left the box of Li's weird attack shit in the trunk!"

She watched him retrieve it. "Me? You were the last to leave the car when we unloaded at the hotel. I thought we had everything."

"I thought you were coming back."

"Just open the damn box."

Ronan heaved it to the front and set it between them.

They tore at the box flaps, yanking the duct tape and ripping the cardboard. Li's people had wrapped it as tight as a mummy. Finally, they had the top open.

They removed the packing material.

"Oh my God," Deanna whispered.

Ronan withdrew a black tube, about a foot long. He turned it over in his hands and said, "I'm not sure what to do with this."

The device had no wings or fins, and the nose came to a tapered point like a punch awl. On closer inspection, he saw tiny propellers folded against the side.

He handed it to Deanna and opened Li's app on his phone, which displayed various weapon icons. The instructions were in both English and Chinese.

"Step one, select a weapon," Ronan read out loud. He tapped the icon on the phone representing the black tube, whatever it was.

"Step two, select a target." He aimed the camera at one of the cars in the kidnapper caravan and selected an older, tough-looking woman watching them from the backseat.

"Step three, tap to activate." The tube quivered and powered on.

Deanna threw it like a paper airplane out their Kargaan's smashed window and it buzzed off.

"Where the hell did it go?" she asked.

Ronan glanced around. "It's gone. Try something else."

She pulled out a small pink canister and popped the lid. It was full of black dust. Ronan recognized it immediately. This was a tin of Mighty Mites, like the ones Li had dumped on the conference room table – the pile Ronan had reluctantly poked with his finger. She set the canister gently on her leg, taking care not to touch the dust, and took his phone. She tapped the Mighty Mites icon. The black dust writhed, set in motion by invisible forces.

Ronan felt sharp biting sensations on his scalp and arms. "Dammit!"

"What?"

"I've still got Mighty Mites crawling on me, what the hell?"

Ronan clawed at his arms. He slapped at his hair. He felt as though he'd been sprayed with drops of boiling water. The mites were biting the hell out of him. "I've showered several times since I stuck my finger in them. They are all over me!"

"What do I do?" she asked.

"Did you set a specific target?"

"No…"

"Turn them off!"

She fumbled with the app and hit the Mighty Mites icon with an angry stab of her finger.

The burning stopped.

Ronan's heart raced and he struggled not to panic. Li's gadget box was a bust. Wherever he and Deanna were being taken by their abductors, it was starting to look like they would have to fight with bare hands and any makeshift weapons they might find.

He reached into the box and put his hands around a big thing coiled on top. *Let's try one more.*

Pulling it out, the thing flipped-flopped in his hands, limp and inert. Heavy. Slick with oil. Long dangling legs. His stomach tightened, though he did not know why.

He held the thing gingerly – every edge was razor sharp. Then he realized why it gave him such a visceral reaction.

This was the machine at LikeLife that he briefly saw eviscerate a rabbit.

His hands trembled. He hoped Deanna did not notice. "Give it a target."

The car with the tough-looking woman in the backseat was close. She had been the target of the odd flying tube, but it had flown away. This time, Deanna zoomed in on her driver.

Target selected.

"I'm going to activate it," she said and tapped the icon. "Machine, go get the driver!"

The Rabbit Killer moved in Ronan's hands, the sharp legs beginning to crawl. He noticed it had a mass of eyes, like a spider, looking at him.

He heaved it out the window, sort of a lob more than a throw, not sure what it would do or how. As soon as he tossed it, he realized that unless this thing had wings, it was not going to make it to the adjoining car.

The Rabbit Killer coiled into a tight ball as it dropped, bouncing on the road behind them. It hurled toward a trailing car in a deliberate arc and hit the car's side. The creature's legs shot outward in all directions, hooking onto the car's window edges and door seams.

Then, the thing clawed across the hood, grasping at the smooth surface, and caught the grill.

The Rabbit Killer pulled itself forward.

And then it just sat there on the front grill.

"It's not doing anything, either," Deanna said.

...

At this point, Ronan felt they were no further along to saving themselves. One car had the angry laptop guy, and that car was ahead of them. There was a car behind them with the Rabbit killer chilling on its grill. A couple bikers were back there, too. And finally the car next to them had several occupants, including the woman in the backseat. She was now lowering her window.

What does she want? Ronan thought.

When the woman saw they weren't going to fire on her, she brought the window down further. She seemed ready to duck if necessary.

"Quit throwing shit out the window!" the woman yelled, "or we'll hang you up and gut you alive!"

From somewhere above, the flying tube shot into view.

"Window down" meant *Target available.*

The thing had been keeping up with the convoy and now it smacked into the woman's left eye. The woman grabbed the tube, but a wire circled her head like a snake. At the end of the tube, a bag began to fill with blood. The thing had tapped deep and was power-leeching with industrial-strength suction. The woman screamed.

A mix of head content sprayed into the bag. Ronan's stomach lurched.

The woman twitched and she tried to pull herself inside the car, but the tube disengaged and half the woman's face ripped off. Her head lolled forward, hanging over the window, but most of it was missing. Blood streamed along the side of the car.

Bloodsucker went vertical, propellers out and spinning. A half-gallon of blood and brain tissue filled the gut bag hanging from its posterior. The tube sailed upward into the sunlight and disappeared, heading in the same direction as the convoy, but much faster.

...

This sequence of events got the attention of the kidnappers. Ronan could see them gesturing and shouting to each other. They had no protocol to deal with whatever had just happened. In the adjacent car, the dead woman hung out the back window. He saw several kidnappers checking their rifles. Ronan was sure their kidnappers would just kill them and call it a day. They weren't going to put up with this shit. He glanced back at the rear car. The Rabbit Killer was still perched on the grill, hanging out.

A biker emerged from the back of the pack.

He rode a bleached-out Harley riddled with rust holes. The bike was scarred with abuse and belched smoke and screamed.

Yup, this was the executioner and the motherfucker meant business.

As the biker approached, the Rabbit Killer leapt with startling speed onto the backseat of the Harley.

The biker didn't notice his new passenger. He gunned the bike and drew close, and Ronan got a good look at him. The man was aflame with tattoos the color of an atomic sky, etched everywhere on his arms and face and bulging muscles.

No helmet – he must be against helmets.

Gray hair whipped in the wind.

He smiled. No teeth.

The Rabbit Killer hunched behind him, holding the seat. It was looking at Ronan.

Grandpa the psycho biker yanked a pole from a scabbard mounted on the bike's frame, pulled up to Ronan's smashed window, and pushed the pole at him like a cattle prod. Two pieces of exposed wire poked out the end.

The rod touched Ronan's arm. He grabbed it in defense. *Bzzzzzzzzt...*

Ronan's muscles contracted into a pulsing knot. He was unable to let go of the rod. His lips and eyelids twitched and a deep burning agony shot through his chest. His body shook. A boiling electric current poured through his blood.

Burning and vibrating became one.

Flashing.

Augs burning?

Ronan's body was an organic circuit breaker heading for meltdown. Panic gripped him.

The shockwaves stopped and the biker pulled back.

Ronan lay in a daze, saw Deanna blurry and concerned. He felt her hand on his face, his arms, his chest. The pain diminished. Everything came into focus. He smiled and saw the relief flood back into her eyes. With her help, he eased back to a seated position. He could breathe again.

He looked at the biker riding parallel to their car.

Ronan realized something and the hair on his neck stood up.

The Rabbit Killer was not on the back of Grandpa's motorcycle anymore.

...

Grandpa moved closer for another poke. That crazy bastard was going to kill them with that thing, whether he intended to or not. Ronan couldn't let that happen. The torture was too much to endure a second time.

Ronan aimed his phone at Grandpa and tapped Target and tossed the phone aside and said, "Gimme the mites."

Deanna slapped the can in his hand.

Grandpa was alongside them again, waving that pole. A cord at the other end of the pole trailed back to the bike's battery.

Grandpa was yelling. He was so close that Ronan saw right down the empty mouth hole to the back of his throat.

Grandpa didn't know he was Target.

Ronan tipped the can and set a dash of mites free. They blew into Grandpa's big waving beard and into the man's face. Grandpa slapped at his cheeks and eyes. The bike swerved a little. Ronan dumped out the rest of the mites. A long dark cloud-stream blew Grandpa's way.

The cattle prod dropped to the road but bounced behind at the end of the cord, then snapped and tumbled off.

Grandpa grabbed his face with both hands. A horrible scream came out of the mouth hole, louder than the engine.

If it was possible for a face to be eaten down to the bone by small black specks, that is what Ronan saw, but it was hard to say because a car broadsided the bike and sent Grandpa free-diving into oncoming traffic.

…

The motorcycle accident receded into the distance. Ronan watched it disappear down the long stretch of road, and now he sank back in his seat. He was trembling. His body burned with Mite bites and the neural aftershocks of the electric current. So much information was bombarding him that he could barely process it all.

Who were these people? How had they tracked him and Deanna?

However, they faced more important questions at the moment. They needed to escape this situation, which was rapidly spiraling out of control.

The chaos was working in their favor at the moment, but also made outcomes extremely unpredictable.

The road continued to whiz by at eighty miles an hour, and other than Grandpa, the convoy still surrounded them. The attackers weren't giving up. Ronan guessed they were re-evaluating the entire situation. The pause gave Ronan a moment to think.

But not for long.

There was something on the roof. Ronan and Deanna looked up and heard clawing, scraping.

As they watched, the Rabbit Killer emerged at the top of their windshield and slid down.

The thing was perched liked a giant spider, gripping the hood of their Kargaan.

Ronan stared straight into its eight eyes.

It was studying him.

...

For many seconds, perhaps minutes, no one moved.

Then, as Ronan looked past the Rabbit Killer, he saw something descend from the sky further down the road. As it emerged from the sunlight and came into view, Ronan realized that it was the flying tube, holding the engorged blood bag. It was heading directly for the adjoining car.

The bag hit the kidnappers' windshield and exploded, splattering blood and brains across the glass. The car careened and crashed against theirs, crushing the remains of the woman whose body had been hanging out the back window. As the kidnappers' car continued to swerve out of control, windshield wipers flapping madly, the Rabbit Killer made its move. It jumped to the kidnapper's car and anchored itself. Two of its legs stabbed at the bloody glass, picking and digging toward the driver, the designated Target.

A hole appeared in the cracking glass and the thing tried wriggling in. The driver fired at it through the glass, fully automatic, round after round.

No effect. The Rabbit Killer was inside now. One of the kidnappers in the passenger seat tried a desperate break for safety, even if that meant jumping from a speeding, swerving car. He opened the door, shirt soaked in blood, and perched in a crouched position. A moment later the Rabbit Killer had sliced off his head. Then the machine went for the driver.

The car skidded to an abrupt stop. The rear car in the kidnappers' convoy slammed into it from behind and window glass popped like fireworks. The Rabbit Killer went flying.

The remaining biker hit the pileup at full speed and pinwheeled five or six times over the roofs of the demolished cars before face-planting on the street.

"Damn," Deanna said as this wreckage also rapidly disappeared down the road behind them.

The explosive events had all happened so fast, *bam, bam, bam,* that Ronan wasn't sure exactly what had just happened. However, the result was clear: the convoy had been obliterated. Only the lead car was left.

Ronan and Deanna's vehicle slowed and drifted to the side. It came to a stop. The lead car had pulled over just ahead of them.

They heard a man yell, "Get out of the car!"

Peeking out of their shattered window, Ronan saw the man approach with an assault rifle. Ronan grabbed a machine from Li's box that looked like a bat, complete with bat wings, set the Target, and threw it out the window.

The man with the rifle saw it coming and tried shooting it down with a stream of bullets. But the bat-thing flapped and tumbled in an erratic path, making it very hard to hit, and the man sprayed gunfire in a dozen directions, hitting trees and cars. Unfortunately for him, he didn't hit the bat, which dropped and clamped onto his head, biting and tearing into his face with slicing razors.

Deanna looked away. "Oh, my God."

But the jig was up. Three other men approached, weapons drawn.

One opened the Kargaan's passenger door and lunged with a metal club, hitting Deanna on the side of the head.

CHAPTER 34

A short time later, all of them were gathered at the side of the road. Deanna had a bad cut on her head; blood ran through her fingers as she knelt before one of the kidnappers. Ronan stood several feet away, hands up. He'd surrendered the moment they had a gun on her.

The three armed men were not amused that their slick kidnapping had gone to hell. The biggest of them stood behind Deanna, aiming his rifle at her. A smaller guy with a ton of freckles on his face was calling in reinforcements. And finally, the angry man from the vehicle charging station clutched his laptop, which had presumably been used to turn their car into an obedient zombie. The rest of the posse were dead.

Ronan had been in some tight spots before, back in the army, but this was possibly the most scared he had ever been. Having three nervous and angry kidnappers pointing their loaded weapons at you, with clear intent to kill, made each moment feel like a roll of the dice. What was the right move? There was no way to know.

Deanna caught his eyes once or twice but she was careful not to provoke the kidnappers' suspicion.

Cars whizzed by.

"There are a lot of witnesses," Ronan said, nodding toward the traffic. "How many seconds before the police get here?"

"We'll be gone in a minute," the big man behind Deanna responded. "I recommend you cooperate. We won't hesitate to kill her. We don't need her. The boss wants you."

Ronan noticed that each of them wore leather gloves. Maybe they were keeping their fingerprints off everything. Their forearms were sleeveless and hairy and sweaty, and the gloves looked strange… ominous.

He knew the three men weren't bluffing. They would kill her. But they were also nervous. Li's crazy attack bots had thrown the men wildly off-kilter. They were on edge and waiting for another weird surprise.

"Get in our car," the guy with the laptop said, "Harper wants to dissect you."

"Don't use his name, asshole," the biggest kidnapper snapped.

With imperceptible movements, Ronan pressed his fingers to activate his ocular and requested maximum data and escape suggestions. Deanna's guard, the big one, was tagged ~210 LBS, 5'11, STRENGTH ~77. BERETTA SEMIAUTOMATIC, 20-ROUND CAPACITY. FEAR HIGH.

The laptop guy kept glancing at the sky and road. He seemed to be expecting one of the bots to come galloping up the road from the wreckage they'd left behind. Ronan figured that this kidnapper might be easy to take by surprise, given how distracted he seemed.

The small freckle-faced guy, however, was designated by the ocular as having NO FEAR. He was the one Ronan needed to take out first.

Ronan scanned their surroundings. DEAD CATERPILLAR. SMALL STICK. HAND-SIZED ROCK, DISTANCE 4 FT.

Nothing of value on the side of the road.

He tapped his fingers – God, he hated having to navigate with such a primitive interface.

The ocular provided PLAN OPTIONS A, B, C. He drilled in for detail.

Plan C looked best. Take out the fearless freckle-faced guy; use his gun to kill the other two.

Deanna mouthed words silently, and Ronan's ocular displayed the translation: I'LL TAKE THE GUY BEHIND ME.

He nodded. Ronan knew he could deliver a massive punch, the force coming from his machined legs, the lunge. But he'd never tested it.

There was no time for doubt. He burst forward, punching the freckled-faced guy in the nose with the reinforced knuckles embedded in his hands. The man's leering grin turned into a mass of bloody skin, exposed skull, and a bunch of anatomy that even Ronan's software couldn't identify. The impact killed him. He dropped his pistol and collapsed backwards to the ground. A second later Ronan had his weapon.

The laptop owner was backing up, too shocked to react. Ronan shot him in the heart.

The third kidnapper aimed his rifle at Ronan, but Deanna knocked it away, then jabbed her elbow into his stomach. She soon had the large man on the ground, his arm wrenched up to his scapula, her knee digging into his lower back harder than required.

This big dude was the last of the kidnappers. They had him where they wanted him, and Ronan intended to get some information. He approached and stopped with his boots inches from the man's face. "Are you working for the weird guy on the video, the one who took credit for the Nashville attack?"

"Could be."

"This wacko, Harper," Ronan said, repeating the name the kidnappers had just used. "What's his full name? I want to know who I am dealing with."

"All routes to the leader will be blocked," the man said through gritted teeth, wincing from the pain of his dislocated arm.

"Why are you all wearing gloves?"

The man spoke in gasps, a man on a mission to convert a lost world. "We do not touch technology. It's a mortal sin. Those of us working in the field have sacrificed ourselves to the cause. We operate guns, cars, computers, phones, drones, every evil thing. Do you understand?"

"Not really."

The man looked from Ronan to Deanna and back. "Kaczynski Chapter 9, verse 68: *What makes us feel secure is having confidence in our ability to take care of ourselves. You are threatened by many things against which you are helpless – nuclear accidents, carcinogens in food, environmental pollution, war, taxes, and invasion of your privacy.*"

The man looked around them. "See all this? You think of it as power or progress, but you are more helpless every day. Soon, you will have no power whatsoever. A primitive man had more control than you."

Ronan's ocular flashed. INDUSTRIAL SOCIETY AND ITS FUTURE.

UNABOMBER MANIFESTO, 1995, THEODORE KACZYNSKI.

"I know you don't get it," the man continued. "I don't know why Harper has any interest in you." With his free hand, the man withdrew a slim grenade. He slid the cap with his gloved thumb and pressed the button. *Beep... beep... beep...*

"Watch out!" Ronan yelled.

He grabbed Deanna in a bear hug and jumped, his mind telling his thighs to make it a good one, his prosthetics jettisoning them over the Kargaan. He landed on one foot and they sprawled onto the concrete as the grenade detonated. The car's window glass exploded over their bodies.

As the shockwave receded, Deanna peered from her position of cover with unguarded gratitude and respect. He realized this was the first time she had seen his augs in top form. It was the first time *he'd* seen his augs in top form. He helped her up and they dusted themselves off.

"Let me see that cut," he said. He indicated where the kidnapper had clubbed her in the head. Fortunately, the bleeding had stopped.

"I'll be fine."

He sighed. "We'll need to wash and bandage it, at least."

She nodded. "Should we wait for the police?"

Ronan gazed down the road in both directions. "Why should we deal with this? I'll tell Edward to notify the embassy, the police, and the DIA about the incident. Every dead man here will be identified and might lead to Harper. Meanwhile, let's borrow their vehicle. Our car is bricked."

The dead freckle-faced dude who no longer had a face had a key fob in his pocket. Ronan pressed it and the kidnappers' car chirped. Deanna texted Niko that they were running late. Then they were back on the road, leaving a handful of bodies and smashed cars behind them. Traffic rushed past, full of people caught up in their busy lives, and while some may have slowed as they moved past the carnage, no one stopped for a closer look.

"Are you the good cop or the bad cop?" Ronan asked as they entered the restaurant.

"Just be direct," Deanna replied.

"Yes, ma'am."

Niko jumped to his feet as they approached the table. Pieter remained seated, a wild mix of emotions on his face: SURPRISE, FEAR, DEFIANCE, PANIC.

"What on earth happened?" Niko asked, noticing a bandage on Deanna's head. "Were you in an accident? You should have called."

"We'll get to that in a minute," Ronan said. "Please sit."

"Is everything all right?" Pieter asked, his voice slightly shaky.

Ronan and Deanna sat across from them. "I'm losing my patience, Pieter."

Niko said, "I'm not happy about your tone. What is this about?"

"Several men just tried to kidnap us." Deanna nodded to Ronan. "Go ahead. It's your show."

"Thank you. Our car was hijacked by someone who wants to stop our investigation. That confirms we are close to a breakthrough. We are investigating the right place, Niko. Your lab."

"That makes no sense," Niko said.

"It's simple," Ronan continued. "The terrorists were tipped off early and have been following us. They tried to kill us on our way here from Taiwan. That didn't work. Now we are here, interrogating your employees. The terrorists want to learn exactly what we know. They're getting ready to scatter to the winds. Deanna and I can be sure of several things. First, at least one of them was at LikeLife in Taiwan. Second, a whole bunch of them are here in Johannesburg."

Deanna tapped the table. "In addition, we know the leader is named Harper and that he is in South America." She aimed her stare at Pieter. "Video captured a microdrone at the stadium at the time of the attack. Next, the CEO of LikeLife thought we should talk to you. And ever since, people have been after us."

Niko looked panic-stricken. "This is a witch hunt. This is crazy. No one at Sanar is a terrorist."

TRUE.

Or, Ronan thought, Niko only *thinks* it is true.

"Pieter," Ronan said, "you've gotten yourself in pretty deep here. How long do you think you can pull this off?"

Pieter went on the offense. "How dare you pretend to have any idea what I do? What kind of cock-and-bull theory are you cooking up?" NOSTRILS FLARED. "You just want to nail someone and pretend you solved this case!" AMBIGUOUS.

"I won't stand for this," Niko demanded.

Ronan fixed his gaze on Pieter. "Tell us exactly what you were doing with those men in the park yesterday, what you talked about, and how you knew that mosquito was a drone. Talk."

"I don't know what you mean," Pieter said, leaning back. He tried to appear relaxed. "I guess you've been watching all of us. I understand the gravity of the situation. I'm sorry about what happened in America, that terrible tragedy, but I was not involved. Yesterday, I met some friends at a park. I don't know what you mean about a mosquito. It's summer here. They're everywhere."

Niko looked furious and seemed ready to punch Ronan. More likely, he would grab Pieter and leave.

Ronan stared back at Niko. "I have questions for you, too, in a moment."

"Me?" Niko asked sarcastically.

Deanna said, "Pieter, please continue."

"What is there to tell? My friends and I talked about the game. We're big football fans and we follow the local teams." TRUE. He crossed his arms and tightened his face, defiant.

"Tell us about South America."

Pieter scowled. "It's a land of rainforests, rivers, coffee, Christians. What else do you want to know?"

"We know about your relationship with Harper," Deanna bluffed. "Where is he?"

Pieter's face betrayed shock. Fear flashed in his eyes. He was speechless, but that ended up working in his favor.

Ronan realized they were all over the place with their questioning. The conversation had fallen apart. They weren't synchronized at all.

"I have nothing further to say to you two," Pieter finally managed.

They had been too aggressive. Ronan switched to a fear tactic. "They're probably watching us right now." He looked around for effect and swatted the air.

Deanna lowered her voice. "Thanks to the hit squad, we have a lot more paperwork to deal with. And when they kill you off, that will be more paperwork."

Pieter looked rattled again. "No idea what you're talking about. Why would anyone kill me?"

Ronan shook his head in mock disbelief. "Maybe you asked them to get us off your back. That would indicate you are their weak link. You weren't that dumb, were you?" He gestured to Deanna as if to say, *you explain it to him.*

"You don't get it? They are shutting down every connection to their cell, burning every bridge. You, Pieter, are an enormous bridge."

Pieter shook his head.

"Our people found Siyu Chen," Deanna said, "in a dumpster in nowhere, China. Harper's covering his tracks."

"Enough of these false accusations and threats," Niko said. "You have no jurisdiction here. I will notify the authorities."

Deanna pointed at Pieter. "Let's cut the crap. This man is directly responsible for the deaths of thirty-eight Americans and I won't stop until he is extradited or dead. I don't care which."

Ronan raised an eyebrow. "Nicely stated."

Niko glanced at the other patrons and repeated, "You have no jurisdiction here. We are leaving."

The two scientists rose and left. Ronan and Deanna watched through the window as Pieter got in his car and Niko stood beside the open door. The two were talking.

Ronan sighed. "At least we shook him up. He will be more likely to make a mistake."

"Niko is going to stir up trouble with the South African government," Deanna said, keeping her eyes on the two men outside. "We may be at the end of our investigation here in Johannesburg. And those accidents back on the highway will catch up with us soon."

Ronan raised two pinched fingers. "We are so close. I know it."

He noticed Deanna watching out the window and followed her gaze. Pieter swatted the air, slapped at his forehead, then stumbled out of the car. Niko tried to steady him, but Pieter sprinted toward the restaurant.

They met Pieter as he stumbled into the foyer. Niko was right behind.

"How do you feel? Are you okay?" Deanna asked.

"No, I'm not okay!" Pieter yelled.

"Hold still," Ronan said. He grabbed a nearby menu and swatted at Pieter's shoulder. "You had a bug on your neck."

Pieter shimmied away, scratching at his skin. His eyes searched the floor.

Deanna peered through the windows for any sign of the Kazites.

"See anything?" Ronan asked.

"No."

All of them leaned close as Ronan flicked the tiny, broken body of a microdrone onto a menu. Ronan saw Pieter tremble as the realization sunk in.

"This can't be happening," Pieter said. "I'll destroy those bastards."

"Stay calm. Maybe it didn't bite you." Ronan studied the drone, another mosquito.

Pieter breathed deep, wiped sweat from his face. "Yeah, maybe."

Ronan set down the menu and gripped the man by the shoulders. "They are trying to kill you. We can keep you safe. Please, Pieter, tell us what you know. Who are these guys?"

Pieter wiped more sweat from his forehead. A look of resolution crossed his face and his shoulders slumped with a long sigh. He looked lost in his head. Then he spoke. "They're crazy survivalists. Their big hero is Ted Kaczynski, the Unabomber."

Niko's mouth dropped.

Ronan cut his eyes to Niko, then back to Pieter. "They idolize the Unabomber? Why?"

Pieter shook his head in disgust. "They want to send us back to a pre-technology world. Kaczynski said that technology was destroying society. He said software and machines will control us. In protest, he mailed bombs to industry leaders. He was inept as far as that goes because no one knew what he was trying to prove. But these guys think they can really scare people. They think they can create such fear of technology that it will trigger a mass movement back to a primitive culture. They call themselves the Kazites or some similar B.S."

"That's really helpful," Ronan said. "What do you know about Harper?"

Pieter clutched his chest. "Jonathan James Harper. A real wacko. What an ass. He founded the Kazites, but he isn't funding the operation. The big bucks are coming from somewhere else. China, I think."

Sweat dripped from Pieter's brow. Any information he had might be gone in seconds.

"My chest hurts. It's burning. I've been infected!"

"Talk!" Ronan urged. "This is your chance to right things!"

Niko whispered, "Pieter, what on earth…? I don't understand…"

Pieter collapsed onto the floor, clutching his chest. "I'm sorry. No one listened to me. I had to send a wakeup call. We're on the brink. I was desperate…"

His mouth and eyes contracted as tight as a fist. A gurgle emitted from deep within his thoracic cavity, from a spot that should never gurgle.

"Pieter, for God's sake, tell us where Harper is in South America!" Ronan scowled at the small group crowding around them and held up his palm, warning them back.

Pieter convulsed. He was on his side, breathing hard. "It's eating my chest!" He reached up, hands fumbling, and Ronan grabbed them, clenching tight. "I asked them to get rid of you," Pieter said. "Sorry."

"Where in South America?" Ronan demanded.

Pieter jerked, eyes wide, lips twisted in agony. His limbs slackened. He shook his head in wonder and his eyes rolled. "He's a maniac, but very clever."

Pieter's head lolled.

"Is he dead?" Niko asked. "What do we do?"

More people joined the gawking crowd, pressing closer. As Ronan checked Pieter's pulse, Deanna waved her badge at the onlookers. "Somebody call an ambulance. Tell them to park out front. No one is to leave the restaurant. The parking lot is dangerous."

"He's dead," Ronan said. He spoke to Deanna in a low voice. "We need to get out of here. See if he has a phone on him. There may be a ton of evidence on it."

Deanna found Pieter's phone. She held it in front of his face to unlock the screen, then changed the password and slid it into her pants pocket.

"Niko, we'll talk to you tomorrow. Tell the police you met him for a meal, and he had a heart attack. Please don't mention us."

They headed out to their stolen car, alert for flying things in the air, and left before the police arrived. Several miles away from the scene, Ronan pulled over. "What do you think? Do you believe Niko?"

"He seemed genuinely surprised. My gut tells me he isn't involved."

Ronan sat back in his car seat, head leaning on the rest. Deanna watched him.

They had some fantastic new information. But was it enough?

A phone buzzed. They looked at each other, confused.

Then they both looked at her pants pocket. Someone was calling Pieter's phone.

CHAPTER 36

Harper leaned back and listened to Pieter's phone ring. If the intel from the Outsiders, his remote Kazite field team, was correct, Pieter was dead. Yet Pieter's phone had just moved three miles to a parking lot down the road, according to the app they used to keep tabs on him. The Outsiders were watching from a distance. They reported that Ronan and his colleague, the good-looking tough woman, had stopped at the same location as the phone. Imagine, stealing a dead scientist's phone! *Tsk tsk.*

"Hello?" A man's voice answered.

Harper smiled and leaned back. "Looking for goodies?"

"What? Who is this?"

"You're looking for goodies. You know, Pieter's GPS data, phone logs, passwords, emails, contact lists, app backups... isn't that right, you nosy freak?"

There was a longer pause this time. "This is Ronan Flynn of the United States Defense Intelligence Agency. I know that–"

Harper cut him off. "I know who you are. You are a wanker. Tell me the name of your partner. The lovely woman. What's her name?"

"I'm not at liberty to tell you that."

"I see. You are turning yourself into a machine, but you still like the bump and scratch. You still have primal desires, right?"

"Hold on," Ronan said. "Can we please talk sense? I don't want any more people getting hurt."

"I know you, Mechanica Man. I know about your augmentations."

"I know you, as well. Your first name is Frederick, and you are based somewhere in Eastern Europe."

Harper liked what he heard. Pieter had fed them bogus information. Good job, Cape Buffalo, you knob. You dead stiff. "Well, just in case you are excited by this call, I routed it through a string of anonymous mobile relay services. You will never track me to the source. Your best bet is to randomly knock on doors. You might want to canvas the streets of Bucharest. You may not find me there, but they have pretty castles."

Harper was in the outer vestibule of hell. The outer room was bare except for a single homemade table and a single chair, both split from kapok trees and hand-hewn with a chert axe. A neat pile of cured animal skins lay on the table. One covered his left hand, protecting his palm from the satellite phone resting upon it. The room was a small antechamber to the inner vault of hell, a bigger room that was truly horrific – containing laptops, monitors, cables, hard drives, power cords, more cell phones, and every manner of foul thing that contaminated culture.

He shuddered just thinking about it. Thankfully, the door to the inner room was large and solid, five inches of steel, a concession, and the chamber bolt held it tight.

The line was silent for a long pause. Harper almost forgot that anyone was even there; he was too lost in his own thoughts, in the world as it should be, the world as a place where a spider was a spider and that's all there was to it.

"Frederick, are you still there?" Ronan asked.

"My, you are persistent. You just keep coming at me, don't you?"

"Can't stop. Like the bunny."

"What are you talking about, fool?"

"I was referring to a mechanical rabbit that– never mind."

"Something LikeLife dreamed up?" Harper asked. "Another abomination?"

"I'm glad you brought up LikeLife," Ronan said, trying to get Harper back on track. "How did you and Siyu get hooked up in the first place? I'll admit, your connections are impressive."

Harper laughed. He had been raised in an environment that emphasized sound, and he always noticed the way someone talked. This fellow pronounced "I'll" with the sound *ill*. He could probably predict where this guy lived, based solely on that. "Let's talk business. You are tracking me, and I tried to catch you, a fun little game. Now I am running out of time. Thus – therefore – I have a demand. Would you like to know what it is?"

"We can start there, or you could just tell me where the fuck you are."

"Now, now," Harper said. "Don't use the word fuck with a man you've just met. We hardly know each other."

"What do you want?"

"I want… well, let's talk about that. Excuse me." Harper was tired of holding the phone. He slid his hand out from under the animal skin and let it rest with the phone on the table. He bent down to speak into the microphone, rolling his eyes. "I'm interested in making the world a better place, Mr. Roboto, as I'm sure we all are. Do you know Theodore Kaczynski?"

"Not personally."

"I am referring, of course, to the Unabomber. He demanded, and got, the publication of his manifesto in two major newspapers. How did he do that, you ask? He mailed a bunch of bombs and got everyone's attention. But we Kazites are doing things on a bigger and more successful level than Kaz did. You are connected to the U.S. president – aren't you?"

"Not really. There are nine or ten people in the chain of command between us." In truth, Ronan had met the president several times. Edward could get a message to him quickly if need be.

"Ah, but isn't it true that if I were to draw a straight line on your org chart, starting with you, that when I got to the top, it would be the president of the United States?"

"Yes, correct."

"Well, he's not on *my* org chart. I'd like for you to talk to your president for me. Tell him what I'm trying to accomplish. Get him on the bandwagon. We're taking the world back to the pre-industrial age, a time when things were simpler, when things were right."

"I can't do that," Ronan said. "He wouldn't listen to me even if I did."

"Don't be intimidated!" Harper snapped. "Don't accept how things are. Don't be one of *them*. Be a force of change, like me."

"You're asking too much of me."

"Don't forget, friend Ronan," Harper said, "that I have the weapons to *make* the world do what I ask. I don't have to beg and hope. I'm giving you a chance to be a historical figure. You'll be known forever as one of the good guys who helped re-launch society. A true society, founded in nature, built with hard work and common sense. And now, my demand. Tell your president to shut down the Niagara Falls Power Plant. It only supplies two million people; it's a small, logical place to start. Everyone in Upstate New York will learn in just a couple of months that it's possible to live without all the lights and noisy machines. They'll be better off. Those two million trendsetters will, in short order, prove to the world that we can all do this. We can all live free of the buzzing, beeping, grinding, and glowing monstrosities that have taken over our lives."

Harper waited for the reaction. He had just delivered one of his better pitches, and he often gained ground at this point in the conversation. Who could deny that everything he said was true? Had he not suffered the truth more than any other person on earth? Wasn't he the most convincing and authentic person to communicate the message?

"I have no way of making such a crazy plan happen," Ronan said. "Is there something else you need? Money?"

"If you don't carry out that demand, I will unleash a plague of locusts like the world has never seen." Harper paused. "I don't mean literal locusts. They will be mechanical wasps or some such."

"You're mad."

Harper winced. But what could you expect from a man evolving into a robot? "Every gathering crowd will soon be at the mercy of these do-it-yourself weapons, whether I unleash them or someone else does. There is no way to track, stop, or control them. The machines will infest our world like flies and ticks. You see? Every technology that empowers also enslaves. Good yet bad, yin then yang, real or not real. Which am I?"

"I am fairly confused, to be honest..."

"Then let me be blunt. Our entire civilization teeters on a precarious fulcrum of technology; it tips, we all go! So we must march ourselves back to primitive feudalism; this is the last chance; the lever is shifting and soon falls. We must shut down the power stations, one at a time, giving society a chance to adjust. It may be rough, but the longer the inaction, the more catastrophic the reaction. If you are unable to comprehend this, then it is you who is mad."

There was another long pause. "I'm doing my best to get this, but–"

"You'll shut that power station down by noon tomorrow!" Harper yelled. "If it isn't down by then, I'll unleash hell in fifteen major cities!"

The line was quiet. Was Mechanica Man still there?

"Okay. I'll relay the message," Ronan said. "Anything else? Fries, maybe a Coke with that?"

"Why yes, I would enjoy a little side dish to go with my mayhem. Thank you for asking."

"Go ahead, what do you want?"

"You must surrender to me." Harper laughed softly. "I'll let you know where and when. Take care of my first request. Then I'll call you back. I'm a reasonable man. We'll work something out that will fit your busy schedule." Harper paused and said, "I want to find out what makes you tick."

"May I help you?"

A woman stared back at Edward from the Capital Racquet Club's check-in desk. She was cloistered in a small work area behind antique oak separators and appeared to be in her fifties, with a diamond brooch pinned to the shoulder of her black dress and a single string of pearls around her neck. Her mouth was pinched tight at the corners.

Edward's left sock and shoe oozed ice water from a puddle he had stepped into on the slushy curb outside. Inside the Club it was warm, and he unzipped his Columbia parka. "I'm here to see Nicholas Click. He's expecting me."

Click was the arrogant CIA agent from the morgue in Nashville. They hadn't talked in person since the attack. Edward wasn't thrilled about this visit, but they needed to compare notes.

The woman lifted a leather book from her desk, opened it with the casual air of someone about to recite a poem, found the current page, and stared at it. "Your name?"

"Edward Foster. I'm the head of Management of Emerging Technologies, or MET, in the Defense Intelligence Agency."

"Edgar?"

"No, Edward."

Her eyes searched her desk, then she fished around in a drawer and withdrew a pencil. Thinking better of her selection, she replaced it and took out a pen. She drew a careful line through an entry. "Spell your name, please."

He did.

"Can I see an ID?" She took his card, frowned, handed it back. Pulling a box from under the counter, she said, "You need to wear a tie."

"Here? Isn't this a racquet club?"

"Are you here to play?" She gave him a once over, noting the lack of a gym bag.

"No."

"Our dress code requires a tie after five. This is a formal gentleman's club."

Edward surveyed the posh surroundings – the wood-paneled walls, antique chairs, gilt-framed mirrors, oriental carpets, and large paintings of pompous old farts from bygone centuries. "This doesn't look like a gentleman's club. Where are the dancing poles?"

Her pinched expression didn't change. "It's not that kind of club, sir."

"I was joking."

Still no smile.

He took a tie from the box and she waited for him to put it on. As he flipped the tie into a knot, he scanned the neatly arranged books on the inset shelves. *The Letters of Thomas Jefferson. One Nation For All. Foundations of a Federalist Republic.* "Well, I know where to come if I want to read a good book," he said.

The lobby lady was not amused and she pointed without looking at him. "Mr. Click has a squash court reserved. He should be finishing up. Take the Grand Hall stairs and follow around to the observation deck. No cell phones."

"Thank you, ma'am."

The ascent up the sweeping staircase made him feel like a visiting dignitary, at least until he reached the top stairs and a woman decorated in diamonds cut a glance his way; apparently, she wasn't digging his parka and jeans. These old men's clubs were a strange mix of functions, he thought. You could work out, take a shower, and then join everyone for a gala event in the ballroom.

The hallway headed in two directions, and seeing no signs, he followed the right-hand path and wound around to the back, where a series of plexiglass windows looked down on a row of squash courts.

Click stood directly below him at one of the courts, talking to another man. He caught a glimpse of Edward and nodded. A few minutes later, he sauntered into the hall from the stairwell, wiping his face with a towel. His tan was immaculate.

"Edward! Nice to see you again. On our first meeting, I believe, you were feeling ill in the morgue. How are things going at MET?" Click had wrapped the sweaty towel around his neck. He extended a hand.

"Pretty well, I think. Nice place you have here."

"You like it? It's a great club." Click headed down the hall as he talked. "We have world-class facilities and wonderful networking opportunities. You know, I could sponsor you if interested. I could wrangle a couple votes on your behalf."

"I'll have to decline, although I appreciate the offer. This place is above my pay grade." They passed an intimate alcove where framed photos of presidents and senators stared down on several chairs and a small table.

"Nah. It's money well spent. The Club would elevate your standing, create opportunities. Think of it as an investment in your future career." He leaned in. "It's mostly older men. They're well-connected on the Hill and they like to mentor rising stars. You don't want to be leading a small unknown agency forever."

Edward forced a smile. "We agree on that. Technology is evolving faster than our agencies can keep up. The terrorists will always have plenty of new toys and they're getting deadlier every day. I expect a higher funding level going forward."

Click nodded and poured himself a glass of ice water from a decanter in the hallway. "Well, one step at a time. It would help if you could identify who attacked us." Pointing with the hand holding the glass, Click said, "You need a win. Come, let's go in here and talk business."

They entered a room lined with books, portraits, and a scattering of small tables, everything bathed in the warm light from a small chandelier. Heavy curtains hung across the windows, emphasizing privacy. A baby grand dominated the middle of the room and antiques filled every niche, including two eye-catching bright blue vases on the fireplace mantle, which looked to Edward like they could fund his immediate retirement.

"I like to have private meetings in here, rather than at Liberty Crossing, where you never know who may be listening. Russians... Chinese... Democrats... Republicans... coworkers. Everywhere you turn in that place, you've got phones, laptops, monitors, television sets – know what I mean? The place is infested with microphones. Even the SCIFs are compromised. Here, no one is trying to listen in. No one uses a phone."

Edward glanced at the collection of antiques and artifacts, then fixed Click with an impatient stare.

His host set the glass down and lowered his voice. "I've read your reports, but I wanted to hear it straight from the horse's mouth. Tell me your theory. Keep it short and simple. Explain like I'm five."

"Okay." Edward collected his thoughts. "It's like this. The victims of the Nashville attack were killed by a designer bio-agent developed by Sanar, a biomedical research lab in Johannesburg. The bio-agent specifically targets heart tissue. Somehow, one of the scientists, Pieter Heynes, got hooked up with Harper. We believe Pieter identified deadly variations of otherwise useful drugs, then handed the synthesizing instructions over to Harper's gang."

"Clarify that part about synthesizing instructions."

"Harper has desktop machines that make these molecules, these nanites. He gets the ingredient list and cooking instructions from Pieter, and the machine pops out a weapon."

"Yes, interesting." Click was pacing the room.

Edward continued. "Maybe Harper injects batches of the nastier stuff into people to see what will happen. To infect someone, you can just stick a needle into them. But to wreak havoc out in the world, he needed a fancy delivery mechanism. The latest microdrones are perfect for that. Commercially available printers can stamp those out by the zillions."

"This guy Harper must be a genius to figure all this out."

"I'm glad you brought that up. There's no reason to assume this guy has any brains at all. In the video, he expresses an anti-technology stance and talks crazy. We don't think he is the real brains behind the attack.

Pieter was killed right in front of my two operatives, Ronan Flynn and Deanna Pirelli, with the same apparent mode of death. Before he died, Pieter mentioned a network of other terrorist cells and a funder in China."

"Hold that thought. Keep going – after Pieter died, Harper called us on his phone, right?"

"Correct."

Click shook his head and sighed. "That's one crazy story. Look, to be honest, our original theories aren't panning out. There's no evidence a weaponized bacteria or virus was used in Nashville. The facts don't stack up. The investigation is in disarray and no one can keep track of all the moving pieces. Over a thousand agencies are involved and I don't think a single person knows the big picture. We have entire groups chasing down poison manufacturers in Baghdad, we have teams interviewing every biological weapon specialist we can get our hands on in every friendly country. Little by little, though, your name has been coming up. We've been following your reports, and one by one everyone is concluding that you are right."

"Thank you. I appreciate that."

"I'm not saying I'm fully on board with the nanoweapon-delivered-through-a-microbot idea, it all sounds a little weird, but I have to admit it's starting to fit the facts."

"This is our world now," Edward said.

"And I'm glad your team is on top of it. Maybe we got off on the wrong foot. I appreciate your summary. How certain are you that this theory is correct?"

"One hundred percent."

Click's eyes lit up. "Why so sure?"

"Ronan records everything 24/7. He recorded the phone conversation with Harper, and we matched the voice to the man on the video. We just finished the analysis two hours ago. It's the same guy. And he obviously killed Pieter the same way he killed the people at the Nashville stadium. It's simple and straightforward. I have no doubt left."

"That's great work. I hope you're right. But we still have the most important question – where the hell is Harper and his group?"

"Exactly."

"Other than the video, do we have anything that might give a clue about where this guy is?"

"According to Pieter, somewhere in South America. We all need to get on the same page and find this guy, fast."

"Are you referring to his threat that he will attack again if we don't meet his demands?"

"Yes."

"Well, we are not shutting down the Niagara Falls Power Station."

"That goes without saying, but we need to put every resource into finding Harper and then this Chinese funder and the other cells."

Click stopped, staring down at a porcelain figurine on the piano, which depicted a woman in Victorian dress looking in a vanity mirror. He crouched closer to it. "I don't remember this."

He held the piece toward the light and examined it, peering close, then set the object back on the piano and threw his towel over it. Giving it a wary look, he continued. "We're all looking for Harper. I'll help, Turlington will help, everyone will start shifting focus and scouring your information. That guy Niko? We're shutting his lab down. The president is putting heat on the director of the South African Security Agency. I expect that to happen soon. As for this idea of other cells and a mastermind in China, that's harder to buy. Your only evidence is the claims of a dying terrorist."

"I think his claims ring true – there is someone else in charge beyond some crackpot hiding in a jungle."

"But we don't have anything to go on. That angle is still largely up to you." He clapped a hand on Edward's shoulder. "You'll get more funding if you can get a win here. That's how it works. Forget China and help us find Harper."

"That's our main goal at the moment."

There was an awkward pause. Click wiped the sleeve of his shirt across his face and took another sip from his glass. With his back to

Edward, he said, "There's something else I want to talk to you about."

"What?"

"There's a complication. It turns out that the president pushed for nanoweapon funding. That's not well known, so don't pass it on. He believes enemy states are getting further ahead in this area and was able to get a sizable amount of money funneled into the DoD, hoping the U.S. could take the lead. Once your nanoweapon theories started circulating and began to look correct, it got major attention from the top."

"I see. You're telling me that once people know that nanoweapons were used in the attack, it's going to make the president look like he's on the wrong side of the issue."

"Exactly. If he funded nanoweapons, and nanoweapons were used against Americans, it doesn't look good. The White House doesn't want this becoming a topic of discussion, you know what I mean? In fact, the channels of communication among the intelligence agencies are starting to shut down. The information in this investigation isn't flowing freely anymore."

"Great, one more thing to deal with."

"I need you to do something for me. Get your people to retrieve some of Sanar's instructions for making Harper's weapons. Or at least samples of the stuff. Anything interesting, before the South African authorities get it all. At the very least, that could help build a case that the president's hunches were right. The U.S. is lagging in a major new weaponized technology and needs to keep up."

"Sure. I'll need to know who is officially approving this request."

"Sanar is going to be torn apart. We don't have time for paperwork."

Edward got the point. "I'll make sure you stay in the loop on everything from our end."

"Thank you." Click extended his hand. "I'll do likewise. It was good to get to know you a little better."

CHAPTER 38

After a long call with Edward, Ronan and Deanna had finally made it back to their temporary headquarters, The Michelangelo Hotel. They went across the marbled foyer, up the shiny elevator, and down the fancy hallway. They were exhausted. The hotel's vibe – Men are the Measure of all Things, or, at least, men with money – was no longer fun. Where was a grimy first-floor bar when you needed it, a place to relax and think about what they had been through? They had fled the scenes of several fatal vehicle accidents, a roadside shootout, and a scientist's death.

They had left Niko behind at the restaurant. Unless he got out of there as fast as they did, he would be interrogated by the police. Niko probably didn't have anything to worry about. The police would assume that Pieter was just some guy who had a heart attack. They would never imagine the man's connection to half-ass villains hidden somewhere in the world's endless tracts of rainforest, playing with populations as game pieces.

Ronan crashed on the couch.

Deanna went into the kitchen. "Tell me again what Harper said about you."

He played the recording back and repeated the exact words Harper had used: *You must surrender to me.*

"That's not a serious option."

"Maybe Edward will want me as bait."

He heard the fridge open and he called out, "Anything non-alcoholic in there?"

"There's a jug of something called Amasi. I'll pour you some."

He heard the crack of a plastic seal and the tinkle of glasses. She reappeared with a gin and tonic for herself, while his glass contained a thick grey goop. On closer inspection, he saw white chunks floating on the surface that reminded him of cottage cheese. He almost gagged. But he sipped cautiously and found it appealing, like tart yogurt.

Instead of sitting in a chair, she plopped down on the couch next to him. They clinked glasses.

"That crackpot would kill you, Ronan."

"I wouldn't just roll over and let him shoot me. I was in the Army, remember?"

She lingered on the edge of her glass. "Afghanistan, right?"

"Yes. Five years, plenty of missions. A lot of it was just trying to help the locals survive the war."

"Any serious combat?"

"Occasionally… things were always dicey. You never knew when a situation would unravel." He remembered crisscrossing the rocky valleys, one narrow dusty road after another in an endless, serpentine stretch of grey-brown drabness. He'd had a few exchanges with small groups of Taliban fighters, but most of the time he was simply bored.

She'd raised her eyebrows. *Dicey? Let's hear it.*

God, he hated telling stories.

"Once, as part of an initiative to stabilize the region," he began, "I was sent to a small village in one of the eastern provinces, a steep hilly area. The villagers' shallow river had dried up, so they needed a water pump. A couple of us arrived first with a truckload of equipment. We had a small satellite rig, solar kits, a drilling machine, and medical gear. Mundane stuff. None of it was for fighting. The end."

He took a sip of Amasi and studied the glass.

She laughed and kicked his leg.

The day was coming back to him – the panic, the raw fear. "This was a simple drop-off, nothing dangerous about it. We even brought a large LED video screen made of synthetic fabric that we could hang anywhere to maintain communication and training after we left. I thought about using it to give the villagers a movie night. Shortly after we arrived, though, we got word a hostile convoy was headed toward the village. At the time, the Taliban was trying to regain control of the region, and they'd pop up here and there, killing everyone in their path."

Ronan remembered the faces of the elders when they realized who was headed their way. "The villagers panicked. There was nowhere to hide, few weapons, and no way to make a reasonable stand. The men were worthless; they were all addicted to opium. The women were crying, begging me to help. One of the elders told me that there was a natural cave nearby, in the hillside, with a small entrance. The townspeople called it – I don't remember – it meant the 'place of birth' or something. But she warned that the cave was easy to spot, and if the Taliban soldiers found them in there, they would be trapped. It would become the place of death."

"Damn."

"Yeah. We had an hour at most before the convoy arrived. A few of the village men, I believe, were planning to kill us for our guns and truck. Knives were appearing. We considered getting the hell out of there."

"I might have done that. What happened?"

"I was struck with a simple solution. I told them to grab their belongings, any evidence that the village was occupied, and get in the cave. While they did that, we hung the LED tarp over the cave entrance, hammering it into the stone with tent stakes. Then I took a photo of the hillside for the tarp to display. I couldn't believe how well it worked. The image perfectly camouflaged the cave entrance. You couldn't detect the tarp or the cave unless you were within ten feet."

"I take it the Taliban didn't know about that cave."

"Hell, there were thousands of caves in the region. The convoy arrived. For two hours they hung around, rummaging for things to loot. Then we heard them leave. They never looked for us. They must have decided the villagers had deserted because of the dry river. I have to tell you, I got a lot of hugs that day."

"I'm impressed, Ronan."

"How about you?"

Deanna leaned back in the sofa. She'd been facing him, but now she gazed off toward the windows, glancing back to underscore certain points. "Army Intelligence. I made Senior Analyst my final year. By that point, I was leading and training hundreds of officers as well as enlisted personnel. They weren't all specifically under my command, but I often ran the show."

The room had good sunlight, and as she looked away, he noticed that her hair had a hint of red. He'd thought of her hair as brown, but realized it was closer to auburn. She had it pulled back tightly behind an ear and swirled over the other shoulder. Being so close to her was a little unnerving, just sitting together, not working, but he wanted nothing more at the moment. She was smiling and glancing at him a lot.

She gestured with the glass. "Let me tell you how I met Edward."

"It seems you've known him a while."

"What happened is that I was helping the CIA locate a cabal that was supposedly planning to assassinate a Syrian government official. I was in a safe house in Syria near the border of Turkey, while embedded ops poked around a nearby town. Everything was good for a couple weeks. Then everything and everyone went silent. Our operatives vanished. On drone footage, we could see the mood of the whole town had shifted. People stayed inside. A creepy quietness settled in. Slowly, information filtered out. We were told not to move. We were alive because they didn't know where we were. But they were hunting for us."

"Who were they?" Ronan asked.

"The Syrian government. A few of the national leaders had been planning to knock out a pro-American local official. One of our ops returned with that information. But they'd followed him. A fleet of Hum Drones arrived at the safe house, intercepting our comms."

"Ah, yes, Hummies. Fun times."

"We thought they would bomb us down to a pile of rubble, as usual. But instead the Hummies shot through the windows and came inside. We realized that their goal was to kill us with minimal structural damage. Scariest moment of my life. They were flying around in the corridors and blasting doors, executing everyone. We called for an airlift. A team from

Turkey arrived within twenty minutes. By this point, the area was swarming in Hummies. The smallest ones I've ever seen – flying handguns and explosives, essentially. Flocks of them, moving in coordinated waves."

"The chopper dropped a line and hoisted us from the rooftop, right through the swarm. Even though I was inside the cabin in ten seconds, I was hit fifteen times on my way up. Legs, arms, back, and ear."

"Hell, that beats my story." He clinked her glass again. "Let me guess – you lived."

"I was the luckiest soldier in the world that month. I was out of the hospital in a couple weeks. Most of my team was not so lucky."

"And that led you to Edward?"

She nodded almost imperceptibly and set her glass down. Her eyes were always intense, Ronan thought. They showed her making calculations, always thinking out the next few steps. Alive with the thrill of the hunt. She rarely smiled, but she had a hint of a smile now, and it was a relief.

"Edward immediately understood the tactical significance of those small Hummies. And he saw that this stuff was going to get smaller and smaller, and that weapons would soon be produced cheaply in vast quantities, and that someone needed to prepare for terrorist attacks with those weapons. Edward asked me to assess the risks, and I started to watch a handful of companies closely."

"And LikeLife was at the top of your list?"

Deanna nodded. The smile was gone, but her eyes still captivated him. "You saw for yourself. They were making the most significant advances in miniaturization. They can crank out a whole dust storm of attack weaponry, not to mention an endless stream of specialized devices."

She looked away.

Ronan contemplated the last drops of Amasi in his glass. What was the next move? He had no idea. It certainly seemed possible that the human race was going to destroy itself one way or the other, because every year there were more ways to do it. He knew there had to be survivalist groups that saw this future, too.

"I'm sure that Pieter is telling the truth," Ronan said. "Someone out there wants to scare us all back to the stone age."

She finally looked back. "Of course they do."

Clarence Bailey was monitoring water flow when the phone rang. The final hour of his shift was almost over, and he used his index finger on a tablet to sign off on the status of each system. Scribble, *tap*. Scribble, *tap*. He stood on a small yellow catwalk inside the enormous cavern of the power plant near Niagara Falls, New York. Thirty-six million gallons of water from the upper reservoir pounded down through the generators every minute, sending electricity out over a rickety grid to two million homes and their televisions, laptops, and microwave ovens.

He answered. "Assistant plant manager."

"Are you flowing as normal?" a voice asked.

"I'm sorry?" Clarence thought he heard a laugh over the line, but the hum of the machinery, including thirteen massive turbines, made it difficult to tell.

"Are your pipes wet or dry?"

Clarence put his finger to his other ear. "Repeat yourself, please. I can hear you now."

"Is your plant functioning as normal?" the voice demanded.

"Yes, sir," Clarence shouted above the turbines. "Of course. Who is this?"

"Are you planning to cut the power?"

"Excuse me? I'm having trouble understanding your questions." Clarence glanced at his watch.

"I'm talking about bringing one system down to force the transition to the next. Have you and your coworkers not been told? Controlled destabilization. A movement away from everything you power. A return to primitive, healthy, regenerative lifestyles. True control. Values and ideals you know nothing about. Can you try to imagine?"

"Let me forward you to the operator."

"Never mind," the voice said. "Have a spectacular day."

"Nut case," Clarence mumbled and hung up.

...

Jonathan James Harper leaned back in his chair and faced First
Lieutenant Graham Bolton. "They didn't listen to our demands."

"The United States says they don't negotiate with terrorists," his
lieutenant said. "They lie about everything, so I believed the opposite. Is
that what you thought, sir?"

Harper stared from his chair like the frozen image on a bad video
connection.

The lieutenant shifted uneasily, waiting.

Harper lifted his hand and placed it absently into his bowl of fertile
earth. He swirled a finger in the dirt, feeling the coolness. Heaven or Hell?
It was anyone's guess how all this would play out for a tired planet
crawling with humans.

After some time, he looked up at the anxious man. "I thought they
cared about their lives and their futures. I really thought they cared more."

He rose from his chair, clutching the bowl of earth, and threw it
against the wall. It shattered into shards and dirt dust. Bolton twitched.

"Is everything still ready on that tourist trap, the island destroying
the ocean ecosystem?"

"Yes, sir."

"I'm ready to move on it. Are the black things all set?"

"Yes, sir."

"What about those weird balls Siyu got from LikeLife?"

"Packed and ready."

"They work, right? Otherwise we look like wankers."

"Pick up a ball and it's game over. They are heat activated."

"Look, the balls don't matter. We just need to spray the black shit on
everyone. The tourists, the locals. Make sure we hit the kids."

The lieutenant nodded and moved to leave, glad the meeting was over.

Harper pointed to the broken bowl on the floor.

"Clean that up, lieutenant," Harper said. "Then initiate Project Spankem."

CHAPTER 40

Flashback to Harper's Dreamlike Childhood

...and his simple path to suddenly becoming one of the world's most wanted criminals

An illustrated interlude

At the time of Harper's birth, his parents were academic researchers who specialized in virtual media theory. Immersive digital worlds were exploding in popularity, with each new breakthrough product promising increasingly lifelike, yet fantastical, experiences. Harper's parents were huge proponents of the life-changing benefits of these products, and they often advised corporations, politicians, investors, and journalists in the near-term opportunities for entrepreneurs bold enough to take users ever deeper into these worlds.

His parents loved the attention, and they carefully crafted their public image. Eventually, they decided to build a permanent legacy for themselves. In a move that was part global publicity stunt and part psychological experiment, they announced that they would be the first couple to raise a child entirely in virtual reality.

Their only child, Jonathan James Harper, was delivered at home into a bathtub of dark water. Before he had time to see natural light, they whisked him from the water and swaddled him in a warm blanket. They wrapped a device around his head and eyes that projected color, faces, and images. The device whispered into his ears.

His mother dressed him in pajamas embedded with sensors. The fabric squeezed him. Warmed him. Vibrated his soft little back and butt.

...

Harper's brain developed strange sensory-motor responses, such as heart palpitations upon seeing the colorful avatars of his parents. These avatars often jittered and shook in his field of view because the stability of his virtual world varied depending on how well the processors worked that day.

He learned symbols and played with electronic blocks. Electric pulses kept his muscles from atrophying.

His parents sent haptic hugs and told him to be free. "Explore your worlds, my beloved," they said, which he heard through tiny ear buds. He had an entire universe to explore and many digital companions of his own creation.

...

As he grew older, he still had never seen the real world – but when he sometimes expressed curiosity about it, his parents explained that he was lucky to spend his entire life in an immersive feedback system that catered to his every need. The system would deliver experiences to optimize his imagination. His environment would always adapt to his moods and thoughts, and thus was far superior to the bleak and painful physical world.

So Harper spent his days and his years in a world of rolling hills, intense suns, dark caves, floating eyeballs, and rat feces.

...

When he was 17, he reached a day when he despised his world so much that he would kill anyone or himself to end it. He ripped out the headset straps that were embedded in his skull and saw his mother for the first time.

She was not colorful or vibrant or pretty. She was haggard and fearful, her mouth hanging open like a moron, staring at the blood dripping from his head. She was much, much larger than he had anticipated.

Afraid of her body, with its skin stretched over the bones of her face and hands, he ran throughout the house, stumbling and falling. Every object he encountered was hard, painful, solid.

In a room cluttered with debris, full of objects whose purpose he could not guess, he saw a metal pipe. He wrapped his fingers around the bar and gave it a swing. The weight and heft in his hands seemed miraculous. Someone entered the room, a man he presumed to be his father; the man appeared upset. Threatening.

After cracking his father over the head three or four times, he re-traced his route, seeking his mother. She was standing in the same spot, her mouth still hanging open. When she saw his bloody pipe, she snapped out of her daydream and turned to run. But Harper jumped on her back and beat her skull until large chunks broke free and he found himself pounding into brain tissue.

"How was that, my beloved?" he asked as he stood in a growing pool of blood.

...

Harper needed to strengthen his body so that he could experience this exciting and new immersive world. His arms and legs were frail, and his back ached from the workout.

He'd been eating vitamin solutions and modulated protein since birth. Swinging a pipe took a lot out of him, and to maintain that kind of activity, he'd need to eat better – *a lot* better. He found food in the kitchen.

Bread. Peanut butter. Yogurt. Cookies. Cheese. Cereal. Bananas.

He knew enough about the real world that you couldn't murder your parents and just sit around waiting for the police to show up, so he packed a knapsack and joined the legions of homeless people on the outskirts of the city. He blended in well, and the authorities didn't know what he looked like: he'd had a screen strapped to his eyes his whole life, and his parents had not allowed photos to be taken of him.

Years passed...

He had no livelihood, but he was free.

He studied every small detail about the world around him. The other homeless people gave him plenty of space, especially since he was prone to long angry rants about virtual reality, but sometimes he would entertain them with his ability to recognize people by hearing them speak a single word. As a child he had developed a remarkable attention to sound.

Meanwhile, he learned to grow food in hidden nooks and public parks. He built all of his own makeshift tools from various discarded refuse.

He found people who, like him, wanted to live off the grid.

Most of these people were criminals. Some were actively running from law enforcement, others maintained illicit businesses, and some just hated everything about modern society. They became obsessed with the Unabomber Manifesto, written by terrorist bomber Theodore Kaczynski, with its call to action against the technological age.

They moved to a rainforest, which provided an abundance of running water, food, and secrecy.

They called themselves the Kazites – the followers of Kaczynski.

One day, a man came to them. He was wealthy and looking for like-minded anarchists. He wanted to fund terrorist groups to carry out violent attacks to warn about the dangers of technological self-destruction.

"Want to change the world?" the man asked.

The man's name was Siyu Chen.

"We will turn people against technology," he claimed. He pointed to an instrument sitting in the back of his vehicle that had many hoses and tubes. "This machine is our weapon. It creates molecules that rip up people's bodies."

Harper was skeptical.

"Use technology to stop technology?" he asked.

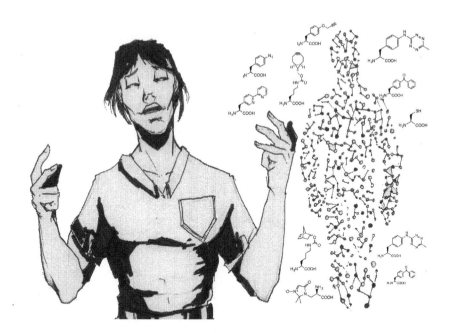

"Yes," Siyu explained. "People allow devious technologies to permeate every aspect of their lives. Maybe they will finally resist technology when we infect their bodies with it."

Harper considered this idea. Siyu waited for his reaction. Finally, Harper broke the silence.

"That's brilliant," Harper said. "This speaks to me. But how do we keep the infection from spreading all over the place and killing us, too?"

Siyu waved his arms as if the answer was miraculous. "The little molecules are not contagious. They are like drugs. We are going to use little biting machines to get the molecules inside people. I need people like you to orchestrate the attacks."

Harper's eyes lit up like a forest fire. "You have no idea how much I want to do this," he said. "Count us in. Do I get to pick the targets?"

Siyu nodded and smiled broadly. "Yes, indeed. We will supply you with all the equipment and instruction necessary to carry out the attacks. You and the Kazites will lead the way, but I am starting many other groups around the world. Might I suggest one thing? Go big. Make a spectacle too weird to ignore. We can shock every nation-state into submission."

Harper began to fill with grim fantasies.

Siyu knew that he had picked the right man. His eyes narrowed, and he concluded, "If people do not follow your orders, rain death upon them with merciless brutality."

PART TWO

St. Bonaventure Island was tropical, sunny, and warm, inching toward hot. The streets of the tiny Caribbean island were far busier than usual, as throngs of locals and tourists gathered for Sea Fest, an annual celebration that lifted the remote drop of land from off-season obscurity to a destination of Great Family Fun. Here, adventurers became great fishermen. The festivities began with a magnificent parade of floats, after which the tourists would captain a flotilla of yachts to seed the clear-blue waters with tagged krill. Everyone would bask in the sun and drink pina coladas. Upon the sounding of the horn, they would discharge their colorful nav-hooks, and the ocean would give up its bounty of snapper and mackerel.

The event brought the island to life, stirring it from a sun-baked slumber. Vibrant crowds poured through the streets, visiting the makeshift shelters of street vendors hawking bright wooden fish souvenirs and tropical fruit. Those who weren't out on the streets were gathered in kitchens and backyards, cooking and preparing for the festivities.

Seda and her children, six-year-old Franco and eight-year-old Luna, left a pastry shop and joined the hundreds of others gathered on the sidewalks to await the arrival of the floats. Banners flapped in the breeze. Vendors worked the restless crowd, selling pastries, fried fish, and water bottles. Children chased each other, tossed balls back and forth, and cheered at the occasional explosions of firecrackers. Several police officers patrolled on horseback, but the island had little crime, and these men were viewed as friends and family more than enforcers of law and order.

Seda called to her children as the first of the floats came into sight, lumbering their way from the warehouse at the harbor. Franco and Luna came running, giggling. They gathered at her side and watched, unable to stand still.

"I wish Daddy was here," Franco said. "Is he going to make it?"

Seda cringed. She hadn't explained to Franco that his father wouldn't be joining them. The boy still thought his father was on a long fishing trip to the Greater Antilles.

"Of course he's not going to make it," Luna burst. "They don't let people out of prison for celebrations."

"What?" Franco said. "What do you mean?"

Seda knelt beside them and pointed at the approaching floats. "Look! See how big they are?"

The crowd moved out of the way as the floats crept closer. Firecrackers shot off like gun rounds. Bottle rockets sizzled skyward and screamers zipped and burst.

The small high school marching band arrived first, blaring and booming a song of hope and freedom.

Seda saw Franco's expression turn to joy as he quickly forgot about his father. Thank goodness, she thought. Sometime soon she would attempt to explain. Not now.

People riding the floats threw candy to the onlookers. Children rushed forward to snatch the pieces from the air, then rushed back to their parents and friends. The floats were impressive: a swaggering fisherman, a swordfish with rolling eyes, a crab with claws that clicked. Then they saw an enormous black tarantula, representing the hairy spiders found all over the island. The spider's legs trembled as the driver piloted it over the cobblestone street. Covered in furry fabric and painted in a black gloss, the towering spider looked more real the closer it came.

"That's scary!" Luna yelped.

Seda became aware that the spider's driver, a long-haired young man covered in tattoos, was staring at her. When their eyes met, he didn't look away. He eyed her with a predatory leer.

Three men on the back of the float tossed soft spider eggs into the air, fuzzy balls the size of cantaloupes that the children retrieved with extra enthusiasm. All of the men had long hair and tattoos, which was common on the island, but this group looked dangerous, she thought, like men who'd just broken out of prison. Seda was lost in thought when her kids returned to her side, bouncing up and down and asking if she wanted some of the tasty candy they had collected.

"Not at the moment," she told them.

She'd brought a carry bag, and the kids dropped in a stream of chocolates and mints, along with a couple large spider eggs, then rushed off to get candy from the next float.

She reached into the bag and withdrew one of the spider eggs. It was heavier than she had expected. Tapping a fingernail on it, she hit a hard shell under the fuzzy coating, which was perhaps metal or thick plastic. She looked around to see if anyone had opened theirs.

A young boy nearby shook his egg with two hands. He held it to his ear. "Something is inside," he said to his parents. "It sounds like sand. How do you open this?"

His parents shrugged. Seda gave her egg a little shake and listened.

The boy jumped. "It's vibrating!"

As Seda watched, the boy's egg clicked. With a small *pop* it fell neatly into two halves, revealing a mass of black stuff on the inside of each half-shell.

There was a moment when no one, not the boy nor his parents nor other onlookers, knew what to make of it.

Then the black stuff started writhing, stirred to action as if energized by the bright sun.

Before the boy could react, the delicate black fluff was caught by the breeze. Some had blown onto his arms.

Seda's brain tried to make sense of what she saw. Small black bugs crawling rapidly up the boy's arms. He was soon covered in them. His mouth was frozen in a scream-less O.

She realized she was still holding her egg. She dropped it.

Someone nearby screamed. "What the–?"

Seda processed what had emerged from the eggs: spiders.

An army of them moved along a man's arms, crawling and jumping and blown by wind. She saw them in his clothes and hair. A few were close to his open mouth.

Pop. Pop. Pop.

Other eggs opened. Flying things came out, as big as horse flies.

Children flailed their arms and screamed. Others ran as though on fire. She saw the tiny spiders crawling on faces and leaping person to person. A parent slapped at her son's arms and legs as the boy screamed and cried.

Seda snatched her kids by their collars and ran from the chaos. She stopped nearby and knelt to inspect their clothes and skin. A couple spiders clung to Franco's shirt sleeve, but this was all she found. She swatted them away and smashed them with a stomp of her tennis shoe.

As the screaming grew louder, a shopkeeper rushed out with cans of bug spray tucked under each arm. He passed the cans around and launched a feverish attack on the spiders, gassing them in thick clouds of spray. From what Seda could tell, the spray had no effect whatsoever.

Now many of the spiders had been brushed off and the street was crawling with them. A stompfest ensued for the next several minutes. Everybody got into it. The spider-crushing didn't end until, after many inquiries, someone asked if any were left and, finally, none were.

Other than a few people knocked over by the short-lived panic of the crowd, nobody seemed hurt. Children complained about spider bites and cried as their parents hugged and comforted them. Seda bent for a close look at one of the spiders. It looked... fake. Mechanical. But it was too small to tell, exactly.

"Where did those float operators go?" an officer asked.

"I don't know," Seda replied. The float had stopped; the men on it had disappeared.

"Is anybody hurt?"

"I don't feel so good," a child said, approaching her.

"What's wrong, sweetheart?" she asked.

"I'm cold."

"He's shaken up," the officer said.

Screams erupted.

A young girl dropped face-first toward the ground, hitting like a sack of fruit. As her father lifted her in his arms, Seda saw that the child's eyes were glazed and unfocused.

"What's happening to the spider float?" someone asked.

The float trembled. It rattled upon its base.

As Seda watched, holding her children tight, a whirring of awakening motors filled the air, and the giant tarantula split like a piñata. A man stood within, holding a large hose. And from it sprayed a blackness like nothing Seda had ever seen.

A tsunami of creatures showered onto the crowd as the man swung the hose left and right. Spiders of all types rained down, but also fleas, midges, bedbugs, flies – the revelers near the float were engulfed by the sheer number of black things pouring onto them.

The police officer climbed onto his horse. He lifted a pistol at the float driver. Seeing the tsunami, he yanked the reins. The horse backed into several children, knocking them into the spider-wave. Parents ran for their children and they, too, were covered.

The horse, now crawling with spiders, galloped madly, reared in panic, and threw the officer from the saddle and into the wave of blackness.

The entire area was alive with crawling movement. Bigger spiders moved among smaller ones. Things flew in the air.

Seda could only stare at the chaos around her. Another police officer, coated head to toe with spiders, shot his pistol in random directions. A dog rolled uncontrollably. Spiders entered every orifice: noses, ears, mouths. A homeless woman beat at the spiders with a newspaper. The breeze had blown black things everywhere, like pollen. People scattered in all directions. Children were trampled.

Seda clutched Franco and Luna as the throngs stampeded toward them. They were going to be crushed. The black things were landing on people only a few feet away, as if by deliberate attack.

A man held open a shop door. "Get inside while you can!" he yelled.

She grabbed her kids and rushed into the store. The man slammed the door and threw the latch as the crowd outside pushed against it.

She heard shouting and screaming and – *Wham!* – someone pounding on the window. Seda watched the chaos on the street. Her heart hammered. Spiders were jumping on the glass. Flies crawled across it. The windows darkened.

"Let me in!" someone shouted.

Others pounded on the door.

"What should we do?" Seda asked, turning to face the man.

He was the float driver.

She gasped.

He reached for her. Flicking something from her blouse, the float driver stomped the ground, then pinched the tiny thing in his fingers. A grin spread across his face as he held it close. She saw a flattened spider, a tiny wire visible.

"They're not *real*," he said, eyes wild.

Seda shrank away, pulling Franco and Luna close to her sides. "What do you want?"

The tattooed float driver laughed, exposing tooth gaps. "Me? Oh, this isn't my doing. This is because the man failed. He's the one responsible. I'm only the dotted I, the crossed T. That's all I am."

"Friend, what the hell are you talking about?" a new voice said. A young man rose from behind the counter. He held a bong in one hand and a bag of chips in the other. His hair was tousled as though he had just awakened. "What the hell is going on out there?"

With a slow swagger, the float driver approached the man. The driver stopped inches from his face.

Stoner Dude stepped back.

The driver lunged, grabbed the stoner's head, and slammed it on the counter. The stoner dropped his bong and chips.

"No!" Seda yelled.

The driver threw the young man to the floor.

"Fuck," the stoner said.

"Shut up!" the driver ordered.

For the first time, the stoner noticed the spiders crawling up the store windows. He noticed the pounding and the screams. "Holy mother of Jesus. What the–?"

The door was cracking and splitting, as though forced by a crowbar. A window shattered and slung shards across the tile.

The door burst inward. People fell inside, gasping and screaming, bringing with them a mass of jumping blackness.

Seda dragged her children as she bolted for the back of the store. The float driver was ahead of them. She heard the stoner stumbling somewhere behind. They rushed through the store and down a rear hall to a single door beneath an exit sign.

The float driver tried to force the door open. He looked out through a small, grated window. "Sorry folks, there are crates stacked against the door. This is as far as we go."

"I was gonna move them," the stoner said, as if remembering something on a to-do list. "We could hide in there..."

He pointed to a utility closet. The float driver opened the door and yanked the light chain.

In a glance, Seda saw things hanging from pegs: gardening tools, rags, a scuba mask, cleaning supplies, a machete.

A loud crash ripped through the store and the building trembled. The lights went out.

Darkness.

"Jesus and Mary help us," Seda whispered.

The sun filtered through the back door window, but the closet was a dark hole. The driver pulled out a knife that flashed briefly when it caught the light.

"Get in the closet," the driver said.

A stampede approached.

Without another thought, the stoner took a step into the closet.

"Not you," the driver said and slit his throat. The stoner crumpled into the shadows.

A man emerged around the corner, then a woman, both screaming, out of their minds, covered in black things.

Seda grabbed Franco and Luna and pushed them forward into the dark closet. The driver followed them in.

He closed the door.

She heard a bolt slide into place.

Over the screams in the hallway, she heard the laugh of the float driver.

Edward was fifteen minutes into his weight-lifting routine at the District CrossFit Gym on Half Street. For years he had been coming five times a week like clockwork, but he was slowly falling off his game. Lately, it was three times if he was lucky. His heart wasn't in it anymore. It didn't take much energy to move the mouse on his desktop computer. His only reason for coming to the gym lately was a fear he would turn into a blob and lose his will to live entirely.

The hunt for the Kazites hadn't helped. He'd been on the clock since the Nashville attack. He needed this workout to clear his mind.

His phone buzzed. Cutting his eyes to where it lay nearby, he saw a text appear on the screen, then vanish.

Edward lowered the barbell onto the rack and slid off the bench. He wasn't expecting anything urgent, but it was an excuse to take a break.

The text was from Click, the CIA guy. He was in the lobby downstairs.

Edward wiped his face with a small towel and threw it on the floor near a wall. He took a sip from his water bottle. Then he hurried downstairs.

The lobby was full of wet slush and blobs of snow melt that had piggy-backed on the shoes and pant legs of people coming in from outside.

"Nicholas," he said. "You could have called. I'd have met you at the Pentagon."

"I needed to see you immediately. In private. Can we step outside? Grab a coat if you need it, but this will be quick."

Edward hesitated. He was wearing gym shorts and a t-shirt. He caught sight of the snow kicking up against the glass doors leading outside. Eight-twenty in the evening, nothing but blackness out there, temperature plummeting. He briefly considered retrieving his coat from the locker room upstairs. Instead, he nodded.

As they opened the door, the wind blew into them, cold and icy, enveloping Edward's body. Worse than expected.

Click led the way, away from the main doors a few paces, and looked around to verify that no one was hanging around outside in this nasty weather. No one was.

Across the street, an old auto repair building sat in snowy silence. At this hour, and in this temperature, the building was locked, dark, and empty. Three rows of lonely cars had been squeezed onto the wide sidewalk in front of the garage doors, their features disappearing under the rising snow. The workers had left hours ago.

Click turned to face Edward. They stood in a patch of light from the gym's outdoor floods. Click was wrapped in a tailored cashmere overcoat and scarf. His tan seemed to have deepened since their conversation at the racquet club. How was that possible? The tan looked sun sourced, with no hint of goggle marks or synthetic tints.

The sleeves of Edward's T-shirt fluttered. The cold attacked his flesh, but he acted casual, as if exposing bare skin to biting wind was like sunbathing in Belize.

Keeping his voice low, Click said, "I assume you've been fully briefed on St. Bonaventure Island?"

"Yes. Harper said he would attack, and he did."

"A crazy attack. Pure theatrics."

No doubt about that, Edward thought.

Click smiled, flashing teeth top and bottom, bleach-white and polished. His teeth were perfectly aligned in a neat row, like the bone-colored drawers in the Mustermann morgue, where Click and Edward had first met.

"We have one of the float drivers in custody," Click said.

Lucky break for Click. Locked up in the captive's head were details that might lead straight to Harper. Unfortunately, the CIA would get those details out of that head, not MET.

"Learn anything?" Edward asked.

"No, but we will. I promise you that."

Edward shivered. Glancing toward the front door to verify that no one had emerged, he said, "What's next?"

A shot of wind blew between them. Click squinted. He smiled and gestured at the night air. "Wind is good. Makes parabolic recording difficult." He lowered his voice even further. "The shutdown of Niko's lab is underway. Sanar's research work is over. The place is getting stripped to the studs. Sometimes I am proud of how fast we move."

Click pulled at his scarf. There was nothing unseemly about adjusting your scarf from the wind, Edward thought. That was just common sense. But shivering when you wore no coat, that was for little boys. He steeled himself and willed his body not to shake. No luck.

Click hunched his shoulders and put his hands in warm pockets. "Tell Ronan to stick around the lab during the lockdown and watch for anything suspicious."

"I'll notify him immediately."

Click pointed a finger at Edward. "Did you ask them to grab what they can, no paperwork?"

The pointing hand returned quickly to its pocket. Click had no direct authority over Edward, but the power strata were cemented in place. Edward's position was many levels below Click's, and while it was within an entirely different agency, MET was still a ghost, an inconsequential square in the jumbo org chart of U.S. intel. Edward would do what Click requested or he would risk having a powerful internal enemy discredit him.

"Yes, I told them."

Click smiled again. Teeth that straight, Edward figured, arose from either jackpot genetics or a brilliant orthodontist. Men like Click usually got them the easy way, through pedigree, but if needed, a credit card worked nearly as well.

"Within the lab, Dr. Pieter Heynes was almost certainly a lone wolf," Click said. "At least, that's what makes sense, until evidence suggests otherwise. We believe he did this to create a scandal, to destroy the president."

Edward clenched his teeth, in part to prevent their chattering in the wind. The CIA still didn't believe that there were other groups and cells involved.

Click waited for a rebuttal. The corners of his mouth hinted that he was pleased by Edward's silence. Speaking as a wise man might to a student, he said, "What does a renowned researcher have in common with our crazy survivalist, a nobody? Why would Pieter join forces with this guy?"

"I'm not entirely sure. He said he was desperate and out of options. But I don't see what they have in common."

"How about this: they are both afraid of technology."

As soon as the words entered the icy air, Edward's annoyance at Click evaporated. Here was an idea he had not considered.

Small flakes of snow twirled between them, catching the light.

Click continued. "Pieter wrote a paper about the dangers of nanoweapons. He gave it to a few key governments, including ours. He tried to convince a congressional subcommittee not to support this type of work... but President Hammami persuaded key representatives in both houses to push legislation through. Instead of shutting down the research, they increased funding."

Click was shining new light on Pieter Heynes. The idea was provocative, and Edward berated himself for not considering it first.

"Harper's mindset is similar," Click continued. "He is using advanced weapons as a tactic to scare everyone about where technology is ultimately headed."

Edward scratched his chin. Perhaps *batshit-crazy Harper* thinks he can scare the entire human race back to the stone age by using more aggressive and dangerous technology than the simple mail bombs employed by his hero, Ted Kaczynski. But Pieter had a more realistic goal.

One that now made more sense. While Harper had a general hatred of *all* technology, Pieter was laser-focused on a specific upcoming threat, one that perhaps could be prevented.

"You know," Edward said, "it's like Pieter was trying to *inoculate society* with a small dose of nanoterrorism to protect us from a bigger, unexpected attack."

Click nodded. "Nicely stated. He warned the U.S. about the dangers of this technology, and he warned a few other governments, but no one listened, so he provided a demonstration. He realized innocent people would die, but he knew how bad it would get if unchecked."

"He must have been extremely scared to take those kinds of steps."

"I agree. He risked the chance that his activities could spiral out of his control. But he deemed those risks worth taking. I suppose those are the calculations that most terrorists make."

At the end of the street in the gloom and snow, Edward glimpsed cranes and construction, entire complexes of earth-moving machinery and makeshift metal scaffolding. Beyond that, just a block or two, lay a branch of the Potomac river. And beyond that, through the snow that settled on the frozen river, lay DIA Headquarters.

"One more thing I should mention, by way of background," Click said. "But don't mention this to your team. The president's second term is coming up and he needs to look like the hero who got the bad guys, not the person responsible for causing this fiasco in the first place. Remember when I said the president was pushing nanoweapon funding?"

"Yes. That complicates his re-election chances."

"It's not just that he funded nanoweapons in general. NIST, a subdivision of the Department of Commerce that funds innovation, funded a company to scale up production of nanomaterials, and that company designed the desktop synthesizer that Sanar is using. The company has made several hundred units and they're gearing up to crank out a lot more. Apparently, the company didn't consider the scenario of a cheap synthesizer in a run-down hellhole cranking out enough nanoweapons to unleash havoc on the world."

"You're telling me that the terrorists' synthesizer was essentially funded by our government, thank you very much to our president's agenda?"

"Correct. And here's something even more inconvenient. We have evidence that the president and the secretary of defense may have invested in this company through overseas shell corporations. The market for nanotechnology is exploding. If it's true he invested – and that comes to light – you can see why the president is getting anxious to find Harper. If we find and eliminate Harper's terrorist nest quickly, the public will think the issue is over and move on. But the longer the investigation drags out, the more the press will start connecting the dots."

Edward detected a delicate change in Click's voice, a subtle shift that indicated the conversation was almost over.

The message was clear: If Edward's agency didn't *actually find* Harper, they had gained very little from their involvement. Besides, the other agencies would have eventually figured out that nanoweapons were involved, without MET's help. MET would soon be forgotten again, lost in the ferocious waves of the next phase of the investigation. For Edward, that meant no end to his short vacations and low paychecks. Maybe unemployment.

"Bottom line, Edward. We need to find these guys and get rid of them."

The words cut. "Agreed," he said.

"Remind Ronan. If he sees valuable weapons intelligence in that lab, take it. Get it to us without delay. Otherwise, thank you for your help. Maybe we can work together again someday."

Edward felt anger surging. For the first time, those emotions were aimed at Ronan.

For all Ronan's expensive embedded gizmos, he had not found the critical evidence. What good was solving half of a jigsaw puzzle, if you then got stuck and someone else had to finish it for you? That summed up Ronan: half-assed.

Deanna was smart, but she was just one person, up against

thousands of investigators in other departments and agencies.

Click was going to find Harper first. Click was going to stick an electric dagger into the captive terrorist's head and push all the answers right out of his mouth.

Edward and MET would disappear back into obscurity.

Damian Hernandez awoke to an immense headache. He opened his eyes and looked at the room around him. As he slowly came out of his fog, he saw monitors, electronic equipment, and wires... *lots* of wires. Most were leading out of him. He was in a strange bed and the room was air conditioned, which was a novelty.

He realized he was in a hospital room.

What the hell had happened?

Other than his head, the rest of him felt pretty good. He struggled to remember what had brought him here. Nothing came immediately to mind. He tried to turn his head, but was unsuccessful, so he slanted his eyes to the left and saw a military guard sitting on a chair, asleep.

Damien tried to recollect recent events.

What was the guard doing? Protecting him? From what?

The pumps, bags, blinking lights, and control panels offered no clue. All that sophisticated machinery made him queasy. The whole damn room was contaminated.

With that thought, his memories started flooding back.

Harper had sent him on another mission. To an island. A place where hundreds of people were gathered but security would be light. He had sprayed a deluge of light-activated biting machines onto the crowd, infecting them with death.

He remembered that he was an Outsider, a Kazite field worker who interacted with the world and its technology, who had made the sacrifice to wield that technology to spread fear and chaos.

Damn, his head hurt.

It was a symbolic attack. A tiny glimpse of a world overrun by machines. By now, those little spiders had blown and drifted to every corner of the island. They'd be turning up for years. No one would ever go near that pitiful little sun-baked island again.

How had the mission ended? He remembered a lady in the crowd staring at him like a condescending bitch. It was always the same with women. They never did like him or trust him. Instead of blowing himself up like the mission dictated, he had decided to get a little revenge first.

He remembered getting her alone. Then what?

Something had sliced into his stomach. Yeah, it was all coming back. The crazy bitch had grabbed him in the dark, locking on to his arm like a vice. Before he could react, she had cut open his stomach. He had instinctively grabbed at his gut and felt his insides flowing out. And then she kept stabbing.

Moments before the stabbing began, there had been a flash of light: a glimpse of the inside of a closet. A glimpse of a machete on the wall. Damn. He had been planning to use that machete on *her*. Why had he wasted time locking the door? While he did that, she was already grabbing the machete.

The guard stirred. Damien squinted his eyes and feigned sleep. The guard rose from his chair and left the room.

Even though he appeared to be in custody, the island attack was a huge success. Yes, the attack would really get them thinking. World leaders would take notice. Smug people everywhere, in every suburb in the world, would be on edge. They'd never seen anything like this before. And much more was coming – so much more!

The Kazites had Siyu's fabricator cranking out biting creatures of every type, stamping them out by the hundreds of thousands, and every unit was armed with a deadly payload. They had tons of manufactured mayhem waiting to be dumped hither and yon. Some of the latest machines were as tiny as dust. They called that stuff "powder that bites."

The Outsiders were working on bigger stuff too. They were printing birds and bats, and packs of rabid dogs, though in much lower numbers.

The Kazites needed more fabricators. Siyu had promised that more units were on the way. But what they really needed to get their hands on was a *fabricator* fabricator.

Soon, the world would be overrun with biting, stinging, attacking things. But it didn't need to be this way. As long as everyone saw the light, that future could be avoided.

The door opened. A man in scrubs entered, possibly an orderly. He had wild blond hair and a devil tattoo on his neck, too sketchy to be a doctor or a nurse. The orderly came to his bedside.

"I see you are awake."

Damien stared.

The orderly surveyed the room. "What do you think?"

Damien moved his mouth. He wanted to say *loss of control*, but nothing came out.

The orderly looked over Damien's body, inspecting the setup. "That woman got you good. Stabbed you over and over. Chest, stomach, side of your head, legs. She turned you into a pincushion full of bleeding organs."

Damien couldn't see his body, only a limited view of the machines around him. With great effort, he shoved out a few words. "How... bad?"

"See that machine over there?" The orderly pointed at a rack of five machines and a bulging bag of blood surrounded by a thick mass of hoses and tubes. "That's your heart. And that one?"

Damien followed the blood tubes to a tall device with dials and switches.

"That's your kidneys." The orderly pointed to other machines. "That's your liver. That's your bladder. She punctured all your vitals. Oh, those bags are your new lungs."

Damien grunted.

The orderly nodded. "Want to know how I got in?" He pulled a blood-streaked scalpel from his pants. "Security around here sucks."

Again, Damien tried to move his mouth. Halting words struggled out. "Security... always... sucks."

The orderly laughed. "That's right!"

"Who... are you?"

The orderly leaned close and whispered. "I'm with a different group.

Same cause. We are in this together, my friend. There are many of us here. I deliver food to the Centro Medico here in Rio Piedras. This is the most advanced hospital in Puerto Rico."

"Puerto Rico?"

"That's where you were airlifted."

"I can't feel my body."

"Most of it has been removed."

"Huh?"

"You're just a *head*, dude." The orderly laughed.

So, society had caught him in its electronic traps. They'd reduced him to a phantom in hell.

"They must really want you alive to spend this much money on you." The fake orderly paused and looked to the door, listening. He continued. "That lady said you had driven the float. It leaked to the news – they got one of the Nashville killers. That's you. You are their main lead, man. Somehow they kept your brain alive, and they gonna squeeze your secrets out of it."

Damien's head knew what that meant. The only thing he could manage to utter was a windless, "They'll learn our plans."

"Oh, you got that right. They gonna *squeeeeze* it all out!"

God..

"But you are in luck, my friend," the fake orderly whispered. "I won't let them. You won't reveal our secrets."

The orderly withdrew a needleless syringe. He glanced at the door. "You are American, yes?"

"Born in Miami."

"I am curious how you became affiliated with the cause. But do not speak. There are security cameras, microphones."

Damien's head tried to nod. The room might be full of recording devices, tracking every little thing – every motorized breath, every piston pump of his new heart.

"You ready to get this over with?" The fake orderly asked.

"Yes."

The man glanced at the door one last time. "You will be remembered as a warrior for the cause. When we return to the pure-natural world, when we are back in control of our lives, people will praise you."

He shoved the syringe deep into one of Damien's nostrils and plunged the contents.

"Thank you," Damien whispered.

The fake orderly left the room.

Damien waited for the nanites to circulate in his brain. A fitting end for a martyr, he thought.

Ronan was asleep on the couch. Under his closed eyelids, a grid of thumbnail images scrolled across his eyes. He felt a nudge on his shoulder and he awakened, drowsy and confused. Deanna stood over him. The images played across his vision, and most of them featured one person, the woman he knew would never leave his mind. He had fallen asleep watching the photos, some of her looking his way, her eyes captured in all their ethereal beauty, and others of her at work or play. Deanna was leaning awfully close, but she could not see the images from his ocular. He tapped his finger to close them.

"What is it?" Ronan mumbled. "I'm exhausted."

Behind her, the TV was replaying the knowns and unknowns of the Sea Fest massacre.

"I just got off the phone with the South African Authorities," she said.

He shut his eyes again and resumed the picture scroll. The images flashed by his vision, stirring glorious and agonizing memories. Finally he opened his eyes. She was still standing over him.

"What did you learn?" he asked.

"They are shutting Sanar down. The authorities are taking everything. There is nothing left for us to do here."

He rubbed his eyes. "Should we head back to the states?"

"I think so. I am out of ideas. Other teams will have to take the investigation from here."

"Have you talked to Edward?"

"I haven't been able to reach him. He won't be happy. But what choice do we have?"

Ronan sighed. "Can you hand me my legs?"

The limbs were sitting near the wall on a charging pad. Their lithium-sulfur batteries lasted for days of steady use, but he re-charged them often. He liked them at one hundred percent.

She picked one up and made a gesture of weighing them. "Damn, these are heavy."

"Try walking around with them all the time." He took it from her and began strapping it to his thigh.

"If you don't mind my asking – did you lose your legs in Afghanistan? Land mine?"

Ronan looked out the window at the drab high-rises of Johannesburg visible through the vague smog.

"Sorry, that was a personal question," she said. "I don't need to know."

He took a long time to respond.

"About three years ago, while on leave, I drove my girlfriend up the Blue Ridge Parkway near Asheville on my motorcycle. We stopped for a picnic at a breathtaking overlook, a perfect spot where we could see for miles. I told her I had taken hang-gliding lessons on a spot very much like that one. She recalled being a camp counselor and taking some city kids to a similar view, where they watched a distant lightning storm. We stayed the whole afternoon and swapped stories until the sun set. It was one of the most lovely and romantic moments of my life."

"That sounds beautiful." By the tone in Deanna's voice, Ronan knew that she was uncertain where the story was headed.

He smiled. "I proposed. She accepted. Then we got on the bike and headed back down while there was still light. She had her arms wrapped lightly around me. The wind was kicking up. I'll never forget the leaves blowing up off the road and how cool it was to drive through them. The universe was going out of its way to make the day amazing and special. I was thinking about this magical moment when I felt the bike slide. We must have hit gravel, and I instantly realized how fast I'd been going. I lost control. The bike hit the ground sideways and spun, and I saw her hit the road and then pop into the air."

"Oh, God…"

"Something yanked my right leg, twisting my body apart, then slammed me against the guard rail. I woke up in the hospital. According to the bike's data recorder, I hit that guardrail at ninety-four miles an hour."

"How was your girlfriend?"

"Chloe didn't make it."

"Wait… I thought you were talking about… oh, I see."

"She died from internal injuries."

"Oh wow, I'm sorry." Deanna laid her hand on his knee.

"I can't get the image out of my head, her falling and hitting the road like that."

"I don't know what to say. How horrible. I had no idea."

He nodded. He felt the raw emotions rising to the surface, coming into his eyes.

"I wish I could go back to that perfect moment, with the leaves blowing in the air and her arms wrapped around me. The last moment of my old life. I kept thinking, Did I drink too much? Was I driving too fast? Not watching the road? I kept coming back to one thought. I didn't have Driver Assist activated. The bike itself would not have killed her. The bike would have kept us at a safe speed and recognized the gravel in the road long before we hit it. I realized the bike's technology was better and safer than my own judgement and skills. I had been a fool to override it. We should let technology take control. I embraced this idea with fervor."

Ronan hunched over, remembering all his regrets, the what-ifs, and the obvious conclusion: he had to leave his human stupidity behind. If he didn't, then he deserved to live in hell, pain without escape. He couldn't bring Chloe back, but he could reject his old self. He could transform into something better, like an insect leaving behind an old shell. The old Ronan no longer existed.

Deanna put her arm around his shoulders. For several minutes they sat like this.

"You miss her."

"I do. But the pain is too much to dwell on. I shut it off so that I can function. I have to move on. She would have wanted me to, and that is what I've done."

"It wasn't your fault."

"Of course it was. I was reckless. I have always been reckless. Even you said so. Which means I still have work to do. Recklessness can be removed. It's just a matter of research and money."

"Well, Ronan, don't take my comments so seriously…"

"You meant what you said. You call things as you see them. That's the Army in you." He saw that hint of a smile that she sometimes allowed. He continued, "To be honest, you remind me of Chloe. You have the same adventurous spirit. You rise to every challenge and never give up."

Deanna leaned back and he regretted the words immediately. A mixture of expressions crossed her face, none obvious, just small tells that suggested a variety of potential responses about to escape her lips.

But she said nothing. Instead, she drew closer to him and wrapped an arm around his shoulder, to comfort him, perhaps. She pulled him tight.

He found himself looking in her eyes, and she did not look away. She smiled, a slight sad kind of smile.

Ronan leaned in, slowly, drawn forward irresistibly by the closeness, and his heart beat faster when she leaned in, too.

This was something he'd longed for, even if he hadn't wanted to admit it to himself, even if he had never consciously thought about it. The anticipation felt natural and amazing and electric.

An alert popped up on his ocular to let him know it had no Internet. SEARCHING FOR A CONNECTION.

"God, these alerts."

"Where?"

"In my head."

INTERNET CONNECTION FOUND.

"Why don't you just turn it all off?"

"What if I miss one that is important?"

She shrugged. The moment had slipped away.

"I'm sorry. I need to think." He stood.

"Maybe we should talk?"

"I don't want to make any mistakes." He went into his bedroom and returned with his keyboard bag. "I'll be back."

He left the suite and shut the door behind him.

In the corridor, Ronan kicked the wall with a bang. He pulled his shoe from the hole he had just made, a jagged puncture in the ornate wallpaper. A puff of flaky debris spilled out. He stomped his foot to knock off the dust, then glanced back and forth. Nobody around. Ronan gritted his teeth and headed for the elevator.

CHAPTER 45

Ronan wandered in the dingy forgotten places of downtown Johannesburg. What had just happened between him and Deanna? He had not seen that coming. He doubted that Deanna had expected it, either.

He had a girlfriend he loved at home. A girlfriend who, he thought, loved him.

He also had a critical job to do right now, one that became more urgent with every passing hour.

Everything was swirling together into one big mess. On top of his immediate worries, the unyielding burden of his guilt had just reared its head again. He had killed Chloe. He had thought they would live together a long time, protecting each other from anything life might throw at them, but she had been his fiancé only twenty-three minutes.

He could distract himself with new relationships and work, with a heroic mission to save the world, with technologies that would bring him beyond stupidity and recklessness, but he couldn't change the past. Future perfection would not erase past failings.

He walked, block after block, through the shadows of abandoned buildings. He passed windows covered in plywood and walls with dull, spray-painted graffiti.

Workers shuffled here and there. The late afternoon sun had fallen behind the buildings as the crowds dispersed; everyone wanted to begin the weekend closer to home.

So many depressing things to worry about.

Priorities. What was number one?

He knew the answer. It wasn't his girlfriend Lisa or Deanna. It wasn't the guilt that buzzed within him like electricity overloading a circuit breaker. He had to focus on one thing.

Finding Harper.

Everything else could wait. All the broken pieces would land wherever they were going to land. In the meantime: someone out there was calling his name. *Focus on him.*

Harper. Who *was* this guy? What the hell drove his crazy attacks?

Harper was fueled by a deep-seated hatred of technology. And he wanted to meet Ronan. Face-to-face. The primal versus the transcendent. Harper must be thinking, *Here's a guy who loves technology. Someone who has put his full faith in complex, man-made systems. Someone who believes those systems are better than the men who made them.*

Ronan realized that Harper would see him as a lost, misguided soul. Maybe even sacrilegious or evil.

Harper doesn't see a viable path beyond human.

If Harper was right, if Theodore Kaczynski was right, we were all killing ourselves as we advanced, collectively as a species.

The attack in the Caribbean showed just one of an infinite number of fucked-up futures. Poisonous bot infestations forcing authorities to evacuate one region after another. Refugees moving from place to place. An endless process – shave the hair, hose them down, burn their clothes. Repeat.

In less than an hour, the tropical paradise of St. Bonaventure Island became an unlivable wasteland. The media dubbed it the Tropical Chernobyl. The wind had blown hundreds of thousands of deadly micro-machines across the island, into every nook and cranny. Activated by light, the spiders crawled around until they stumbled into some dark place, where they remained dormant. Every millimeter of the island would need inspection.

This had been pulled off by a guy wearing a home-made Tarzan costume.

This guy hadn't invented anything.

He hadn't done anything smart or clever.

Hell, he probably didn't even know how any of the technology worked.

This guy had simply taken our own tools and weapons and thrown them back in our faces.

And now Harper laughed. Because it didn't matter how we responded. As far as Harper was concerned, the world was headed back to the stone age regardless. Whether willingly or through our own absurd hubris, we would one day find ourselves in much smaller numbers, living as we once did in the wild.

An image flashed in Ronan's mind of tribes in the Amazon, people who lived entirely in the natural world. Reading the stars. Reading the ground. Jabbing their spears as planes flew overhead.

A bright yellow icon flashed. INCOMING CALL. Ronan connected. Edward appeared on his ocular.

Not what Ronan needed right now, unless it was good news.

"Ronan, we've run a hundred programs on the video, analyzing Harper's statements. We've analyzed every data point. We can't find shit. We have no idea where he is."

Edward had cussed. He was in a bad spot.

"We just have to keep looking and hope for a break," Ronan said.

"But what do they have planned for us next? Spray Washington with blood-penetrating dust? The fear is through the roof. Everyone up the chain of command is on the phone right now, debating every option you can imagine."

"What do you think we should do?"

"We're going to have to serve you up to Harper like he asked."

"That's a nice choice of words. I'm not crazy about being *served up*. I think he wants to dissect me. I don't want to be dissected."

"Then you need to find him soon because we're out of options. The CIA will get all the credit."

Ronan said nothing. He could hear his boss's desperation, and that ruled out a rational conversation.

Edward's voice became more strained. "You told me that *man-plus-machine* is better than *man*. This was all your idea. I dumped all that crap in you. Ability to read faces. Built-in alerts. Lie detection. You were my big hope for the agency. But it hasn't made you any better."

Ronan said nothing.

"Maybe we should pull all that crap out of you."

"It might leave a few ugly holes."

"I'm not joking."

"I know."

"I'll take the legs back."

Ronan remembered the first prosthetic limbs he had been given, back in the foggy aftermath of the accident. A cheap wobbly pair... worse than stumps.

"You've nothing to say to that, I guess," Edward said.

"That hits me hard."

"I'm sorry to be blunt."

"We're making headway, Edward. There is going to be a breakthrough." Even as he said this, Ronan knew it wasn't true. The opposite was true: he and Deanna were giving up.

"Ronan, listen to me. Our funds are nearly exhausted. If we cannot move forward, they'll shut us down."

"I understand."

"You want to go back to where I found you? In a state of worthless despair? You were clinging to this idea of human 2.0. I'm starting to think your idea is crap."

Ronan's vision of transcendence was collapsing.

"Ronan, we are out of time. You are out of time. I've got no more cards to play."

"I hear you."

He could almost hear the energy drain from Edward.

Ronan wanted to say something but couldn't. Edward had nothing, either.

The icon changed to a dull brown.

DISCONNECTED.

Ronan was now moving in a quick stride that took him nowhere.

He stopped on a curb. *I'm a fool*, he thought. The hardware had failed him, and everyone thought he was a clown. Even Edward had lost faith. Not one of them believed that humans would merge software and hardware and wetware into something new.

Maybe they were right.

Rip everything out of me, Edward? Then I would be a pockmarked nothing, back to being a loser, a man who lost everything and learned nothing.

Ronan waved his arm slowly through the air. Everything felt robotic. Across the street, he saw a glowing logo: Mini-Tel Quick Sleep.

In the lobby, an old man studied the sad-sack joker that had just walked into his run-down bed rental. The man leaned to the side, trying to see past Ronan, because people rarely entered alone.

Ronan recoiled at the pungent smellscape. Urine plus fish, maybe. "Here." He watched himself handing over his credit card. The old man handed it back. Done. One room, one bed, and one light. The Steal-A-Deal special. Be out in three hours or we call the police.

Bending low so as not to bump his head, Ronan squeezed into the tiny plastic cell. It smelled like Lysol had been sprayed in there 10,000 times.

Didn't matter what it smelled or looked like. He needed to think.

A password was written in ballpoint pen on a small sheet of paper with stains on it. Under the password, the word "Why-Fy." The letters were bold and dark originally, as if to leave no doubt about the purpose of the password, but they were faded now. The account was probably in the hands of every hacker in town.

He wouldn't need to connect. Noticing a tiny fridge beneath the desk, Ronan tried to open it. No go. He saw the credit card slot, slipped his card through, and selected a Pepsi.

"Can't remember the last time I drank one of you," he mumbled. He cracked it open and sat on the bed, hair touching the ceiling.

Sweat dripped under his clothing. He ran his card through the slot on the crappy AC unit and cranked the dial to HIGH.

The AC made a cacophony of pained mechanical sounds and sprayed a thin jet of warm air on his face.

He shut his eyes.

A scene flashed into his mind. He forced it away. It popped back. Chloe on the hill, kissing him before climbing on the bike. A casual hug from behind. Such a wonderful memory, all one could ever ask for, turned into such a terrible one. Her last smile, her last hug, and she never saw it coming. *I took her life.*

Memory was misery ever since.

Okay: nihilistic fatalism was the exact *opposite* of what he needed right now. He needed energy, focus, and heroic determination.

He felt his right hand unbuttoning his shirt sleeve to expose a bump on the left forearm, as if his hand had a mind of its own, as if he had no say in the matter.

Without further reflection, he pressed the tiny God button. The small medical pack just under the skin of his arm was supposed to inject epinephrine, give him a boost of kick-ass, and indeed it did that, but he had spiked it with a micro-dose of BLiSS.

He held the button to keep it pumping, make sure it got every drop…

He might have drifted off to sleep briefly but opened his eyes when he felt the clouds disappearing and a deep fountain of clarity and love start to take its place.

Chloe appeared. "Follow your gut," she said.

She meant intuition. The human brain was the smartest object in the known universe, so why not trust its deep subterranean logic? Because, he countered to her, the brain's wiring was a tangled and unpredictable mess, no match for software that delivered near perfect behavior.

Chloe was gone. A dark presence rose swirling in his mind. Like evil, or Satan. An iconic scruffy face: Theodore Kaczynski. Genius, PhD in theoretical math, seeker of pure truths, youngest math professor in UC Berkeley's history, the Unabomber. He *knew*.

Kaz knew that when it came to humanity's future, nothing outweighed our relationship to technology. Not religion, social norms, or the insights of artists. Technology would define everything.

Today we were toddlers playing with loaded handguns. Tomorrow: riders of spacetime.

Ronan pulled up the Unabomber Manifesto.

The opening line was a detonation: *The industrial revolution and its consequences have been a disaster for the human race.*

Paragraph after paragraph, Kaz criticized the destructive and unsustainable nature of our technological society. Everything was going to collapse sooner or later.

And it was entirely the fault of the technophiles.

That would be me, Ronan thought.

But the BLiSS had given him the clarity he needed. He would not be persuaded by such dour arguments.

He did not feel fear or regret or guilt.

He had PURPOSE.

In a universe of expanding and infinite knowledge, the only way to go from Alpha to Omega was to cross all points in between, and everything we valued now would be crushed in the process.

To take that path, he had to make a decision. He had to willfully commit to replacing his mental functions with higher algorithms. That had been his vision, and it was still his vision.

He must be all-in. Fearless. First.

The Winner.

...

Ronan opened his eyes.

Something rattled around in his brain. How much time had passed?

The universe was no longer a gaping vista of radiant truth.

He was back in a small dim coffin, a pay-by-the-hour sex or sleeping slab with a small jet of warm air.

Something bothered him. Something about that damn video. *Something* was there.

Two things in his brain were trying to connect, groping for each other. One was the video. He couldn't figure out the other one.

Tap, tap.

The video appeared, a glowing micro-thin curve of light.

Why did he want to look at the video again? He'd watched it over and over. There was nothing there. Or was there?

Ronan lay in complete darkness in the Mini-Tel room, eyes shut. The video of Harper taking credit for the terrorist attack played on his ocular, hovering against the darkness of his lids.

He had been over the video at least ten times. With each replay, he had scoured the background for clues.

In the video, Jonathan Harper stood next to his horse on cleared land, with the edge of a forest behind him. The investigative team had had high hopes for that backdrop – a dense tangle of vines, ferns, shrubby bushes, creepers, hanging lianas, bole climbers, and tree-choking stranglers. Wall-to-wall leaves. Surely one of those plants could narrow the geographic region. A team of botanists had scoured every frame.

Unfortunately, the tape was focused on Harper, not the background, and all those trees and leaves were in poor resolution. The team had managed to identify dozens of species, but all of them were run-of-the-mill tropical rainforest vegetation.

The trees extended beyond the upper frame and were impossible to identify by their trunks alone. They seemed to be *Euterpe precatoria*, a palm tree as common as the house fly; there were five billion of them in the Amazon alone, and their range extended all the way up to Panama.

The botanists had, at least, ruled out similar rainforests in Central Africa, South Asia, and the South Pacific. Ronan would take their word for it.

The investigators believed that the terrorists were building a community somewhere in South America, deep in the rainforest, living as primitives, away from prying eyes. But where?

Finding a needle in a haystack would have been far, far, easier.

At a loss and feeling lonely, Ronan tapped his fingers, selecting his way to his contact list. He paused. This was against the rules, but the hell with it. He needed this.

He tapped Lisa.

Hi babe, he texted.

A minute passed. Then, the notification sound: *tck.*

Hi! She answered.

He spoke his words into text. *Can't talk. Wish I could hear your voice. I miss you.*

You okay?

Yes, but ready for this to be over.

Same here. I miss you too.

Harper's video played behind her words. The trees, the leaves, the occasional butterfly.

She added, *We can go on vacation as soon as you are back.*

Ronan saw a flicker of yellow in the trees, so brief he had completely missed it before. Tapping his fingers, he advanced the video in small increments.

She added, *We can get some sun and just relax. Go to some great restaurants.*

The yellow blur was a bird, visible for no more than two seconds.

He responded: *Can I go bird-finding?*

You can hunt all the birds you want.

Will you join me?

Maybe! Maybe not LOL.

Lisa typed something else, but now he was reading the analyst report. In the bio inventory, the bird had been identified: *yellow-margined flycatcher*. The report did not list any possible alternative species. This struck Ronan as a little odd. He knew flycatchers were notoriously hard to tell apart. An ornithologist from Sao Paulo had made the ID.

Are you there? she asked.

Sorry, I'm just distracted.

Are you safe?

Very

Whatcha thinking about?

Birds, actually

Ronan did an image search and compared the bird on the tape. Despite the blocky resolution, this was clearly a yellow-margined flycatcher: grey crown, green back, black triangle on the wings. *Etcetera.*

And common throughout Central and South America.

Another dead end. But given that no other clues had emerged, and because he actually had some expertise in birds, he wanted to be absolutely sure the ID was correct.

He found the flycatcher's calls online and sat in the dark, listening carefully. Then back to Harper's video. He isolated the bird's call as best he could, looped it, and listened.

Wait. It didn't match.

The bird on the video made a sound like a harsh vibration. It didn't fit.

Lisa, love you! I have to go.

So soon?

I'm sorry - will call you as soon as I can

He shut off the texts.

Sitting up, almost hitting his head on the low ceiling, he plowed into the literature on yellow-margined flycatchers and turned up a new piece of information. A similar species, *Tolmomyias Sucunduri,* was sometimes found in a few isolated areas of the Amazon. The variant looked identical, but it made a sound like someone striking a washboard.

That was the sound of the bird on the tape.

As his heart rate picked up, he retrieved a map of the bird's sightings; they were all clustered around the isolated city of Manaus, Brazil. A few had been spotted in the dense forests south of the city, along the Amazon River, a few more on the Uatuma River tributary, and one was sighted on the Jatapu River which fed into that.

Within minutes, Ronan had the ornithologist on the phone.

"Did you ever analyze the bird's call?" Ronan asked.

The man on the other end of the line sounded sluggish, as though he had just awoken from a deep sleep. He snapped to attention, becoming serious and accommodating. "No, I based the ID on its visual markings. The sound quality of the recording was poor. I didn't hear any vocalizations."

"I'm sending the isolated call to you now. It's a banging noise. Maybe everyone wrote it off as a video artifact or a man-made sound. But I'm pretty sure it's the yellow flycatcher on the tape. If true, we can focus on a small area to search for the terrorists. I need your expert opinion. Please get back to me as soon as you can."

The biologist agreed.

A text came back an hour later and shot across Ronan's vision. *I agree with you 100%. This is Sucunduri. Great job! You are a world-class birder.*

That was it. One speck of data, one big answer. Harper's compound was somewhere in the vicinity of Manaus, deep in the Amazon.

Ronan smiled. His dim little compartment suddenly felt nicer.

The intelligence community would soon be scouring every inch of the surrounding jungle. Harper was going to get ripped out of his hidey hole. Vengeance would be delivered. MET would be rewarded.

The final steps were falling into place.

Walking quickly through the city streets, Ronan re-traced the route back to the hotel, amazed by how rapidly a situation could change. A couple hours ago, he was at a dead end. Now they had the break they needed. He wanted to tell Deanna first, before informing Edward and the rest of the intel machinery.

He reached the hotel, wiped sweat from his face, and plunged into the air conditioning. The Michelangelo was cold. After spending the afternoon in a suffocating rental cubby and then walking for miles in the heat, the blast of cold was refreshing.

"Guess what?" Ronan called out as he entered their suite.

No response. She was in her room or taking a shower. Her bedroom door was open a few inches, but the light was off. *Was she taking a nap?* He pushed the door wide and saw the empty bed.

Her bathroom door was open, the lights off in there, too. Ronan stopped, puzzled. He lifted his phone to text her, but as he glanced back to the common area, he froze. Something had caught his attention.

With some trepidation, he returned to the common room and flipped on the light. There was something sitting on the table. *A note.*

He sat on the couch to read it.

Ronan,

I'm heading back to Washington. I will be more help there at this point.

Earlier I saw a side of you I'd never expected. I like that part of you. In that moment, I felt like getting closer to you. And I have to admit my relationship back in the states is not great right now. But after you left, I realized I am not ready to leave him. I don't know if there could be anything between you and me, but I'm glad you're not ready either.

Regarding Edward, he's not cruel or spiteful. No matter how much he yells or threatens, I don't think he would take back the technology he's installed in you. He knows your value. He knows you represent the future. Even I admit that.

For now, remember that you are never going to be perfect. You can't stop every bad thing from happening. I hope you forgive yourself.

See you again sometime.

Ronan lay the note on the couch. His phone vibrated.

It was a message from Niko: *Please come to Sanar. I need help.*

Careening down the M1 highway, feeling a strange mix of euphoria and trepidation, a map alert flashing his upcoming exit, and thinking of the love of his life, Ronan was multi-tasking his ass off. He held his phone in his right hand and called Edward.

His boss picked up. "Ronan, what are you up to?"

"On my way to Sanar."

There was a pause on the line. Ronan sensed Edward looking for his next words. "Hey, I'm sorry I got a little heated earlier. It's just that..."

"Apology accepted. That's not why I called."

"What's going on?"

"I know where to look for those idiots."

"What do you mean?"

"Manaus, Brazil. They're within a 120-mile radius."

"You sure?"

"One hundred percent."

"If you're right," Edward sang, "do you know what this means?"

"Talk to you later, Edward. Got a date with Niko. Pulling into the parking lot right now. Keep me updated on the search."

He hung up without waiting for a response.

...

The Sanar laboratories were in chaos. Men and women in black uniforms carried computers, packed equipment, and hauled off notebooks. The State Security Agency was dismantling Niko's world.

Ronan walked the halls, temporary access badge dangling from a lanyard around his neck. The busy security personnel knew he was with

U.S. intel and didn't question him. On his way to Niko's office, he peered into the labs and offices, now stacked with rows and rows of boxes. Hazmat teams had taped off some of the labs, but he could look inside. He saw workers dumping assay trays into industrial garbage bags decorated with biohazard symbols. All the cancer research – packed up, shut down, gone.

He arrived at Niko's office. The door was half-closed. After a pause, he rapped and pushed it open.

Niko sat at his desk. "Ah, Ronan. My agent of doom."

"I'm sorry this happened."

"I don't blame you for it."

Ronan glanced over his shoulder in the direction of the hallway. "I got your text. I'm surprised how much they are gutting your lab. Sorry… bad choice of words."

"No, you're right. They are gutting this place. They're taking every laptop and notebook, stripping every room to the floor." Niko's voice had no spark or life, and his eyes seemed dead. "This reaction is not just because of Pieter's activities. Sanar had political enemies, people afraid of the technology. People who never took the time to learn about it."

"With all due respect, didn't Pieter validate their worst fears?"

"Pieter was –" Niko sighed and sank in his chair. "Maybe. I don't know."

"Have you figured out exactly what Pieter did?"

Niko nodded. "He gave the worst people in the world the plans to synthesize the scariest, most body-destroying agents on the planet."

Ronan shook his head and noticed for the first time that Niko was holding a vial. A second vial sat nestled in a small rack on his desk, and Ronan reached for it.

Niko stopped him. "The lid is tight, but if one drop gets in any open wounds, you've had it."

Bending close to read the label, Ronan asked, "What does Groot Gemors stand for again?"

"Big Mess. Get this stuff inside your body and you will just dissolve.

It binds to every cell and… destroys everything. Heart, lungs, hands, eyes."

"Good God, do you think Pieter gave them the synthesizing instructions to that?"

"Not according to what we've found in the logs. But there's no way to know."

"What are you doing with these vials?"

"Looking at them," Niko sighed.

"Not thinking of packing it in, I hope?"

Niko watched a bird flitting around a tree outside the window. After some reflection, he said, "Is that an American expression?"

"You are, then?"

"Ronan, this place represents twenty-five years of my research, all swirling down the drain. Every long night, every weekend. All of it getting flushed as we speak. I might as well have spent the time golfing."

"This is just a setback. You can pick up the research somewhere else."

Shaking his head, Niko's tone turned menacing. "If I'm not in prison. Do you have any idea how long it will take to get through the legalities of this situation? I could be in court the next twenty years. Pieter ruined my life, he screwed the employees, and he hurt everyone we were trying to save. Setback? No, this is a tragedy. There is no going back. The authorities will tie up this research and keep it from moving forward. The media will run with stories of fear." He toyed with the vial, rolling it between his thumb and index finger.

"Put that nasty stuff back, Niko. Put the vials back in the freezer. That's why you texted me. To talk you out of killing yourself."

Niko smiled and continued staring in a daze. Finally, he rose. "I believe you understand. Your words mean a lot."

"You'll start up again. I know you will."

Niko's eyes showed a hint of tearing. "Maybe. For now, I'll put these back."

Several men appeared in the doorway. "Dr. March," one said. "They want to speak to you in the lower conference room."

"Ja, fine," Niko answered, collecting the two vials from his desk.

"We need to escort you, sir. I'm sorry for the inconvenience."

Ronan followed them out. Niko stopped at the freezer, tapped the keypad, and went inside. When he emerged a moment later, he no longer had the vials. He looked at Ronan and nodded. Then he and his escorts were gone.

There wasn't much left to do. Wandering the halls, Ronan watched workers remove all the glassware and instruments, stripping the place down to a skeleton of steel shelving, like army ants pulling apart a dead lizard. Ronan passed two men carrying a desktop centrifuge and spied an open door. The animal lab.

Almost everything had been cleared out in there, too. The shelves were empty, most of the cages gone. The only animal left was the monkey, still sitting in its cage on the far side of the empty room, staring at the floor. It didn't look up when Ronan entered.

His phone rang. It was Edward.

"Deanna arrives tonight," Edward said. "We have a large debriefing session first thing in the morning with all the top intel stakeholders. The CIA has an enormous team scouring satellite shots of the Amazon for possible clues in the target area you identified. I am holding out hope we will soon have something to act on."

Edward was in a far better mood. Ronan was in his good graces again.

"I hope I can make it in person," Ronan said. "There's no point sticking around Johannesburg."

"We're still scouring your footage of the car hijackers. Several have been identified, but we have no useful leads yet. Their bodies were gone from the highway. Witnesses said armed men arrived and removed all the evidence of the attack. And we are trying to track down the remaining St. Bonaventure attackers. Tourists recorded them on dozens of phones. The one we had in custody was killed. We're trying to locate his assailant."

"How long will Deanna be in DC?"

"Not sure. She'll be re-assigned once she files all the reports."

"Okay." Ronan felt a wave of disappointment. He wasn't going to see her again. No time soon, anyway. "Hey, don't you know a guy who works with the zoo?"

"Huh?"

"A guy on the board of the National Zoo?"

"Alexander Rice? Why do you ask?"

Ronan saved the name. "I have a monkey here in Johannesburg that needs a home. You owe me a favor. We nailed this investigation."

After a pause, Edward said. "I'll contact him."

"You need to do it in the next thirty minutes. They are tearing this place apart and that monkey doesn't have long."

Workers emerged from a stairwell to retrieve the last of the room's contents.

"The monkey is going somewhere else," Ronan told them, flashing his ID. "Leave him. I'm waiting on the shipping address now. Approval is coming."

They shrugged and collected a few last extension cords and feed bags. The monkey watched through the bars of the cage, its black leather fingers wrapped around the grille.

Ronan smiled. "Hey buddy, just a little while longer. You're going someplace a lot better than this hell."

Back in the hall, he glanced at his watch. Workers crisscrossed the corridors from room to room. Edward had asked him to "acquire" anything interesting. The synthesizer files would be invaluable, but those would be too hard to access. Was there anything he could take to Washington that would be better in U.S. hands than those of the South African government? *Anything that might give American military researchers insight into the advances in nanotechnology here?*

Entering one of the labs, he scanned a table stacked with boxes and cords and spied a stainless-steel container about the size of a small penlight. It was embossed with the Sanar logo and had a small touchscreen. He tapped the screen and it glowed to life; when he pressed one of the buttons, the top of the canister popped open. He peered in.

What does this do? he wondered. After a moment, he understood the purpose of the device. It kept lab samples frozen so they could be carried around.

This canister, he realized, could easily slip into his pocket.

Now that he had a storage device, he realized there *was* something he wanted to take. But… should he?

No. Too dangerous.

The temptation grew. Should he do it?

He snapped the lid shut.

Yes.

If you had to swipe something, go big.

Ronan returned to the hallway and mingled with the workers. He had one more task before leaving Sanar for good. The freezer might have been raided by the workers already, but there was still at least one sample inside, and he knew the password.

Thousands of unblinking eyes watched the planet.

A network of satellites pointed their telescopes earthward, orbiting far above the clouds. Their cameras captured the human activity below, the people unaware, dumb as insects.

As the satellites passed overhead, they transmitted a stream of encrypted photos to ground stations around the world. Every square foot of the planet was captured in crisp detail, stored by the National Geospatial-Intelligence Agency, and updated every four days, creating a vast repository of images of every road, pole, Walmart, Mosque, pool, air strip, and clothesline.

Few people within the CIA had access to the data. Geospatial Operations Analyst Erin Lucas was one such person. She had the entire NGA database at her fingertips.

She flipped through the images, poring over miles and miles of the Amazon. Where were the Kazites in this monotonous jungle? No sign of them yet. She glanced at the clock. She was tired and finding it harder to stay focused. On to the next set of photos.

Someone at the DIA had narrowed the search to the area outside Manaus, Brazil – a small region of mostly uninhabited rainforest within a vast sea of uninhabited rain forest. While there weren't any Walmarts here, there were fragile towns and overgrown villages and isolated outposts and cleared tracts of land and a variety of other ways that civilization tried to encroach on the wilderness.

The photos she examined were generated from a search using the following criteria:

1. Within ten miles of the Amazon, Uatuma, and Jatapu
    rivers and their small tributaries.
2. Cleared land at least one mile from developed villages.
3. One large building or multiple dwellings.
4. Large gardens or livestock.
5. Absence of large machinery.

There were hundreds of photos for her to analyze.

The most detailed shots came from the latest enhanced imaging satellites, fifteen-ton machines that aimed a lens as large as the Hubble telescope toward the artifacts of human life. Erin loved finding personal moments caught in time, little gems hiding in the terrain. If a Crystal photographed someone relaxing on a wooden dock, the image could reveal a logo on a coffee cup.

Cool as hell, yes, but Erin figured her days analyzing satellite imagery were numbered. Every time an important assignment like this came up, her worries bubbled to the surface. Her problem wasn't a lack of skill. She had plenty of that. She could look at something from a bird's point of view and determine, for example, that a large white circle was a covert radar dome and not a geodesic greenhouse. She was able to see past the tricks of relief inversions, shadows that looked like holes, and dozens of other illusions.

And the problem wasn't that the people around her produced better results. In her own humble opinion, she was the best on the team. Who stayed an hour longer every night? Who tackled the most challenging analytical problems? Her.

Nevertheless, her job was under attack on several fronts. First, she and her colleagues had written so many scripts to automate image analysis tasks that they had almost coded themselves out of the org chart. In a year or two, someone with no experience whatsoever would be able to initiate a GIS program, enter descriptors, and wait for the software to find the best match.

Second, and this problem was even closer at hand, the spy satellites of earlier generations were reaching their expiration date.

Who wanted them anymore? Drones of all shapes and sizes were ready to be poured into the world in exponential numbers, to crawl, skim, and soar through every nook and cranny from every vantage point. The world would soon be crawling in tiny eyes, hiding in every tree, bush, gutter, windowsill, and dark corner, and the amount of data would be overwhelming.

There would soon be trillions of eyes watching the planet.

She simply didn't have the skills to interpret that kind of data, and there was no way a team of humans could keep up with it all.

She had heard the rumblings. They were going to shut down the satellite program. Even her bosses couldn't justify the expense. After all, each spy satellite had to follow a specific orbital path, trying to record inch-level detail from hundreds of miles up, and once it left an area, the damn thing couldn't photograph the target until it circled all the way around again. Not to mention the $400 million price tag and the fact you needed a rocket to blast it into position. How efficient was all that?

She had heard of new programs, well-funded efforts that would drop massive waves of tiny eyes into the world, perhaps to hide until they were needed, or conduct covert surveillance, or simply snoop around until they broke down.

Worse, all that data wouldn't be flowing through NGA data processing centers. It would be flowing through the arteries of thousands of commercial entities, private intelligence organizations, and world militaries.

So... she was pretty much screwed. Putting those thoughts out of her mind, she forced herself to get back to the task at hand. The terrorists who had launched two major attacks, and who seemed capable of many more, were lurking somewhere in these images. Hiding in the rainforest. Hiding right in front of her. And she could be the one to find them. She could make a difference in the world. She could alter history.

This mission might be her last hurrah.

Twenty other analysts were scouring the same images. A few had gone home for the night, but most were still in nearby cubicles, tapping away. Nicholas Click from the CIA was riding their asses; he didn't care who found the Kazites, as long as one of them did. His unstated promise: whoever found their hideout was on the fast track to a fantastic promotion, which Erin knew might be the only path to long-term job security. Out of photo-gazing, into senior leadership.

She needed to think like a Kazite. What were they like? What shapes would they build? How would they live? What were the geometries of their lives?

The key to locating their headquarters, the GEOINT team thought, might be their primitivist philosophy. No one knew whether they lived according to their ideals. On the one hand, they publicly espoused a back-to-the-earth approach. But behind the scenes, they used cutting-edge tech to kill. That was a puzzle of incongruent shapes. Which were they – radar dome or greenhouse?

Where and how did such odd people live? Find their shelter, their method of transportation, or their food and water sources, and you could catch them and lock them up.

She ruled out sites linked to farming, ranching, logging, and gold-mining. The GEOINT team did not think Harper's group would use heavy equipment to disembowel the environment. If Harper's statements on the video were correct, he was on the side of nature.

The Kazite's compound was probably along a river, for the same reason that most primitive cultures lived along rivers – they were a reliable water supply for drinking, sanitation, cleaning, and boat transportation.

After several hours, she had narrowed the list down to twenty-seven sites that strongly matched the five key criteria. Most of the sites probably harbored fugitives, outcasts, drug dealers, preppers, and others wishing to keep a low profile.

A few sites stood out. One had gardens and horses, but no buildings. Another was a ramshackle cluster of tents with a large black flag on a makeshift flagpole. She doubted the terrorists would be that obvious, but you never knew.

She rubbed her face. Her boss would be checking on her soon. He had been hovering like an Apache helicopter among the cubicles, hunting for hot leads. Unfortunately, narrowing these candidates further could take days, maybe weeks. That's assuming it was even one of these sites.

She needed coffee.

The room at the Michelangelo Hotel was dark and quiet. Ronan flipped on the light. Deanna's note remained on the couch where he had left it.

He sat on the bed, reached into his pocket, and withdrew the pencil-thin container that he had pilfered from the lab. He stared down at it. Edward had wanted him to grab something, anything, of potential value to U.S. intelligence, and the sample inside certainly fit the bill. He ran his finger across the embossed letters on the brushed stainless-steel exterior. SANAR. The outside was sleek and cool to the touch. The inside was 0°F and filled with a polymer gel that kept samples frozen for up to one week, such as the small microtube of material currently nestled inside.

He would soon be getting on a military plane for an overnight flight to DC, and this wasn't likely to get past security. He unscrewed a panel in the lower section of his leg, exposing a narrow space between the leg's outer carbon-fiber shell and the interior titanium frame. He slid Sanar's container into the space and re-attached the panel. His legs were full of electronics, and he doubted anyone would dismantle them, especially after he proffered his DoD ID.

Time to pack up, head home.

Gathering all his things from the bathroom and bedside table, he dumped them on the bed. He held a mirror close to his left eye. The tiny circuits, camera lens, and display screen embedded in his eye were the same blue-grey color of his iris and blended in almost perfectly. To the untrained eye, they looked natural.

Tossing his head back, he placed a drop of immune booster in each eye, designed to keep his eyes from becoming irritated by the electronics or rejecting them entirely.

He lifted his shirt, and probing his skin near the hip, found a small metal rivet. He jacked in a pressure gauge. The oxygen-boost canister was at 98%. No leak. Good.

Next, he inspected his knuckles to make sure the titanium reinforcements were not causing issues. No separations or bruising – *check*.

He unfastened the straps of his left leg and removed the prosthetic. He felt the *weight* in his hands. He slid his hand across the smooth surface. Then slowly and with great care, he used a felt cloth to polish it, buffing the surface shiny and bright. Edward had given him these kick-ass legs to replace the cheap ugly ones he'd received after the accident. He loved the aesthetics and was awed by the technology of this thing in his hands, but he did not like what the limb articulated personally.

Loss. Death. Chloe.

When he realized that no amount of further polishing would make any difference, he set the leg on the floor.

He removed his right leg, polished it slowly, then placed it on the floor next to the other.

After the accident, it had been a dark time. Discharged from the Army. Nothing to live for. No light, no laughs.

Months had gone by. At the time, it felt like years. Nothing but a black hole. His brain didn't work. He couldn't get perspective. Couldn't plan for anything in the future.

Day in and out, he ate and slept. Sometimes he took a shower and dressed.

He probably went on errands but had no recollection to confirm whether that was the case.

Then one day, for some reason, maybe just a subconscious desire to reboot a hint of life within, he decided to go to the mall.

He could get dressed, he had thought, comb his hair, strap on his crappy artificial legs, drive to the mall, and maybe buy some new clothes like normal people.

The mall was bright and alien. People everywhere. Talking about things that made no difference. He saw product displays in every store, each more absurd than the last. ON SALE signs. What was the point of those? Paying less and buying more stuff – that mattered?

He tried on some pants. He brought a pile of them into the dressing room, having selected mostly loose boot-cut jeans. Making sure the door was secured, he pulled a leg off and slid it into each pair for a quick check of fit. Many were too tight. Once he narrowed the pile down, he replaced the leg on his thigh and worked each pair of pants over the limbs, followed by a struggle to get the shoes on, stand up, check overall fit, and reverse the process. After the fifth pair of jeans he was exhausted. He tried a shortcut by pulling the pants over the shoes and it all got stuck.

He caught a glimpse of himself in the mirror. He hadn't looked at himself yet since the accident. Avoiding his own eyes, he looked at the half-way body that ended in stumps and then continued as cheap beige plastic the rest of the way to the floor.

He ripped off the shoes and pants and got dressed and gathered up a few to buy and left.

Back out in the mall, he boarded an escalator, bags in hand.

The escalator was trickier than he'd expected. The slats separated and he adjusted quickly, almost losing his balance. *Stand completely still*, he told himself. Don't move.

And that's exactly what he did, all the way to the top, where the slats slid back together and disappeared into the floor. He just stood there, brain not connecting to machine, blanking out, what am I supposed to do, why am I here, why did I live, what next, how do I move, until his legs hit the floor abruptly and he pitched forward.

This wasn't a casual stumble where you quickly recover and save face with a smile. No. This had been a face-first, bags-flying, loud and painful floor-smash.

He just lay there, unsure of what had even happened. Where was he?

A smiling woman had been right behind him on the escalator, and she was helping him up, saying something, but he wasn't listening.

Sure, I can stand, thank you.

She was asking if he was okay.

He adjusted a leg.

Others were looking too.

If he jumped over the railing from this height, headfirst, could he kill himself?

The woman was still talking to him. He focused.

Maybe you need to sit down, she said.

True.

She led him to a table. He sat.

She sat, too, and regarded him with concern.

I'm sorry, she said.

About what?

They were talking, and that seemed to go on for a while.

They moved from the table by the escalator to a coffee shop, and they bought coffee.

After some time, she said she had to go. She texted him, so they could stay in touch.

When she walked away, he looked at his phone. *Lisa Hutchinson.*

...

Ronan found himself lying on the hotel bed staring at the ceiling.

Lisa was so different from Chloe. By day a dog groomer, at home a lover of books and TV shows, plump from inactivity, with no capacity to have adventures with guns in foreign lands. Just warm, accepting, and comforting.

She had saved Ziggy, a Welsh terrier that she had rescued from a dismal dog pound, and then she had saved him.

Because soon they were dating, his mood lifted, and things started to make a little sense. She knew of his loss but never brought it up, not because of jealousy, but because she knew his pain.

By then, he had realized that technology was going to save humanity. Technology could do everything consistently, tirelessly, reliably. Technology could overcome human imperfections. Mastering technology meant taking *control*.

He joined Edward's team and asked for any augmentations that might prove valuable to field officers. He wanted to be the first to find solutions. He pitched the vision of human 2.0.

He got better legs.

He improved his eyes.

Even his hobbies became technology-driven: it was fun trying to identify birds with his new-found powers. The little bastards never sat still, just flitted around behind leaves or soared overhead, shadows against a backlit sky.

He found ways to catch all of them in his crosshairs. Freeze-frame, zoom-in, contrast boost, cross-check diagnostic features against a database. Bam, add another one to the list.

She laughed at his bird obsession, even seemed annoyed by it, but she had her obsessive hobbies too. She watched a lot of sports. She spent hours analyzing player InstaStats, looking for an edge of one team over the other as a game progressed, trying to predict the outcome with a long list of biomarkers for nervousness, confidence, and other mental and physical states.

It had never dawned on her that she, too, was embracing the power and control that technology provided.

But Lisa also cared for the players. She was a Burlie B fan, and Ronan knew she was hit hard by his death. The Nashville attack would have her on edge. He knew she was worried about him, and worried about terrorism, and worried about things in general.

He knew it was time to head home.

Lisa was waiting.

Erin glanced at her watch. The tapping from the workstations around her had slowed to a trickle. Her boss had gone home. Another hour had gone by and nothing had jumped out at her. She practiced how she would deliver the bad news. Even though the DIA had narrowed the site down to a relatively small area of the Amazon, it still amounted to hundreds of square miles. They might have to send ground drones to every one of her priority locations.

She plopped herself back down in her seat to go over the photos once again.

The caffeine had given her mind a shot of clarity and determination. This time she paused on the site with the gardens and horses, but no buildings. What was going on here, anyway? There was a large clearing surrounded by dense old-growth forest, the Amazon barely held at bay. Maintaining a clearing took a lot of effort. If left alone, the vegetation would have grown over the site in months. There was a sizable cluster of trees in the center of the clearing, too, but now Erin noticed that these were new growth. The owners of this plot of land had let the jungle grow back in the middle of the clearing, for some unknown reason, creating the approximate shape of a doughnut. The entire area was located on a hill, and drainage ditches ran down its length. There were narrow dirt roads, but no vehicles.

The whole setup was odd. She scrutinized every pixel of the satellite shots. And then something *did* leap out at her, clear as day: a black square, nestled among the new-growth trees. She couldn't be completely sure, but the size and shape looked an awful lot like an open skylight. She searched harder and soon found others.

Within ten minutes, Erin had found a dozen of the tiny squares. Their surface wasn't glass; some looked like open holes, while others were lighter and appeared to be covered with wood.

It was almost as if someone had dug chambers in the ground and then added a hole for light or ventilation, right there among the trees they were allowing to grow back.

Anything unusual like that was worth a much closer look.

She retrieved satellite photos taken ten years back. At that time, the entire area was old growth. No clearing, no signs of any human activity.

She went back five years – same thing.

She went back three years – and hit the jackpot. The satellite photos showed trees being cleared, although there was no sign of any land-moving equipment. Just a dozen people whacking away at the woods.

Three months later, the site had a maze of trenches in the ground, half the size of a football field.

Again, swarms of people were on the site, with no sign of any excavators, loaders, bulldozers, compactors, or other construction equipment.

They were digging the damn holes by hand.

She flipped through the entire sequence, saw rooms large and small take shape on at least three levels.

Erin sat up. The implications were immediately clear. A large group of primitivists had built an enormous structure, fed skylights into it, and then piled dirt on top and covered it in trees and brush. They were living under the jungle.

They were hiding their home.

And it had almost worked.

The snow had turned into crumbly chunks of ice and was slowly melting. Allen Pond Park was full of dog walkers and joggers enjoying the nicest Saturday in Bowie, Maryland, since the first frigid snowfalls of late December. Edward walked his border collie, Emma, around the pond and took in the fresh smells adrift in the air.

They kept to the sidewalks, which were dry and bare, the snow scraped into heaps along their sides. Emma sniffed at the benches glistening in wet ice and inspected the drips plopping down from them.

A chilly breeze brushed against his cheeks but was defeated by the warm sun rising in the sky. Some of the park's visitors wore heavy coats, but others donned sweatshirts or lighter clothing. Many of them, like Edward, worked inside the beltway. They were here to relax. Washington, and all the stress and craziness that went on there, was just fifteen miles away.

On the surface, nothing about the crowd seemed unusual, but Edward knew everyone was thinking about the same thing. The attack on St. Bonaventure Island was a disaster that woke up the half of the world that hadn't already been shocked by Nashville. Fear ran rampant and governments were spending fortunes on internal investigations, initiatives, agencies, and preparations. Still, the word "nanoweapons" had not yet blazed its way across the media and social networks. Everyone was focusing on the emerging risks of microdrones and miniaturized robotics, which had previously gone largely unnoticed in the public eye. *Wait*, the world seemed to be realizing… millions of these things can be produced in any shape or form? And they can swarm and attack you?

Soon, though, word would get around that the victims hadn't died from a run-of-the-mill poison or virus. When people learned that manufactured infective weapons smaller than a virus could target specific internal organs and blow them apart with ruthless savagery, well, even the word *panic* seemed insufficient.

Edward had predicted that problem long ago. So had Dr. Pieter Heynes. The technology was inevitable, it was here, and now it had to be dealt with. But that was a problem for another day.

His overarching emotion was joy. Of the untold numbers of experts who had poured over Harper's video and other meager clues, an operative in *his* department had made the crucial discovery. The Kazites were located somewhere near Manaus. Now the CIA could find this guy Harper, track his every move, monitor Kazite communications, and find all the other terrorists around the world that were involved.

Edward reviewed the events that he and his team had pieced together so far. He didn't have all the details, but he could make educated guesses and fill in the gaps.

Everything had started with Siyu, the Chinese investor at LikeLife who had sabotaged Ronan and Deanna's flight from Taiwan. Siyu was a fervent anti-technologist. To Siyu, the world was barreling toward push-button, dumb-headed annihilation. But Siyu had no idea how to shock the world into paying attention. He did, however, have access to big money from a Chinese patron.

Siyu had read Pieter Heynes's paper warning that terrorists could take small attack devices, like those made by LikeLife, and arm them with incredibly dangerous nanoweapons, such as those being developed at Sanar. Together, these two technologies allowed you to do whatever you wanted to whomever you wanted. *Wow*, Siyu must have thought – *this will get everyone's attention!* He became an investor at LikeLife to get closer to their scariest bots. Then, he recruited a variety of anti-technology groups, including Harper and the Kazites, and got them all hooked up with the device printers and synthesizers. Now they could deliver some serious havoc.

Siyu, Pieter, and Harper were all of a like mind. The three believed the world needed a major wake-up call, a series of deadly events that would demonstrate just how fast everyone was tumbling into the technology meat grinder.

But Siyu had been bumped-off by one of his allies. Maybe the wealthy patron had become nervous. Or maybe Harper had done him in, just as he had killed Pieter. The bottom line was that Harper was the main threat at the moment. Harper was a dangerous idiot, and he was running unfettered with Pieter's ideas and Siyu's machines.

At this point, the story was becoming clear. Unfortunately, there were still unknown actors at large. No one knew who the Chinese funder was, or how many other cells were sprinkled around the globe. The next stage of the investigation was critical. By covertly watching Harper, they should be able to uncover the necessary trails and leads. They could, with proper diligence, mop this whole thing up in four to six months.

He took Emma across the bridge and up the steps to the gazebo that overlooked the pond. The snow there had not been cleared as often, and the ground was slippery and crunchy.

Leaning on the railing, he breathed in. Spring was coming and with it the blossoming trees, the excited twitter of the birds passing through on their way north, the smell of the soil, blue skies.

Funding was coming, too. MET would grow. Edward's salary, stature, and power would increase. Maybe he'd even join Click's stupid club.

Emma looked at him with loving eyes faded by age. She had glaucoma; she could see well enough to walk around, but not enough to fully appreciate all the visual stimuli of a park alive with activity.

He bent and scratched her head. This old dog had been with him from the beginning of the founding of the agency and all the stresses over the years. How many times had they walked in this park as he fretted about internal politics or justifying his budget or a dead-end investigation?

When the problems of work followed him home and he needed to clear his head, he'd jump in the car with her and head to this park. Emma did not ask questions; she just let him think while she enjoyed the walk, regardless of sun, rain, snow, or heat.

Gradually his current problem rose to the forefront. He couldn't ignore it.

Click wasn't returning his calls.

Their previous conversation was unnerving. On top of everything else the intelligence community needed to worry about, there seemed to be wheels of politics spinning within the many wheels of the investigation, and it was entirely possible that some of the motivations within the various groups were at odds with the overall mission.

If Click wasn't getting back to him, that meant Edward was being kept out of the loop for some reason. Deanna was in town; Ronan was in flight and due to land soon. Edward needed answers so that he could keep them involved in a meaningful way.

His anger flared and he forgot the peaceful lake, tugging at Emma roughly as he stormed out of the gazebo and back down the steps. A few minutes later, back at the main sidewalk, he slowed and took a breath. He looked down at his dog. He bent and rubbed her chin, studied her cloudy eyes.

Why were they playing games? These attacks harkened the most serious threat since the rise of the nuclear arsenals. People like Harper were unleashing a terror that could savage the biological world. Turn your heart into goo. Your lungs into molasses. Whatever they want to do to you, they'll do it. Once the biters were as small as spring pollen, they would be everywhere, infecting everyone. The biter and payload would fuse into one tiny molecular machine, like a virus.

He tried calling again.

This time, Click answered.

Edward was relieved. "I've been trying to get through to you. What's the latest news?"

He watched Emma sniffing a frozen bush that had been visited by other dogs. Two joggers passed, talking to each other in loud voices. As they retreated, Edward said, "Can you repeat that?"

Listening to Click, Edward smiled. "That's fantastic!"

The CIA had located the terrorist cell.

He stroked Emma's head. But then, as Edward felt his spirits soar, Click gave him shocking news.

"Why? What are you saying?"

He paced. "Sure… *after* we conduct the surveillance and check out…"

Edward broke into a fierce stride. "Nicholas, you've got to help me knock some sense into them."

Edward stopped. "What? When?"

A few seconds passed.

"Tomorrow?"

Edward disconnected, sent a few texts, and sprinted for the parking lot as fast as Emma could keep up.

CHAPTER 54

CENTER FOR THE MANAGEMENT OF EMERGING TECHNOLOGIES
DEFENSE INTELLIGENCE AGENCY
WASHINGTON, DC

Ronan entered Edward's office at DIA Headquarters, located in the southernmost section of Washington. He had landed at Dulles three hours ago and was anxious to head home to see Lisa. Then he got the text from Edward: *As soon as you land, come straight to see me.* There had been no explanation. That was the last thing he needed right now. With a six-hour time change and a dismal night's sleep, he was already jet lagged.

Ronan knew from the moment he saw Edward's face that he wasn't going to like the conversation. He didn't know what was about to transpire, but he could tell that Edward was agitated.

"Welcome back, Ronan."

"What's going on? Have we located the Kazites yet?"

"Have a seat."

Edward walked to the small fridge he kept in his office and removed a cold water bottle. After a moment, he put it back and removed a can of Red Bull. He set the drink in front of Ronan and popped the top.

"Not thirsty," Ronan said. "What's this about?"

His boss plopped himself down in his creaky old chair. "Thanks to your breakthrough, we found the compound."

Relief flooded over Ronan. *They had done it.* "That's wonderful news."

"The terrorists are located in the low mountains of the Serra Acaraí, deep in the Amazon, on the eastern bank of a small river about 185 miles north of Manaus, Brazil, just like you said. We dropped a recon drone. The primary structure is on a sloping hill. There's at least one basement level and two stories above ground. The entire thing is camouflaged – they covered it all with dirt. Vegetation and trees grow on the roofs. The dirt roads are overgrown, and they rely on horses for transportation. Real primitive. They live what they preach."

Well, Ronan thought, this was the best possible outcome. He didn't yet see why Edward had the look of twisted pain on his face, but, he assumed, they would be getting to that.

Edward continued. "We're not sure how they power their electronics. Maybe generators. The place is extremely isolated. The only people in the area are primitive Indians and a handful of illegal gold miners. There isn't a phone, TV, or flush toilet for a hundred miles in any direction."

"I'm waiting for the punchline. I can tell something's not right. What's the problem? Did they find the president's nephew living there or something?"

"As we speak, the U.S. is preparing to launch a tomahawk cruise missile from a navy ship off the coast of Guyana. We're going to blow that shitty little building out of existence. The entire side of that foothill will be gone tomorrow afternoon. Any microbots will be obliterated along with all the Kazites."

Ronan bolted upright. "Wait–"

"Our country is not going to risk another catastrophe like Nashville or St. Bonaventure Island. We are going to hit the Kazites fast. Destroy them before they relocate. Strike time is 1200 tomorrow. That's in twenty-seven hours."

Ronan shook his head. "Hold on. Pieter said there were other cells. We should stay in stealth mode and identify those connections. They may have laptops and cell phones in that location. We can't bomb the evidence."

Holding up a hand, Edward nodded. "I know, I get it. But the CIA doesn't think your human intel is reliable. And maybe they're right. Our theory is on shaky ground. Harper is loopy and impulsive. He doesn't fit the profile of someone taking orders from a guy in China. We have no real evidence. The CIA is of the opinion that these Amazon survivalists are acting on their own."

Ronan sank back in his chair. Dr. Pieter Heynes had warned against other terrorist cells. Ronan thought an anti-technology vendetta might be motivating groups worldwide, almost like a spiritual jihad. "I believe Pieter knew that other people are planning similar attacks, with or without Harper."

Edward fixed his eyes on Ronan. "How sure are you? Do you think we should send a mission to recover any electronics from the compound?"

"Yes."

"There wouldn't be adequate prep time, and it is safe to assume the Kazites are loaded with weapons. We would be putting our soldiers' lives in danger."

From his years in the military, Ronan knew what it meant to trust that his commanders were making the best decisions. He would never casually put another soldier's life on the line.

Edward waited for an answer. He clicked a pen.

"Yes," Ronan said. "If they won't delay the bombing, I think it is worth taking the risk."

"Are you willing to put yourself on the line for this?"

Ronan paused. There it was! The source of the pain on Edward's face. The question took Ronan by surprise. "I've been out of action too long. And I've never been trained in special operations. There's no point in sending me."

"I disagree. Harper wants *you*. So let's deliver you to him, just like he asked. Your presence could provide critical leverage if the operation goes awry."

For the first time since the initial attack, Ronan felt fear and shakiness in his stomach. He tapped through his contacts. Lisa's photo popped up and hovered over Edward's desk. He looked at her smile, the bright cheer in her eyes, the delicate swish of hair. He hadn't seen her since the night of the Nashville attack, when he had given her a quick hug and sped off without another word. At this moment, she was only twenty-five miles away.

Ronan tapped and she disappeared. "How would we get approval? I don't think the president would go for something like that." He glanced at his watch. "And we've just lost five critical minutes talking about it."

"I've already got approval and a SEAL team is preparing right now. The bombing is a joint mission between the CIA and DoD. The Secretary of Defense secured approval to send an advance team. When we arrive and attack, Harper and his people will hunker down inside their compound. They won't have time to bug out. Our team will drive them into their building. If we find any electronics, we grab what we can. Then we get out before the missile strikes. But if the whole thing goes south, my head is on the chopping block, and no one else's."

Ronan zoomed his ocular to give Edward an unsettling stare. "If the whole thing goes south, we could lose men. If I'm there, *my* neck would be on the chopping block."

"True."

Rising, Ronan paced. "I don't know if I would be an asset. More likely, I would just get in the way."

His boss's eyes hardened. "There's one other thing you need to know."

"Shoot."

"Deanna is going. She jumped at the chance. She is gearing up now."

"What? Why would you send her?"

"To make you go too, of course."

"I don't understand this at all. Why would you do this?"

Edward threw the pen on his desk. "Dammit, you know I don't take this lightly. I want you there to get face and iris scans of the Kazites, alive or shot dead, before their faces are bombed into oblivion. Close ups if you can. Fingerprints too. Get any biometrics that could open their computers and devices. We put a lot of tech into you, Ronan. So far it's been a waste of money. It's time to put all that smartware to use. And if you're caught, negotiate with Harper. He seems keenly interested in you. Get in his head. Make him spill important information. Get him to react. Do the thing you do with everybody else – throw him off guard!"

Ronan mulled this over. *If I'm caught?*

The thought of Deanna heading into the jungle made his stomach feel worse. Ronan put a hand to his chin and paced. He desperately wanted to go home to Lisa, but now he pictured Deanna next to him on the couch. What if she ran into trouble?

"Khatib wants you to go, too," Edward said. "Given that you left her jet contaminated and worthless, she thought it would be a nice gesture to accompany the mission and help out."

"There's no way she said that."

Edward shrugged.

Ronan continued pacing. He rubbed his forehead.

"I need an answer," Edward said. "Are you going with them?"

"You know I am."

Edward leapt to his feet. "Every second counts. Let's hustle. I'll take you to the staging facility." He handed Ronan the Red Bull. "Drink up. You'll need it."

Ronan grunted, tight lipped. There was no movement in his eyes. "Do I have time for a call?"

"No. I have a lot of information to go over with you. We'll review the plans on the ride over."

Ronan nodded.

Noting his expression, Edward said, "Cheer up. I have a present for you."

"I can't wait. Is it chocolate?"

"Much better." Edward held the door for him.

Upon arrival, Edward introduced Ronan to two military personnel, wished him luck, said goodbye, and left. Ronan's escorts led him to the staging area, a cavernous hangar dominated by a large white plane with black windows. Ronan recognized the plane as a new Boeing Constrictor, a long-range transport aircraft with the wings and sleekness of a stealth bomber, but the bulbous belly of a python that swallowed a pig.

The workers moved with determined speed and ignored Ronan as he crossed the floor. He stepped over power cables and hoses that snaked across their path, the tangle leading to the underside of the plane and electronic instruments sitting on wheeled carts. Powerful lights poured down from the lattice of girders high overhead and reflected off the shiny floor.

Nearby, a team of Navy SEALs packed their gear, pulling equipment from heavy plastic bins that had been rolled up and locked down. The SEALs were focused and barely spoke. Most looked to be in their twenties. Several had their gear arranged on a long table – knives, grenades, electrical tape, battery packs, glasses, gloves, and dozens of other items, waiting to be packed.

He spied Deanna. She was talking to a man in full fatigues who seemed to be explaining some of the gear to her. She didn't notice Ronan.

A row of chairs had been arranged in front of a whiteboard. Beyond the chairs, a dozen large pieces of equipment had been stacked like spoons, each unit about five feet high and shaped like a curved kite. They had been deposited near one of the open bays on the plane.

Ronan had been on his share of deployments. Military operations were always supremely organized, with outgoing equipment on well-marked pallets, personnel filing around in precise patterns, RFID chips for tracking everything, and senior officers calmly directing the efforts. SEAL teams trained and practiced relentlessly together and could carry out an op almost entirely without verbal communication. They were always ready to go at a moment's notice. But even by SEAL standards, this mission had a *last-minute* feel to it. The effect was subtle. Despite the obvious order and systematic movements of everyone around him, a closer look revealed sloppiness, an edge of frenzy. Boxes picked up, moved, quickly set back down; people hustling across the floor, turning, hustling back.

This prep is way too short, Ronan thought. He tried to interpret the faces of the men and women hurrying around him. None looked concerned. They knew what was needed, even if they didn't have enough time to do it *right*.

The escorts led Ronan to a bare spot at the table and immediately took his measurements for a full uniform, including helmet, body armor, and boots. They tapped on their phones as they worked head to feet. They had just started explaining the gear and weapons when they were joined by the older man who had been talking to Deanna.

"I'm Lieutenant Elliott," the man said, shaking Ronan's hand. "I'm leading the squad going out to the compound. Welcome to our team."

"Just so you know," Ronan said, "I was discharged over two years ago."

"It's going to be okay. We've brought non-military on ops before. We'll keep you positioned toward the back. Just yell if you see anyone behind us."

Ronan smiled. "I can handle that."

"Also, Edward left this for you." Lt. Elliott retrieved a weapons case from under the table and flipped the latches. After removing a sheath of packing foam, he withdrew a rifle and handed it to Ronan.

"Unusual. What is it?"

"Edward called it an X-Rifle, a gift from Leckham Technologies. A prototype. The hardware uses corrective aim by syncing with your ocular."

THE HAVOC INSIDE US

Ronan gave it the once-over and glanced at Lt. Elliott. *Please explain.*

"Once you look at your target," the lieutenant said, "just pull the trigger. As long as you are pointing in the right general direction, the barrel corrects and makes a perfect shot every time."

"It's a dummy-proof way to kill people."

"Perfect for you, huh?"

Ronan hefted the gun to his right eye, then stopped.

Lt. Elliott rested his hand on it. "There's no scope. You don't lift it up. Get it synced up with your ocular and make sure the barrel is responding."

Ronan looked down at the dull black steel of his gun. It felt much heavier than a typical military assault rifle. The weapon might be a pain to lug around, but he felt he could handle it. He was intrigued. The barrel didn't disappear into the handguard like other rifles. Instead, the barrel lay across the top, attached to a block-shaped receiver. If he understood correctly, the barrel and receiver would pivot on any axis and adjust the aim automatically based on whatever he was currently looking at.

"Thank you for this," he said.

He looked up.

Lt. Elliott was gone, having moved on to the next member of the team.

...

"Hey, partner," Deanna said, approaching the table.

Ronan swung the barrel into the default position with a quiet *click*. "Hello." He met her eyes. "You left rather abruptly. Just a note?"

"Edward wanted me to brief all the intel chiefs."

He stopped checking the gun. "Why did you let Edward talk you into this?"

"We need the data. You know that."

"They have Navy SEALs to get the data."

She gritted her teeth and readjusted her belt. "Why are *you* here?"

"Same reason."

She grunted.

Ronan tried to smile. "Let's hope we find what we're looking for."

Deanna returned the smile. "We will."

Nearby, a middle-aged man in fatigues set a plastic case on the table, about the size of a laptop. He opened the lid and gestured to one of the SEALs.

"I didn't get a chance to congratulate you on finding the Kazites," Deanna continued. "Now I see why Edward hired you."

"I'm at my best when time is short."

The man with the case withdrew a thin strip and placed it on the SEAL's forehead. He tapped a screen inside the case.

Deanna nodded toward them. "He's taking vitals. We're next."

Reading the SEAL's metrics, the man said, "Resting heart rate 52, stress low, fear low, blood pressure 105/70, temperature 97.6. Are you feeling as good as this data looks?"

The SEAL nodded. "I'm going to feel a lot better when I'm flushing the filth out of that compound."

The checkup man pulled the strip off the SEAL's forehead, dropped it into an envelope, and withdrew a new one. Without a word, he gestured to Deanna. He fixed a strip on her. "Resting rate 88, stress medium, fear medium, blood pressure fine, temperature on the nose. Congratulations, you passed."

Next, it was Ronan's turn. He swallowed and took a deep breath as the cool strip was pressed against his forehead. For a moment, the man stared at it, saying nothing.

"How'd he do?" Deanna asked.

"Resting rate, blood pressure, temperature all good." He pulled off the strip. "Stress high… fear high."

Ronan avoided Deanna's reaction.

"Don't worry, Mr. Flynn," the man said, snapping the case closed. He smiled reassuringly. "From what I've heard about this op, I'd say you've got the best results."

...

The entire team sat in the folding chairs. Ronan had met a few of them. Buckley was a large guy in his late twenties with a head like a block of cement. Word had it that Buckley had actually died during a breaching exercise, when five pounds of C-4 plastic explosive went off next to his chest, significantly impacting the physics of his heart. Ramos, another member of this op, had performed CPR on the spot and saved Buckley's life, transforming him in five minutes from lying flatlined to standing upright. The two had a deep, quiet friendship, and they were tighter than a clenched fist with rigor mortis. As a result of Buckley's resurrection, the SEALs sometimes called him Zombie. And as with any good soldier, Buckley the Zombie accepted his nickname, whether he liked it or not.

Zombie and Ramos were equally close to a third SEAL, a guy name Owen Wu. Ronan thought Wu looked kind of small and wiry, maybe better suited at a computer navigating a drone strike than running toward gunfire. Maybe that's why they called him Wuss. He clearly had the team's respect, though. They said he could kick the balls off a man wearing pants.

Zombie, Ramos, and Wuss formed a solid core to the team, having spent more years together than the others.

They all watched Lt. Elliott as he took a position in front of the group. A well-worn topo map of South America was taped to a whiteboard. The map was dominated by Brazil, overwhelmingly flat and filled with rivers and swamps. "This briefing will be short. We leave in thirty minutes."

Ronan cut his eyes at Deanna, sitting next to him. She returned the glance but did not smile.

"Our target is in the upper corner of the Amazon basin," Lt. Elliott said, "the beginning of hilly terrain that eventually becomes the Guyana Highlands. This region is incredibly remote. Almost no one lives there." He tapped his pencil on an area bordering Guyana. Unlike the rest of the Amazon, the target area showed hilly gradients and deep ridges. To the north, the hills became steep mountains.

"Most of what we need is already packed. The plane has two pilots, a prep crew, two navigators, two intel, and a comm. Flight time is eleven hours, fifty-five minutes. If we had our choice, we would land at Buenos Aires and transfer to a helo. Unfortunately, that's not feasible. We will fly to a point ten miles from our target, far enough to avoid detection, and deploy from the plane."

He pulled off the map, revealing another underneath. The second map was an aerial photo consisting almost entirely of trees, with occasional glimpses of ravines, streams, and rivers. A label in bold yellow said: 250 SQUARE MILES.

"K-92 automated TurboGlides will carry us to a location three miles from the compound." Lt. Elliott circled an area of trees that looked no different than any other part of the forest.

Gliders, Ronan thought. *That's what those things were next to the plane. What did I get myself into?*

"From the landing site," the lieutenant continued, "we will proceed through dense vegetation. Sergeant Amelio, please raise your hand. He joins us from the Brazilian special forces. He is our guide and will help us bushwhack to a usable path." Lt. Elliott circled another area of trees. "Which we will follow to the compound."

Their destination differed from the surrounding area. It resembled the letter "O," a thin, bare circle with a patch of forest in the middle. Lt. Elliott removed the map and revealed a third sheet. This one contained ten or twelve photos in a grid. They all showed a large structure, clearly man-made, but overgrown with jungle. There were no windows and only a few doors.

"We have a surface drone fixed on a tree near their compound. The Kazites cleared a low hill that sits at a twelve-degree angle. There is a single large structure, 360 feet by 310 feet, with three levels. Because of the angle of the hill and the way the compound is built into it, the bottom level is partially submerged below ground. Drainage ditches carry rain runoff to the Jatapu River at the bottom of the hill."

Lt. Elliott tapped various photos with his pencil.

"We estimate that roughly fifty to sixty men live in the structure. We don't know exactly what the interior looks like, but we have some idea. It will be cramped. There are probably dozens of small sleeping cells. Lots of narrow corridors. A handful of larger main rooms. Lots of ventilation and light shafts, open from the top to the basement. They close these off when it rains. Many of the walls are interlocked, hand-hewn lumber. The Kazites were clever. They appear to have kept many of the existing trees for support. The biggest trees growing out of the roof are the support core of the structure. A ravine lies about a mile away, with an old foot bridge. The ravine is full of rocks, and they appear to have used a lot of those in the construction as well. It's part underground treehouse, part large Celtic stone tomb."

The SEALs exchanged glances. They had extensive experience and training in tight quarters, in buildings made of concrete or plywood, of both shoddy and solid construction. They had seen it all. None of them looked concerned.

Ronan stared at those photos. It was going to be hot in there. Hot and dark and foul-smelling. And the place would be full of angry, armed terrorists, like a big mound of biting red ants. The SEALs were going to kick it open to see what spilled out.

"Outside, there isn't much to see. They have several horses, no vehicles. They plow the ground manually and have a garden, which seems to be raided at night by animals. They placed wooden spears around the perimeter. Other than plants, they also seem to eat bugs, snakes, lizards, and various mammals. The roof of the compound is completely covered in trees and vegetation. By all appearances, they are living an extremely primitive lifestyle. We may be fighting the equivalent of cavemen."

"Nice," Zombie said. "The engagement may be over in ten minutes."

"On the other hand, we know they also launch sophisticated attacks with microdrones and nanites. We have to watch for that. Every inch of your body must be covered. In other words, we assume they are low tech, but be prepared in case they are not."

Lt. Elliott circled a door on the side of the structure.

"We have three hours to hike to the compound. If we haven't been detected upon arrival, we will breach without resorting to explosives. We anticipate a straightforward penetration and extraction process. We enter the compound and move room to room, neutralizing attackers as we go. We hope to take them by surprise, but we don't know what to expect. They may ready to fight. As we press forward, we believe survivors will retreat to the interior, giving us the ability to complete the mission objective."

"While we sweep each room, look for electronics. Our goal is to recover laptops, phones, thumb drives, hard drives, DVDs, anything with data on it. We are joined by two DIA officers, Ronan Flynn and Deanna Pirelli, who have final decision on what we take with us. Ronan and Deanna, you will carry packs, screwdrivers, cutting tools. The team's goal is to surround you, protect you, and get you out safely with the assets."

"At 1120, we exit the structure. We will rendezvous in the forest and secure the perimeter. If anything tries to crawl out, destroy it. We don't want anyone running for the woods. Terrorists tend to reproduce like mosquitos. No one gets away. At 1145, we pull back to a safe zone. The missile strikes at noon. We sweep the area for survivors. A helo will be waiting five miles from the site, and we will notify it for pickup."

"To be clear, the DOD's top priority is to completely destroy the terrorist cell. We are not looking to take prisoners. Our data recovery mission is a secondary priority. When we return, there will be a lengthy decontamination process. All equipment and clothing will be destroyed – everything but the Kazite's electronics, which will be stored in secure containers. The helo will land at NAMRU-6 in Peru, a biosafety facility operated by the U.S. Navy. We'll be inspected for any weapons that might be crawling on our bodies, clothing, or equipment. It will be like checking for ticks."

Wuss raised his hand.

"I'm sorry," Lt. Elliott said. "We don't have time for questions, but we will talk further on the flight. Get your gear. When you hear the horn, you have five minutes to be in your seat on the plane."

…

Most of the SEALs had carried their equipment to the glider assigned to them and stowed their supplies inside it.

Ronan, who was a few steps behind everyone else, reviewed his kit. He was familiar with the handling of most of the gear. MK18 close quarters select-fire assault rifle. SIG MK25 sidearm. Digital fuse stun grenades. Six-inch stainless steel Navy knife.

His body armor, clothing, and helmet had been delivered. He pulled his t-shirt off and replaced it with the compression top they had supplied, designed for staying cool and dry in the jungle heat. He donned the camo shirt, then the combat pants, pulling them over his prosthetics. The fit was tight across his chest and in the crotch, but there was nothing he could do about that now. He glanced at one of the large digital clocks mounted on each wall. Twenty-five minutes.

He threaded the belt, pulled the boots on his Flex feet, laced up. Finally, he slid into the body armor and connected the straps, pulling the vest tight. The body armor was composite resin, maybe Zylon and other fibers mixed into a hard shell. Multi-hit. Normally these rigid torso protection plates were custom ordered, but he'd been given an extra one from inventory. It felt tight across his chest, worse than the shirt. This might cause serious movement problems.

Again, nothing he could do about that now.

He loaded up on ammo. Three mags in pouches across his front, one mag on each side, and one in the gun. At thirty rounds each, he had a total of one hundred and fifty rounds of ammo for the X-Rifle. He positioned the sidearm for easy access and grabbed a spare mag for that – forty-two more rounds. If he had to take even a small fraction of that many shots, it was going to be a horrible day.

The helmet had a snug and comfortable fit. It could protect his brain against a spray of forty-four magnum rounds. The helmet's high cut was going to be far more comfortable for a long trek to the site than a full-cut helmet would be, and it made communication easier, but it exposed a lot more of the face, sides, and neck. The headset cups sat a few centimeters from the ears and could be snapped into place when needed.

They had given him an assault pack, and he scanned the contents. Tape, flashlight, multitool, signal mirror, iodine, skin wash.

Ten feet of nylon cord.

Evidence collection bags.

Backup power.

GPS beacon.

Compact breathing system for chemical attacks.

Bottom line: fifty to sixty pounds of gear, a heavy load to lug through a dense, hot jungle.

He removed the helmet and body armor.

One of the SEALs stopped by to help. "Hi Ronan, I'm Sergeant Michael Fulsom. I'll be the point man inside the compound. I'll help you get your gear packed into the glider."

"Thank you. I need to sync up my rifle. I'll bring it over in a minute."

Fulsom nodded and left with Ronan's other weapons and equipment.

Someone laughed. Sergeant Amelio, the Brazilian operative who would be their navigator in the Amazon, was standing next to him. Amelio was built like a tank.

"You look like you just got dropped into a whirlpool with your hands tied."

Ronan returned the smile. "I'm fine. Glad you'll be with us. How familiar are you with this region?"

"I've been through the area. I paddled down the Jatapu River."

"What's it like?"

"Rough. A handful of indigenous people live there, completely wild, no contact whatsoever with civilization. We won't see them. They hide in the shadows. Other than a ton of animals and bugs, there is nothing there but rain, heat, trees, water, more water, and more rain. There's no infrastructure, nothing but a few paths and a river that winds through the rocky hills."

"Sounds like a tough hike."

"One of the toughest on earth. It's nature's last stand."

...

Ronan flipped the rifle's power switch. ACTIVATED. A red dot hovered in his vision. The sync was automatic. He smiled.

As he looked from person to person in the room and aligned the glowing dot with their head or body, the barrel moved in three dimensions, rotating and swiveling as needed. Ronan confirmed that all he had to do was aim the rifle in the general direction of the target. As long as he did that, the barrel lined itself up for a perfect shot.

He discretely swung the rifle around the room at waist level, looking at open mouths, creased foreheads, ears, legs, chests. The barrel adjusted each time. *Works like a charm.* He set the rifle back in its case.

His helmet had an integrated comm system. He adjusted the chin strap and ear shell and powered the unit. As he flipped a dial of connection options, a robotic voice said, "radio one," "radio two" ... then "cellular," which he selected. The cell connection number flashed on the ocular.

He glanced left, right. Everyone was too busy with the last of their packing to pay any attention to him. Most were heading for the plane. He tapped his thumb.

A contact list opened on the ocular, with his girlfriend's number at the top of the stack.

Tap, tap.

Connecting.

Lisa answered the call, her image superimposed over the X-Rifle, a ghost hovering over trigger, stock, and barrel. Her smile radiated from the digital ether and her eyes sparkled in boosted ethereal blue. Her eyes, he thought, were much prettier in their subdued real-world hues.

He picked up the rifle, turned it over, set it back down, a pretense that he was wrapping up his inspection. People hurried in both directions in front of his table.

"Where are you?" she asked.

He spoke in low tones. "I can't say, but I am close. And I have good news. I am on my way home."

"That's fantastic. When will I see you?"

"Two days, if not sooner."

"I can't wait. Ziggy misses you."

The enormous door to the hanger clanged and reverberated and began to open.

"What's going on?" Her brow had furrowed.

"Unfortunately, I can't say anything about that either, honey."

"Is it dangerous?"

"I will be fine."

"Okay. I trust you." Her smile faded. "You sound really stressed."

Deanna was gathering the last of her gear at the end of the table. *She shouldn't be doing this*, Ronan thought. *I shouldn't be, either.* "I'm fine," he said.

Someone had set two ammo cans next to Deanna. One of the SEALs grabbed a bandolier and loader and hustled off.

"C'mon," she said. "You have to sound more convincing than that."

Lisa's ghostly smile glowed over Deanna.

Ronan looked away. Lisa's face trailed with him, across the crates, the plane. The sinking feeling was threatening to overcome him. He needed to get his shit together. Lisa blurred as his eyes watered slightly.

She kept talking, but now he had trouble focusing on her words. She was talking about work or Ziggy, and he glanced back at Deanna.

Lisa asked, "Is Deanna still with you?"

Deanna had headed across the open floor to the plane.

"She's around."

"I can't wait to see you again," she said.

The horn sounded.

"Gotta run, honey. We're having a meeting."

Lt. Elliott strode over. He tapped his wrist.

"Love you," Ronan said.

"Love you, too."

"Say bye to Ziggy for me."

"Bye?"

But Ronan had disconnected and was hurrying to the plane. Last to board.

Lisa examined a pair of nice leather Chelsea boots and glanced at the price tag. They were cool as hell, and Ronan would look great in them, but they were two weeks' salary. Maybe it was too much. But he would love them.

She guessed he would probably arrive home within a few hours, so she shouldn't take too long to find him a gift.

If there was one gift that always seemed to go over well, it was a new pair of shoes.

She spied a pair of black combat boots. *Wow, look at those.* They were rugged, slightly worn looking, not all shiny and new. Zipper up the side. Oily laces. All leather. $550. You could kick some ass in them, she thought, and look good doing it. *Maybe these could help remind him what it was like to be in the military.*

He had been honorably discharged from the military by the time they had met. She remembered back to those days. He was barely holding it together and all the action-hero stuff had drained out of him. In fact, he had been just a few steps away from hitting rock bottom.

She had been riding behind a man on the escalator. He hadn't been paying attention as he neared the top, and when his feet hit the floor, he had pitched forward.

The moment came back to her in horror. Not because he had landed hard on the ground, but because of what she had said to him. She'd simply hoped to relieve his embarrassment.

Hey, she'd laughed. Did you just learn to walk or something?

Then he'd turned and looked up at her with the strangest gaze, one that chilled her to her core. Just complete emptiness.

He was talking but seemed in a daze. Like a robot.

No, I just got these new legs and I guess I'm still learning how to use them.
The words had cut right through her.
Oh my god, let me help you up! She led him over to a chair.
See? he said, pulling up a pant leg. A piece of beige plastic protruded from his pants, a metal rod extending to the shoe.
What happened? Of course, it had been rude for her to ask, but it just came out.
Motorcycle accident.
I'm so sorry about the joke, I had no idea.
What joke?
About learning to walk.
I didn't even hear it.
Say, are you okay? Did you bump your head? You seem kind of out of it.
And on it went from there.

There was something about this guy, despite the dazed look, that seemed genuine and deep. He was also rugged and good looking. She wanted to talk a bit more.

One thing led to another, first dates, then more dates, then falling in love, then moving in together and fights and make-ups and Ronan having night terrors, screaming in the middle of the night, flailing his stumps, overly paranoid about vehicle safety, especially motorcycles.

And he went off on long trips for work. He found a job as a technical officer for the DIA, which gave him a taste of excitement, but he promised her he was never in danger. He was just a "data collector." He said he was like the guy who comes to the door to ask about the census. He asked questions and filed reports and that was it.

She loved him, but it was stressful not knowing where the hell he was or when he would be home.

What, she asked herself, was she looking for in a relationship? Maybe not someone who jetted off at a moment's notice for indefinite periods of time.

Most importantly, his augmentations weighed on her. At first, she didn't think anything of them. The first ones were necessary. He'd lost his legs, so he needed artificial limbs. She didn't mind them.

But gradually she had become aware of something else. The way he viewed technology was almost religious. He'd installed a couple things that hadn't quite made sense. At least, not for a census collector.

Oxygen booster? Reinforced knuckles? What was up with that? He had said he had left his military fighting days behind.

So why?

He'd said he was testing a vision, an idea. Possibilities.

Beyond that, he didn't say much. Maybe he didn't know himself.

Or maybe he wasn't being totally honest with her.

It was so hard to figure out where he was coming from…

She knew his former fiancée had been in the military. She'd been tough. Ronan had shown Lisa some pictures of Chloe, photos of the two of them that he had saved, and Lisa would never have asked him to delete those photos. Memories were important, even memories of a former love.

But when she had searched for "Deanna Pirelli," his new partner on this mission – she was unsure why she'd searched in the first place – she noticed something immediately. Deanna was a tough chick with a shockingly similar resemblance to Chloe.

She had suddenly panicked. Ronan was going to be spending a lot of alone time with someone who seemed a hell of a lot like his former fiancée.

Didn't she trust him?

She wasn't sure. But why not?

Because there was a chance, maybe, that they weren't right for each other after all.

She wasn't sure what to expect when he came home. She hated doubting their relationship.

But she did.

Turbulence rocked the jet as it flew through the thunderstorm. Lightning flashed and Ronan glanced out a rain-streaked window. Thousands of feet below, though he could only catch dark glimpses, the Amazon rainforest stretched for endless miles. The birds and animals and insects would be hunkered down, taking shelter among the wet leaves, waiting for the rain to end. The deluge, he knew, though no one wanted to say it, was turning the Brazilian forest into gloppy mud. Cutting through that mess was not going to be fun.

In the adjacent seat, Sergeant Anton Amelio, their guide, noticed him looking out the window. "This weather will be over soon," Amelio said over the engine and wind noise. "The storm complicates things, but at least the clouds will help give us cover in case they have scouts with long-range scopes."

A member of the Brazilian Special Ops Command, Amelio was the team navigator from landing point to the compound. He had been in the states when the team was quickly assembled and had agreed to join the operation to lend his expertise on the route's terrain and vegetation.

The plane shuddered, dropped, stabilized. Thunder rumbled and lightning flashed.

The team members were strapped into their seats along both sides of the cabin. They avoided each other's eyes, each running the mission over in their mind. The eight SEALs, led by Lt. Elliott, would lead the advance into the interior of the Kazite's compound, improvising the route from room to room as needed. The compound's inner layout was unknown. There was no telling who or what they would encounter inside. Sergeant Fulsom, a serious young man with an intense stare, would take point during the entire operation.

Deanna and Ronan would play a backup role if they engaged any hostiles. Their primary job was to prioritize the retrieval of hardware, paper records, and other evidence. And Ronan would be there to talk to Harper, if needed. Like some kind of friendly hostage negotiator.

Lt. Elliott checked his mic, called everyone's names, verified comm. He had already checked twice before during the flight. The gear and weapons were stowed away in the gliders, so there wasn't much to do but sit, wait for 0735, and test the comms one more time.

Ronan glanced at his watch. Ten minutes to jump time.

He had to take a serious piss. *Too bad for that.*

The TurboGlides were secured to the floor in single file. Each consisted of a rigid, clay-colored stealth shell with two short wings. It mounted on a soldier like an enormous backpack, creating the look of a streamlined, aerodynamic beetle. The hard shells encased and protected not only the soldier, but the weapons and supplies as well – assault rifles, battle rifles, grenades, water. Everything snapped up tight in the underside of the shell.

The TurboGlides used four microturbine engines to boost their glide capacity, giving them a range of forty to fifty miles depending on jump height and wind speed. While this op would use a slow approach, they could be punched to 125 mph if needed.

For Ronan and Deanna, the most important feature of the TurboGlides was that they required no training. Each unit would supposedly – *hopefully* – stabilize itself during free fall, settle into a glide, boost when needed, take them to their destination, and identify an ideal landing location within the target area.

Lt. Elliott had reassured them that the units were completely self-sufficient. "If a child was strapped into one and pushed out of a plane," he said, "the unit would land itself with no input from the child whatsoever. But if you need to juice the speed or steer it a little, go ahead. When I give the signal, we'll coordinate our landing by hitting this button here."

"What about a two hundred and twenty-pound guy with another

seventy pounds of equipment?" Ronan had asked. "Will this thing be stable with a load like that? I don't want to spin like a top."

"They'll carry three times that weight without problem."

Ronan's X-Rifle was secured inside the glider, along with the rest of his weapons. He was itching to try the X in the field, but he wasn't itching to engage the enemy. Their mission was to collect leads and get out. Let the missile do the killing. Ideally, his gun would go unused. But it was pretty damn cool. He didn't even need to get the crosshairs on the right body part – he had pre-set the rifle to *headshot*, and a perfect headshot it would be, every time.

If those techno-hating Kazites attacked, they were going to get their asses kicked.

Ronan smiled, imagining this. He loved experimental weapons...

Deanna was sitting on his other side, hands in her lap. She hadn't spoken or moved in ten minutes. She hadn't spoken or moved much during the entire flight. He wasn't sure why he had come on this mission. Was it to get the leads? Watch her back? Make sure she survived? Or maybe he just didn't want her to get all the glory? Or maybe he didn't want to let her go?

Lt. Elliott studied his watch carefully. He unbuckled from his seat, stood, and said, "Five minutes to launch. Take your jump position."

The SEALs lined up with Fulsom in the lead spot. Sgt. Amelio took his place behind the SEALs, followed by Ronan, then Deanna. Lt. Elliott took the back.

Ronan crouched into a sitting position and slid into his glider as they'd demonstrated. He pulled the straps across his body and snapped them into place. *Click, click.* He pulled the air supply from the side of the unit and secured it to his mouth. He adjusted his helmet strap and mic, tugged his body straps, lowered the visor, and checked the glider straps again. His hands briefly tapped the pistol strapped to his belt.

He secured the visor. His heart rate increased.

"Go time," Lt. Elliott said.

The jump door opened at the rear of the plane. Wind and rain tore into the cabin as it lowered, drenching the walls. Ronan was back far enough that only a few drops sprayed against his exposed cheeks.

At the front of the line, Fulsom stood and grabbed the guide wire. Ronan watched over the row of gliders in front of him, seeing only the wings and body of Fulsom's glider moving up and down as he took position at the edge of the precipice.

A moment later, Fulsom's glider dropped from view.

Ronan felt a knot in his stomach. Like Deanna, he had extensive military parachute training. He had dropped from many planes in simulation exercises, but he had never executed a strike operation launched from the air, had never leapt into a storm like this, and had never worn or operated a TurboGlide.

One by one, the SEALs stepped forward, their heads hidden behind their gliders, and dropped out of sight.

Sgt. Amelio was next. He stood, found the guide wire, and made his way to the jump platform. He hesitated, shifting the enormous glider on his back. With no one else between them, Ronan had a clear view of Amelio's legs as he steadied himself and prepared to jump. There was no point in adjusting before the leap. You were either strapped in or you weren't, and the glider would either get you safely to the ground, or it wouldn't.

Sgt. Amelio jumped.

Ronan stood and worked his way forward, with nothing now between him and the enormous black stormy hole. His heart raced. *Showtime.*

Deanna would be watching him advance, readying herself.

On the platform now. *Steady, don't hesitate, just go.* Ronan's legs were jelly. *Nothing wrong with that, nerves were normal.* He inched closer to the edge, gripping the guide wire, the rain and wind slamming him, saw the endless stretch of forest racing below, shifted his glider on his back. He saw his left foot perched on the edge, the very edge, and that was it.

He stepped into the maelstrom.

He fell, whipping and flipping and turning in the wind and rain and blackness, water flying off his flight suit.

His visor streaked and fogged, but he could see the dark blurs of the men below him. The jungle canopy careened into view, and he instinctively grabbed for a ripcord that wasn't there. Then he calmed enough to tuck his arms and legs close to his sides, and the TurboGlide – *thank God* – took over as promised. The unit stabilized, jet pack on top, him underneath facing down.

One by one, the gliders below him activated their engines, blue lights ringing the exhaust ports on either side of the beetle shell, and the men slowed in their downward plummets and leveled off.

As the trees raced toward him, gnarled and dark and wind-whipped and angry, his glider's own engines kicked in. He leveled off and the unit began a confident glide.

Tilting his body, the wings lifted, and he caught sight of Deanna speeding past him against the dark clouds above. Lt. Elliott was below, a blur through rain streaks. He gave Ronan a thumbs up, which Ronan returned. Moments later, they had all leveled off and were speeding over the tops of the trees, close enough to reach out and touch the branches, close enough to evade radar. The mission was underway. Seven miles to go. Then, they would drop to the forest floor and approach the compound on foot through three miles of dense forest.

Deanna spoke in his ear. "Thank God these things know what they're doing."

The others laughed, but Lt. Elliott chimed in, "No chatter. Five minutes of flight time remaining."

Ronan looked behind him and confirmed he was last in line. He opened his fly and took a long, satisfying whizz. Rain streamed off his helmet. Deanna was right. Good thing the glider knew where it was going because visibility was terrible.

Activating PulseView, he set the frequency to 60 GHz and the radio waves whipped through the raindrops to the trees below. He saw the jungle pop into stark relief, a massive tangle of black and white forms, dense with birds and animals among the leaves. Switching back to normal view, all of it disappeared into sheets of rain.

Moments later, the rain slowed to a drizzle. They were flying away from the storm.

Ronan tapped the thrusters and shot ahead of Lt. Elliott. He watched the speed display inside his visor and brought the glider to 95 mph. He scouted the canopy for any sign of Deanna. The sun was breaking through, but now fog billowed up from the hot jungle floor.

He spotted her, jacked his speed and caught up. The line of flyers ahead disappeared into fog rising in thick swirls from the canopy.

Ronan tapped his fingers and a status summary floated over the trees: 7:48 am local time. The helmet monitor indicated they were getting damn close.

He emerged from the fog and saw Deanna cruising just above the branches, keeping a low profile. Startled birds blasted out of the trees behind her.

"Yo, Deanna. Pull up a bit. You're making noise."

"Sorry." She angled up and leveled off ten feet above the trees.

"You're good," Ronan said.

"Two minutes." Elliot's voice crackled over the comm. "Red eagle to silver, do you copy?"

"Roger," Fulsom responded.

Lt. Elliott confirmed a comm connection with each member of the team, then said, "Red eagle is in lead position. We land in 1,000 yards..."

The trees rushed below them, sparkling in their newfound rays of sun.

"900 yards..."

"800..."

Ronan placed his hand on the large button on his shoulder strap, as instructed.

"Zero... activate land function!"

Ronan hit the button.

Immediately the team streamed off to Ronan's right without him, their units heading toward some unseen break in the trees, an open area that would serve as a soft and safe landing area.

Ronan's unit continued straight ahead. He craned his neck to look backward, hoping to see if anyone was with him, but they had all veered off together.

"What the hell...?" Ronan mumbled and pressed the land button again. The unit immediately descended into the trees. "Not here!" he yelled.

"Ronan, what's your–"

With a crash, Ronan hit a massive tree limb, taking the full impact on his prosthetic legs. He felt both legs rip free as he careened down.

A second later: *Impact.*

Chapter 58

The Amazon
3.1 miles north of the Kazite compound
4 hours, 10 minutes to missile impact

Ronan writhed. His back was in searing pain and his arms felt as though they had been pummeled with baseball bats. The flight suit was shredded and his thighs burned like they had been de-skinned with a power sander. The back of his head throbbed, too. It had whipped backward and smashed against the glider when he first hit the trees.

He groaned and unsnapped himself from the harness. He pulled away from the glider and gave the unit a shove. *Piece of shit. Couldn't handle the rain on its sensors.*

He found his canteen locked safely in an underside compartment and took a swig, then removed all his weapons, his binoculars, his battery packs. He laid everything out on the damp leaves of the forest floor.

Beep!

A voice called over the headset. "Red one to Red nine, you copy?"

"I'm here," Ronan answered. "Had a rough landing. Alive but assessing damage. My equipment looks like it was well-protected by the glider. I wish I could say the same for myself."

"We have a read on your location. We'll come there. Stay put."

"Roger that," Ronan said.

He unzipped his flight suit, pulled himself out, balled it up, and tossed it into the bushes. The suit was waterproof and most of his clothes underneath were still dry. Glancing around at the water pouring out of the canopy above, dripping down from limb to limb to the wet muddy earth, he knew he wouldn't stay dry for long.

His leg armor was banged up and empty, hanging from his torso like spent balloons.

He felt helpless. There was nothing to do but wait. And scan the trees for legs.

As he lay there, looking up into the dripping trees, he saw a flash of bright yellow. It moved from branch to branch, stopped, then continued behind the leaves.

Was that...?

He propped up for a better look and zoomed in, but when he did so, he lost his bearings in the monotonous spread of leaves and trees. He zoomed back out.

It had looked like a flycatcher, maybe. He caught another glimpse. Sure looked like a flycatcher. Gone now.

After about ten minutes, he heard crashing and thrashing in the trees. Ronan grabbed his assault rifle and aimed it toward the sounds. The movements didn't indicate an animal: too much whacking and shuffling. He heard voices, but couldn't tell what they were saying, couldn't identify the language.

He kept the gun trained on the sounds until Fulsom appeared, followed by Lt. Elliot, the other SEALs, and Deanna. They all looked fresh and ready to go, as though they had taken a first-class flight to the jungle.

"Goddamn, Ronan," Fulsom said. "This is how you should look at the end of a mission, not the beginning."

They gathered around him, watching the woods. They were still pretty far from the compound, surrounded by miles of dense vegetation, but you never knew who might be lurking.

One of the SEALs saw Ronan's leg-stubs and couldn't contain his horrified reaction. "What the fuck happened?"

Deanna pushed through the men and knelt beside him. "He has prosthetics."

"*Had*," Ronan corrected. "All right everybody, I never thought I would say this: fan out and help me find my legs."

The team split up and canvased the area, searching through every fork in every tree, every dark space under dripping bush. They soon found the exact spot he had careened down from the heavens, snapping everything in his path, and focused their efforts on the immediate surroundings.

"Here's one," Lt. Elliott said. He reached up and pulled the appendage out of a tree. It was scratched and dented and covered in mud and leaves.

Ronan forced it on. "My legs took a direct hit. Good thing they weren't real."

"Will they even work?" Deanna asked.

Ronan shot her a concerned glance. "If not, I'm not going very far."

The other leg was retrieved from a gloppy puddle and passed man to man to Ronan.

Deanna helped him secure both legs and stand, wobbly, back to his feet. Then she made him remove his helmet and conducted a thorough examination, her face close to his, her breath on his cheek, evaluating a large cut on his forehead. She ran her fingers over his hands, flipping them over and studying several gashes sustained when he had held his hands in front of his face during the crash.

"Thank you. I'm fine," he said. "Let's get the hell out of here. We are wasting a ton of time."

"Correct," Lt. Elliott said. "We are fifteen minutes behind schedule. Let's move out."

They headed into the woods in single file, back in the direction the team had come, following the cleared space they had just made. The air was stifling. Water plopped steadily from the branches, and birds and animals were now out in force, flitting and scampering overhead. Sunbeams had started to pour through the trees. It was getting hotter by the second.

...

Soon they were back at the team's main landing point. They collapsed their hardshell gliders and stowed them in the brush. Each unit would send out its location with a recovery signal and be retrieved later. They were far too expensive to abandon. The operatives covered the units with branches and spread the leaves around on the ground as much as possible, covering their tracks and other evidence.

"The Kazite compound is about three miles that way," Amelio said, gesturing boldly with a chop of his arm. "There's a trail about one mile from here. Once we find that, we'll take it the rest of the way. We can't bushwhack all the way from here to the compound. There's not enough time. We'll take our chances on the trail and hope they don't have any scouts hiding in the trees."

Several of the team nodded and everyone lined up single file to continue the trek.

"The jungle is harder to navigate after a rain," Amelio added. "The mud will make it rough going."

Lt. Elliott glanced impatiently at his watch as they disappeared into the forest.

···

They took turns at the front of the line, whacking the trees with machetes. Ronan's legs were glitchy and didn't bend smoothly, and the fit was loose. He fiddled with them constantly, thinking they might fall off at any moment.

The torrential downpour had turned the paths into slick mud. Everyone slid and slipped.

Because a sniper might take a shot at them at any point, they kept their helmets on. They had brought mesh face wraps, but they hadn't donned those yet. It was too damn hot. They would put them on before entering the compound to protect their skin against microdrone attacks.

Ronan eyed the swarms of bugs in the air. To take his mind off the millions of flying things around them, he scanned the trees for snipers.

The flycatcher was back. Ronan spotted it in the trees about ten feet off the ground; he zoomed in and fired off a series of photos that captured all of the bird's diagnostic features. Positive ID: *Tolmomyias Sucunduri.*

"I wonder if anyone has seen the flycatcher this far upriver?" he wondered out loud.

"Oh, my god, Ronan. Really?" Deanna said over the comm.

He didn't respond. Instead, he tapped his fingers and banged out a quick text to Lisa. *Lk what I found.*

Less than a minute later, her reply popped up on his vision: *awesome honey.*

That will keep her from worrying, he thought.

...

2.2 MILES TO COMPOUND
3 HOURS, 34 MINUTES TO MISSILE IMPACT

Bushwhacking, Ronan soon learned, was extremely slow work made even slower by the ever-present clock ticking down in your mind. They had been going for twenty eight minutes and were already showing signs of significant fatigue. Ronan wondered if Elliott and Amelio had underestimated how long the trek to the compound would take.

Amelio stopped. He swatted flies away from his face.

"Why did you stop?" Croft asked. He was a burly guy with three rifles and a grenade launcher strapped to his back. He scanned the trees.

Amelio completed his assessment of his surroundings, nodded to himself, and announced, "The first stage is complete. We made it to the trail."

Ronan and Deanna looked around. "Are you sure this is the trail? There's no difference."

"In the rainforest, the plants grow very fast." Amelio answered. "This is the trail. It is better, a little."

They kept going, following a path that Amelio swore was a trail, continuing to slash the path with machetes, too focused for conversation.

Their trek took them up and down small slippery hills. The forest occasionally showed glimpses of a rocky ravine on their right. Streams and streamlets born from the recent rain wound down from the left, crossed the trail, and found their way to the ravine. The group crossed these streams with slow cautious steps; even their jungle boots could not prevent a nasty slip. Listening carefully over the buzzing of insects and the calls of birds, they heard the trickling of small, spontaneous waterfalls.

"You see that ravine?" Amelio called out. "We will cross that soon. The sides of the ravine become quite steep as it cuts over to the northwest. The bridge there is a key landmark. At that point, we will be only one mile from the compound. We should put on our face wraps soon after. Our risk of being detected will increase exponentially."

...

As they stumbled along in silence, the machetes whacking in constant rhythm, Ronan became more vigilant. He scanned the bushes and trees for any sign of human movement. According to Amelio, it would be easy to detect the movement of a human ducking behind a tree. The jungle was full of busy birds and other creatures that moved within the chaotic pattern of trees and branches, but if a person shifted against this backdrop, it would be like a flare going off. So he watched, and so did the others.

He tried to identify differences among all these trees and leaves. Most of the rain forest was nondescript, just endless branches and bushes, but the standouts were the giant kapok trees, which fanned out like rocket fins at the base, shot up 200 feet and blasted out of the canopy with an explosion of branches and vines. Someone could hide up there and rain hell down on you, Ronan thought.

The pungent, earthy smells of wet leaves and rotting wood surrounded and enveloped them. The canopy above was full of light and life, but down here on the ground, it was death and darkness. This was the home of moss and mushrooms.

The team marched along the trail past massive fallen trees, now just hollow trunks with nooks harboring scores of species. The trees, the endless piles of leaf litter, the creatures that had died and fallen from the treetops, all the detritus that had collected on the forest floor around them was being eaten. Fungi, bacteria, termites, and worms by the billions were working away at it, breaking it all down piece by piece.

Ronan could not stop thinking of all the bugs and felt the urge to get a better look at the world around him. He turned on PulseView at the highest sensitivity. Anything bigger than a gnat that moved was now rendered in sharp contrast to the dead surroundings. Immediately he was overwhelmed. He knew there were millions of species of insects in the Amazon, but it was one thing to read about it, and quite another to actually see all that shit crawling around. Now that the rain had stopped, countless species emerged from their hiding places.

There were centipedes large and small and other multi-legged things he didn't recognize. Some of the centipedes were huge, hanging from leaves, waiting to catch birds. And ants – there were ants everywhere, marching in great hordes to devour everything in their path, crawling everywhere, eating, being eaten.

There must have been millions of spiders skittering on leaves; they were everywhere too, and every one of them watched with a headful of eyes that PulseView highlighted in hyper detail. There were jumping, hairy spiders crawling among the fallen litter, hunting mice. Dozens of smaller spiders dangled and twisted like circus performers from massive webs that engulfed entire trees.

He flipped off PulseView. Looking at all that stuff had been a dumb idea, he realized. He liked the forest a lot better when all he saw were trees.

The mosquitos grew thicker. The team had entered a cloud of them, and soon every bare hand and cheek was covered with the biting insects. Why were mosquitos landing on skin sprayed with one hundred percent DEET? Were these not mosquitos? The thought was reason enough to panic, but no one did: they brushed them off with feigned indifference, as quick as their SEAL coolness allowed.

Ronan had been bitten repeatedly. He began to imagine he had been infected, that nanoweapons were circulating inside him, pulsing through his blood vessels, searching his body for a target organ. Finally, he said to

Deanna, half joking, "I think I feel them inside me. My body is tingling."

She smiled. "No, that's just because I'm here."

He smiled and kept trudging forward, eager to get out of this godforsaken, bug-infested place.

...

1.3 MILES TO COMPOUND
2 HOURS, 52 MINUTES TO MISSILE IMPACT

They were a half hour behind schedule but getting close. The group proceeded with more caution.

The trail had never become a trail, and the group at the front continued to slash with machetes. Ronan and Deanna took a turn to help.

Bushwhacking was not quiet. They were probably announcing their approach. After a few minutes, Ronan's arms burned, and he returned to his place in line toward the back. Damn legs were still acting up, too, wiggling this way and that.

The humidity had become nearly unbearable. Sweat trickled down his back, arms, chest, and cheeks. Why would anyone, even an insane terrorist, deliberately pick such a godforsaken shithole to call home?

A small spider crawled up his shirt sleeve. He smashed it and bent close. He had crushed it too violently to identify what was left. Nothing looked like wires, plastic, or metal.

He took another swig from his canteen.

...

1 MILE TO COMPOUND
2 HOURS, 12 MINUTES TO MISSILE IMPACT

They were hacking through the jungle, vine by vine, stepping forward root by root, and the clock was ticking down at warp speed. They might never reach their destination at this pace.

"We are at the bridge," Amelio said over the comm, looking at his GPS.

Ronan was surprised. They were? The bridge? Where? Then he saw the rotting, wooden beams peeking through the foliage here and there, around them and under their feet. The bridge was covered in so much dense overgrowth, he hadn't even realized they were passing over it. The bridge was just a series of rough-hewn planks with no railing, covered by moss and leaves. Tall bushes had grown up from the sides and through the slats, creating a darkened tunnel little different from anything else they had navigated so far.

Amelio had crossed to the other side. "It's sound, but watch for gaps and rot."

They all advanced carefully, guiding each other, offering hands to steady the way.

Ronan didn't see the river, but heard it, crashing through the ravine beneath them.

Judging by the sound of the water splashing over the rocks, they were thirty or forty feet up. He was careful not to step on any soggy boards that looked particularly weak. The planks looked like they hadn't been put to the test in years.

Ronan wondered how old the bridge was. Maybe they should have crossed one person at a time. He zoomed in and noticed fresh notches on some of the planks. The notches secured vines that disappeared into a nearby gap. Peering through the gap, he saw that hewn poles supported the bridge underneath, but these were bound with taut vines that stretched off at various angles.

Just as he stood to inform the others, he heard splitting sounds from below. The bridge rocked with a stomach-turning twist to the left, then rocked the other way, then collapsed.

CHAPTER 59

As the footbridge gave way, Ronan lost his footing and grabbed at the overgrowth. Just ahead of him, a SEAL named Schroeder toppled over the side. The man never made a sound, just fell through the vegetation and disappeared.

Ronan soon realized that the bridge had not fallen into the ravine, but dropped only a few feet. He clung to the vines and small trees to steady himself and quickly assessed the situation. The wooden structure seemed to have dislodged from the far edge, but the thick tangle of vegetation held the structure in place from one side to the other. Many of the underlying boards had fallen away. The group was hanging suspended on a living bridge of plants. Like him, Deanna was lying on her side, clinging to the vines. Their eyes met and they gave each other a thumbs up.

Lt. Elliot, Fulsom, Amelio, and the others crawled to a better position on the tight twisted mass. It rolled a bit as they pulled themselves into place on top. One by one, they nodded to each other and got their bearings.

Amelio spoke first. He was somewhere ahead. "We should not have crossed at the same time. This thing could collapse at any second. Fulsom, proceed carefully while the rest of us hold still." He had stated the obvious in a lecturing tone and it wasn't his place to give orders. The SEAL team members had long ago worked out their protocols for most situations and they could make their next move with minimal communication. Nevertheless, they had just fucked up and they knew it.

The structure felt too unstable to lean out and try to determine Schroeder's fate. He could have fallen into the river and been swept downstream, or might have hit rocks, or maybe was clinging to the underside. They would have to figure that out once they were safely on the far side.

At the front of the line, Fulsom was proceeding forward while the others held their positions. Three of the SEALs had binoculars out, looking, Ronan assumed, for an approaching ambush. The only clear view was the sky overhead. The rest of the team had their weapons at the ready.

Ronan stood on wobbly legs and pulled some of the brush back. This gave a limited view of the ravine's edge. He switched to PulseView and scanned the forest for hostiles. The radar unit embedded in his forehead sprayed radio waves outward, rendering the lush green trees and brush into black and white. He removed stationary objects to bring moving forms into stark relief. Figures shifted in the bushes. At least a dozen of them.

Black and white streaks sailed through the air in their direction. "Incoming!" Ronan yelled.

Flaming arrows hit the bridge in dozens of spots. The team members clung to the structure and tried to shoot through the vegetation at the same time. Ramos' rifle jammed; he threw it in disgust and pulled a second one off his back.

The entire leafy structure was soon ablaze. Despite the recent rain, there was enough dead, sheltered vegetation to catch fire. Ronan made his way to Deanna and together they navigated the flaming patches where arrows had hit. The structure leaned one way and then the other as the team scrambled forward. None of their movements were coordinated. Billowing smoke burned Ronan's nostrils. The SEALs inched ahead, flaming arrows hitting around them, some dangerously close, others whistling past and disappearing into the ravine.

Fulsom was almost to the far side. A chopping sound echoed through the ravine, then a violent snap detonated. Ronan heard cracking and splitting and the sounds of leaves ripping and tearing. An enormous tree emerged from the forest. It missed the structure and tumbled into the ravine. A massive chunk of earth and roots tore free along with it.

There was another severe *snap*, and another tree, this one coming from behind them, crashed downward. It hit the mass directly, crushing bushes and ripping vines from the ravine's edges. The footbridge shuddered with the impact. Ronan pitched forward into a flaming patch but managed to stumble through it and grab on tight again. The other team members also held firm.

The tangled mass felt tighter and more stable. The SEALs were securing better holds and firing more confidently into the trees, although the angle was not ideal. Lt. Elliott detached a drone from his pack and tossed it into the air. The machine rose, arrows whistling past it, and once above the gorge, unleashed a short burst of gunfire. It rotated left and right, spraying into the brush.

The drone flew into the woods and continued shooting. The drone was small and didn't hold much ammo. With luck, Ronan thought, it would find and kill those who had ambushed them before they could signal the others in the compound. But the SEALs couldn't count on such luck.

They had all made their way across the footbridge and now pulled themselves up the side of the ravine, grabbing ahold of small trees, bushes, and roots. They regrouped at the top. Only Schroeder was missing. Fulsom dropped a pocket drone into the ravine. They soon found him motionless on a rocky patch in the middle of the river. "I'll go down for him," Ramos said. He paused, processing the situation. "You guys keep going."

As they resumed their bushwhacking on the overgrown trail, a small patch of trees shook, and a man took off running. The SEALs opened fire and let him have it in the back, shredding the leaves and trees around him into pitiful strips.

"No longer matters how much noise we make," Lt. Elliott said. "Shoot anyone you see."

"Copy," Fulsom agreed.

They continued toward the compound, now less than a mile away. They were banged up and rattled and down two men. They were pissed and ready to unleash hell on anyone who got in their way.

CHAPTER 60

Ten minutes later they found the drone caught in a net tangled around the upper branches of a Kapok tree. The machine was too high to retrieve quickly, and they couldn't use it in the compound, so the SEALs simply pointed and marched on.

Ronan paused to zoom in for a closer look. The net was fashioned from thin vines and homespun fibers twisted into tight cords that interlocked every few inches, with golf ball-sized rocks bound into the edges. The tangled mess hung among the leaves as if the net had been thrown from the ground, and Ronan marveled that the Kazites had somehow managed to catch the drone at such a height.

Soon after, the dense jungle gave way to a large, open field. The team got their first view of the imposing compound – wide and low, built from sturdy, split logs bound with cords. Several narrow wooden doors were spaced out along the front wall. The doors looked simple, not reinforced, and wouldn't be hard to breach. Ronan made a quick measurement of the building, the dimensions glowing in his vision: 362 feet wide, ten-foot walls, another fifteen feet of dirt and vegetation on top of that. The depth of the building could not be determined from his vantage point. The roof was alive with trees, bushes, and a dense tangle of weeds and grasses, as though the jungle had hopped over the field and taken root on top of the compound, devouring and hiding it from above.

Damn this thing was huge.

The area directly in front of the building looked like some sort of meeting area. Tree stumps had been arranged in rows, and a target was set up at the front, a hatchet sticking out of it. Something hung from the target.

Further up the hill, Ronan saw large holes everywhere. The Kazites probably had tunnels running all over the place.

The SEALs gestured to each other and took positions on the periphery, crouching low behind the brush. Ronan listened on the comm as they confirmed their next moves. To his left, Lt. Elliott scanned the compound. "No movement," he said.

The SEALs prepared for the attack with well-rehearsed procedures, adjusting their Zylon armor, checking weapons, loading ammo, and storing away their binoculars. Ronan and Deanna helped each other prepare.

Everyone wore a high-cut helmet that left the lower face and neck exposed and vulnerable. So before going any further, they retrieved their face wraps. These stretched across the nose, mouth, and neck, providing a twenty-micron nylon mesh that made it possible to breath, but would keep out any weaponized microdrones, including a mosquito with a forty-micron proboscis. Of course, the face wraps did nothing to protect against bullets, knives, or any other traditional weapon.

The team pulled on plasticized gloves for additional skin protection. The face wrap and gloves made the jungle even hotter and itchier.

Ronan activated PulseView. "Hold on, there's a shitload of them on the roof."

"Where?" Lt. Elliott adjusted his bins. "Can you tell what they're doing?"

"Nothing. Watching us."

The SEALs exchanged glances and gestures. They adjusted position.

"We could shoot a 4-50 up there," one of them said in the comm.

Lt. Elliott shook his head. "Negative. A detonation would kick the anthill, rile them up and compromise the integrity of the structure. Shoot three gas grenades onto the roof."

Two men emerged from the trees about a hundred yards away, riding horses, seemingly unaware of the SEAL team in the woods. Ronan and the others froze. The men stopped at a makeshift hitching post and dismounted. After a few glances around and a study of the woods in the general direction of the SEALs, they hustled inside a door.

Lt. Elliott spoke on the comm: "Plan review. Stop to the left of the

nearest door, breach, then enter the compound. Clear each room, proceed
to the next, push the Kazites further in. Look for any place where records,
material, electronics, or other objects of interest might be stashed or stored.
Flynn and Pirelli take lead on prioritizing and retrieving any material
deemed worthy of bringing back for analysis. We need to be out by 1130.
Check your face wrap periodically in case we see any flying bugs in
there."

On signal, Croft launched a canister of tear gas into the air. It landed
in the roof-top jungle and spewed a noxious purple cloud through the
leaves of the brush. With a whistle, the next canister landed twenty feet to
the north, and then another landed further beyond that.

Ronan studied the trees. "They're disappearing. Yup, all gone. Into
the anthill."

Lt. Elliott fired smoke grenades onto the field and the team, with
Fulsom in lead, ran in a crouch across the open space, past the horses, and
gathered near the door that the two Kazites had just entered.

Toward the rear, Ronan and Deanna sprinted and flopped themselves
against the wall next to the SEALs. Ronan's heart pounded and sweat ran
into his eyes. From here, he got a better look at the Kazite's outdoor
meeting area – the rows of tree-stump stools, the target board with painted
bullseye, the embedded hatchet, and a hairy human head hanging like a
black mop. Flies dotted the face.

Lt. Elliott was last to join the group. They pulled down their night
vision goggles and Ronan activated PulseView. Moments later, a strip
charge burst the door inward with a loud crack.

They entered the compound and fanned out. As Ronan stepped in, an
arrow flew from a dark corner, and he flung himself against the left-hand
wall. Deanna joined him. Fulsom and Croft, the first in, shot everything
that moved. Three or four Kazites, crossbows raised, twitched with each
hit and crumpled to the ground. A hulk of a man appeared in a doorway.
Ronan zoomed in on the man's tattooed face and saw the word
FREEDOM on his cheek, but the word transformed into a bloody bullet
hole.

The room became smoke and flying debris and popping lights and deafening sound.

The remaining Kazites tried to escape, but were hit with single shots – *pop, pop, pop* – and they dropped like shell casings to the floor. Several more emerged from the doorway in a suicidal run and loosed arrows on the SEALs, but their heads jerked back with each bullet from Fulsom and Croft, who took them out as easily as a child pops soap bubbles with a finger. Afterward, the SEALs lifted their goggles, pressed on their LED rifle lights, and surveyed the room. The bodies lay soaking red on the floor, the glint of their blood sparkling in the focused beams.

With speed and precision, the SEALs cut fingers and scalps and hair. Every DNA sample was a lead. Ronan opened the dead Kazites' eyelids and scanned their irises in high-res. These images might give biometric access to any devices salvaged from the compound. He scanned faces and fingertips as well.

The team, Ronan noticed from the back of the pack, was advancing in a controlled fashion under Lt. Elliott's silent guidance. Within the first twenty seconds they had killed at least a dozen of the enemy, and now they were sweeping room two, destroying it with the brutal onslaught of their semi-automatic weapons. The Kazites fired off a few arrows but were soon backing away in hasty retreat or dancing in gunfire.

Ronan and Deanna held their weapons at the ready, but did not fire, letting the SEALs do their job. Ronan was okay with this arrangement. He had no intention of getting into any volleys if he could help it. The situation was surreal, watching the action occur around him as though he were immersed in a VR game.

A minute later the battle was over and the team re-grouped.

"Crossbow versus MK18 assault rifle," Croft laughed, patting his weapon. "This is a massacre."

Several of the crossbows were lying in the blood. They were simple devices with few parts; the stock was thick and sturdy, the cross-piece thin and flexible. A shallow notch held the string taut. Fulsom picked up an arrow, inspected it, then tossed it down.

"Anything to worry about?" one of the SEALs asked.

Fulsom nodded. "Sure. If they hit your windpipe or carotids."

The team glanced around at the arrows on the ground but seemed little bothered by them.

Tense but ready, Ronan scanned the room and doorways, wondering from which direction a threat might approach. The walls, constructed of wood and stone, were grungy and moldy and covered in artwork – genitalia, stars and comets, flowers, mushrooms, bushes and trees, and a whole kingdom of stick figures standing or sitting in groups. Something hung from the wall. As best as Ronan could tell, it was the dried skin from someone's face, stretched by hooks from the eye holes and mouth.

Taking advantage of the lull, Ronan reached for a small water pack on Deanna's belt.

"What's the matter?" she asked.

"Nothing."

"What?"

"Nothing..."

"Did you put a tick on my water?"

"Yes. If you get separated, I can find you."

She ripped off the water pack. "You take it, in case I need to find *you*."

"No."

She threw it on the muddy floor.

Ronan looked at it. "You need your water..."

"You swore you wouldn't do that again."

Ronan said nothing.

She turned away. "Don't worry about me. Watch your own ass."

There was no time to argue. Lt. Elliott gestured for them to shut up. The SEALs had lined up to head around the next corner.

CHAPTER 61

Lt. Elliott placed his shoulder against the wall and lifted his rifle. He and two SEALs eased around the corner. As the team worked their way into the next room, one of the soldiers jerked and stumbled backward.

The SEALs opened fire. Ronan helped the injured man to the floor and saw a slender arrow lodged in his neck. His name tag read Nunez – Ronan had never actually spoken to the man. Blood spurted from the gash, which Nunez touched once or twice, then he slumped, motionless.

Once the firing stopped and the Kazites disappeared, the SEALs looked to Ronan.

"He's dead," Ronan said. The shock of the moment hadn't fully settled in yet. He had briefly activated an LED light on his helmet, and now he saw the look in Lt. Elliott's eyes. The SEAL team had no doubt worked together a long time; they had just lost a brother, a man they trusted with their lives, as he had trusted theirs. But Lt. Elliott's stare was resolved, professional, almost emotionless. Almost. He said, "We'll recover him on the way out."

Lt. Elliott motioned for everyone to get back in their line position. Ronan flipped his light off. Croft launched three smoke grenades down the hall and proceeded into the cloud. The rest of the team followed, keeping close.

Ronan's heart hammered. He could make out nothing but stone walls, axe-hewn beams, and smoke, even with boosted PulseView. The enemy had excellent aim and Ronan felt much more aware of his mouth and neck, unprotected except for the mesh wrap. Lt. Elliott fired in short bursts, then others shot once or twice, although Ronan didn't think they could actually see anyone. The corridor seemed empty.

Wrong. Shapes moved in the dark.

Arrows from nowhere, fast as light. Then banging flashes and running forward and shit flying everywhere and more arrows way too close to the face.

Then quiet. All still.

The smoke thinned as it drifted through the corridor and into open doorways on both sides. Everything smelled of dank mildew and sulfur.

"Where are they?"

"All over the damn place. Dozens of them."

The archers blended into the never-ending darkness of the place. They had covered themselves in black stuff that thwarted the team's night vision goggles and had littered the place with glowing piles of red-hot rocks that messed with infrared. Rats threw off more false alarms. Amid all this background noise, the archers hid behind walls and waited, nearly invisible. In this oppressive darkness, Ronan felt like the SEALs faced an army of phantoms.

As the SEALs moved along the corridor, they peeked into each open room for a quick survey. Ronan had only a moment to assess each room and thought the team might be moving a little too fast. But he was rattled by Nunez's death and hustled along with the others, unable to think clearly. Inside the rooms, he glimpsed little more than primitive beds, makeshift tables, spear poles, rocks in various states of being worked into weapons. No paper, no files, nothing resembling electronic equipment.

A net fell out of the smoke and darkness, dropping from the ceiling.

The net missed most of the team, but engulfed Croft. Screams from the Kazites pierced through the hallway from both directions. Arrows whistled. Ronan ducked, slamming into Deanna's back.

The SEALS bunched around Croft, firing at doorways and dark areas. Their rounds hammered and destroyed everything around them, the noise deafening. Ronan took out his knife and sliced through the net, an arrow whizzing past his arm. Where the hell were these guys hiding? Deanna knelt to help. An arrow glanced off her helmet.

Croft pulled himself out. "Appreciate it," he said, slapping Ronan's shoulder and taking Deanna's hand.

Ronan was about to respond when an arrow lodged effortlessly into

Croft's cheek, buried deep. Croft's eyes widened and the two glanced at one another.

"Oh, shit," Ronan said.

Croft squinted. He opened his mouth to say something, but only gurgled. He rose into the raining arrows and unloaded a clip on full automatic. When that was out, he slammed in a fresh magazine.

Lt. Elliott attempted to pull him back, but Croft walked steadily forward, firing his way into the smoke. After a few seconds, the firing stopped.

The SEALs rushed down the hall toward him, deeper into the corridor. Ronan noticed gaps in the walls and trap doors in the floor, dark hiding spots where the Kazites had fired at them. Lt. Elliott raised his hand and the team stopped.

Ronan scanned the hallway with PulseView and a heat overlay. He saw colors, textures, recesses, protrusions, wet spots, dry spots… but no signs of heat, except for the corpses they'd just passed.

In the middle of the hallway, about thirty feet later, they came to Croft's body, surrounded by dead Kazites. The SEALs circled around Croft, guns aimed outward. Ronan and Deanna knelt beside him and she put her finger to his throat.

"He's gone," she said.

Three arrows protruded in a tight cluster from Croft's neck. *What the hell happened?*, Ronan thought. *We just lost two men. These are primitives. How'd they do that?*

For one thing, he realized, there were a hell of a lot of them. Corridor after corridor of fire ants. And they weren't giving up: they were defending their home, they were on a mission, and they were dying for the cause. With a pang of envy and guilt, he also felt some respect for these guys. They were fighting on their terms, by their principals. But they were crazy, so he wasn't too impressed.

He smiled weak encouragement at Deanna, but she didn't notice, because his mouth was covered by the mesh wrap.

"Keep moving," Lt. Elliott said. "We'll retrieve Nunez and Croft on our way out."

They proceeded another five minutes and came to a section of the corridor made largely of stone, unlike the previous stretches, which had been primarily wood. The ceiling appeared to be stone as well, caked over with mud.

"Why the stone?" Wuss asked. "What are they protecting?"

"Check that door," Lt. Elliott instructed him.

As the others aimed their rifles, ready for anything to come out at them, Wuss pushed the door open a crack and paused. No arrows, yet.

Ronan glanced up and down the corridor, then returned his attention to Wuss, who was carefully pushing the door open. Inside was a small room with a table and a bowl. Something small and thin tumbled down and hit Wuss on the helmet.

Wuss looked up as a great grey blur fell, smashing into the ground with a deafening roar. Dust and splinters blasted outward. The walls shook. When the dust cleared, the tip of Wuss's rifle protruded from under a massive stone block.

"Oh, Jesus," Lt. Elliott said.

Zombie dropped to his knees. He clawed at the ground, trying to remove dirt from under the slab, seeking to make space for Wuss, then realized the foolishness of the act.

Ronan watched Zombie sink away from the cave-in. What a disaster. They were falling for every one of the Kazite's traps. He began to wonder if they should abort the mission, turn and get the hell out while they could. There was no telling what lay ahead. But there was no telling what lay behind them if they retreated, either. He wondered what the others were thinking. He glanced at Lt. Elliott and Fulsom and activated FaceLab. The program took longer than usual, because only their eyes were visible. Then the label appeared. FEAR.

They were getting deep into this place.

"That's a deadfall," Ronan said. "It's one of the oldest known traps. They don't get any simpler than that."

Lt. Elliott's voice wavered slightly. "We need to be more careful."

The instructions seemed obvious and stupid. Ronan debated his options. They needed to get the leads, if any existed. If they kept up their guard, they might make it out with both the leads and no further loss of life. "We have to keep moving," Ronan said and brought his X-Rifle to chest height.

Zombie placed a fist on the ground. He was silent, as if in prayer or respect, or maybe just reassuring himself, then said, "No matter what happens, when we come back, I am getting him out from under there."

Lt. Elliott checked his watch. He pointed down the hall in the direction they had been heading. "Confirmed. For now, we must continue."

The floor trembled as another round of rocks, dirt, and wood crumbled to the floor from the hole in the ceiling left by the boulder. Ronan caught Deanna's glance. Eyes wide, she shook her head: *What have we gotten ourselves into?*

Further down, the hall split into three directions – right, left, and straight down, into a hole.

Ronan approached the hole, X-Rifle ready. A ladder nailed to the side disappeared into darkness. "I'll see if any electronics are down there," he said.

"Hold on." Amelio grabbed Ronan's shoulder. He leaned forward and fired a couple rounds into the hole. No one shot back. Satisfied, he nodded. "Make it quick."

Ronan slowly put his full weight on the top rung. Solid.

He descended. The fourth rung cracked.

"Shit!"

The rung gave way and he felt only air, for a second, maybe two. *Thud.*

He lay on his back on a mud floor. The air was hotter, more humid. He could hardly breathe.

He'd fallen into a pit with dark recesses. The floor and walls were slick with rain. He checked and adjusted his legs. Something moved about in the air – feathers settling to the ground. Around him, bones.

He activated PulseView and adjusted the contrast. The walls of the muddy hole glowed black and gray, but two tiny pinholes of light hovered ahead. Ronan grunted and stood, readying his rifle.

"What's going on, Ronan?" Deanna called down. "You okay?"

"Affirmative," he said. "Give me a minute." He refocused his eyes. The area surrounding the two spots of light took shape. *Animal*. Large. Moving.

"Fuck me," Ronan blurted.

A jaguar lunged from the recesses of the pit, past fallen timbers and mounds of dirt and bones. Ronan jumped out of the way, blocking a claw-swipe with his rifle. The cat bent low and burst forward, growling and hissing, but Ronan sprang onto the broken ladder high enough to scale his way back up. Claws snagged his pants and ripped free. He bolted out of the pit, startling Deanna.

"What the hell?" she said.

Ronan crumpled at her feet.

"Any leads down there?" she asked.

He looked at her, took a breath, then examined his legs.

"You okay?"

He stared. Nodded. Standing slowly, he stepped about. His legs seemed wonkier than ever. "Everything's fine. Let's keep moving."

...

They regrouped in a large room with skylights. It seemed to be a food preparation and dining area, with crude bowls and plates stacked on long tables, a butchering area, and a giant fire pit below an opening in the ceiling. Sun streamed in with bold rays, and the room almost looked friendly.

"Holy cow, this place is huge," Zombie said. His voice echoed.

No signs of movement.

Lt. Elliott motioned for everyone to circle up. "Croft, Nunez, and Wu are dead. With Schroeder back in the ravine and Ramos looking for him, the mission team is down to six."

Amelio glanced toward a dark hallway on their right. "This place is a death trap. Do we proceed?"

Ronan knew everyone was thinking the same thing.

Lt. Elliott thought for a moment. "Affirmative," he answered.

Zombie objected. "These guys are medieval. I don't think they have any electronics in here. Nothing worth retrieving, nothing worth dying for."

"They might have notebooks, papers, other evidence," Deanna countered.

Zombie shook his head.

"We keep going," Lt. Elliott said. "Understood?"

Everyone confirmed, voices coming across the comm in various degrees of confidence. Zombie spoke last. "Roger that."

"Let's head this way." Lt. Elliott motioned to a nearby corridor.

Fulsom took the lead again. They moved slowly, wall to corner, peering, gesturing, crouching, running. Ronan's legs had been further damaged by his fall and he struggled to keep up. But he gripped the X-Rifle, ready to take a stronger role.

Archers appeared, popping out of the shadows. Ronan opened fire and punched through seven or eight Kazites as they tried to scramble into their holes. The X-Rifle took care of the aiming: *flip-flip-flip*. The barrel barely made a sound as it adjusted for perfect shot after perfect shot.

He'd made some kills, but the corridor seemed full of moving forms running back and forth in the dark. Arrows rained down on him, and Ronan delivered a steady stream of firepower in response. As chunks of the wall fell under his onslaught, a text message streamed across his vision: *hi honey! hows it going? i think ziggy is feeling better.*

He ducked as an arrow whistled past; damn message was blocking his vision, but he didn't have time to let go of the trigger to click his thumb and dismiss it. He'd forgotten to disable messaging.

The SEALs fired from their positions, bullets shredding everything. A wall came loose from the impact of the rounds and fell into a heap.

Silence again. Dust hung in the air, but the SEALs could see dead Kazites strewn everywhere and a closed door at the end of the corridor.

"I like that weapon," Lt. Elliott said to Ronan. "I want you behind Fulsom. Let him kick open that door, then take out any hostiles who get in our way."

Ronan gritted his teeth behind his face wrap. Fear and adrenaline – fight and flight. Everything mixed inside him in confusing signals.

Gathering at the door, they watched the ceiling with caution as Fulsom kicked it inward and jumped back. Nothing happened. Ronan scanned for Kazites, but the room beyond was empty.

Deanna grabbed his arm.

"Did you hear someone yelling?" she asked.

CHAPTER 62

Harper called out to the compound's invaders, shouting through an old copy of *Bug Out Magazine* that he had rolled into a tube. "Cease fire!"

Silence.

His lieutenant, Graham Bolton, stood near him. Bolton said, "They stopped firing. I think they hear you."

Harper lifted it again and bellowed the request once more. He listened.

From a hidden viewing spot, Harper had watched the attackers' brutal second-wave assault, led by a large man with an unusual weapon. Several dozen Kazites had been lost in the volley. The evil weapon had mowed them down in seconds, leaving them no time to duck for cover, and now they were lying about with their heads cracked open like walnut shells. The audacity of it all – to come into a home built with sweat and respect, and kill its occupants like bugs!

He had retreated to discuss the situation with his top officer. Bolton held a homemade crossbow at chest level, nocked and ready to shoot, and was decked out with axes and knives that were secured on chest straps. His belt held a variety of other makeshift weapons.

"The tall one has some sort of automated shooting system," Bolton told Harper. "He seemed to be spraying wildly without aiming and yet every bullet hit us."

"I got a good look," Harper said. His eye twitched. "The barrel moved on its own."

The silence continued.

Harper yelled into his tube, "My name is Jonathan James Harper, and I am the one you want!"

No shooting, no sound. The invaders were listening.

"If you agree not to kill any more of us," Harper yelled, "I will surrender willingly. But you must agree to bring me safely to the states and give me one more chance to address the nation and the world with my message. I'm here and my hands are up in good faith."

A hazy avatar of a large man appeared in the doorway on the far side of the room. He was a large, muddy, beat up bad-ass and he was decked head-to-toe in rigid body plates. He held the enormous rifle in a firing position, aimed at Harper.

"Who am I talking to?" Harper asked the intruder. "Will you do me the courtesy of lifting your veil?"

"I'll ask the questions and make the demands," the man responded.

There was a certain way the intruder had pronounced "I'll" that gave Harper pause. Harper had a knack for pinpointing unique phonetic signatures. *I never saw my parents,* he thought, *not until the Last Day, but I always heard their voices. I know voices.*

The man had said more of a slurry "I ill ask" rather than "I'll ask," as though he had started the contraction then changed his mind halfway through.

A realization struck Harper like a hatchet with a sharp blade.

He was the man on Pieter's phone. *He was Mechanica Man.*

Ronan Flynn was right here in the compound, standing twenty feet away.

Other soldiers had taken position behind Ronan, rifles pointed at Harper and a few of his archers.

Harper lifted his arms over his head. "Do you agree to my terms?"

Mechanica Man was quiet a minute. "Okay, Harper," he finally said. "If you cooperate fully right now, with no delay, we will spare you and anyone else remaining. Be warned, we are here to kill all of you, and we don't have time to play games."

Harper nodded to his men. They lowered their crossbows and placed them carefully on the floor.

Mechanica Man said, "I want access to your electronics, cell phones, laptops. Now. Lead me there."

"I will. I agree to those terms."

The man was thinking. Progress!

Finally, Ronan nodded and stepped forward. As he did so, he flapped his arms and fell from view as a massive section of wood flooring dropped away, pivoted like a seesaw, and rose up behind him. Dust crashed down and billowed in the shafts of light. The floor was now at an angle and blocked the other invading soldiers.

"Gotcha!" Harper yelled as the archers grabbed their weapons and ran toward the pit that had just swallowed the machine.

CHAPTER 63

Ronan felt the floor give way and he tumbled into a black hole. He hit cold water.

Opening his eyes underwater, he saw only murky blackness. His headlamp created a narrow beam for several feet. Cold seeped into his sleeves, pant legs, helmet, and boots. All the gear and clothing and armor made it difficult to kick and swim. Thankfully, his augmentations could be submerged without damage.

When he broke the surface and gasped air, there was nothing to grab: the walls of the water pit were smooth, slick, and muddy. He struggled to keep his head up and tread water, and in the process, accidentally let go of the X-Rifle. The rifle sank.

He dialed up his headlamp to assess the situation. He was in a stone well. The walls extended about fifteen feet above him, and rainwater trickled down the sides. He treaded water in thick, scummy muck. The air was rancid and foul.

A section of the wooden floor hung into the pit, while the raised end slanted almost to the ceiling. Cut off behind it, his team unleashed a steady volley of gunfire. Chunks of wood shot across the opening of the pit. The rim of the pit was higher on his team's side, and although bullets were blasting through the thick barrier, a careful Kazite could safely approach from the other side. Clever.

Sure enough, two archers appeared at the edge, hunched to avoid the barrage of bullets, and fired down at him. An arrow deflected off his shoulder, missing his neck by inches. His head was an easy target.

Ronan sucked in a breath and dove, his headlamp penetrating the murk, arrows torpedoing past him and disappearing below.

As he went deeper, a sharp pain stabbed at his eardrums; he squeezed his nose and exhaled gently to equalize the pressure.

He reached the muddy bottom. His headlamp revealed large stone blocks lining the walls. Yanking his combat knife from a thigh strap, he thrust it into the cracks of the stonework. He gave the knife a firm shake to confirm it would work as a handhold to anchor him.

The most pressing problem, more so than the archers on the rim, was air, but he had a short-term solution to that problem – his blood-oxygen boost. His fingers kneaded into his hip and located the subcutaneous activator. *Press* – wait five seconds – *press again.* A bolus of oxygen fed into his blood.

The boost allowed him to hold his breath twice as long as usual and increase his activity at the same time. The oxygen reservoir, implanted just behind his kidney, held another ten hits.

Next, he felt around in the mud for the rifle. It was waterproof to 100 meters and should still work. *Should.*

Moving from wall to wall, he swept his fingers through the muck without success. He activated heat mapping, hoping the rifle would be warm enough to locate. Either the cold water had cooled the gun, or the muddy water messed up the signal, because there was no sign of it.

Blood oxygen dropping fast.

He groped for the handgun holstered to his hip, pulled it free. It should still fire after being submerged.

One, two, three, *now!*

He swam for the surface, breaking through with arm extended, and fired at the first thing he saw.

An archer in mid-pull loosed his arrow weakly and toppled over the edge into the well. Ronan fired again and again – there were now five archers raining arrows down on him. At the same time, cracking gunfire continued to rip through the slanted flooring from his team on the other side.

He took a deep breath and sank below, extending his legs above his body to make another dive. Arrows smacked his legs and crotch. The impacts would cause welts and bruises, but as far as he could tell, nothing had penetrated his armor.

Back to the bottom: his headlamp radiated off the chrome knob at the end of his knife handle, and he grabbed hold of it again.

He would try to hang out down here and wait.

This time he noticed the flow of a gentle current. Must be a drain nearby. Maybe they collected rainwater on the hill and channeled it through here for some reason. Crazy motherfuckers. The well seemed like some kind of holding bin, almost like a settling pond that engineers put in rivers to catch sediment, or like a…

Feeling around in the deep muck, he thought, *this is shit.*

He was swimming around in a *septic tank.*

Screw this. He wasn't going to wait down here, admiring the Kazite's indoor plumbing.

How many more archers could there be? Perhaps dozens. Harper had him pegged as the team leader, so Ronan suspected he was their chief target. They might be able to keep this up for hours. He didn't have hours. He had ten minutes at best.

He could stay at the bottom until his oxygen was gone, hoping for rescue.

Or, he could surface and shoot at them from a heavily compromised position with nothing more than a pistol and limited ammo, while treading water and trying not to sink in all this gear and armor.

He didn't like the idea of running out of oxygen underwater.

He took another bolus of oxygen. An arrow drifted past him and stuck in the excrement.

Up he went.

As he broke the surface, a dozen Kazites, crossbows drawn, loosed their arrows. He instinctively covered his neck with both arms as the arrows slammed into his armor.

A lasso tightened around his armpit and neck and his body lurched. He clawed at the rope.

Harper appeared, crazy-eyed and hairy. "Haul him up!"

The rope bit into Ronan's neck and he choked. They dragged him upward.

"Get him there with the blubber hook!"

Poles swung near him. Something gouged into his side and yanked him upward.

"Hand me the monkey belt…."

Ronan flopped, his full weight bearing on the lasso, unable to catch air, the oxygen boost running low. He swung like a pig on a butcher's rack.

"Anyone have the head strap?"

"I got the throat chain."

Bouncing against the wall, vision flashing, trying to aim his gun, firing aimlessly…

An ear-wracking explosion rocked the room. *Breaching charge.* The enormous wooden seesaw blasted apart. Debris crashed down and ricocheted in all directions from the walls.

In a blur of splintered wood and rock, Ronan fell and hit the water.

Flailing and trying to swim with his neck and arm cinched, he saw Kazites jumping in death-twitches under the onslaught of his team's gunfire.

CHAPTER 64

As the last gunshot echoed away, Lt. Elliott and Deanna appeared at the rim. Ronan had been pummeled by a rain of small chunks, one of which hit his right eye. A flashing light zig-zagged across his vision. He got his hand under the noose and pulled it away enough to breathe as the last of the oxygen boost petered out.

A knotted nylon rope from his team smacked into the water. He grabbed it and strained to pull his weight upward. Wet clothes and all the gear added eighty pounds, at least. He was exhausted.

"Make a foot hold," Lt. Elliott yelled.

Ronan tied a bowline knot and placed his foot in it for support, and the five remaining members of the team hauled him up. Deanna kicked a dead Kazite into the pit to give him room as he approached the top.

As he collapsed on the edge of the pit, they removed his helmet, shook out water, then fastened it back in place. They pushed a dry Glock into his hand. Without the X-Rifle, he would need to aim by sight, but the flashing light in his right eye was growing worse, not better.

He lay in debris from his team's demolition of the wood barrier. As he tried to assess his surroundings, he saw Kazite bodies on the floor, but where was Harper?

The SEALs gave him no time to recover. He stumbled to his feet and got back in line as they continued their inward push.

No one spoke.

The interior looked grimmer, if that was possible. They were deep inside the structure and had lost track of their position. They had a compass bearing, but that was no help in navigating the correct path through the maze. The visceral remains of archers lay strewn about the rooms and corridors behind them. The way ahead was deserted.

Progress was slow. The dark corridors cutting one way and then the other had a disorienting effect. The place can't be as big as it seems, Ronan thought. Surely they would have reached the other side by now. Maybe they were doubling back.

His wet clothes chafed his back. His ruck was heavy and dripping water. The bright zig-zag lights from his right ocular had become cacophonous, almost a strobe light, and he noticed a sharp pain on the surface of his eye. Gingerly, he reached up and felt with a fingertip, and realized half of the augmented lens was hanging out.

Nothing he could do about it.

He stretched out his arms and spoke into the comm. "Is the corridor getting narrow?"

Deanna said, "Affirmative."

Fulsom, at the front of the line, stopped. He held up a hand to halt their advance. "It's getting tighter, and the way forward is full of debris."

Ronan and Lt. Elliott joined Fulsom to assess the path ahead, their lights reaching into the darkness. Ronan's left eye, which was the better of the two, drifted out of focus, then snapped back to sharpness. A little further down, the narrow space was jammed with dead branches and leaves, tangles of dry grass, and other vegetation that seemed to have been cast aside. Ronan spotted rotting fish on the floor.

"Looks like their dumpster," Ronan said.

The team was faced with a decision: keep moving ahead through a tight, cluttered space, or return the way they had come.

"Did anyone see any other corridors we could try?" Fulsom squawked over the comm.

"Negative."

"I didn't see anything."

The team contemplated the two options. Their lights criss-crossed the space as they searched the branches for combatants or other dangers.

"I don't like the look of it," Zombie said.

Lt. Elliott aimed his light further into the darkness. "It takes a turn in about forty or fifty feet."

Ronan didn't feel any more confident than Zombie, but he didn't want to turn around empty-handed, either. "I vote we proceed down this corridor. Maybe one of us can clear a way for the others."

Lt. Elliott gestured *negative*. "No time. And it's dangerous to touch anything."

Fulsom held his rifle with one hand. "Fuck it, let's just keep going."

After a few moments, Lt. Elliott said, "Confirmed. Proceed. Look for tripwires and be careful where you step. Watch for snakes and traps."

"I can go first," Ronan suggested. "My legs are less vulnerable."

The SEALs looked among themselves, signaled their agreement with his reasoning, and moved aside. Lt Elliott made an okay sign and pointed at him.

Ronan's light cast crazy patterns as it cut through the brush piles, the shadows of branches extending across the walls like a jagged web. As soon as he was among the debris, he realized it was impossible not to touch anything. The ground was littered in crunchy leaves that stuck to his wet pants. Small twigs poked him at every angle. He contorted his body to avoid brushing against the debris, using his left eye to watch for strings or other warning signs, but there was too much clutter to have any confidence that it wasn't loaded with traps. The smell of dead fish began to turn his stomach.

He went as slow as he could bear, aware that the team needed to get out of the compound soon. Or more accurately, *escape* the compound. He felt his heart beating. Above his head, he saw dark ventilation holes in the ceiling, but they seemed covered at the surface. No light slipped through. No fresh air came down.

He finally reached the corner. Leaning around it, he let the light slowly inch across the corridor beyond.

Nothing different. The corridor was full of branches and leaves for another ten feet, then widened and cleared out.

He signaled for someone to join him.

Amelio, the Brazilian guide, started forward. He mimicked the same approach that Ronan had taken, twisting to avoid touching what he could, taking the same path as best he could remember.

About five feet away, Amelio stopped. He reached down to examine something.

"What?"

"Just a pile of turtle shells."

"It's garbage," Ronan said into the comm. He regretted his tone, but he was so tense he felt he might snap like a dry rubber band.

Amelio now held some of the vegetation between his fingers. "This is pampas grass. No idea why they are throwing it here."

"I'm going on."

"Right behind you."

Ronan inched around the corner. He decided to stick close to the wall. His movements were quicker and more careless, but he couldn't help it. His heart raced faster.

A minute later he emerged from the mass of debris and kicked his legs and brushed everything off his pants and shirt. He realized that the Kazites could simply have dumped Mighty Mites into all that clutter, and it would be game over for all of them. No sign of mites, however. He watched Amelio round the corner.

Unlike Ronan, the Brazilian headed straight down the middle of the corridor.

Ronan clenched his teeth, watching. It wasn't smart to forge multiple paths, but Amelio hadn't been able to see around the corner to watch Ronan, and it was too late now to say anything.

Amelio stopped to pull a branch that had snagged on his armor.

He set the branch free, took a few more steps, and was soon standing next to Ronan.

"We're both clear," Ronan said into the comm. "No sign of anyone. While the rest of you come through, we'll go a little further down."

...

Compared to the dumping ground they had just navigated, walking in the open corridor felt like freedom.

The feeling was short lived. This corridor ended in a dark square opening. Amelio arrived first and leaned in, sweeping the space with his rifle. "What the hell's this?"

Ronan did a cautious survey of the inside and his heart sank. The Kazites' compound was getting weirder by the minute. This room was wider but had less headroom. Stakes had been driven into the floor, the walls, and even the ceiling, poking out from all directions. They appeared to be used for drying animals.

There were lizards on the stakes, snakes on the stakes, and random skulls and fur and lizard bodies scattered about on the floor. Some of the stakes were empty. All were streaked with blood.

As Ronan's light cast a cautious beam on the repulsive scene, he saw nasty stuff stuck to the points – stringy strands, maybe tendons or muscle. He saw frogs stretched and wrapped with twine.

He also saw a dark tunnel exiting on the far side.

"We should stop here," Amelio said. "Too dangerous."

Ronan tried to identify any possible safe route through the room, but it looked too much like the open mouth of a crocodile. "Agreed. This has danger written all over it. The ceiling would probably collapse and crush us."

"Let's tell the others. Maybe we'll find another way."

They headed back, but Ronan was surprised to meet the entire team already arriving. They had moved through the debris quickly. The countdown was getting too urgent to ignore.

Lt. Elliott and Deanna went to assess the stake room for themselves, and the others followed. Soon all of them were taking turns peering in while Fulsom covered.

After a minute or so, Lt. Elliott spoke. "Anyone think we should continue? If we head back now, that's it. We leave. I'm done exploring."

No one said anything. As he looked from person to person, they each gave the signal to leave. Regretfully, Ronan did, too, and then Deanna. It was over. There was no time left to keep searching for communication devices that might not exist, or if they did, might have little value. The mission objective was not achieved, but this was the right call. They turned and headed back toward the dumpster corridor.

"Smoke ahead!" Deanna called.

They picked up their pace and soon found themselves in billowing clouds of dusty smoke. Fires crackled further on.

"Damn corridor is on fire!" someone said.

Coughing, they scrambled to pull particulate masks out of their rucks and strap them over their ears. Ronan's ruck was soaked and hard to open, but the mask was factory sealed and still in workable condition. He saw that inside the corridor, the dry pampas grass was ablaze. Twigs, leaves and branches were catching fire and the smoke burned his eyes. Already the heat was intense.

"Can we get through it?" Ronan asked. The filter muffled his voice over the comm.

Lt. Elliott's voice was strained. "Not a chance."

A mass of burning wood and leaves emerged from one of the ceiling vents and hit Lt. Elliott's shoulder. Sparks blasted off him.

"Son of a bitch!" he yelled.

They brushed him with their gloved hands, knocking embers and oily leaves off his body.

Lt. Elliott swung his rifle upward. "While we've fumbled around in here, some of them are on the roof building fires. Watch those vents."

The SEALs shuffled to ensure they were not directly underneath any of the ventilation holes.

"It's like Waco," Fulsom said. "These guys are burning their place down. As far as they are concerned, this is the end."

Ronan guessed what they were all thinking, and voiced it. "If we can't go through the furnace, we have to go through the stakes."

Fulsom said, "Can't we just blow out a wall and get the hell out of here?" His calm demeanor was beginning to succumb to the stress.

"Negative," Lt. Elliott said. "We are surrounded by tons of dirt. The ceiling could cave in."

Without any clear signal, they started to move out of the smoke.

Ronan kept up. Once again, they were hustling back the way they had just come, rifles out.

They arrived back at the room with the stakes and stood at the entrance, lined up on each side. The air was clear here, so they tossed the filters.

"Go fast and watch your step," Lt. Elliott said. He checked a data panel on his arm. "We are running out of time. Go in groups of three. Ronan, Amelio, Fulsom – you're first. Now!"

Ronan charged inside, flanked by the other two, heart pounding. He scrambled over the obstacles in the room, arching his body and legs to clear any stakes poking from below, while also ducking the ones pointing down. His partners did the same. On every surface of the room, Ronan saw graffiti of bones and corpses.

Something dropped out of a vent and twisted on the ground. A snake.

"Watch out!" Fulsom yelled.

The snake hissed and coiled. Pit vipers and coral snakes began dropping out of the other vents, along with spiders, centipedes, something hairy that snarled, and other crap Ronan didn't recognize.

Ronan cursed and picked up his pace.

Fulsom jabbed his rifle into a vent and unleashed his anger, the rounds thumping into stuff above. Bloody chunks and insects fell out of the hole. Ronan couldn't tell what they were.

With new urgency, Deanna, Zombie, and Lt. Elliott entered the room in a mad dash, bumping into each other in their desperation to avoid getting bitten or impaled. They scanned the ceiling for signs of an impending collapse.

Fulsom's rifle strap snagged on a stake and ripped it clear out of the ground. He yelled, "Watch out!"

After a frozen moment, they saw that no trap had been triggered, and they all launched into forward motion again. Shit rained down on them. Bugs and rocks and burning coals and boiling sewage. The SEALs fired a few warning shots up the small tubes. Things were crawling around them on the mud floor.

Amelio cried out. His foot had collapsed into a small pit.

Ronan was closest. He grabbed Amelio by the arm and tugged. "C'mon!"

Amelio winced. "I'm hooked on something."

Ronan saw that the pit dropped a foot and was full of spikes, a punji trap in the manner of the Viet Cong. One spike had entered Amelio's leg at the ankle, just below the shin armor. Ronan reached in and grabbed the stake with one hand, Amelio's leg with the other, and yanked them upward as a unit. The stake pulled from the ground. Amelio wrapped his arm around Ronan and cursed and they stumbled forward.

Fulsom was the first to make it out of the stake forest and was approaching the dark opening on the far end.

There was something in there.

Ronan boosted the contrast. A bunch of Kazites crouched in the dark.

Fulsom immediately began firing. Figures emerged from both sides with knives and spears. Someone dropped from the ceiling. Fulsom popped at least three attackers, but the man who landed on him brought him down. The man stabbed at Fulsom repeatedly.

Ronan was at Fulsom's side within seconds. He popped the attacker's head, *bam*, gone, but two others lunged at him from opposite sides. He fired the last rounds from his pistol, taking out the man on the left. The other attacker collided into Ronan's side, a man as big as a linebacker, and Ronan was almost knocked out.

Kazites flooded in and the SEALs fired in all directions, muzzle flashes bursting from their rifles. The man who had tackled Ronan was hit countless times and collapsed backward in a dead heap. Deanna stepped past Ronan, firing into the melee. He saw more of them emerging from their hiding spots. They were all killed mid-lunge. Ronan leapt to his feet but was still dazed and almost fell.

The skirmish was over in less than twenty seconds. Amelio lay on the ground nearby, holding his hands to his face. Blood poured through his fingers. The stake poked from his leg. Fulsom was bleeding from an arm and leg, having been stabbed multiple times.

Ronan helped check their injuries. Amelio had been stabbed in the throat and was only semi-conscious, his body bathed in sweat. Working quickly, Lt. Elliott fished a first aid kit from his ruck. Deanna helped him apply tight bandages to their wounds. Ronan grabbed a full mag, slid it into his handgun, and watched for anyone approaching.

Lt. Elliott stood and surveyed the surroundings, rifle in hand. Further down, a large skylight splashed sun on the dirt floor. "We have to get out now," he said. He consulted his data panel. "We were supposed to start securing the perimeter two minutes ago."

"Won't they delay the missile launch if they don't hear from us?" Ronan asked.

"Negative," Lt. Elliott said. "We're assumed dead in that case. The last thing they want are Kazites escaping into the jungle. If anything, they will get nervous and launch sooner. There is an acceptable amount of friendly fire, especially in high-priority bombing campaigns. We all volunteered to enter the kill box with the understanding that the primary mission would not be compromised."

"Amelio is dead," Deanna said.

"What…?" Lt. Elliott dropped to his knees. The bandages on Amelio's throat were soaked through and his eyes did not react to a penlight. Ronan saw Lt. Elliott struggling to control his emotions – shock, sadness, stress, fear. Amelio was not a SEAL and had never trained with Lt. Elliott's team, but he was a brother in spirit, and his death was a blow.

"We're not leaving him in here, so close to a way out," Lt. Elliott said. He grabbed Amelio by an arm pit and immediately Ronan took the other side. They dragged him the twenty yards to the patch of light.

The skylight was three feet in diameter and rose two stories to the outside. The walls were smooth and fashioned from packed dirt and stone. Ronan saw blue sky and clouds drifting across the opening. His reluctance to leave without the Kazite's electronic devices vanished. He no longer cared. He wanted out.

There was also no way they would recover the bodies of the other

SEALs before the missile hit.

Lt. Elliott interlocked his fingers and Zombie stepped on them, then as Lt. Elliott lifted him, Zombie grabbed a branch nailed into the ceiling and pulled himself into the shaft. He pressed his legs against the opposite wall of the shaft, pinning himself into place, then began shimmying upward.

Ronan pointed his firearm at the empty rim at the top of the shaft. "I don't have a visual on anyone, but they were just dropping shit down their murder holes. They're up there. If anyone peers over the side, it will be the last thing their face ever does."

...

Zombie made good progress. When he was within five feet of the top, he paused by a root embedded in the dirt. He carved a space around it with his knife, then took hold and pulled hard. The root held fast. Satisfied that it was deeply anchored to a tree somewhere, he slid a nylon cord around it and dropped both ends to the floor below. Then he withdrew a small packet of foot powder and poured it on the root. The cord slid easily across it. He worked without speaking into the comm, not wanting to alert anyone above of his presence.

Below, Fulsom stood carefully on his good leg while Lt. Elliott looped the cord around his chest and secured it with a slip knot. He tugged the cord and gave an okay sign. Lt. Elliott took up the other end in a firm grip to help pull.

Zombie tied a butterfly knot in the middle of the cord, put his foot in the loop, then worked his way back down the shaft, using his body as a counterweight to help lift Fulsom, who reached up with his good arm to pull himself into the shaft. The lighter of the two, Fulsom ascended easily.

Dirt toppled from the top and trickled down the shaft in the bright sunlight. They all looked up.

As Ronan watched, Deanna pointed at the rim to draw his attention to something. A large rock seemed to be moving. It was wiggling back and forth, and as it separated from the wall with more dirt falling downward, they could see that it was massive.

"That boulder is shifting. You have to come down, now!" Deanna said into the comm.

Ronan fired up at the rim but no one was there; the Kazites were obviously using a lever to work the massive rock free. He heard them grunting and shouting. No doubt the boulder had been placed and positioned for just this purpose, was probably unstable to begin with, and thus needed little coaxing.

Dirt rained down.

Zombie suddenly reversed course, shimmying back up toward the surface so that Fulsom could be lowered back down.

Lt. Elliott was frantic. "Let him fall! Slip out of the cord!"

The boulder was clearly breaking free and enormous loads of dirt poured into the shaft. Zombie began wiggling his foot out of the cord, and as it slid free, lost his leverage against the opposite wall.

Before he dropped, the boulder crashed into him.

Everything gave way. Dirt, debris, Zombie, and the rock all piled onto Fulsom below.

The rock hit the ground with a loud *thunk*. Dirt billowed in the air.

To Ronan, Deanna, and Lt. Elliott, the result was horrifying. There was no question about what they were looking at.

Fulsom's head was partly under the rock, and his skull was cracked, and his head's insides were now outside.

The rock was the size of a refrigerator. Zombie was almost entirely underneath it, but his head and neck protruded, and the wide eyes and blood seeping from everywhere signaled unequivocally that the rock had just pushed several gallons of blood up his torso and out every orifice.

Lt. Elliott sank to his knees. He put his ear next to Fulsom's nose and mouth and felt for a pulse. His voice wavered. "I've lost all of them."

Ronan gripped his pistol and looked around the room, half of his vision crazy with electric white noise. He trembled with panic.

An arrow hit the back of Lt. Elliott's neck and emerged halfway out the other side through the man's nose.

Ronan and Deanna took off at a full run, shooting wildly, arrows flying. They reached the far wall and stumbled into a black opening.

Chapter 65

They stopped to catch their breath. Several minutes passed. They heard no one pursuing, nothing moving in the walls, no murmuring in the dark.

Deanna whispered in the comm, "I don't hear anything."

"Neither do I."

"Should we risk a light?"

He answered by flipping on his headlamp. They had emerged into another large, dank room, full of tree trunks and branches. Moisture dripped from overhead, smacking into muddy puddles on the earthen floor. As the light moved across the room, shadows played against the walls. One stack of branches leaned against a far wall, still covered in bark and leaves, while some piles had been cut down to rough poles, beams, and spears. Animal pelts stretched between wood frames. Plants and vines hung in various states of processing, on their way to becoming usable ropes and twine.

Ladders extended upward throughout the room. Examining the ceiling, they saw numerous skylights and what appeared to be utility shafts, possibly for lowering things in and out, but these were covered, the sun completely blocked out.

Ronan tried to activate PulseView for his left eye, but it was dead. Pulling a small pair of binoculars from a pouch, he searched the wood piles and shadows for any sign that someone might be hiding among them. Nothing.

They stared at each other in the dark.

"I'm sorry you got sucked into this," he said. "You aren't even supposed to be here."

"What are you talking about?"

"They only wanted you on this mission so that I would come."

She tried to maintain a cool exterior, but he saw raw emotion flare up. "How could you even say that? That's pretty arrogant, Ronan. What a nice vote of confidence now that it's just the two of us."

Ronan sighed. "It's true."

She was silent. Ronan avoided her eyes.

Then, with purpose, she began walking. "We have thirty minutes to get out of here. Let's check this room for evidence, then find a way out."

They moved among the piles, searching for anything hidden among the beams and branches, scouring the walls for a doorway they might have missed. The earthen floor was slick with rain, the suffocating air rank with mold. What a miserable cesspool of a place. The Kazites thought this would be the birthplace of a better world?

At the far side, as Ronan turned back, Deanna blurted, "What's that?"

He followed where she was pointing, squinting his left eye to overcome the blurriness. There was a small nook with a little table and chair. Further down, a crude sign hung on a wall, partially hidden by a stack of leafy wood that had been propped against it. He cleared off a few branches and tried to decipher the sign through his compromised vision, but before he had it figured out, Deanna read the words aloud. "Cleanse your mind, then enter Hell."

They exchanged baffled looks, then pulled away more of the debris, which exposed a large sheet of metal in the wall – the first machined surface they had seen in the entire compound.

Removing the rest of the brush, they discovered a giant vault with a keypad on the side.

"Bingo," Ronan said.

They paused to listen. Still quiet.

"I wonder what they are doing?" She asked.

"I don't think many are left."

Glancing at her watch, she said, "This is where they store their computers and phones, I am sure of it. But we're out of time. The missile strikes in twenty-six minutes."

The vault had no biometric entry, just the simple keypad. But the team had known that gaining access to secure areas would be tough, so they had brought along an arc cutter that could turn thick metal into atomized molten spray. Deanna was already unhooking the transformer from her gear. Given the odds of being severely burned, this was a last resort.

Ronan began typing on the keypad. "One second. The CIA suggested a few passwords. Let me try this odd word that Harper used in his video threat: Terrycloth."

He tapped quickly.

They heard the door unlock with a click.

Shocked, Deanna grabbed the handle.

The door to Hell opened.

"Wow, those CIA people are good," Deanna said, pulling the door open. "What does *terrycloth* mean to Harper?"

"I'll tell you inside. I looked it up during the flight down here."

The vault was packed with electronics – laptops, cables, backup drives, drones, webcams, battery packs, satellite puck, and a disassembled watch.

Ronan cleared a spot on a table, set up a small lantern, and turned it on. They had been in the dark for so long that the bulb seemed as bright as the sun.

Deanna recoiled at the sight of him. "Holy shit, your eye looks terrible."

"It needs a touchup."

"It's hanging half out."

The ocular was separating from the cornea on his right eye, damaged by debris in the water pit, but his left eye was usable. They each withdrew a collection bag from their ruck and opened it. They began sweeping the devices off the tables. There was no time to evaluate each piece – all of the smaller devices went in the bags, which had an aluminum layer to prevent electronics from being remotely wiped.

"Leave the desktop machines," Ronan said. "We don't have time to rip out the hard drives."

"Agreed." She was forcing a laptop into her bag. "I'm almost done. What's the significance of the word terrycloth?"

Ronan zipped his bag, yanking the drawstring to secure its contents. "In the video, Harper used the phrase *terrycloth mother*, which is a reference to experiments conducted on monkeys in the 1950s. They would take a baby monkey away from its mother forever and put it on a wireframe robot thing covered in soft terrycloth. They wanted to see what would happen to the baby."

"What happened?"

Ronan held up his hand, listening.

Then he said, "It would cling to the machine in desperation. As the monkey got older, it couldn't develop any connection to other monkeys… it had no trust, no perspective, no framework. Some were violent. To the monkey, everything was a threat."

Ronan didn't know why Harper had made the reference. Just a simple statement about the bleakness of technology perhaps, or maybe there was a connection to his mother. Or both.

Something squeaked.

"The door!"

With a bang, the vault door slammed shut. Bolts slid into place.

"Someone is out there," Deanna whispered.

A mosquito flew into view and they both recoiled. Then a second bug appeared, then more.

"The vault is booby trapped," Ronan said. "They didn't care if we came in."

"So *terrycloth* wasn't the magic word," Deanna groaned. "I take back what I said about the CIA."

Within seconds, brown clouds of biting machines rose from the piles of electronic clutter and made toward them.

They pulled the mesh wrap over their eyes and hunched over as the bots landed on their helmets, vests, arms, and legs.

"Oh my God," Deanna whispered, slapping at her neck.

"You okay?"

"I think so."

"Continue with the plan."

Deanna grabbed a few more things that would still fit in her bag and snapped it closed. They hoisted the bags on their shoulders.

"Ready?"

"Yes. Let's go."

Deanna handed him the punch gun for the arc-cutting system. He shot leads into the door arranged in a large square, then dumped the battery out of his ruck and jacked in the wires. He was thick with mosquitos.

"Let's max it out," he said, tapping the power up to one hundred percent.

"That may be too much."

"We don't have time to run tests and compare and contrast," he said.

Deanna turned away as he briefly flipped the switch. A massive blue flume arced across the metal door and melted a foot-wide hole. With his wonky remaining eye, which he opened after the burn-through, he briefly saw someone in the outer room with a surprised face disappear into the dark.

"There are still vermin running around this rat's nest," he said.

Four leads had fired. Sixteen left. He turned away.

Then he melted the Doorway to Hell into formless molten slag.

Chapter 67

They ran in dark corridors and met no resistance, stumbled past bodies and walls torn by gun fire. They ran through smoke. The heat and humidity were unbearable. Ronan eased against the wall and peered around a corner, just one more corner in an endless string of corners. He heard Deanna scraping against the wall behind him.

"You're stumbling," he said. "You okay?"

"I can't breathe."

"Take a minute. Want the last of this water?"

She shook her head. "We need to keep moving."

The mosquitos hadn't been able to keep up, but he smashed a few that remained on his sleeves. He scanned her protective covering and confirmed that her face wrap was secure. Her pants were properly tucked, strapped, and sealed. He checked her arms. He found a rip in a sleeve, and caught his breath. He pulled it back gently with a finger. Bare skin.

She glanced at it and shrugged. After a minute her breathing calmed. With a nod, she took off again. They wanted to avoid ending up back at the furnace, so they took a route that went in a different direction. Smoke lingered in the air.

They hurried down a corridor and followed as it turned to the right. "There's no rhyme or reason to these corridors," he yelled, because the comm wasn't working.

"What the hell?" Deanna answered, coming to a halt. "It's turning right again! That heads back the way we came, deeper into the building. It doesn't make sense."

Ronan strained to see down the corridor while Deanna slumped to the ground, her back to the wall. An endless stream of data flowed across his vision. Nonsensical alerts. FEAR. $LYING. 20 FEET. MONKEY. THE TY$$#3 FEELS MUCH BETTER. Sharp daggers of pain poked deep into his right eye, along with ripping and tearing and blasts of static and color.

"This corridor only goes a short stretch," she said, yanking her face wrap off. "Then makes yet another right."

"That would intersect with the corridor we were just on, but we didn't pass an opening."

"I know. Maybe it's a dead end and doesn't connect." Deanna rubbed her eyes. Sweat trickled from her brow. "Even if it did connect, we'd be going in circles."

Ronan ignored his time readout and stifled the panic welling up within him. "We need to pick a wall and throw some grenades. Blast our way out of here."

She nodded. "I agree. But if we aren't near an outer wall, that could take time. And we can't risk heading inward. Can we blow up the roof?"

"Probably won't work. As Lt. Elliott said, it has tons of dirt and trees on it."

"Fuck this. What's that grinding noise?"

At the far end, where the hall turned right, the wall started to move, sliding in the dirt, opening a dark corridor beyond. It stopped halfway. Ronan aimed his pistol while Deanna fumbled to pull out a frag grenade.

A voice shouted from beyond the new opening. "The walls move, fools. There's no way out." It was Harper. Ronan fired into the dark.

"Try again!"

Ronan tried to process this new information. Kazites had been moving the walls around, scooting them around at intersections, opening new corridors and closing off others. It would be impossible to find a way out, at least in the time they had. No choice but to blow up their prison. Fast.

Harper shouted again. "You killed most of my men and that wasn't very nice. Looks like you're running low on firepower. When is your backup team showing up?"

"Any minute now."

"Yeah? We'll see. You'll be waiting for them, skewered on a post at our front door." His voice echoed in the empty corridors. "You didn't talk to the president, did you? Now I've got to adjust my plans. My next lesson will involve the whole world. No more little wakeup calls. It's extinction time."

A hulking archer appeared directly in front of them, holding a massive crossbow. Ronan shot wildly and fell against the wall. The man disappeared.

"What are you doing?" Deanna gasped.

The image had been an artifact, a replay from earlier – an electronic ghost. "I'm seeing things," Ronan said. Lightning flashed in both eyes. He stared at her. Either she was shaking violently, or his ocular was jumping and skipping.

"Something's wrong with me," she said.

"We'll get you help."

She laughed quietly.

He turned toward Harper and yelled. "Why don't you come out so we can talk?"

"I'm more clever than you. Have I not proven that?"

Ronan knelt next to her and put an arm on her shoulder. "I'll run down and try to kill him. I'll throw grenades every which way."

Harper's voice careened down the corridor. "It's been nice chatting. I'm heading off to approve Plan B. Please continue this debate with my coworkers."

Deanna said softly, "I was bit."

Ronan wanted to refute her. "You can survive this."

"Yeah, right." She readjusted against the wall, breathing choppy, and pulled out a grenade. Ronan didn't stop her.

He helped her to her feet. His headlamp caught the glistening paleness of her face.

"Please tell Max I love him."

The finality of the comment hit him hard. He wanted to yell at her to run with him, to try to get out, but those words stuck fast.

She squeezed his arm and looked away.

"I'll tell him, Deanna. Of course I will."

"Thank you." She held up her pistol with her other hand. "I can see three or four of them behind that section of wall they just slid back. I'll charge them. As soon as the grenade goes off, run down there like the machine from hell."

"You know I can do that."

She slid off her bag of the Kazites' electronics and handed it over. He hoisted it to his other shoulder.

And then she was off, running under his cover, protecting her head. When she reached the opening, Ronan took off in a sprint, legs wobbly, looser. Through his flickering left eye, he saw her stagger, an arrow protruding from her throat.

The grenade went off. The blast nearly kicked him off his feet, but he fell against the shaking wall and held on.

As the smoke cleared, he saw that the sliding wall had been blown askew.

The corridor ahead was empty. He didn't see her or Harper.

All was quiet.

He was alone.

CHAPTER 68

The grenade had scattered the men, but he didn't see any sign of them. Deanna's body lay on the floor, destroyed, with an arm, maybe a leg, lying nearby, and a lot of blood everywhere.

He couldn't look. Stifling a retch, he surveyed the path ahead. The walls looked intact. The grenade hadn't blasted any holes.

Absolute quiet. A black void in front and behind. Time left: sixteen minutes. He couldn't find his pistol. He'd dropped it in the explosion. The pain and fear were joined by a deep sense of regret – about Deanna and Lisa, the SEALs, and all the people who would die if MET and the CIA couldn't track down the remaining tentacles of this crazy group.

He started to head down the empty corridor, the shadows from his helmet light flickering on its surfaces. The beam caught symbols scrawled on the walls – swirling suns, knives, enormous cocks and orifices, and tormented phrases written in the blood of jungle animals. His ocular sprinkled copies of the symbols across his vision.

Glancing back, paranoid of an attack, something about the wall caught his eye. He returned to the point where Deanna's grenade had exploded.

A piece of the wall was damaged, and a length of split wood now hung loose. He grabbed the piece and pulled. The board moved with effort, but only a few inches. He put his head close to the crack and saw an area beyond, the light from his helmet shining through and illuminating a narrow section of an adjacent room.

Something lay in the dirt. He moved his head to readjust the beam and the light fell squarely on the object. Deanna's water bottle.

She had thrown it on the ground after they had cleared the first room. This corridor was close to the exit, after all. The water-bottle room led directly to the outside door. He tugged on the wall, yanking, gasping, coughing, and sweating, and pulled the rough board a few more inches outward, but not enough to crawl through. He paused, mindful of the time ticking down, down.

Whispers and scuffling. Men approached. He sensed them moving along opposite walls, stalking him, careful but approaching fast.

He patted his shirt and pants, but knew the pistol was gone, the knife was gone; he had no weapon. In desperation, he lifted his pant leg and opened the small panel on his prosthetic where he had stashed the thin canister from Niko's lab. He withdrew it, the SANAR logo catching the beam of his helmet, and pressed a button near the lid. *Pop.* Cold air brushed his skin as the lid opened. He let the small plastic tube inside drop into his left hand, and he shoved that into a side pouch. Finally, he threw the canister into the darkness in the direction of the approaching men.

It clattered to the stone floor somewhere beyond. He heard them stop. The feint was the oldest trick in the book and wouldn't hold them for long. They would brace for an explosion, but after a few seconds, realize he was only stalling them.

Grabbing the broken wall board with both hands, he planted his feet on either side and willed his legs to push. The myoelectric connections between his thigh and prosthetic were loose, but his legs flexed and the leverage worked and the board gave way a few more inches.

That might be enough. He pushed each bag of electronics into the room beyond, ripped off his helmet and tossed it aside, and started wiggling.

His head and right arm went through with no problem, but the left arm wedged tight. With more kicking and thrusting of his legs, shoving at the ground to push forward, he gained another foot. Now he had both arms on the other side and used the wall to push away as he kicked.

He felt someone tug on his leg. In response, he burst into a flurry of kicking and wiggling. He was halfway through the wall, and stuck. Laughter erupted in the corridor behind him.

"Lieutenant Bolton, look what we have."

Two sets of strong hands gripped his legs. The men yanked roughly to pull him backward. A moment later, he heard something being shoved through the open gap above his chest.

"Kiss your girlfriend, you fuck."

Deanna's lower face slooped through the crack. Ronan flailed and pushed and kicked. His body advanced another inch.

"His legs aren't real."

"Take them off."

Ronan heard a blade tearing through each pant leg below his buttocks and the clothing separated. Bare legs, now. The hands clambered at his thighs, digging where the prosthetics met his flesh, yanking and pulling. A leg came free.

"Got one!"

He kicked with his remaining leg, catching one of his attackers somewhere, maybe a chest or head. The man swore. A knife plunged into his thigh, above the prosthetic. Ronan screamed and yelled and pushed. He got a little further through the wall.

"Pull that strap!"

"This one? Stop kicking you motherfucker!"

With a snap Ronan felt the other leg disengage and all leverage was lost. His legs were gone. He wiggled.

Laughter. "Now what are you going to do? Oh, shit."

Ronan slid forward and flopped into the adjoining room, leaving the attackers behind. They'd be on him as soon as they got through the nearest door or sliding wall.

He pulled himself along the ground, one arm through the loops of each bag, past the water bottle, flopping like a fish on the back end, up to his chin in dirt and mud and blood, past the bodies of the Kazites they had shot on the initial stage of the mission. Breathing through his nose, clenching his teeth, he followed the sunlight.

He crawled over a pole that had fallen from the wall during the SEALs' barrage. It was an enormous carved phallus, smeared from the top with blood. He kept crawling.

The next room led to the outside and he saw that the door was off its hinges, in the same position as they had left it after Fulsom had detonated the strip charge.

And just like that, he was outside in the brightest sunshine he had ever experienced in his life. The sun boiled the air and bugs swarmed.

Ronan crawled in the dirt.

In his crazy jagged peripheral vision, clouded with letters and numbers and swimming in color, he saw both men emerge from the compound. The shape of their bodies danced in data and heat.

"Okay, fun's over."

They were on him again. Harper and another guy. Kicking his head, gouging him with a spear. The henchman unzipped his pants and began pissing on Ronan's head, spraying his face and hair. Ronan clenched both bags of electronics to his chest. They laughed. Harper beat him with the spear's shaft.

He couldn't think straight. There was nothing but agony and the sense of a giant timer counting down to zero.

"I'll bet you're kicking yourself now," Harper said, clubbing Ronan with one of his own legs. "Look at you. Turning yourself into a machine. You are not even fighting it, the horrible future Kaz outlined in his Manifesto. Kaz didn't know how to get the world's attention. He mailed a few bombs here and there. That didn't scare anyone. *We* know how to scare people. We know how to execute. Electricity feeds the machines. I'm turning off all the electricity."

Ronan had caught his breath. "You are electricity, Harper. Electrons head to toe. The whole *universe* is a machine. *You're* a machine."

He couldn't see Harper's expression, but there was a pause.

"That's hitting below the belt, Mr. Flynn," Harper said. "Can we keep this gentlemanly and keep the name calling out of it?"

The henchman, who was far larger than Harper, his face covered in crude homemade tattoos, climbed onto Ronan and raised a fist high in the air. He hit Ronan on the side of the head with tremendous force, knocking Ronan's brain sideways. Purple lights flashed. Greens streaked. Yellows zagged and aquas zigged. His ocular retracted.

As Ronan managed to refocus his left eye, he saw the muddy fist raised again, and again felt the massive impact, the blow hitting his hair and skin, wet with urine.

This is it.

The struggle to refocus took longer. The fist came into view again, raised high. It went out of focus. Ronan tilted slightly, focused, and the man's face came into sharp relief. Tattoos. Missing teeth. Dirt. Broken lip. *Crack.* Loud noise, bang. Crack. The henchman's face broke open, spraying gunk everywhere, and he toppled hard on Ronan.

What – ?

Ronan tilted his head and Harper was running crazy, stumbling – fleeing into the shadows of the building.

He tried to lift his head. Searing pain.

That's my name.

He rolled to his side, and looking out across the clearing, he saw someone, a man emerging from the forest.

Ramos. The SEAL who had stayed behind at the ravine to look for Schroeder. Now running, rifle scope at his eye, advancing quickly toward him.

CHAPTER 69

Harper had disappeared.

Ronan gestured to the advancing SEAL, *go back,* but his hand flopped in a feeble wave and Ramos kept coming.

Ramos squatted next to Ronan. He rolled off the dead Kazite. "Where's the other hostile?"

"That way – out of time."

Ramos scanned the surrounding walls, turned back to Ronan. "Are you all that's left? You are seriously banged up. How can I help?"

"Electronics. Two bags."

Ramos crouched low and retrieved the bags lying several feet away.

"Get out of here," Ronan croaked.

"I'm not leaving you."

"Go… now. Before he comes back."

An arrow hit Ramos in the mouth and he lost balance. He fell back on his ass, the arrow protruding as though he were clenching a long cigar in his teeth.

The soldier slumped to his side, listless.

Harper approached, his jagged image moving in a four-legged scramble like an animal. "You got any more of them hiding in the woods?"

He dragged Ronan by the arm to a spot sheltered by the giant wooden target. The rotting head hung from it. "Where was I? Oh, yeah…" He crouched on his heels, examining Ronan's eyes, his hot stinking breath in Ronan's face. "Fascinating. You came all this way into a bullshit jungle to kill me and my people? What do *you* have to gain from this?"

Ronan groaned.

Harper leaned over him like a crazed jungle animal, huge eyes ablaze, face burned with tattoos, hair a long wild mess, and snarled, "Huh? Answer me. Oh, you're not going to say anything? You plead the fifth? You represent everything that is wrong. You *embody* what is wrong, you traitor. You are rebelling against our nature, with all its glorious limitations. You are a complete violation. You don't talk much do you?"

Harper stood and steadied himself against the target, then ducked as though he remembered he might be in a line of fire. "Sorry. I have an undeveloped vestige."

"What…?"

"What do you mean, *what*? Oh. You're right – I mean vestibule. I confuse those words. Vestibule. Exactly." Harper paused. "You are correct!" He kicked Ronan.

"Oh, God." Ronan wiped a hand over his eyes, which were stinging in sweat and urine and ripped optics, and looked around, hoping to see a weapon. The static had settled in his vision. Just little pops and zips now. His head throbbed in agony.

"Pay attention. I'm trying, Mr. Flynn. I'm trying. Now, where did I drop my spear? Ah. Over there."

As Harper shuffled off, Ronan unzipped the side pouch to withdraw the small sample tube from Sanar. Groot Gemors. *The big mess*, now thawed to a liquid.

His shaking, bloody fingers gingerly popped the cap. *Don't let one drop get inside you*, Niko had warned. Ronan almost spilled it on his face.

CHAPTER 70

Harper gathered his spear from the ground where he had dropped it in his mad dash for cover. Returning, he took a good look at his best friend lying on the ground, face shot to hell.

They had known the risks. They had always known. Still, this hurt.

The Engineered Man, the violator, Ronan, was nearly dead: beat to shit, one eye hanging out, legless torso limp like a rag doll, now watching him approach through his remaining eye – that abomination of an eye.

Hoisting the spear to waist level and gripping tight, Harper clenched his teeth. Revenge would be easy. Like spearing a fish on the dock. He lunged forward and his enemy held up his hands in futile defense. Harper took another step, then plunged the spear into the enemy's side, pinning him.

The mechanized freak whipped his hand and Harper instinctively covered his eyes. Something splashed across the back of his hand and forehead.

After a moment of shock, Harper sneered. "What was that?" He spied the small plastic tube in Ronan's hand. The bastard had some kind of toxin. Then he realized it might be from Sanar's lab.

Harper laughed. "You needed to get that stuff in my eyes or mouth. My blood stream! You missed." He wiped his hand on a monkey-pelt pant leg.

The enemy, the machine man, checked to see if anything was left in the tube, then tossed it aside. Harper pushed harder on the spear.

His antitheses, Ronan Flynn, grabbed a broken arrow lying in the dirt among other debris and held it out. The splintered shaft was no more than six inches long.

"If you can kill me with that, I deserve to die," Harper said. He kept his full weight on the spear. Beneath him, Ronan waved the arrow in pitiful defiance.

"Now, now," Harper scolded. He drew back. How to finish this dirty work? He studied the situation. It was best to simply hold the digital man at a distance with the spear, then grab the arrow when he wasn't expecting it.

He lunged for the arrow, but Ronan saw the move coming and slashed the air.

Harper felt a sting and turned his hand over to see a red slice across his palm. "Look at that. You got me. Now I'm pissed."

He would wait for Ronan to let his guard down. Contemplating his palm, he said, "Society is dying by a million small cuts."

No response. He twisted the shaft. That got a reaction.

"Maybe," Ronan whispered.

Once Harper got that arrow away, he would strangle this fool, wrench his head like a dinner cock.

He felt a stirring, a tingling deep in his arms, and worried he was getting too low on energy. The battle had taken more out of him than he had thought.

"Plan won't work," his enemy said.

The Techno Guy was in a judgmental mood, but his voice was weak, like a dying pulse. Harper pushed and twisted the spear, driving it deeper and wiggling at the same time.

His enemy gasped and opened the good eye wide in desperation. The other eye was worthless, the implant separated from the blue part – the iris? – just danglin'.

The tingling in Harper's arms had grown, turning into needle points, pricks of pain now spreading into the rest of his body, a burning, a spreading heat.

The enemy recognized his distress. That good eye watched.

Beginning to panic, Harper said, "I didn't feel the solution get in my eyes. Have I been invaded somehow?"

"Before throwing it in your face," Ronan groaned, holding the arrow high. "I dipped this tip. You've been cut."

Harper reeled back. "You....?" He looked at his bleeding palm. The pain had spread to every inch of his body, every muscle, every organ. He retreated further, withdrawing the spear, and let go, too weak to hold it.

"I'll be damned," Harper said. He staggered as the enemy propped himself up, still holding the broken arrow. Harper stumbled for the right word. "Touché." Was this real? Or not? A ruse? Or not? More information needed. "What will I die of?"

"Everything."

"I mean, heart? Lungs?" Harper heard his voice tremble. "What's it going to do?"

"Nothing specific."

That didn't sound so bad. Not so painful. Was this real? "What does it attack then?"

"The whole enchilada."

Harper squinted. "I don't understand."

"Every cell in your body is going to pop like a zit."

Harper felt his left eye twitch. The full weight and meaning of his situation began to sink in. He kicked at the ground. The people must know he was not afraid. "I will return to the earth from which we come, to which we go. Kaczynski Chapter 45: If the system breaks down, the consequences will be very painful. But the bigger the system grows, the more disastrous the results of its breakdown, so if it is to break down, it had best break down sooner rather than later. *Ah, shit*!"

Collapsing to his knees, Harper winced. "Chapter 52: it is not possible to make a lasting compromise between technology and freedom, because technology is by far the more powerful force! Oh, God, Mechanica Man called me an enchilada! Chapter 14, *the technophiles are taking us all on an utterly reckless ride into the unknown*. Fuuu–!"

He realized he might be melting. Reaching to his chin, he felt gaping holes, dripping stuff, his jawbone. He felt the jaw itself dissolving. "Shyth!"

Staggering, flapping his dripping arms, he attempted to steady himself but toppled over. His vision was falling apart. Mechanica Man was disappearing into the blur. That fuck!

In the swirl of color around him, his skeleton hands slid forward on the ground, mere bones and tattered muscle. Blobs fell to either side. Perhaps they were ears or clumps of hair.

Every cell in his body felt like the sun. Someone with a blowtorch, perhaps God himself, was burning his way from the inside out, melting the doorway to hell.

Darkness! His head hit the dirt, and though everything seemed disconnected, he no longer cared. His eyes were gone, all dark, but somehow he was still thinking, waiting for the final attack.

His brain tingled and burned. Jackhammers pounded but there was no fear, just awareness. Acceptance. *C'est la...*

He continued dissolving. Nothing more than molecular spaghetti. Then, not even that.

CHAPTER 71

Ronan crawled out from the shadow of the compound into the wide yard overlooking the river. The sun had peaked in the sky and he shielded his eyes, although he could only see out of his left; the right ocular dangled heavily from his cornea and produced a disorienting stream of fragmented images, flashing colors, and noise. Every blink brought pain. He concentrated his left eye on the horizon and searched. No sign of the missile. Good thing. Once it appeared, he would only have seconds.

He took one heavy bag of electronics in his mouth and clenched his teeth. He left the other behind. Then, slithering and groping through the mud, he pulled the weight of his body toward the post where the two horses were tied. Ocular flash: TWO-MINUTE W#$RNING.

The horses shuffled as he approached. They eyed him. They'd probably never seen a bloody legless man with an eye hanging out slithering toward them before.

He had no knife to cut the reins and no legs to kick the post over.

As he drew close, they moved back as far as their reins would allow. He got a good look at their tack. The bridle appeared to be homemade, a crude twisted leather, and the reins were attached to the bit by a makeshift fish-bone hook.

He grabbed the reins of the nearest horse and tried to hoist himself for a better look, but only rolled on his side. No legs, no leverage.

The horse pulled against the reins, drawing the cords taut. He struggled to apply his whole weight on the cords, hoping to snap the bone. Nothing.

He knew the missile launch was counting down. Just seconds now…

The fish bone was about the size of a small comb, thin and flat with a hole in the center that the reins and bridle passed through. Around the hole, there was a quarter inch of bone.

He wrapped an arm in the loop of the bag.

As he gripped the reins, he lifted himself and bit down on the bone, as hard as the pain would allow, biting until he thought his teeth might break, harder, until it snapped.

The horse reared as the reins fell away. Did the horse realize it was free?

Ronan inched closer.

The horse shifted.

"It's okay," he said in the calmest voice he could muster.

He slithered and crawled and soothed the horse with his most horse-seductive voice.

"Good, so good," he said.

Glancing at the sky, his heart seemed to stop. Across the clearing, above the treetops, a bright slice of flame burned in the distance.

He snatched the wood base of the horse's stirrup and gripped the bag. The horse shook and took off.

He clutched the stirrup and screamed and swore and cursed like a demon from hell, and the terrified horse shot to a full gallop and dragged him across stick and stone and the trees and sky swirled around him in a blur–

Out of the corner of his eye, he saw a streak of light. A deafening roar ripped the air itself.

The ground behind them exploded. The trees shook with a reverberating boom as the forest shuddered, fire exploding upward in a massive plume, shit flying everywhere, dirt raining down–

The horse ran and ran and ran.

Beat up and pummeled senseless, Ronan let go and heard the horse race off into the brush.

He sank his face into the dirt. Minutes passed. The stunned creatures of the jungle slowly regained their senses and a bird called.

Insects buzzed.

He lifted his chest off the ground and tossed the bag of leads aside. Rolling onto his back, he pushed the sagging ocular implant in, but it wouldn't stay. He wiped the back of his hand across his other eyelid.

Patting his vest, he fished around and found a pouch and pulled out a small GPS beacon, flipped it on.

And waited.

Waited for extraction.

CHAPTER 72

"Open your eye, Sleeping Beauty."

A hospital room came into fuzzy focus, and Ronan saw Edward beaming down at him.

Ronan winced. Pain surged through his right side. His thighs ached and throbbed. He felt like he'd been dragged over rocks and tree stumps. Wait – he had. His scalp hurt. His lips hurt. His entire face hurt.

"Glad to see you're back," Edward said. "You might want to lie still. In addition to your stab holes and broken bones, we've removed all of your technology."

Edward carried out his threat? He took away all my augs?

Well, screw him then.

"Your left eye is okay. Your right eye… will need something, not sure what." Edward slapped the table and the sound hurt Ronan's brain. "There's so much to tell you! Your video coverage of Harper's face unlocked many of the devices. The forensic teams have extracted reams of data. The leads are flowing, Ronan!"

Ronan lifted a hand. "Edward…"

"Every contact is connected to more contacts. We've found affiliated cells in Morocco, India, Vietnam, Philippines… and money trails pointing to China." Edward bounced with enthusiasm, but Ronan's vision was blurry. "The common thread isn't clear yet. We don't know whether the cells all consider themselves 'Kazites' or whether this is just a loose confederation of people with vaguely compatible anti-technology ideologies. I bet you're as anxious to discover the answers as I am."

Ronan groaned. Let it stop. Let all of it stop: the pain, the memories starting to come back, and especially Edward talking.

"…we have identified a bunch of politicians that Harper had planned to kill – and there were a lot of them. We're going to find these Kazite bastards wherever they live and destroy them, one by one."

A shooting pain in Ronan's hand implied that someone had smashed it flat with a sledgehammer. Stitches crisscrossed the yellow and purple skin of his palm and the back of his hand.

"You've noticed how messed up your right hand is," Edward said. "I think the horse stepped on it."

Why hadn't they given him enough medication?

"You were stabbed in the gut. You were covered in blood. No worries, though. The doctors will get you back in shape. Do you want a reinforced abdomen that isn't as easy to cut? By the way, we are ready to juice you up with far better augmentations."

Ronan could only tilt his head in Edward's direction. It hurt just to talk.

"We have a new oxygen boost. This one is a synthetic organoid, a device with a fabricated surface containing your antibody profile. We'll surgically embed it into your abdominal cavity. It can expand your lung capacity by thirty percent and is completely automatic, kicking in with exertion or low blood oxygen."

Reaching to the left side of his head, Ronan felt a wire. He could feel where it disappeared under his skin, but he couldn't tell if it went through the skull. "What is this?"

"We embedded a temporary electrode array. I wanted you to see how it worked. It's kind of like a cochlear implant, but it hooks up to your temporal lobe."

"For what purpose?"

"It whispers information to you, in your mind. Instead of having to use those text overlays on your eyes." Edward must have sensed Ronan was losing strength and attention, because he felt the need to clarify. "We also gave you a new navigation controller. Thought-based EEG variations are grouped into discreet actions. Use it to command your information systems. No more finger navigation. Give it a try."

"Any risks?"

"Oh, you know. Bleeding, swelling, inflammation, seizures, nausea, rejection of the device. The usual."

"Sounds wonderful."

Edward crossed his arms and smiled. He gazed deeply at his field officer. "Ronan, do you know the name of Orville Wright's first passenger?"

"No idea."

"Lt. Thomas Selfridge."

Ronan tried to snap his fingers sarcastically, then remembered that every bone in his right hand felt pain. "How'd he like the flight?"

"Who knows? They crashed and Selfridge died on impact."

"That was a short story."

"We're at the very edge, Ronan. The very edge. There are no guarantees."

"I know." Edward was watching for any sign of a reaction. This was all too much for Ronan to think about right now; he wanted to go back to sleep, but his boss was aglow with enthusiasm, so he stayed with the conversation. He touched the wire. "Can you turn it on?"

Edward came to his side and lifted the screen on a laptop. His fingers moved on the keyboard. "I'm typing you a question. I'm asking how you like it."

Tap tap tap tap.

"I don't know what–"

Edward smiled. *Tap tap.*

"Wait… what? This is weird!"

"We call it WhisperWords. Like it?"

"It's like I'm thinking to myself! I can't tell the difference!" Ronan paused to process and study this new sensation. "I'm not actually hearing anything. It's just… thoughts bubble out of nowhere like they always do, but I can't tell if they are my own…"

"*Do you like it?*" Edward stopped typing.

"I don't know. Do I want this voice in my head?"

Edward held up the finger pads that had been removed from Ronan's hand, the wires hanging down. "Ronan, you need to leave all these technology add-ons behind, this bolted on baggage. You need to merge with your tools. You may be the first person to transform into something else, a being that is not simply human anymore."

Edward tapped a few more times. Ronan turned his head and shut his eyes, listening.

"Excited?"

"I guess, but…"

"No buts. You must want this. Where's that passion you had for breaking new ground?"

"I'm sorry. I'm just… struck by the invasiveness of this."

"Learn to control it. Our enemies will have this soon. We need to be ahead of them. You can sync up to someone and have a silent conversation. If you are ever captured, you can discuss your next move with a resource in another country."

Edward started typing again.

In the medicated fog of Ronan's consciousness, seemingly from nowhere, Edward's words passed through his mind, vocalized yet silent, tonal but soundless. *We need to know, Ronan. Do you want all this technology or not? It's your decision.*

Ronan weighed the options. Clearly, they wanted to operate on him and install these new technologies immediately. He wondered if his thoughts – just weighing his decision – were going back the other way, into the laptop so that Edward could read them. Edward's face, however, betrayed no hint that he knew what Ronan was thinking. He was staring, waiting.

What to do?

Harper had made some good points about where the future was headed, everyone disappearing into technology, completely dependent on it until disaster ended the human era. He remembered Kaczynski's warning: "The technophiles are taking us on an utterly reckless ride into the unknown."

Reckless… the exact opposite of why he had wanted technology in the first place.

Maybe it was time to abandon his goal… give it all up…

Technology didn't necessarily make us better – it just raised the stakes. And kept raising the stakes, over and over.

But what was the alternative? Go back to stone tools and primitive huts, like Harper and Kaczynski wanted?

Impossible. You couldn't even *halt* the development of new technology, let alone go backwards. The progress of technology was inevitable.

He sensed Edward watching him. Waiting.

Damn! Ronan saw the truth as plain as if it were in large capital letters on his ocular.

There was no "decision" to be made about whether to accept the surgeries and take the technology as far as possible. He had no decision to make about whether to merge with technology.

Because there weren't two possible paths.

Not for humanity, and therefore not for him.

Blip... blip... blip...

Ronan awoke for the fifth time that morning, having endured another brutish nap. All was dark. The air in his hospital room was chilly. Medical equipment hummed around him, a sound not quite audible, but it was there, if he really listened. *You notice lower frequencies when you can't see anything,* he thought.

Was he alone?

"Lisa?"

The act of speaking tugged the wires strapped to his chin and throat.

He had a serious headache. He'd been enduring one operation after another. The doctors had removed his oculars and what was left of his eyes, leaving sockets covered in gauze. His new oculars, which hadn't arrived yet from Tokyo, would feature deeper zoom-ins, ghost tracing, magnetic field overlay, scent detect, and smarter overlays. They would connect to his optic nerves. They would withstand gushing water currents, hurricane-force winds, even close-range explosions. His eyes would have to be blasted out of his head before the new oculars broke.

Cold air gushed from an overhead vent. He tried to shift under his flimsy sheet.

I can't feel my arms!

Wait, yes, there's a twitch. Whew.

All the older stuff had been removed... oxygen-boost canisters, titanium knuckles – all of it broke-ass, all of it unhooked from bones and internal organs, pulled out of his insides with wires trailing...

His body was getting a total overhaul. Muscle injectors and tensors in his arms and thighs. Synthetic webbing in the skin for durability. WhisperWords.

Excruciating pain blasted from his crotch to his neck, despite the full-strength Neuronatil dripping into his veins.

A horrible image of Deanna entered his mind. He forced it away.

He would make sure, as long as he had any fight inside him, that her death would mean something. If MET needed Ronan to track down the other Kazite groups, he would, down every hole. He would wipe every analog trace of them off the planet, every knife stroke and hatchet mark.

The door opened. The rustling of a food bag. A cup on the table. Lisa was back with her lunch. *Oh yeah, Lisa went to lunch.*

It was really amazing what you hear while waiting for your new eyes.

Footsteps. A kiss on the cheek.

Fingers stroking his hair, then hands entwined. He squeezed her hand.

As she leaned against him, sparks of pain shot up his sides.

She was complaining about the cost and quality of the hospital's food court options.

His new ghost tracing ability would display the face and name of anyone who had recently visited his immediate vicinity. The surgeons would have to remove a kidney to fit the battery needed to power that superpower, but that wasn't going to matter; they were going to compensate by installing a nephron MicroPac distillation filter, a tenth the size of the absentee kidney. The device only needed a filter change once a month.

"I wish I could read your thoughts," she said.

"That will be possible soon."

"With more implants?"

"Yes."

"I wish you would get rid of them. All of them."

"So did Harper."

"What does that mean?"

"He wanted us to retreat. He saw that we may lose touch with everything that once grounded us. But we must take technology as far as we can. We have no choice."

"I don't agree."

Ronan squeezed her hand. "This is the path I have to take."

She was quiet. Listening, maybe. Maybe not.

"You're going to get yourself killed," she said. "When we met, your job wasn't dangerous. You just wanted a few tools to help your investigations. We have plans to make, don't we?"

"Vacation?"

"I'm not talking about vacation and you know it."

"Yeah."

"You can't let them treat you as expendable."

"I have a job to do."

"So now you are battling terrorists?"

"I have to play my role. I have to master these tools, adapt to them, become them."

He felt her lean away. "How far are you going with that idea?"

The faint hum of the machines could be grating, just going and going, such dismal sounds. He could use another bolus of Neuronatil. Lisa probably thought that he had missed the question, or that he was ignoring her. "All the way," he said.

"What will be left of you?"

"I'm not sure."

The bed shifted as her weight slid off. Their fingers were no longer touching.

He heard the footsteps on the floor.

"Are you coming back?" he asked.

Silence.

Would she see that his path was inevitable? If not, would he be able to go on without her? He did not think that he could lose her, too.

"Yes. Of course, I am."

The door shut. She was gone, for the moment.

He felt a surge of hope.

Reaching for his left arm, he felt around for the drug pack, but discovered that it had been removed. Just a hole now.

He breathed deep.

At least he had tubes with happy gas going up his nostrils.

Things looked grim. But he had a role.

He was ready.

It was going to be a wild ride.

Thank you to our readers

Thank you for reading *The Havoc Inside Us*. If you think others might enjoy the novel, please add a quick review and let them know why!

Reviews are critical to a book's visibility and we really appreciate your support.

Greg Juhn and Matt Yurina